ANOTHER
KIND OF
MADNESS

ANOTHER KIND OF MADNESS

A NOVEL

ED PAVLIĆ

MILKWEED EDITIONS

Published 2019 by Milkweed Editions
Printed in Canada
Cover design by Mary Austin Speaker
Cover photo by Michael Putland
19 20 21 22 23   5 4 3 2 1
First Edition

Milkweed Editions, an independent nonprofit publisher, gratefully acknowledges sustain-
ing support from the Ballard Spahr Foundation; the Jerome Foundation; the McKnight
Foundation; the National Endowment for the Arts; the Target Foundation; and other
generous contributions from foundations, corporations, and individuals. Also, this activ-
ity is made possible by the voters of Minnesota through a Minnesota State Arts Board
Operating Support grant, thanks to a legislative appropriation from the arts and cultural
heritage fund, and a grant from Wells Fargo. For a full listing of Milkweed Editions sup-
porters, please visit milkweed.org.

Library of Congress Cataloging-in-Publication Data

Names: Pavlic, Edward M. (Edward Michael), author.
Title: Another kind of madness : a novel / Ed Pavlic.
Description: First edition. | Minneapolis : MILKWEED
EDITIONS, [2019]
    Identifiers: LCCN 2018016849| ISBN 9781571311283
(hardcover : alk. paper) |
    ISBN 9781571319678 (ebook)
    Classification: LCC PS3616.A9575 A83 2019 | DDC
813/.6--dc23
    LC record available at https://lccn.loc.gov/2018016849

Milkweed Editions is committed to ecological stewardship. We strive to align our book
production practices with this principle, and to reduce the impact of our operations in
the environment. We are a member of the Green Press Initiative, a nonprofit coalition of
publishers, manufacturers, and authors working to protect the world's endangered forests
and conserve natural resources. *Another Kind of Madness* was printed on acid-free 100%
postconsumer-waste paper by Friesens Corporation.

For Stacey Cecile, Milan Edward, Sunčana Rain,
and Mzée Yanour Shahiri—

CONTENTS

Book One: Neutral Corners 3
Book Two: Stolen Hands 93
Book Three: Inflation 177
Book Four: Archipelago 281
Book Five: Angel, Unarmed 397

Acknowledgments 487

I need you. But that's another kind of madness.

—CHAKA KHAN

ANOTHER
KIND OF
MADNESS

They came around the tip of Paté Island. The coastal channel gave way and she felt the rhythm of the sea begin. Ndiya tasted salt on her lips. Trade winds filled the sails and the boat lunged. Shame slept. After midnight, the clouds parted revealing diamonds, a milk of stars. Ndiya had checked the map. She figured six more hours, Kiwayu was midway between Lamu and Ras Kamboni. "At the coast," the captain had confided to her, smiling and with a motion of his hands as if releasing invisible doves, "the border doesn't exist at all."

Malik had said something like that, "Take a dhow, go to Kiwayu, there are no borders there, you'll find, between the sea and the sky. You always feel like you're gliding."

The mate had unrolled a mattress across the mangrove slats in the open boat. Ndiya watched Shame sleep under starlight. The open sea woke him. He sat up and she leaned against him, thinking. That thing about gliding. Malik must have meant during the daytime. The waves were soft and black to the east, the border was very clear. At the horizon, the stars turned red before, all at once, they ceased. Something about that horizon, something in the ceasing made her say,

–You know we have to go back.

Ndiya felt his head nod. The bandage on Shame's arm against the dark, like exposed bone.

–How far?

–I mean all the way back.

–Chicago?

–No, I mean farther than that.

BOOK
ONE:
NEUTRAL
CORNERS

Cold, endless summer days . . .

—CHAKA KHAN

A nd after how many speeches to herself about what *not* to do? Things not to do such as, first and foremost, meet anyone, much less someone, at a basement party? After all of that, Ndiya Grayson met Shame Luther at a basement party. It was the Fourth of July, a Sunday. Well, by the time they met it was early Monday morning. Over the next month she'd seen him twice. This night would be the third time. Ndiya promised herself to review the two previous occasions so she could make the third time turn out different. What does that mean, "turn out"? "At least give it a chance to happen," she'd thought to herself. As for Shame, OK, she thought, "It's some-kind-of-his-name." That's what it said on the flyer Yvette-at-work brought to show her on Tuesday, after Ndiya's email about having met him at the party: *Night Visions*: Catch Shame Luther: Wednesday Nights @ the Cat Eye. The glossy card featured a yellow cat eye superimposed over a piano. She slid it across Ndiya's desk without a pause in her step, "*This* your basement boy, girl? Watch yourself with musicians." And no she didn't just keep walking.

Musicians? Shame hadn't mentioned the music part when they met. He said he was a laborer. He recited it as if standing at attention: "International Laborers' Union, Local 269." She had no idea what that meant. As they shook hands on the porch, she'd managed, "Yeah? Where's that?" She noticed the callused skin of his palm and the thick, smooth feel of his fingers. His hand felt like it wore a glove of itself. "Well, the local's in Chicago Heights. But for a few more weeks," he said, "*that*, the work, is a wire mill out west up on Thirty-Eighth Street." "*Up* on Thirty-Eighth?" she thought. He said the name, "Joycelan Steel." She remembered the name because she didn't know what a wire mill was and because the name, Joycelan Steel, sounded like a person she'd want to meet. Names: Shame Luther and Joycelan Steel. The union, the local, the work? None of it sounded real. On her guard that first night, she didn't ask him anything more about what or where or why he did whatever he did. She didn't ask. She was trying to keep it simple. She failed.

■

And at night, the city arched its back. Its eyes faded to slits, front limbs stretched out. The claws became invisible, likewise the scars. The heat eased as the day gave up. Motion ensued where everything except scars rests. Scars took over and attempted to redeem the day. A telephone pole begged the cleat take back its divots. Things no river could forgive vanished. They didn't disappear. Just slipped up inside of wherever they were for a while. It's like the way you fold a piece of paper in half, trace your thumbnail down the crease until it's sharp enough that the missing half of the page fills the room and there's nothing else to breathe. They say a person experiences a rush of pure elation at the exact moment of drowning. At twilight, in the summer, the day drowned in the dark. Pieces of elation came alive, parcels of fugitive heat. Invisible streams of it moved around, lolled about in the streets, paused without pausing on stoops.

So for a few minutes at dusk the city opened. It was as if all the promises of invisibility existed without the terrors. The terrors came later, of course, enough to break a bent beam of light. But for a half hour or so around sunset after a hot day, it was pure drowning.

Ndiya Grayson would get off the bus to go see Shame Luther at twilight. She stepped into this place he'd found to live where elation hung out longer than it did elsewhere. Where life was wound into what happened on the missing half of the page. It's why she arrived by descending degrees, presence terraced. It's why she was already gone by the time she found she couldn't leave. Had never left. Long gone and never left; she held, as it were, the American ticket.

To tell it means to unfold the untold. The sky glowed overhead, the orange clouds of a night in late summer, Chicago. The hiss as the bus knelt down. It dipped its bumper into the huge puddle left over from the afternoon's gushing fire hydrants on three of the four corners at the intersection. It's just a few world-changing blocks east from the corner of Sixty-Third and King Drive, a few minutes' walk. As she'd learn later, a few minutes' walk into a past she'd never had, her past. There was no place in the city like it and no place in the city was close. No police of place, fences buried underground. She noticed it right off. She remembered it with the feeling that it was remembering her.

She'd ask Shame about it when she and Mrs. Clara's Melvin finally got inside his door. He'd take Melvin's goggles and her thigh-length linen coat and try not to notice, just yet, her soaked high-heels and dripping skirt. He'd say, "Yeah, this is where all the city's twilight comes to stay the night. And, do you know, there are places that have none at all? We get theirs too. Isn't that right, Melvin?" Melvin was oblivious in his red swim trunks with blue sailboats. He rocked back and forth on the outside edge of his sandals and held one yellow rain boot by its pull-on loop in each hand. Shame: "A little payback." And she: "Payback? For what?" And Shame, smiling at the hallway outside the open door behind her: "Come on in."

All of that was still a bus stop and a three-block walk away. It'd seem to her that it took half her life to walk those three blocks. In a way, she was right about that. But for now she was still on the eastbound 29 bus. She was still dry, hadn't felt the fitted glove of air. So she hadn't asked herself anything yet. Yet. The word seemed laced into all her time with Shame. Call it "time." Hers with him seemed to be built of delay. Every moment shackled to its mirror in a kind of tug-of-war between this and that, here and there. Things took forever to happen. They happened when they happened and never felt late. Then the bizarre part, they happened again and again—and so *really* happened—later in her mind. Ndiya's memories of time with Shame stood out like colorized scenes in a black-and-white film. No. They were like parts of a movie that she'd encountered first as music and so could never really take the movie version seriously. It'd be weeks before she asked herself much at all about Shame Luther. But when she did she'd find music where she thought there was vision, touch where she thought there should be music. And whenever there was supposed to be touch she found a part of her life that had nothing to do with him at all.

She hadn't thought it through, refused to in fact. So she knows all of this in a way she can't tell herself about. Known without the telling to self. Words evaporated into what lay behind them before her brain caught the voice. Absorbed, maybe. But—then what? As she moved up the aisle to the back door of the bus, she felt like she was already in the street. The crushing heat of the afternoon was gone. She loved the summer heat at night, the way the whole city stretched out in strings of light, turned its back and breathed long and quiet.

■

Breath in slow motion. Easy as this here. The mute pressure of heat lightning. The way a city slipped its pulse into you. This was a South Side summer night and the difference, that is, the memory, struck her immediately when she'd come back at the beginning of the summer.

Ndiya had sworn she wouldn't come back to Chicago, not until they tore The Grave down. Somewhere in herself she believed they never would. From all what they'd stole into her as a child, she'd assumed they never could come down. From all what they'd torn—in her mind, something in how she'd been sent away had made the buildings indestructible. Now they had come down. It was national, international news when they'd decided to tear down the projects where she'd grown up. It was journalism; she had her doubts. But here she was. True to her word.

True to *the* word. "Here" she was, back in this city that she'd forced to forget her name. So she thought. Immediately upon her arrival, she'd found that "here" was a verb. She felt "hered." The first thing she noticed about this verb was that it hurt. And the hurt twisted into colors, a kind of bouquet in her arms and legs. The bouquets changed her pulse, sharpened her vision until the colors in the world began to switch places: blue bars from the city flag on a police car swooped up into the sky; red from the stripe on a passing bus caught and wrapped around parked cars; silver green from trees in the park blown into the air made the wind momentarily visible. Here was musical. When the colors "hered" their way around playing musical chairs, she noticed, they didn't hurt anymore. Here bristled and sparkled. But it wasn't pain. She learned that all kind of things, voices in daily, anonymous speech more than anything else, had the power to here her. All summer voices in crowds of people jousted about until she lost track of which voice came from which face. "Where is this here?" she repeated to herself as she checked to see if the strange lightning in her arms and legs was visible to people around her. Didn't seem to be.

More than twenty years she'd lived in other places. She found that "there" was a verb too. She'd felt all kinds of "theres" and "thereings," the ways people could unknowingly there her. All kinds of ways. At every new job, people asking her the question and—without noticing

Ndiya's face—answering, "Chicago? Great place. Oh, I *love* Chicago, the Art Institute, and we have friends in"—fill in the name of whatever suburb. Or it was, "My daughter lives near Wrigley Field." Ndiya wondered how everyone's fucking daughter could live near Wrigley Field. At first, she'd attempted to halt these "thereings" by stating merely and matter-of-factly that she'd never been to the Art Institute nor had she ever seen Wrigley Field. But after a few rounds of those "thereings," she found herself frightened by the accumulating urge to smash the visibly confused face staring back at her over a cubicle wall or via a favorable angle in an anonymously glossy, marble-veined women's room wall or mirror. For years, in self-defense, she called it pleasure, the way those there-smiles she wore felt hammered on her face with hot nails. This was the period of her life she called Ndiya-Walking-Away. It didn't last. And, reluctantly, she'd conceded that she'd gotten nowhere walking away which, in a way, felt to her like a virtue.

■

Looking out the windows of the bus as it inched through traffic east on Sixty-Third Street, Ndiya could smell it. "Here." Chicago laid out on its back, its chest rising and falling as if lying next to a midnight blue lover. The lake. She thinks of the lake as Chicago's unmapped East side. "Forget State Street," she thought, "the dividing line between east and west is Lake Shore Drive." As a child, she studied "Chicago" in the encyclopedia. In third grade she found a map of the city in the *World Book*'s volume *H* under "Hydrogen Bomb." She traced it carefully into her notebook. There was a map of the city with a hydrogen bomb blast marked by a black dot in the middle. Concentric circles of destruction radiated outward. She asked her teacher where exactly on the map *they* lived and Mrs. Cross had swiftly taken the book away from her. It didn't matter, she had it in her notebook. Years before she'd ever really connected it to the actual lake, she found a fold-out *National Geographic* map that showed the contours of the bottoms of all the Great Lakes. She'd mark her way east off the edge of the city and imagine herself a mile out, floating eight hundred feet above the earth on the sound of the invisible water.

Not the waves on the lake—her map showed the shape of all that space under what you saw on the surface. All that cold, dark water plunging down and away from anything anyone could ever know. While she stared at the map, she traveled as if she was underwater where sound comes at you from all directions at once. Suspended in this unknowable sound, her own index finger with the mocha moon-sliver at the top of the nail traced the darkening shades of blue on the map. The shades told its depth. Once, in second grade, she filled a five-gallon pail for their box-garden project and found she couldn't move it at all. Her teacher, Ms. Willis, had to pour half away so *she* could carry it. "So, it's heavy too," she thought, narrowing her eyes. She checked both corners of her vision as if she'd just discerned a crucial secret. For weeks after that, she went to bed and lay there sleepless imagining how the lead-heavy depth of the whole lake would feel if it was her blanket and how nobody—not her mother, not Principal James, not the mayor—would be able to move it.

Nothing in Chicago ever made sense to her without the lake. Strictly speaking, nothing much made sense with it either. But with the lake floating out there, in her mind, it didn't matter as much. She remembered the Fourth of July when she was little. They'd go to the lake. It seemed that the whole South Side lined up along the shore. She always wondered if they ("We?" she thought now) thought the lake would open up and everyone just walk away. When memories like this came to her, it felt like she could blink with her arms and legs. It was as if her whole body closed quickly then reopened. To herself she called these memories body blinks. No music in Chicago makes sense if you can't feel the Moses effect in the song: the pulse-way people arrive but never *get* there, depart but never *leave* a city. No sense, not sense to feel, that is, if you can't hear that. You have to follow a song out over the lake at night till the sound of all the spilled light of the city disappears into the waves. If you've done that you know that the light is the gloss of all the never-lostness and not-foundity, the used-to-be-somehow and the not-quite-ever-again-ness of the people, of even one gone-person. When you do that you, that used-to-be or could-have-been but now-never-again version of you blows off with it.

For Ndiya, no matter the pronouns and prepositions, every song was really sung to that unknown, invisible weight. And she had the chart on her map. She listened to her clock radio at night, volume down so low she used it as a pillow to hear the songs played by her favorite DJ, Misty after Midnight. She'd listen with her eyes closed and then open them up and place each song on her map of the emptied-out lakes according to something she thought of as the depth of the sound. The depth of the sound was the weight of a song. Sound never lost, songs without a trace.

As she rode the 29 bus, Ndiya heard Deniece Williams's "Free." In her memory she saw her ten-year-old finger catch the red glow from the digits in the clock face. Her finger pointed at the blue-black center of the lake's terraced shape. She still thought of "Free" as Chicago's *heaviest* song, an impression she couldn't shake or believe, find or lose, until she heard the song again and it was as plain as never is always plain. The way Niecy's voice stood alone among the instruments. The way she floated and dived. The way the song was, on one level, so simple. The way she sang the filigreed frailty of what she knew and her point-blank refusal to take any refuge in it. Blue silk stitched around an ice cube. So clear the cold it held felt like a mouthful of high-altitude sky, almost empty. The song was a dare: "Go ahead, *melt*. Give up your shape against the smooth blue skin of it all." Ndiya held that song in her mind like a low moon rising up. Kept it in her mouth like a cherry gumdrop full of venom. Walking down the aisle of the bus, she tried and failed to remember ever hearing the song played in any other city. She knew she had, of course. Still, she wondered if it was possible to hear this song outside of Chicago. What could it possibly sound like with no poisonous moon low over the lake's impossible weight? She figured it must be possible. For someone maybe, but not for her.

At night, in the summer, she thought, the city got its breath from the cold bottom of the lake. It heated the air in its lungs, took what it needed, and breathed the rest out invisible. She imagined body heat blowing out the open window of a car speeding down South Shore Drive. She imagined the weight of the whole lake balanced on the head of a pin. She'd never actually been on the lake in a boat, but thought it must actually move like her uncle Lucky's big old burgundy sedan. "My ninety-eight," she remembered him saying. She didn't know what that phrase had to do with a car. She decided, vaguely, it must mean something chrome and cursive.

It didn't matter. She remembered Lucky's cut-eyed smile, the way he wore his hat pushed back on his wide forehead so it made him look like he'd always just been surprised and was always, anyway, ready for more. Rusty-haired and freckled. That phrase, "ninety-eight," floats on loose struts. "Hair on fire," he'd say. In his voice, it sounded like "hay-own-fie." Uncle Lucky drove with his right arm laid across the top of the passenger's seat so he could wave at people without looking at them. His left wrist draped on the wheel to coax and nudge the loping chassis through the curves. She used to think he steered that car the way you do a friend with your shoulder and an elbow in the ribs when you pass a secret joke between the two of you. She felt both her arms blink at the term "ninety-eight."

Ndiya looked at her face in the bus window, "The two of you." Then she thought, "The both of you." She recognized her reflection in the smudged glass, the girl under the lake disappeared under that suspended blanket of sound. The word "disappeared" echoed into static and traveled down her arms and legs. To keep her balance in the aisle, she thought of Lucky and his falsetto "ninety-eight." She thumbed a bassline on her thigh and heard it in her chest, *boom-bomp*, "Riding High." Faze-O: Lucky's theme music. Ndiya blinked her whole body closed, hard, and opened back to the present. Her voice evenly split between plea and command: "All you colors back in your places."

To focus, she reminded herself that this bus took her to her third date with Shame. That name? Just then she heard three sirens, all of them in the distance. "These aren't dates!" she scolded herself as the siren of a distant fire truck caught her ear. The clear sound of its bell bounced off the bus driver's rearview mirror and came straight down the aisle. The distant clarity of an emergency cued a thought that she didn't know this man all that well. Didn't know his neighborhood at all. She thought, "Shame? Is he serious?" She'd heard more bizarre names, but this one seemed to sit on its owner a bit too much like the crushed rake of a loud velvet hat. Yvette-at-work's warning about musicians had gone all "red zone" when Ndiya showed her Shame's address: "This Negro lives *where*? And you don't *ee-ven* know his name?"

She had been "here" before. Now she wonders if she means "there"? That was date number two. This thought broke a rule. She'd vowed not to admit to herself that date number two had happened: "Mind off number two, nothing happened, *never* happened." But even if it hadn't happened, she *had* ridden over there with him on his cycle—"*Ah, ah!* Mind off that, never happened." In any case, this *was* her first time coming to see him, here, by herself. She allowed herself to think about that because if she really thought about the last time, she wouldn't *ee-ven* have agreed to come back. She liked to think in that voice even though she knew better. She felt the epic adrenaline in that voice. She felt the power of that idiom and the betrayal of her disappearance into static as a child. She shook it off and thought safely about language.

Moving up the aisle, she held the thought under her tongue in her mind; she could taste the difference. "Here" and its grace-note silent *t*. The way the word "even" arched its eyebrows and appeared in her face. "Chicago," she thinks. Even the way you say "*ee-ven*." She felt the meaning push up from beneath while the sound of the word held both ends down. Ever since she'd been back, her arms and legs blinked on their own. Tones in simple words pulled them apart from the inside. Words, or whatever they were, played through her body like a flashlight waving around underwater. Chicago. A place where you could taste words. Ndiya stared at her reflection in the window. She turned away, eyebrows up, body closed. Then she whispered to herself, "Call it even."

■

At night, the sirens tie the city together in a web of ascending and descending sound. Sirens in the daytime tear the city limb from limb. Audible ones lash the ears. Doused in daylight, the scars hold fast to the people who wear them. At best, people attempt to steer their scars, to ride them like invisible, runaway trains. They aim the remaining pieces of themselves at whatever they do. Twilight changes that. At twilight, you might not think it's comic, but it is: no one owns the scars. By night, you might call it tragic, but it's not: the scars change back into wounds. Wounds do most of the owning. After as much daylight as they can get and as much nighttime as they can take, people, like a vast clockwork of diagonals, javelin themselves into sleep. Listen to a million icicles diving into hot sand, the sound of a city going to sleep. The night-sirens only appear from far away, a map of non-arrival, an otherness, an order. A dark blue depth so deep inside it sounds far away. Distant, that is, until they're too close, too deep, too quick. Until what's not you *is* you and so it's too late. During such a night, a dead scar opens into a living wound like a night-blooming blossom.

Ndiya was in the aisle of the bus when it stopped at her stop. At once, the distant fire truck turned, another body blink broke the ricochet and the thought vanished taking Yvette-at-work's warning from her vision before she realized she'd seen it. She didn't feel it. Distracted by the joust between "here" and "there" for less than the time it takes good luck to turn bad, she missed the worn-chrome handle at the edge of the bus seat. Instead of the handle, for a whole stride, she held on firmly to the slumped shoulder of a sleeping old man. As her left hand reached for the next handle, her right released its hold on the nearly worn-through fabric of the old man's jacket.

Her fingertips grazed his as he reached his arm up from the heavy plastic bag in his lap. He was dreaming. Her hand had sharply squeezed the thick shoulder beneath the thin cotton when Yvette-at-work's warning about musicians appeared to her like a distant siren. When their fingers grazed, the touch of Ndiya's hand nudged the man's dream. His wife's hand pressed his shoulder at the breakfast table. He dreamed his wife waking him up and handing him a lunch box. Her face in his dream turned into a flock of crimson gulls: it was some kind of warning. Without knowing it, Ndiya had touched a life in whose dreams "here" meant "gone."

Esther Brown's lovely face. Half a million black women Ndiya never knew; women she'd refused, without knowing it, to become. It was the first time in years that that man had touched a woman's fingers. And he'd missed it. If he'd been awake, he'd have magnified and replayed the texture of tiny washboards from their glancing fingerprints in his mind. He'd have chosen a minute and a place in his apartment in which to keep that accidental texture alive. He'd have played that off-chance touch until he could hear her fingers move the air aside and taste them in the ache from the delta of swollen glands in his throat. Where this man lived, to say nothing of where he worked, such a touch from such a woman was a sacred thing. It was a prayer, in fact, a here that's hardly there at all, a here that tells gone where to go.

If he'd been awake, he'd have had one more thing to hide from his partners at the job. And that's what he figured he needed, more things in his life that he couldn't possibly tell to the men at work. While Esther Brown was alive he'd have said just the opposite, "Why don't we never *do* nothing, never *go* nowhere?" But now he knew different. She was right. What he needed was more things in his life he couldn't tell the men at work, which is why that touch was a prayer. Or it would have been if he'd been awake. As it was, such touch was a dream. As far as he was concerned, that was close enough to a prayer and, anyway, he wasn't talking about either one to those fools at the job.

Jay Brown, sleep. He rode the bus home two hours late. He tried to pretend he got off work at five instead of three thirty. Jay Brown faked like he got paid on Friday instead of Wednesday. So, he wore an old gray suit, his only suit, and kept his work clothes and boots in a plastic bag in his lap. He rode the number 29 bus with an old briefcase full of work-worn tools wrapped in newspaper under his seat. The kid at the job years ago asked Jay Brown: "Why you wear a suit home from work?" And Jay Brown: "So maybe knuckleheads think I get paid on Friday." The kid: "Why?" And Jay Brown: "Why? So, rob me on the wrong day, that's why!"

■

With a light touch on the brushed silver of the pole, the rear bus doors jerked open from both sides. Body blink. The first thing Ndiya saw was a little girl. She had bright barrettes for each braid on her head and lay facedown on the sidewalk. Her hands were cupped into parentheses around her eyes and binocular'd her view straight down in the ground. Her toes drummed lightly against the crushed concrete as she lay on her belly. Ndiya, feeling as if she was viewing her own innards through reversed binoculars, thought, "What, exactly, *does* that to concrete?" Her eye traced the frayed edge of the faded black, cutoff T-shirt. The girl's face popped up from her cupped hands and she yelled, "Fifty!" In Ndiya's vision, the orange sky brightened as the broken line of rooftops across the street darkened. Somehow, with no transition, the little girl went from lying still to full stride down the way and around between the buildings, "Get-gone or get-got here I come Imma *get* you, Lester!"

When the little girl popped to her feet, Ndiya glimpsed the message on the cutoff shirt. She called back the image after the girl had spun and vanished. Above the frayed and curled edge, two stick figures held hands, one with dizzy-circles around her head. In Gothic script it read: I'm Allergic to My Sister! Without moving, Ndiya shook her head the kind of way you do when you agree with something you know is wrong.

Ndiya's body blinked again. She recalled how it felt when, in the third grade, she tripped little evil little perfect little Tara Davis and ended up giving her a temporarily busted-up lower lip and a permanently chipped front tooth. The diagonal-chipped-tooth effect had somehow perfected Tara's face in a way Ndiya and everyone else envied forever for always for the way, years later, it made the older boys love her. Now, for the first time, with a shudder, as she stared at the darkening line of rooftops and the brightening night sky beyond them, Ndiya felt the gravity of what all that attention must have been to that perfected, injured, and targeted little girl. A cloud of static sizzled across her body and Ndiya shook her head, again. Avoiding the mirror in her body, she thought, "Jesus, Tara Davis," said, "Thank you," to the driver and stepped off the bus.

Her weight shifted just before she checked down for her step to the curb. Inverted directly beneath her, she saw the buildings across the street and the bright sky beyond. She watched the reflected sole of her shoe as it came straight up at her. A streetlight's glow spread across dusty, liquid skin of the surface. Her eyes told her that she'd stepped from a plane, not a bus. The dream-fall feeling bloomed behind her eyes and she heard Yvette-at-work's voice: "You a *mess*. By the way, you *do* know that was a *man's* shoulder you had your hand on back there on the bus, right?"

She rode a ribbon of air for a moment—before she found herself splashing into a puddle with both feet. Even with her heels, the water was over her ankles. Misjudging the step by a thousand feet or so caused her to land with her left leg perfectly straight, shooting pain up her spine and nearly popping her kneecap off. The splash vanished back into the oily murk as the bus leveled itself and went on. The departing bus stirred a wave of hot water that hit the back of her legs just below her knees before it washed over the broken curb and across the ruined sidewalk. She felt the warm wave pull at the hem of her pastel teal, cotton-linen skirt. The dreamer with the long-fingered shadow on his shoulder went away too. He dreamt on in a dream as thin as the camouflage his gray suit provided his life. Rainbows gathered themselves around Ndiya's legs as she stood beyond-ankle deep in disbelief. "What next?" she thought, "Dolphins fly and parrots live at sea?"

Single drops of oily gutter water ran down her legs. She felt a few ash-colored drops on her arm. A single drop slipped down her neck and disappeared into the collar of her coat. And then another body blink. "There, no, *here* he was," she thought, "Junior." She once knew a strange little boy, Junior Keith, who called drops from these puddles gutter-pearls. "Little nasty, little big-headed, Kodak-glossily-jet-black and girl-attached-to-eye-having Junior Keith," she thought. Hydrants open. He'd wait on the sidewalk. He always somehow avoided getting wet himself. She had no idea how he stayed dry but she knew exactly why. His Grandmama. Junior loved to sneak up behind girls and, depending on their height, he'd lick their arm, shoulder or sometimes even the back of their leg. "Hmm. Mm, Gutter-pearls!" he'd say, and run off down the block and across the street to the safety of his grand-mother's raggedy old porch. There his sisters Lynn and Vanessa were usually lurking ready to pounce on some-body and call it protecting him. Those girls were hell on sequin roller skates: "Na-ah, Grandmama," they'd say, "we wasn't fighting, just protecting Junior from that boy down the block—ooh, he think he bad." Ndiya felt the wet skirt clutch her legs as the air made its way through to cool the fabric. And she thought, "So much for casually anony-mous arrivals. So much for 'at least give it a chance to happen,' to 'turn out.'"

She hadn't seen Junior coming. He didn't just arrive. Nor was he alone. His image rode a roar of static, a hot numbness. This body blink felt like an empty flame. Ndiya felt it burn but refused to acknowledge the heat. With a precision so complete it masqueraded as innate, though it had been systematically learned, honed, and deployed, Ndiya coexisted with a rare thing about which both— maybe all—of her selves agreed without agreeing. This deal of nonengagement was as perfect as water poured from two pitchers into one pail. Except there was no pail. So the deal was pure *pour*, forever. As in, if you throw a sea turtle into an infinite well, you might as well call the turtle a seagull. This was her method of control, of avoidance. A method she'd used to make this city forget far more than her name. Twilight in Shame's neighborhood meant Ndiya Grayson wasn't alone. This fact was precisely why she'd come back and exactly what she'd lived her life avoiding.

And the city had forgotten nothing.

Then there appeared a bright, capsized yellow boat. It had a blue rudder and a red propeller. The border of Ndiya's vision widened to include a pair of tiny yellow boots and two impossibly large eyes. These eyes didn't appear to recognize anything in their sight as much as they appeared to house the whole scene inside themselves. It was as if the tiny owner of the huge eyes had bypassed vision altogether and beheld the world as if it was all a matter of inner vision. She felt like he could bypass her skin and soaked-through clothes and x-ray each crook and notch in her spine. "Big, aquarium-eyed little boy," she thought.

Then, she thought, "Again. *Again.*"

An old woman was crocheting an expression across her tight-lined face by lamplight. She warned, "Look out for the water, honey. *Dirty.*" Then her voice changed color, "That's enough playing tsunami by the bus stop, get yourself on up out away from there, now, Melvin." Ndiya: "Too late I'm afraid, ma'am." The crocheted knots beneath the old woman's eyes looked like someone was pulling them open and closed from behind. Slack for her, tight for him. "Come here, boy." Then, "Oh, honey, that's a shame." Next, "Here, Melvin, now!" And again, "But it'll dry child, it'll dry." And, "Over here, *before* now! Before you get yourself into . . ."

But Ndiya's mind had tipped like if you try to carry a wide, inch-deep tray of water with one hand or balance it on top of your head.

Here she was somewhere between ankle- and knee-deep in what was looking like a third fiasco. And she hadn't even *started* her review of fiascos one and two. After meeting Shame at the party, each time they got together began with some farcical incident precisely calibrated to prevent her from feigning any dignity or self-assuredness. Ndiya had plenty of both. She knew it and for as long as she'd been grown she'd been bothered that she couldn't account for where or how she'd come by any of it and what, if any, good it did her.

So, with Shame, she thought she would experiment, maybe improvise. What was to lose? She met him, after all, at a basement party she knew better than to go to anyway. Somebody's friend of a friend named Renée had thrown herself a Fourth of July birthday party that was supposed to be a reenactment of one she'd had in 1985 or something. Ndiya's plan with Shame was to act like she had the false, everyday kind of confidence and protect her secret. She'd act *normal*. Brilliant. But it didn't work. After the first few seconds of their first date, she needed the secret kind, at least.

There was the first meeting at Earlie's Café. Ndiya made it clear beforehand, this was not a date. She'd rushed—if it was possible to rush by bus?—to her brother's place after work to grab her oversized and always overstuffed canvas handbag. She'd left it over there on a rare visit the previous night. Wanda, Malik's girlfriend, answered the door. She blocked Ndiya's path and handed her the bag. Aiming beyond Wanda's attitude, Ndiya called, "Can't stay, gotta meeting!" to the blue room the TV lived in, and bolted back to the bus stop thinking, "It's time to empty this bag." Traffic was bad, she had to transfer twice; she was at least an hour late. She kept reaching for her phone and then remembering that Shame didn't have one. When she arrived he was waiting for her outside the café. He sat facing the street and leaned back on his hands on the top of a stone picnic table with his feet planted wide apart on the bench. "There he is, with his feather-light brown self," she thought, "and there he'll stay." From across the street she let him know that she'd seen him with half a smile aimed at the ground in front of his feet. Then she focused on the door to his left while holding him in her sight. She thought, "OK. Keep him *there*."

Ndiya tabulated her quick survey from her peripheral vision: "V-neck T-shirt (bad sign) and faded jeans (neutral and leaning on what's next like a spare in bowling) that rode up to reveal his unpolished (thank heavens) brown boots (the kind with the metal ring at the ankle, that could be OK) and what looked like a brown leather jacket on the table beside him." From across the street she noted that his clothes all seemed too loose to fit but weren't baggy. She thought, "It's been a while since I've crossed a street for this kind of thing." The dusk of the street and the blue light atop Earlie's awning traveled the lines of Shame's face. The shadows made it seem like his face had been sewn together from a haphazard assortment of three or four faces. She searched for the sloped lines she subliminally depended on when meeting people and found precious little to work with. She didn't remember this from the porch at the party. "Not good," she thought. "He damned near looked white." But this wasn't quite a thought. It was more like an itch near the corner of her mouth.

All that changed when he got up to shake her hand and said her name: "Enter Ms. Ndiya Grayson." First of all, he got it right. Áh-ndiya, accent on the first syllable and the *a* pronounced soft like the opposite of "off," not sharp like the *a* in "candy." No one got all that right, ever. He read the surprise in her face and said he knew the song. "That's good," she thought, because she didn't. "What song?" He laughed and she remembered his easy smile. "A little too easy," she thought. She noticed first, then, what she'd learn in stages later. Shame only looked like himself when he moved or when he spoke. And his voice sounded exactly like he looked; it was uncanny. When he sat still, pieces of his face and body pulled against each other. Then, she'd learn later, there was his life: his before-work vacant-self; the with-kids dude; the chef-Shame; and the piano man. In his life Shame was a kaleidoscope. He changed into a third, fourth, fifth person altogether. "One, two, three," he'd say sometimes, "which Shame you want me to be, which kind you want from me?" He said it was a quote, or almost. She asked from where and he didn't say. Her first, zero-sum impulse was to wonder where were the people whose faces he'd stolen, pulled apart and put back together. But she cut herself short before that. She was still on that whole "give it a chance to happen" thing.

Still in the street, she replayed his voice from the night they'd met: "Gosh, I guess every day *is* Wednesday, right?" And she: "What?" And he: "If I'm not mistaken, you just said hello *to* me and looked *at* me with both eyes at once. That's rare around here, that's all." And she: "If you say so, but—Wednesday?" And he: "*The Mickey Mouse Club*, you know, Wednesday: Anything Can Happen Day?" She: "Oh, OK. That's cute." And now, outside Earlie's Café, she thought, "*There* he is," and, seeing her reflection walking in the window behind him, "There *you* are. There you both can stay. *Here* can sit this one out."

When they shook hands she felt the thick skin of his palm again. He said, "Thanks for coming, I like your ride." His open tone left no room and less need for her rehearsed, frustrated, CTA mass-transit-hell excuse for being late. Shame led her by the hand through Earlie's as if the place was a tight, dark cave. In fact, the space was the opposite of cave-like, tall windows and high ceilings. Ndiya's first impression, however, had been a kind of softness about everything in there. She followed closely. Shame's right shoulder interrupted her view of palm trees, bushes, and shrubs of every size. She quickly forgot her trip over there, crazy-always-guarding-the-door-ass Wanda, her lateness, and her neutral corners rationale for asking him to pick a spot near where neither of them lived. She'd even forgotten the silly day-of-the-week thing about Wednesday.

The softness came from what the music at Earlie's did to the space she felt around her. At first, she didn't hear anything. The sensation was that she had entered through a door in the wide hip of an upright bass. She heard Shame's voice and saw his head gesture this way and that. He didn't turn around. "I come here for the plants, the wood, and the sound. I can't really hear the music anymore, but it's good to know it's there." He continued while she followed thinking, "Maybe this corner isn't quite neutral enough." Shame said, "This place always makes me feel like ordering a Scotch so old you can't even drink it, you have to just tip the glass, close your eyes and inhale it into your lungs." He continued, "It's the same with the sound. Do you know an amphibian hiccups to breathe under water?" Strangely, she did know that. But she let it blow by.

Maybe Shame was nervous. He went on, "Do you know who Reggie Workman is? Red Garland? Wynton Kelly? Otis Spann? Errico Beyle?" "Ah, musicians?" Ndiya managed. He said nothing in response. He might have nodded but that could have been a way to silently say hello to someone at one of the tables. They came to a corner table between two windows looking out at a small garden, a courtyard. On the table stood a white card with "S. L., 7:30" written on it in black marker. The time had been crossed out and "8:00" had been written in; the "8:00" had been crossed out and, this time in red marker, "8:30!" had been added. Ndiya winced.

Immediately after they arrived at the table, Shame sat down, swept the card into his back pocket, reintroduced himself and, before she could sit, asked if she had a tissue. Ndiya thought to herself how glad she was that he hadn't made a big act out of pulling out her chair, etc. She asked if he had a cold and he said the tissue was for his glasses though he wasn't wearing glasses. She rummaged around at the bottom of the bag. Playing off her surprise at feeling the slim plastic packet without having to go in after it headfirst, Ndiya assured him, "Of course, sure, here you ar—"

Then the scene dropped like if she'd stepped backward off a ladder she didn't remember climbing. When her hand emerged from her bag with the pack of tissues, a Velcro patch from her brother's busted-open house-arrest ankle cuff caught her sleeve. The ruined hunk of plastic and wire leapt as if it had hurled itself out and landed on the table. It bounced once and turned over the sugar bowl and toothpicks spiraled across the dark grain of the floor and through the aisle coming to rest strewn about the feet of the couple at the next table.

Shame sat looking at her with one hand on the tabletop. His other hand was extended toward her to take the tissue. He hadn't flinched, he hadn't moved at all. Judging by his relaxed posture, nothing strange had happened.

Ndiya's ears reduced the room to the sound of the flat-line, we're-losing-her tone. The jolt triggered a kind of survival mechanism she had employed many times in her life but knew nothing about. Her body leaned into the immediate present, her brain snapped back and became surgically abstract. It all happened without her intending, and it worked. It was kind of the way her brothers and their friends used to discuss running from the police. You never run in the same direction. They called it fifty scatters. They described it all in comic, managerial tones:

"Now, police show up, we *out*, fitty scatter on they ass. Meet up later and assess the situation."

Ndiya felt her body fifty scatter. Her mind abstracted, analytical: "No matter the length, all instants are exactly the same size. It's the shapes that never repeat. Some twist and recede, some gape and come right at you, others, furtive, listen around corners." She took account of the instant. The objects before her eyes on the table made no sense. She thought perhaps the place had been bombed. Maybe the toothpicks were splintered wood from the roof? Her mind a-twirl, the room somewhere bent and concave in the chrome mirror of the still-revolving sugar spoon. She couldn't recognize the broken-open cuff of plastic on the table. Obviously, she had no idea Malik had hidden the damn thing in her handbag. As if laying down cover, her brain told her that it wasn't a bomb. Her eyes recognized the torn blue flag with its four red stars, of the CPD. Her mind filled the instant with Malik's milky-eyed, laughing, beautiful face.

Ndiya watched her vision like a foreign film as it hopped from the broken cuff across the toothpick-strewn tabletop and landed on Shame's face, Ndiya watched her vision like a foreign film. Then he did react. Ndiya's mind backed away and took in the scene as if it was printed in subtitles at the bottom of the screen. Shame's eyebrows lighted into an asymmetry of pure surprise and sheer pleasure. Ndiya watched as her mind leapt in to abstract the anomaly of Shame's expression. She decided it was actually wonder and that, for Shame, at least, wonder must be a subset of pleasure. "Or maybe vice versa?" her brain asked itself. "No," she thought as Shame's expression replaced Malik's face in her mind, songs pinned all over it, like a depth-chart of Lake Michigan with no water in it, "Definitely, Shame's wonder is inside pleasure." Ndiya's mind continued on: "Pleasure's the wider circle. Wonder is the deeper blue." It concluded, "Shame's wonder gets deeper as its surface area gets smaller. That's about pressure. So the formula: wonder equals pleasure under pressure." Then her brain gave up its finding: "In other words, this man is trouble."

Her analytical brain circled the wagons. Tactically, she could feel that retreat wasn't an option. So, Ndiya's body stood its ground before the absurd scene. The absurdity was her brain's problem. The rest of her was right there. To an observer it might have appeared that showing up late and tossing a busted-up house-arrest bracelet out on the table was how she usually began a conversation with a man she'd just met.

Ndiya heard Shame laugh in words, "Well, hey now!" And she felt his extended hand take hers, lightly, and guide her down to the chair beside him. She wasn't blind, exactly. There were bowls of light playing in and out of each other. The whole plan about acting normal, about the false and real confidence was out the window. She remembered thinking, "Another *blown* date. *So* blown!" Another page of life had been slashed diagonally across the middle and torn from the book.

All this was trivia, however. The real trouble was that the push and pull of Shame's stolen faces was totally gone. A familiar play of curves appeared, somehow, from under the angles of his face. Her thought just then wasn't a thought, it resolved a melody in her body. It was like a sound in her hands or a turbulent feeling around them as if she'd reached into rushing water. She sat down and turned toward a pair of eyes that looked like leaves on the bottom of a clear pond. Light brown, flecked with dark spots. "Sunspots," she thought, as her brain informed her that sunspots are actually huge magnetic storms. Shame's voice: "My cousin used to use an electric can opener and a Bic lighter, looks like you just slammed yours fifty times in your car door or something." He looked under the table and laughed. "Is your *ankle* OK?" Then he turned to the waitress, who looked as if she was afraid to approach the table with the piece of wreckage on top of it: "Angela, may we have two Blue Labels, please, neat." Ndiya saw the waitress staring at her out of the corner of her eye. The waitress said, "Right, Shame, sure."

This date was *so* blown. *Oh* so blown. Somewhere, she'd already begun to type the postmortem email to Yvette-at-work. Email. This thought brought with it its own waves of disbelief, but that was the story of date number two and, for now, that was *too* much. And, remember, date-by-whatever-name number two hadn't *ee-ven* happened.

Ndiya felt music around her. A distant song played, something about no mountains and no moving, no tides and no turning. She couldn't quite hear it. Or maybe it was thunder? Shame's voice was stuck in her head among the clanging sounds. She heard echoes of the phrase Bic lighter over and over. Then Shame's voice: "Ever notice the tiny dude with the huge Afro on Bic lighters?"

Shame's honey and molasses accent. "*Here* I am," she

thought, "deep, in denied territory." And Shame: "Let's have a drink." And she: "You already ordered." And he: "So I did. Done! I stay away from expensive liquor, but in this case." Her eyes focused on him again. She felt like he'd curved himself across the upturned spoon on the table. Her voice answered him as if on its own. It sounded like she'd whispered it into a wind tunnel: "No. No car door. I, I ride the bus." He: "I know, remember, said I liked your ride, your carbon footprint?" He laughed. She: "It's not mine, it's my brother's." She saw Shame's lips move but she didn't hear him. She felt the music again, nearer. She nodded at whatever he said while a song too far off for her to hear chimed: *Just as sure as I live, I will love you alone. . . .*

■

Since that first house-arrest bracelet night, Ndiya kept a still shot of Shame's face looking up from the table to hers. Obscure details like this burned into her memory. She replayed the instant between the points of his eyebrows and the tone of his voice, "Hey now . . . Bic lighter." It had happened a thousand times: Shame's voice with sunspots in his eyes, some far-off song holding on to her by her shoulders. She listened for the Doppler effect. She looked hard into the from-somewhere memory. She searched for Shame's retreat but found nothing. There was only his wide-open face.

The way that tangle of wire and plastic hit the table and Shame's face fell through those pulled-apart lines and into itself, it was as if he appeared from nowhere. Ndiya had much too much experience with nowhere to trust it. And she prided herself on not being taken off guard. She depended upon that forewarning. She didn't appreciate things like beautiful faces falling through themselves and appearing, unannounced, before her eyes. She searched his face again for the way people do their eyes, the eyes behind their eyes, like they're pushing back from a table getting ready to stand up and turn away. It wasn't there. Each time she recalled the scene her thought was, "OK, I'll catch him this time." But she couldn't. The expression, the voice, the bit about his cousin with the Bic lighter, none of it added up. The shape of the instant appeared as itself, different every time.

If she were paranoid, she thought, she'd be sure he'd planted the bracelet in her bag. If she'd gone crazy, she'd remember that happening very clearly. There'd be evidence filed in the precinct of certainty. She wasn't crazy because nothing was certain. Or almost nothing. Later that week, she'd gone into a corner store and checked; there really is what looks like a little dude with a huge Afro on a Bic lighter. It *was* an instant in time. She had proof. So she halfway thought her sanity, or at least a kind of clarity, depended upon her ability to make one instant in time be itself. Be still.

She tried but she couldn't do it. What scared her was elsewhere. Somehow, despite all of her expert deployments of abstraction, it took no effort, in fact, for her mind to fix itself on the image of a man who looked like Shame—that damned name—who could watch a house-arrest bracelet tumble out, catch a shower of toothpicks in his lap and the first thing that comes to mind is a description of a tiny blip of a mark with an Afro on his cousin's Bic lighter? No matter the abstract expert, there was no man like that. What appeared was him, every time. Shame. His apparent ease, the clarity and concision disturbed her. The timing. But there it was, undeniable. No, she hadn't known anything like it, like him. And she told herself out loud, repeatedly, she didn't want to.

She began to wonder what that cost him and where he'd paid. Then she banished the thought before the pressure had a chance to do its thing. "Wonder be damned at the bottom of the lake," she thought. "Dolphins and parrots can go on and live wherever they want." Somewhere else—or in the same somewhere, it didn't matter—she didn't want to know such a person existed. Not in Chicago, not across town, and certainly not with no random sunspots happening at the bottom of a clear pond just across a table from her.

■

Ndiya had accepted that it was some kind of personality trait she'd come by through genetic mutations. She had a knack for getting into bets with herself that forced her to sacrifice pledges and vows she'd made in the mirror. Here was another one. In no uncertain terms, she'd pledged, however impossible she knew it was, to erase all evidence of date, meeting, whatever-it-was number two with Shame Luther. She'd also vowed a new level of self-scrutiny that, she reasoned, was the only way to avoid disasters in her personal life. This was necessary now that she apparently had a personal life in which she wasn't the only person. She'd promised herself that she'd go over all impressions of her brief and catastrophic times with Shame Luther before she'd see him again.

Partly because she feared if she did it sooner she wouldn't show up at all, she'd put off the emotional inventory until she was actually on her way to his place. Then, the splashdown off the bus. She'd had the impulse to cross the street and get on the next thing smoking that would debit her metro pass. Right then and there, as she stood in the water, Ndiya shook her head at her soaked Nine West heels and her sodden skirt. "Ain't this just a crying sha— oh hell, OK, here we go, step number one, *date* number two."

The second date hadn't begun as a date. Fact. That was true as trouble in mind. It had started like sudden sunlight through the back door. If not a fact, it was at least a fluke. A chance meeting that caught her in a bad way, followed by a bad decision that precipitated a personal, public relations disaster. That disaster set a system in motion that would change her life, then several lives. Still, as she stood on the sidewalk, soaking wet, Nydia felt like she was over most of it now. That was another troubling pattern about the time since knowing Shame: the bigger the disaster the easier it was to put away. But little incidents and impressions of incidents would dog her. Yvette-at-work said, "Ndiya, you should talk to someone, you know, a professional." She figured date number two must have been bad because, as she sloshed away from the puddle and down the block toward Shame's building, she found that almost none of what she recalled had to do, strictly speaking, with him at all.

She remembered his unzipped jacket as she'd seen it from across the street, his cycle. U-turn. His offer and then his shoulder against her chin as she sat behind him and watched Chicago lean away from them with the high-pitch, first part of the S curve and then back toward her as they leaned away from the lake on the second curve. The engine cleared its throat, lowered its voice, and the city disappeared behind her back and into the wind. She remembered the sweet-salt smell inside his helmet that she wore and the texture of the way tiny points of hair lay down smooth against his shaved head. She felt her hips learn how to balance on the cycle without falling off the back. Meanwhile her arms tried to avoid holding on to his waist tight enough to feel his belt buckle and his torso beneath his jacket. She feared if she got too close and he hit the brakes she'd butt him with the helmet in the back of his bright, bald head and they'd crash. She remembered biting the upturned collar of his worn leather jacket.

Memories flipped in a series of images, some of them blank. Sunpool on his scalp. Burnt-down candles on an old piano. A Frank Lloyd Wright–looking daybed with mat-thin cushions. The warm, amber-and-blue glow from the thing he called a tube amp on a low table across the room. She remembered almost nothing else about the room except that it was filled by the sound of some oud player Shame seemed to worship. She thought it was strange that he turned *off* the music when he got home. She can't even remember exactly what he'd said an oud was.

"You gotta love that, playing tsunami," Ndiya thought, as she walked down the block beyond the old woman crocheting prophetic comments into a doily in her brain. She passed Melvin with his plastic boats in the gutter. A young man slipped through a set of double doors across the street. His denim jacket opened in the warm breeze and interrupted her recollection. Surprised at her pleasure in the even rhythm of her memory through which flowed a level of detail she could taste, she noted the slightly electric, morning-coffee and cigarette effect. She decided date number two couldn't have started out as bad as she'd recalled. Maybe. But it got that way. Then she wondered: Maybe disasters happen in reverse? They wash over you, move back into your past and then flow forward dragging it all along with them like historical flotsam into the future. "Maybe we don't have a chance, maybe we're all playing tsunami," she thought.

E yes straight ahead, what you do is focus on something about twenty miles away. This allows you to see everything and gives no one the impression that you're actually looking at them. Having found it an effective way for a single woman to negotiate city streets at night, Ndiya had actually learned to do this confronting dining halls at college. "Whitecaps today," she'd chant to herself as she blurred her vision and looked for a round, dark pool that would be one table of black students with whom she'd eat. While eating, she'd focus so hard on each face that the chalk-faced waves and wan-toned voices surrounding them disappeared. The background turned into what she'd seen the weatherman standing in front of when they'd gone to the TV studio on a field trip in fourth grade. "WGN's Roger Twible," she had kidded herself then, "and the pure, blank blue he keeps behind him." And now she thought again, "Ain't mad at him." Then she realized how uneasy she was on this street because she was doing it again. Her eyes strained against her peripheral vision as she followed a man's progress across the street without turning her head to watch.

The bus disappeared into the darkening distance and she saw the young man undo the denim flap on his jacket. He inserted a tightly wrapped packet of plastic in his breast pocket. He appeared to her and then disappeared. He had something in his face she wanted to trust. Everything about it was even; there was nothing soft, nothing hard, nothing too round, nothing too sharp. He fell through her sight into the easy, curved play of light on lines and the spectrum of brown out of which she built everything she knew about how, what for, and why to look at people. All the possible ways of being came inevitably from these basic shapes and shades in faces. When there was no human face like that around, those patterns appeared anyway. They turned to her out of trees, clouds, waves at the beach, the froth of a cappuccino. All that led to a static she wasn't going near. She carried that space hidden inside. In that static, a kind of noiseless noise, drifted something she refused to know but knew was true: it's the people you know, that you trust—leave love alone—that hurt you the worst. People you don't know or trust can kill you, or maim you; but that's it. The real injuries that leave you touched and staggering around hiding from yourself come down the hallway, they invite you to come along and you follow. Afterward, they hang there in the torn-open wound of your trust. The arrival of trust is subtle and dangerous, its perils are intimate, vertical, bottomless.

This young man's eyes were deep without the masked howl that she usually saw in the faces of black men with deep-set eyes. Her father's face flashed and went away. Every hair on this young man's head and in his wispy goatee was in place. But he didn't have the razor-coiffed precision of the cuff-linked men at work who stalked about the Loop like perfection itself. She'd see these professional men at lunch meetings; she knew their smell. They walked like they were fresh from the weight room and flashed corporate AmEx cards like they were swords in a divine battle scene in some museum painting. The young man—truth be told he was a boy in her mind—struck her with a grace, an elegance in his stride and the perfect break of his jeans over tooth-white sneakers. For a flash, she replayed her long exile from Chicago in her brain and, against that second's blur, she gave herself to this young stranger. She kept her eyes twenty miles out over the lake and him in her peripheral vision. It was an old technique, let the body ache but refuse to feel it. Wonder your way around the pressure of the moment. Let it sing.

This kind of openness felt very new to her. It had been a long time.

A pastel of music melted in her body. It did a slow, counterclockwise lap in her brain passing by her right ear: *I've got things on my mind.* It disappeared until it reappeared in her left ear and she heard, *I'm not too busy for you.* She knew the song, knew its moves. She loved the song so she turned it off before Kenny Lattimore had his chance to croon her favorite line, *If you're feeling a-lone. . . .* She could trace the gentleness of that line as it moved through her body like a long swallow of hot chocolate at the bus stop in the winter. The kind of warmth that you feel when you swallow, the kind that makes it seem like anything you look at will melt. The song laid the words perfectly along the lines and shades in the faces she saw pass her on the street. With lines like this, she could abstract her way past the masks men wore in public and even past the others she'd found stuck to their faces in private. "Male privacy!" she thought. "It's up there with companion for life and soulmate in the bait-and-switch way of the world."

She mourned the secret war black men fought, must

fight anyway, in places far away from her, quite possibly far away from everyone, with those gentle lines and the fantastic beauty in those shades of brown they carry through life. "Let's not *ee-ven* talk about eyelashes." Black men's beauty and the near-cosmic arrays of violence leveled against it. She began to smile, then felt a rush of tears pressing into her eyes and a lump in her throat. Then she put it all away: "Brain broom, must pan, thought box." She had a hundred tricks like this.

To hasten away the romance, she considered the casualties of this gentleness. This was no trick. She felt her scalp sweat and her eyes harden. The casualties of that gentleness were women. Every time. "And it ain't *ee-ven* gentle," she thought. She remembered something Shame had said to her that first night, out in front of Renée's party on the Fourth of July. They could hear the music slow down, and the dusty sound rose like floodwater in the basement. She was halfway into praising Jesus that she'd come up for air and was outside when the music got low. It was an old song. She knew because the words were overpronounced in a way that made her feel eighteen years old. *Dream about you ev-er-y night-tah, every day-ah*: a city soul singer with a country preacher's punctuation.

"Smoke City," Shame said. "Remember them? I knew this singer, ain't seen him in years and years, but that's a whole 'nother story." Then he said,

–I love music that starts with how life is and then opens up like this and makes life seem like how it *has* to be and at the same time makes it all sound like you know it can't *never* be.

He concluded the thought scowling at the ground:

–All at once.

And she, trying to follow the logic as she repeated what he'd said to herself:

–I'll have to think about that.

–Naw, just listen is all. Otherwise, well, never mind the otherwise.

And she thought to herself, "Who the hell is this?" and to disguise the thought, she asked the singer's name.

–Never mind, that's part of the otherwise.

As he said this, Shame's eyes rose up. He'd been staring at the ground. When he looked to the sky his eyes passed over her face. Ndiya felt a strong pull, or was it a push? As their eyes passed each other, she thought she heard a voice in her ear say, "Careful with that." She must have said it to herself out loud because Shame asked,

–Careful with what?

–Oh, never mind.

–Oh, right, "never mind," that's part of the "otherwise."

But Ndiya thought, just then, that party didn't count as a meeting or a date. So, she was under no obligation to deal with it.

■

Despite being soaked and conspicuous, Ndiya tried to maintain her equilibrium in this unfamiliar street. She thought, "Weather and the blank blue behind it," and blurred her ears from the inside. The song was no more and the young man was greeting another young man and a woman who'd each been shifting their weight from one foot to the other at the corner since she'd passed by them on her way. One eyebrow up, she felt her top lip fold inside her mouth, her teeth scraped across it twice before it popped back cool in the air. OK, here goes.

Date number two. Late July? A Friday? The twenty-third? She'd been invited to a birthday party for Maurice from the firm. Maurice Thomas, Esq. Morehouse, Phi Beta Sigma, Northwestern Law, office 2402. She knew him mostly from editing his briefs. Immediately after they'd been introduced, she named him "*That* Maurice." She couldn't have been back in Chicago for more than six weeks. She was new at the job. Afraid to unpack most of the boxes in her provisional, no-lease townhouse sublet. She had regular urges to tape up the few she *had* opened, call the movers, and spend half her savings on a one-way move to a brand-new nowhere in the big old ABP, her personalized acronym for USA.

Her job was to keep records in the firm, sit in on depositions, prepare forms, motions. The computer did the formatting and the abstract, opaque legalese the lawyers used came naturally to her. "Naturally" meant it was a skill she'd practiced unconsciously in order to survive. She recognized the technique immediately. Just like she did, the legal language surgically and tactically excised its connection with the world outside the precise matter at hand. The point was to create a version of whatever case that guarded against threats. Bring it on. If she could do anything, Ndiya Grayson could do that. In two weeks, she could mouth the words before the lawyers got their sentences out. In three, a few junior associates recognized that she wrote in their world-obliterating tribal language better than they did. Most quickly began to simply list the basic facts of the case and let her do the rest. They'd make a special effort in five-syllable words to say—strictly on procedural grounds, you understand—that they'd need to proof the briefs before they were submitted, but she knew it was all show. They probably didn't even read them until they were on their way to court, if they ever got that far.

She felt a flash of panic when she saw how plainly some people read things about her that she hadn't consciously disclosed. She asked Yvette-at-work about her future as a legal ghostwriter. She was told not to sweat it. "If they know you're smart you'll either get promoted in a little while or fired right away—how long has it been?" She'd started as a temp and, when the temporarily absent person stayed gone, she'd signed a one-year contract for more money than she'd ever thought she'd make. In truth, she thought to herself, it wasn't so much a job as an excuse to get out of bed, shop on Oak Street, and live in a part of the city that meant absolutely nothing to her. "What do you expect," she'd laughed to herself, "going to work in a building that looks like a fifty-story pair of sunglasses?" She imagined that the buppified stretch of townhouses on the near South Side where she sublet her place couldn't mean anything to anyone. She figured that was the whole point. She was wrong, of course, but that didn't matter yet. And if you allowed for travel well beyond the speed of light, and back in time, the neighborhood was just a few blocks east from where she'd grown up.

The message about Maurice's party was the first post she'd received after having been added to the SnapB/l/acklist. This was the secret listserv that trafficked news between the young, gifted, and professional black employees of Gibson, Taylor & Gregory, the corporate law firm where she worked. Somewhere, of course, she knew better than to click to join and RSVP to the list to say nothing of actually showing up to *That* Maurice's birthday party. And worse, Yvette-at-work had written back to the list to acknowledge that Ms. Ndiya Grayson, new colleague and the newest member of the list, would be there and everyone should make it a point to introduce themselves.

Nevertheless. "No, forget the *n*," she thought. "Make it 'evertheless.'" At six thirty on that Friday evening, she found herself in front of a mirror, humming along to the sublet TV's "Soul Salon" and lost in time blending shades of MAC on her eyelids. She checked the rhythm-method calendar of her hair: "It's Friday, second day out of the braids and on its way *back* for the weekend. Sunday evening, back to braids." She made sure the seam in her stockings was straight up the back of her calf. The door of the building said, "Don't!" when it slammed behind her but she shook it off and went down the steps to take the bus uptown to the Violet Hour. Everyone was meeting there for dinner before they headed off to whatever other closet of uptown nowhere the rest of *That* Maurice's party was to take place in.

■

Leaving big-eyed Melvin and his grandmother or whoever she was behind, Ndiya continued walking as the
business strip gave way to residential buildings rimmed
with lawn and living room furniture and old people to
nod and smile at as she passed. In her mind, she continued on with her self-promised reckoning with date number two. The incident. She remembered riding the bus up
South Michigan Avenue, awestruck by the unfamiliarity
of the city and bothered by a strange feeling that she knew
all of the black people she saw personally. Coming back
to Chicago felt like returning to a family of two million
people who lived in, or near, a city that'd embarked on
an aggressive campaign of cosmetic surgery. "Way too aggressive," she thought, as she wondered if what happened
to Michael Jackson's face could happen to a city. She knew
it could. She'd been to Phoenix, an experience—or, more
accurately, the utter lack of—which changed USA in her
mind to ABP: "Anywhere But Phoenix."

Still, this was Chicago. She thought, "It is *still* Chicago,
right?" The miles of empty lots, abandoned blocks, and defunct train tracks that she'd known south of Grant Park
were one place of massive change. And she knew that
what she'd known was itself—for someone else—a bit of
blur that wasn't designed to last either. "Chalk it all up to
America's War on Time," she thought.

Thoughts like these made Ndiya half regret her youthful, vengeful lack of patience and half wish she could feel
it again full force. Then she remembered Art. After college
they'd moved back to New York City where he'd grown
up. She saw herself smile and wince and shake her head in

the window as post-op Chicago wheeled past like it was on a gurney outside the bus. She remembered, though, how her youthful fire had delivered her to dangerous dead ends. "Look at me," she'd told Art. "I can go anywhere in the world and never be mistaken for anything but exactly what I am, NAF, Negro American Female. All I have to do is open my mouth and say a word or two. A person, a language with origins nowhere, no history. Certainly nowhere and no history the world will admit to."

She had looked in Arturo's eyes as they opened up and fell through the back of his head like someone had kicked through the scrub and knocked the lids off of two long-abandoned wells in a ghost town. This had begun to seem like a weekly ritual. Aggravation building, she had thought, "He better not cry because I'm not sure if I'll cover his wide, ever-earnest face with kisses or bust him in his no-irony-having mouth." His tone as cold and clear— and, Ndiya thought, poisonous—as the abandoned water in his welled up eyes, Art had said simply, "You're lucky." And with her response, what had already become a kind of code-phrase for her life knowing Art began to feel like some kind of secret name or destiny; "Maybe I am."

■

As she traveled toward date number two on the bus up Michigan Avenue, still trying to admit to herself that she'd decided to go to *That* Maurice's birthday party at all, she looked down to her left and into the sun. Where once lay strewn and tangled abandoned railroad tracks, she saw new, sapling-studded rows of townhouses and signs: 2 Bdrms of Brilliant Light Starting from the Low-400s. She thought to herself, "Botox and a nose job, and what the fuck does *low*-400s mean?" In the end, she couldn't file the altered landscape under anything resembling "change" in her thoughts. She knew ripples would pour out of the money changing between the same hands and shift the gravity of things. Maybe that *is* change?

Everyone else would be forced to react. At the same time, she wasn't inspired by the, in her ears, delusional howling about gentrification either. "Who the hell got to keep their neighborhoods?" she thought, with a force that made her look around to see if she'd actually said it out loud. If she *had* said it out loud, no one on the bus cared. She hadn't invested in either position. She'd opted out or tried to. So she figured her thoughts didn't really count and that's exactly the way she'd wanted it. For a minute, she even thought about giving brothers like Maurice Thomas a break. Maybe she would. She thought, "Who knows, maybe this party would be OK."

Maybe it was all the maybes. She thought of Arturo again. She'd gone home with him and she'd seen the gentrification wars up close and impersonal in New York City in the summer of 1991. Art had told her about growing up in Alphabet City and it had sounded like Mister Rogers. Of course, it wasn't that way at all but you couldn't tell him that. She remembered the banners and fliers from that summer: Save Tompkins Square Park. The first time she saw one of the placards, she'd asked Arturo, "Where *is* Tompkins Square Park?" He pointed across Avenue

A into a tangle of weeds and bent iron fencing behind which she'd seen all manner of makeshift dwellings and the rhythms of the homeless men and the thin-boned, addicted white girls who, from what she could tell, lived in there. "Save that? Too late, baby," she'd said. Art shook his head: "They just want to clean up the place, Ndiya, are you mad at that?" And she: "Yeah, and clean *you* right up and out of here along with it." But she didn't mean what he thought she meant. As always with Art, she meant, "Maybe I am." She'd walked through the park with him several times already. She'd certainly never had the impression that it was a place to be saved.

She'd recognized the people living in that park. Mostly they were dangers to themselves. Most of the men were vets and other fugitives cured when Reagan cut the funding and "liberated" them from the VA or whatever other kind of care they'd been getting. The girls and their paramours were all, she suspected, from Milwaukee and they couldn't seem to tell if they were being saved by dope or punished by life in New York. "Saved or punished," she thought, "it beat Milwaukee." By Milwaukee, Ndiya didn't mean the town itself. She'd never been there, after all. She thought of it, instead, as the paradigm town of *Happy Days* white amnesia and numbness that silently, somehow, seemed to work like quarantine for the however many hundred thousand black people who lived there. That could be any number of American cities. In Milwaukee, as in Chicago, as elsewhere, it all happened under the banner of the stolen American Indian name and that clinched the cynical deal and made most of what she saw burn down her arms from her young and half–numb struck flame-thrower of a brain.

Riding the bus to Maurice's party, she could see that she and Art both had had it *all* wrong back then. The placards and petitions and protests weren't meant to save or clean up the park. They were meant to prevent the police from occupying it in *order* to clean it up. The white girls she saw who'd left Milwaukee to grow mats on their heads and convince themselves that "life" meant forgetting to change your T-shirt, they didn't want the park cleaned up. They wanted it preserved so that the twisted thicket could remain just like it was. All this was far beyond Ndiya at the time. In retrospect, she was happy to have misjudged it like she did. In a way, by then, her own private pain and the numbness she guarded it with had made her conservative. If it hadn't, she might have really hurt somebody. Likely, she'd have hurt Art, even worse than she did. Art who ordered and gathered his own thoughts by disagreeing—albeit always in the most agreeable terms—with whatever Ndiya said. Art said he wanted a "good life for himself." Somehow this meant he'd convert all memory and things he saw in the present into models of such a good life to be replicated.

Outside Tompkins Square Park and down the block were huge, would-be empty lots full of fragments from broken bricks and pieces of broken window frames. Arturo explained that the buildings had been abandoned and then demolished and the bricks had been mined for use in suburban housefronts all over the country. Not always in that order, either. Often bricks were mined while the buildings stood. He said white men used to come to the neighborhood and offer a dollar for every hundred bricks the kids could load on their pickup trucks and flatbeds. A penny a brick. Arturo and his friends had worked many summer nights until dawn loading down those trucks with bootlegged bricks. The buildings leaned, floors bowed, the walls in the hallways curved. Slats under the busted plaster protruded like ribs of an animal left for vultures on some Sunday afternoon wildlife show. In the basements, the whole structures of shifting, diminishing weight made low moans and sharp coughs. Art said he knew two boys and their sister who were killed when a floor and ceiling collapsed after too many bricks were mined from weight-bearing walls in the basement. At dawn, after those nights, their hands were hot and raw, forearms scraped from carrying bricks stacked in each arm. When the light came up, the trucks drove away up First Avenue loaded down so that the front wheels looked like they barely met the pavement.

Ndiya was always amazed that Art could relate stories such as these and retain a sense of optimistic detachment, as if the moral of all of these stories was that everything happened for the best. At school she'd admired this in him, and she had thought it was a radical kind of focus; at home it seemed much more like a determined blindness.

In these lots cleared by Arturo and them, Ndiya saw where hundreds of people had built shelters. Families lived there. She could see the World Trade Center in the background, and in the foreground lived a shantytown. There was another down the block and there was another around the corner from there. She identified with these people somehow. She'd prayed for the buildings she grew up in to be vacated and destroyed. On a bad day she just prayed for them to be destroyed. She felt something familiar in the dissembled misery she witnessed in these lots. She saw kids playing much like she'd played, getting pain and fun and joy and bitterness and togetherness and betrayal all tangled up with each other in their bodies until, she thought, no one could get them untangled. Anyone who suggested that they could be untangled was an enemy. They'd grow up like she had, until she hadn't. They'd be afraid of all the people they loved until they didn't know if they were in love with fear or afraid of love itself.

Remembering all of this on the bus to Maurice's party made her feel it all again. Most powerful of all those feelings was the truly strange rain of realization that happened when she began to learn that this inseparable tangle wasn't true for everyone. Or that's what they said.

Some people she saw on her walks through Art's neighborhood were addicted already. She recognized them because they were the only ones who walked like they knew where they were going in the morning. Others soon would be. One or two of those kids in the shanties would move though it all just like she had and come out without any visible scars. They'd bear their experience, mostly a series of things that should have but didn't happen to them, like an unintelligible alphabet written in kerosene on their skin. Their lives would swerve between lighted matches that would touch off sketches of flame on their skin and furnaces would roar in chests, fire in their veins. Then, if they were lucky, they'd scramble around lighted matches and call it life. All her life, Ndiya had found she could recognize these people no matter where she saw them. She'd never been able to make up her mind what, in fact, distinguished them from the crowd. She could feel these people recognize her as well. Their eyes would catch and fall open. There'd be a quick nod and then they'd turn and be off.

That's what she had thought in her twenties. None of it was true. And most of her sudden flashes of anger were really about the numb wall she'd put between herself and her actual past. In a way that was even less memorable to her than it was visible to other people, she wasn't one of the spared, to whom things hadn't happened that the odds said should have happened. In fact, as if in a twisted symmetry, things that should never have happened to anyone had happened to her. In just that way, by changes almost as simple as grammar in a sentence, she'd invented a story to stand beside her. This twin person could negate what had happened to her in that abandoned elevator when she was twelve.

All of this, guarded by a sentry, sat behind a wall no one, certainly *not* Arturo Almeida, was going to get behind. In a way that was standing right next to her before she'd seen it approach, and in a way her sentry was incapable of dealing with at all, Shame's reactions to things had awoken something, put something in motion. From the start, part of knowing Shame took place behind this wall in her life story, took place in a part of her life that wasn't in the story. She could feel he was trouble. Nonetheless, she went along with the string of accidental inevitables that happened after they'd met. She didn't know why. With Shame, in exactly that unforeseen way she'd armed herself against, she felt alive close up; trouble, for once, felt like distant thunder.

In New York that summer with Art, some of the adults she saw headed and raised families in these thrown-to-gether shanties often comprised of materials stolen from construction sites, two-by-fours and sheets of blue plastic, with portions of abandoned cars and delivery vans. She couldn't tell how many families lived in a sky-blue US Air Force school bus that had been turned on its side in one of the lots. She'd pass by in the morning as the addicts stalked their singular purposes and the employed adults in the shanties tried to wipe wrinkles from their loose pants and tight jackets. Some stood in line to brush their teeth at the steady trickle from a long-spent fire hydrant near the corner. She appreciated their struggle for dignity, and their misery echoed the wordless and violent melody of her worldview in a way that made her sweat feel like it ran down someone else's skin.

She remembered the protests and the way the NYPD surrounded the park. She remembered no one seemed to care about the families in the shanties all around or the other families, like Arturo's, who lived in the projects that loomed over Alphabet City from Avenue D. It was all about that disaster of a park. She didn't ever see any of the people from the projects or the shanties—too busy dodging matches—at the protests about the park. The protesters were the only ones she *didn't* recognize. But, she thought, she knew them all. For all she knew, every one of them had individually passed her in the crowded but utterly empty hallways and pathways of the college she'd attended. Instead of looking at her, they all intently studied the fucking wall or became instantly obsessed by trees in the distance. The scary thing she didn't learn at college, as she'd find out later, to her horror, was that they basically treated each other and most of all themselves the same way.

And she suspected the difference between the police and the protesters was a matter of competing dialects in the same language. For the people in the shanties and for Art's mama, and for his little sister, the police and the protests, finally, meant the same thing. The police were getting paid to do what they got paid to do. They looked the part. Most of the protesters looked like, and even more, *sounded* like, the whitecaps Ndiya had abstracted into "weather blue" in order to survive college. Most of them had the same ratty T-shirts and jeans on and hadn't rubbed quite enough grime over their suburban accents to cover up their SAT scores. She used to taunt Art mercilessly about this. He'd take her to some newly opened restaurant full of whitecaps and she'd ask him, "How does it feel to be the grime these people rub on their tongues?" His eyes would do the abandoned-well thing and she'd scrape her lip with her teeth.

Neither one of them knew the half of it then. They didn't know that these hopelessly clean people under their precisely wrinkled clothes were protesting desperately to *save* the catastrophe in the park. The park wasn't the point, much less the people. It was the catastrophe that mat-tered. It was the catastrophe they thought could bleed for them and help them walk on the water of their wants to the other shore of what they needed. Transcendent ca-tastrophe, the dark matter, as ever, of self-reliance. When flashes of all this dawned upon her, Ndiya felt possessed by a violence at once very far off and as near to her as the metal taste of anger in her mouth; Art would shake his head at the ground: "You're selling them short, Ndiya." And she: "Yeah?" Her top lip scraped twice on her teeth and then back in the cool air. "Maybe I am."

■

Ndiya paused in the street. She also paused recounting date number two with Shame so she could focus on the end of the "maybe I am" days knowing Arturo. Split be-tween the scene in the street and her memory, she felt something, maybe sundown, warming her back. Or maybe it was the memory-sun through the window on the bus up to Maurice's party? It hadn't come to her in years, and then, just then, there it was.

One wrong afternoon Arturo had to physically pre-vent her from attacking a staccato-syllabled, open-faced young white woman on the street. Looking at it now, Ndiya thinks the woman had done her best to imperson-ate the appearance of the addicted girls she'd seen in the park. Somehow she had stepped out of nowhere, directly in front of Ndiya's next stride. She pushed a squatter's rights petition into Ndiya's face. Maybe it had nothing to do with the park, the catastrophe, or the vacant lots, maybe it was just how the woman ended what she said with her tone of voice pointed up in the air like one person riding a seesaw? Maybe the provocation was simply the collision between the dingy clothes, the militant white-straightness of the girl's teeth and the fashionable angularity of her eyeglasses? Or maybe it was that voice she'd just bought from the Gap? It didn't matter.

The slashing phrases that erupted from Ndiya's mouth echoed in her memory. The scratch-the-surface-and-look-what-you-get look on the struck-open young woman's suddenly old and closed face scared Ndiya all over again for the fresh waves of hatred it inspired when it came to mind. Ndiya prided herself and depended upon her ability to see these people long before they saw her. She'd missed this one and so Ndiya heard herself saying, "You better get your motherfucking hand out my chest, bit—"

Art grabbed her from behind, pulled her back toward the corner hissing, "Hey, hey, hey now, hey now," into her ear through the siren pulsing in her head. On the bus, Ndiya absently bit through the skin on her knuckle thinking about it.

When they got to the apartment Ndiya went straight to the bathroom and double-locked the door. She took Art's mother's hidden cigarettes out from behind the radiator and smoked one and then another, blowing smoke out the small window that stayed open over the chipped tile in the shower stall. Art, bless him, somehow knew better than to bother her with his sapper's kit of mitigating questions and accommodating disagreements.

She sat, frozen, timing her pulse against the duet of drips from the shower and sink. Her eyes followed the joints in the wall between the cinder blocks north, south, east, and west. That summer, Art's little sister, Sonja, had created a mural of lower Manhattan using the tile joints on the bathroom wall as the major streets; she'd begun to color in and label storefronts, vacant lots, schools, and churches. All her friends' apartments were labeled. Sonja had listed the names of the people in them, who worked, and who did what. Ndiya traced lines between these buildings and a key to the map comprised of hearts and stars and frowning faces. A week ago Sonja had proudly told Ndiya that young Latino brothers from Washington, DC, called it a Youth Map and they paid her a hundred dollars per week to do it. Several of her friends were doing their own Youth Maps as well. At the end of the summer, they'd receive a final payment after submitting their finished maps and a written report describing what they'd learned making them.

"Recon," Ndiya thought. The little girl was a double-agent and she didn't even know it. Who would pay how much for the information these kids come up with? What *would* it be used to do? Despite all that, the love in Sonja's mural had calmed Ndiya before. This time, as the pieces fell together, it felt like the eye, the camel, the needle, *and* the last straw. Then her face folded into itself and splintered when she smashed her hand into the mirror as she spit out, "Squatter's rights? It doesn't age well, you know." Then her body broke into convulsive sobs and a sound filled the room that had no room in it for anyone's maybes.

She pictured the woman with the petition, "I'd pay to see *her* petition for her own family's rights to squat in an abandoned building while kids mine the walls for bricks. Her family probably lives in a house, in Connecticut no doubt, made of the damned bricks themselves. Of course they do, it's perfect. I wonder why she won't squat in *that* house?"

An hour later, she came out of the bathroom feeling clean and elegant as brushed steel and sharp and mean as the ivory-handled knife her father had used to cut her slices from his apple. He told her it was a gift from *his* father. At once, in a clear sweat, Ndiya understood that gift. "Maybe I am" was slashed and lay dead on the tiny, white, nicotine-tinted octagonal tiles of Art's mama's bathroom floor. He knew better. But Art asked anyway. And she: "It was *about*, Arturo, what kind of people could imagine what other kind of people, families, kids, Art, kids, deserve squatter's rights." Then she lost it and screamed, "And it's *about* having clue-the-fucking-first and, so, not jumping up in my face with no white-ass-uptilted-seesaw voice, period. Ever!" Even then she could feel that this was about much more than that but she defended herself by blaming that feeling on Art.

With her voice echoing in his screamed-at eyes, Art said that she didn't understand, and she thought to herself, "You're damned straight I don't. No maybe about it." Art held her hand but she could see him try and fail to well his eyes. She asked him, "What if they're people, *real* people?" In that moment of intense and reductive focus, she told herself that she could see Art had no idea what she was talking about. And she could see more clearly than ever that he was determined not to know. At that time, she couldn't admit what all she, too, was determined not to know. As for Art, if he'd known that much, she'd have respected that. He didn't and she could see then that he wouldn't. Blind to herself, she could see that Art was determined to be a certain kind of American, the kind that wants to be an American. Ndiya was equally determined to be another kind of American, the kind determined not to be Arturo's kind of American. As soon as she realized this, of course, she'd need to find another Arturo somewhere, or she'd need to be alone.

She'd heard about medical training and how doctors needed to insulate themselves against all the kinds of caring and feeling that sent them beyond their clinical abilities. This enabled them to perform the technical features of their work. From college English, Ndiya remembered Hemingway's doctor saying of the American Indian woman, "Her screams aren't important. I don't hear them because they're not important." She'd been afraid to ask the professor about it in front of all those whitecaps in the class. But she remembered wondering if the doctor would have said that if the woman was white? What if she was *his* daughter? Suddenly she saw the answer: *especially* then. The answer was yes. If it wasn't, that staccato white girl down on Avenue A could have squatted at home in Milwaukee, CT or wherever-the-fuck.

The police, the protests were all part of the same stage. No one had a home here. That was the way it was supposed to be. She was mad at Art for accepting that. She was mad at him, mostly, because she silently insisted upon an essential homelessness. At bottom, she was mad because she was lying to herself. But all of that was far, far ahead; in a way, all of it led her to where she was.

On her walk to Shame's apartment, buried in her assessment of date number two, she saw for the first time how she and Art were in denial about almost everything. And how they'd covered up those denials by blaming pieces of each other they'd surgically isolated in order to focus upon. Almost none of it was conscious, she thought. In that moment, she decided, it wasn't surgical either. Surgery was conscious; this had been a kind of unconsciously agreed-upon mutual mutilation.

That summer afternoon in 1991, Art, bless his blessèd heart, tried to hold her bandaged hand and she felt all of it getting away from her as the waves of panic turned into motes of flame that strung into lines. The lights lighted up beautiful rounded lines in faces she'd known and faces she knew that she never got to know, faces that never got to know. And she saw the world turn over and all the mirrors began to glow and the heat raged from behind the smoke-blackened glass that hissed when you put your ear near it and, if touched, would have made your hand wish it didn't have fingers.

She remembered seeing Art's mouth moving but she couldn't recall, probably never heard, a word he said. She smelted this anger into a kind of pain. Then she made that pain into the platform of her reality; the pain was safe, the violence in her remained distant. This worked as long as she could see threats in the distance as they approached.

It was how she survived her twenties. She made herself impossible. This impossibility of self made her imperme-able to surprise.

She left Arturo's house the next morning at 6:00 AM with her mother's voice singing in her ear: *I'm going to lay my head on that lonesome railroad iron. Let the 2:19 train ease my troubled mind.* She was surprised to find Manhattan still asleep and the streets to the Port Authority empty as she made her way along the long blocks west. "Somewhere, anywhere, everywhere else," she'd said to herself at the time.

"What the hell does all this have to do with date number two?" she thought. Still not really wanting to know, Ndiya asked herself this as she replaced the layers of time and came back from Manhattan through the bus ride through post-gentrified Chicago and returned to her soaked skirt and cool legs in the Sixty-Third Street of the twilight present. Then, before a beat, back to the uptown bus of her memory.

■

The danger signs had been clear on her way to Maurice's party. The trip back to 1991 had made it worse. But when the mirror started to smoke, Ndiya knew how to stand with her back to the wind. She knew how to survive her-self. She'd gotten good at it. "Hell is where the heart is," she told herself. And she calmly closed her heart's eyes. She pictured the map and told herself where all this had happened and that, yes, it had happened to someone—but it hadn't happened to her, not to *this* her. She pictured a calendar, slowly turned the pages, and confirmed that it wasn't happening now.

She kept it together. The goal was to recall things without experiencing them. She couldn't always do that. But it helped to know the goal. She kept her eyes closed but eased up on the pressure so the tears stayed where they were. She kept her full eyes closed. The way she saw it, things in Chicago and elsewhere in the United States would continue to slosh about, unanchored, and in the end everyone needed it to happen and in the end no one really had any idea what it could mean to them. "Other than the pain," she thought. "We're all squatters," she allowed. "Maybe, finally, *that's* what 'Maybe I Am' was so enraged about. Let's just admit it." It was gentrification, after all, that had brought down The Grave and brought her back to Chicago. "Gentrification had torn down *all* those projects, it sure as shit wasn't no squatter's rights," she thought. Gentrification, greed, and a good dose of pure sha—that name again.

She opened her eyes and let the sun pour into her pupils from beneath a gray bank of stratus clouds somewhere out west over Cicero. When her eyes adjusted and her sight returned, she saw a beautiful, perfect, empty beach. The copper, gold, and blue on her eyelids reflected in the window. The sight replaced the city and her pointless and personal analysis of the politics of gentrification. She knew she couldn't help it; and more importantly she'd learned that the intensity of her reaction to things didn't often match up well with other people's views and ambitions. She called that fact "privacy." So, she went to the beach. The private beach. Her eyelids.

The high and low dust of the metallic colors on her eyelids had perfectly set themselves off against each other. Even though she had added it last and wished she put it on first but didn't have time to start over, she saw that the clear-sky-meets-cold-lake of the blue had somehow found its place beneath the bronze and copper dust; the result was the perfect set of illusions. Water and metal, sky and dust, matte and gloss, surface and depth, sunrise and sunset moved over and under and around each other on each eye as she winked at herself—right eye, left eye. Then she blew a kiss at the perfect pain-beach of a face in the window.

"Pleasure to meet you, my name is Ndiya Grayson," she whispered. "Happy birthday, Maurice." She smiled, "Pain-beach, gosh, haven't been *there* in forever." Maybe it had been since Phoenix? "Put the pain in the water and stand on the beach. Wade in when you want. Small victories," she'd thought. "A little run of those and some luck, I might survive this dinner with the SnapB/l/acklist folks. I might even have some *fun*. Is that a crime?" She knew she'd asked herself this out loud and she didn't care, even though somewhere she knew perfectly well that she thought it *was*.a crime.

As she made her way step by quietly sloshing step east down Sixty-Third Street, on the third and—according to his directions—final block before arriving at Shame's place, Ndiya approached an alleyway that led between the backs of the buildings facing Eberhart to the west and Rhodes Avenue to the east. Most old-time blocks in Chicago had one. She knew what was down there. Broken pavement pulled up by neighborhood plows, chain-link fences leaning one way and their gates leaning the other, maybe stray dogs, an old garage or parking for apartments, maybe a bike thrown down in the middle, trash cans and, starting right about now, she thought, the rats that came with them. She started not to even look. She did. Then she looked again.

Just off the sidewalk, there was a row of black iron bollards with a thick silver chain hanging between them. From the middle of the chain hung an upside-down orange triangle and centered within it was a black exclamation point outlined in day-glow yellow. Part of the alley was grass. Not grass. It was a manicured lawn with ivy at the edges climbing up the walls on either side. Twenty feet from the sidewalk, a picnic table sat crossways in the middle of what should have been an alley. But this wasn't an alley.

Two old men sat on the near bench with their backs to her. Beyond them she could see a basketball court with one hoop. Strings of white-and-blue holiday lights lighted the court area from around the edges and beyond that the far side was a mirror of the nearside complete with two old men facing her from the distant picnic table and Sixty-Fourth Street to the south behind them. Was it a mirror? She looked for her figure on the opposite street but couldn't decide if she could see her reflection or not. She'd never seen anything like it. She'd seen abandoned lots turned into rock gardens and even broken up into plots for neighbors to grow their greens, turnips, tomatoes and peppers in. But a beautiful grass alley, she thought as she kept walking, and a basketball court for old folks? What had Shame done, lied about his name *and* his age and taken up in subsidized housing for the aged? She stopped walking. Those hadn't been old people on the court. Then she did something she never did in unfamiliar territory of any kind. She took a step backward, stopped, and stared directly at what she was looking at. They were *young* people on the court. Or maybe they weren't all young but they weren't old. She saw the boy with the jean jacket and his two associates from down the block sitting against the wall in the grass. She wondered why she'd thought it was for old folks when someone took a shot and the others turned to watch the ball in the air.

It struck her like it had when she'd gone to Comiskey Park and sat in the bleachers. You saw the pitcher throw, the batter swing, the ball react. But you didn't hear the crack of the bat for a half a beat or so. And you could hear each word the announcer said several times. She'd gone first with a group of spelling champions from Chicago elementary schools. They were paraded out onto the field while the crowd had recognized "these Chicago youngsters for their hard work and the excellence they'd achieved in spelling." She could still hear the phrases circle through the stadium like they were surrounded by twelve announcers. She'd never heard the word "youngster." It sounded to her like some kind of furry pet that ran on a wheel in a glass tank. She looked around to make sure the voice was talking about them. And she didn't know anything about baseball but she immediately loved the open arena in the night air. The solidified glow of the false daylight fell dim and bright at the same time. The smooth diamond, the precise line between the brown dust and the green grass. And, most of all, she loved the overlapping and askew play of sight and sound laid out in space so she could examine it. This seemed like the whole point of the game to her.

Inning—another new word—after inning she sat there knowing that the laws were the laws. Sight and sound must behave in this strange way all the time. She knew about thunder and lightning and one-Mississippi, of course. But still she wondered why she'd never been in an arena where you could watch it happen like this in so many ways at once. Who'd hidden this from her? This was what "education" was to mean to her always. There was a rush of discovery followed by an immediate, accompanying, cutting sensation that it had been hidden from her on purpose. The thing whirred in her, a tornado of elation from the discovery and rage at the withholding. Later, she'd wondered if this belly-twisting sensation happened to all the kids she knew. If it had, they'd certainly kept it a secret from each other. She couldn't remember learning how to do it, but she'd converted the hot twists in her belly into a kind of tutor, a partner with whom she rehearsed all the hidden, secret things she learned. Even when Ndiya found that facts in history or certain characters in books were common knowledge to many people, she retained the feeling that, in fact, she and her twisting partner were acquainted with these things in ways only they could understand. "Hide it from me, from us, we'll find it and make it into something only we can recognize," she declared. Staring at the dim-bright distance while the sounds and sights dove and arced, she thought, "If everyone had their own night and night was a fruit and you could split it open when it was ripe," this was exactly what the inside of her ripe night would be like.

The basketball game down the designer alley and Comiskey Park and the tornado effect she'd learned to quell enough to hide from everyone but herself roamed through her again. She couldn't really hear anything from the scene down the alley. She tried to summon up her almanac of ways to "here" and "there" herself and found no familiar cues. The ball didn't seem to make noise when it bounced. She assumed it bounced but she hadn't seen anyone bounce the ball. The shot was the first action she'd focused on. The ball hung there and she got the roller coaster–belly feeling she had waiting for the sound of the hit to catch up to her vision of the swing. But unlike the split-open instant inside her ripe-fruit night at Comiskey Park, this thing went on and on and on and on. The ball was like a singer holding an impossibly long note. It hung in the air like a question no one could answer. From the career described by the ball and the rate of its diminishing speed, she sensed the shot would probably make it to the apex and go down the other side. Then again, it might not.

Three figures sat against the wall. They all focused on one of their outstretched arms. Ndiya couldn't tell whose arm it was that warranted such scrutiny or why. She looked back and the ball was still slowing down, traveling upward. From the first moments of their first meeting, she'd had this sense that things involving Shame Luther took a long, long time to happen and then they seemed to *have* happened while they never had actually been happening. Still, this was another level. The other people on the court walked around each other, placed their hands on the back of the person in front of them; those in front seemed to hold their arms out to their sides like wings as they backed up into the ones behind. They all moved in a two-step, four-beat rhythm.

The players didn't move nearly as slowly as the ball suspended in the air. Suddenly, one man broke the spell and moved more quickly than the rest. He took off his hat, dropped it on the ground, stomped his foot firmly on top of it and walked off the court to talk to the three sitting against the wall. He gestured easily and slapped the hand of the young man with the beard and the deep-set eyes she'd seen on the street. She thought, "They all move like Sunday morning." Easy like her uncle Lucky's voice sounded when he drove her around in his loping ninety-eight, like she remembered watching the trees move from the front porch down in Greenville on a thick summer night full of her great-uncle Clem's music and the electrified skeletal glow from thunderstorms in the distance. The South. Everyone in the alley laughed at something the woman sitting on the ground said and the basketball player bowed to her and ceremoniously removed the hat he didn't have on down to his waist and back to his head as he straightened up.

"Jesus," Ndiya thought, "they're *all* high? All of them? Always were? Lucky, Clem, those splayed-out pecan trees too? Southern thunder is high? Even the ball's high?" Normally, stopping to look at anything in an unfamiliar neighborhood like this was out of the question. The trick was to stare twenty miles off and always, always, look like you had somewhere to go and not quite enough time to get there. At the same time, you never made a rushed or sudden move. Ndiya realized she'd just broken all the rules at once. She was soaking wet up to her knees, in high heels, starstruck still and staring, blind to everything else, at the slow-motion scene down the alley, a scene no one else on the block seemed to think noteworthy at all. "Here I am," she thought, "an easy mark, an open wound."

The player went back to the game. He slowed down as he returned to the court, making exaggerated motions with his arms and hips so that it looked like he was wading out into deepening water when he crossed under the lights at the court's perimeter line. He waded back to his hat and the player dancing in place behind it. He picked up the hat, put it on, and resumed his movements with what, just then, looked like his dance partner in the area just to the right of the hoop.

As she watched the other players, Ndiya wished she'd

paid closer attention to basketball once or twice so she could judge what was going on here. They clapped their soundless hands, rubbed them together and held them out, palms up, at arm's length so that they looked, from the waist up at least, like they were about to meditate. One knelt down low as if to pray, then untied and retied both his shoestrings. One swayed back and forth, holding on to the pole beneath the hoop. Ndiya thought she saw one kiss the neck of the player in front of him. Another, off to the far left by himself, stood in place watching the ball while his right hand worked its way into his back jeans pocket. He removed a pack of cigarettes while his left hand produced a lighter. The decidedly unathletic gesture made her notice that none of them had on gym clothes of any kind, though a few at least wore sneakers. Then she checked quick to make sure the gym shoes weren't all the same like the black Nikes of those crazy Comet Hale-Bopp folks who'd followed that comet up out of here a few years ago. Nope.

The smoking player held both arms extended straight out to either side. His lighted lighter in one hand, glowing cigarette pointed upward and pivoting to follow the movement of the ball in the other. Obscured by her angle of view, Ndiya saw the flame and the glow from the tip of his cigarette while the rapt, stationary player traced the flight of the shot as it moved beyond the apex and began to pick up speed. It looked as if something impeding the ball's progress had been removed from in front and placed behind to push it on its way toward the rim of the hoop which, Nydia now noticed, had a long net of tinsel stars and sequins hanging down from it. She'd seen basketball courts. She'd never seen one with the net hanging down almost halfway to the ground. This hoop looked more like one of those West African crowns worn by kings to obscure their human faces while they performed supposedly divine duties.

Most of the courts she remembered in Chicago either had chain nets or no nets at all. Her brothers had always had their *own* nets that they took with them and brought home when they were done. Just then it dawned on her that the net-thing had something to do with the question of touch. Her brothers had always discussed "touch" like it was some mystical attribute possessed only by gurus. She didn't know what that was about, but she knew her brothers sometimes had to fight in order to leave the park and take their nets with them. For a few summers, they and their friends had talked about it ceaselessly, as if it was an issue they should submit to the UN. Finally, she asked them what they needed nets for anyway and they all turned to her at once and froze. Six boys with exactly the same look on their faces, and no one moved and no one said anything. She turned and walked away, at which point the cursing and revenge plotting resumed.

■

Ndiya stood there revising what she knew about the physics of basketball and thinking how none of this strangeness boded well for her evening. One of the old men on the picnic table turned around and yelled, apparently at her,

—Miss, would you mind and please tell Mrs. Clara to tell Melvin that a shot's about to go in?

Exactly then the other old man interjected,

—No it's not!

He didn't take his eyes off the nearly stationary ball. The first man turned to him:

—Yes it is!

Then he turned back to her:

—Would you mind and see does the boy want to come and watch?

And she did. She minded. It seemed like it'd been two lifetimes since she'd minded someone. She minded him back up the block feeling like she was moving on a sidewalk that was itself moving almost fast enough to get back to where she came from if she kept on minding. She hadn't even thought about which way to go or to make sure she knew who Mrs. Clara and Melvin were. She was just minding.

When she reached the old woman and the tsunami boy, they were packing up the yarn and needles and boats. Ndiya mustered,

—Ma'am, Mrs. Clara, ma'am, the gentleman down the, er, down the alley, I mean in the park?, a gentleman down there would like to know does little Melvin here want to come and see the, ah, the shot go in, or, or not?

Mrs. Clara looked up at Ndiya as if they'd known each other for life:

—You hear that, Melvin? Now go on. This nice young lady, what's your name honey?

—Ndiya, my name's Ndiya, ma'am.

—Yes, yes, I see. Well, Melvin, you go on with Miss

Kneed-in-the . . . you just go on and see does the shot make it in the net tonight or doesn't it, OK?

Mrs. Clara handed Ndiya a small backpack. Melvin moved his goggles up to stick above his eyebrows, this pushed down his brow and seemed to make his whole face frown.

–OK, Nana.

Then he raised up his hand and, taking Ndiya's:

–Let's go!

Ndiya turned, holding little Melvin's hand. She heard Mrs. Clara charge,

–You mind now, Melvin, you hear?

And so, Melvin minding Mrs. Clara to mind Ndiya minding an old man on a picnic table, the both of them sloshed and squashed back to the opening of the alley and up to where the two old men sat concentrating on the shot.

–You all just made it, won't be a minute—

At which point the other old man said,

–Bet it will!

And the first continued as if he hadn't been interrupted,

–before Nesta out there makes his shot and Lee Williams, right here, loses another quarter to yours truly, Lucious Christopher.

Lucious Christopher extended his hand and Ndiya, feeling like she was still minding, introduced herself,

–My name's Ndiya. Ndiya Grayson.

–Grayson . . . Grayson. Lee Williams, you ever known any Graysons?

Lee Williams, eyes drilling the floating ball, answered,

–Used to know some Graysons from visiting my cousins down in Greenville, but that's a long time ago.

–Don't mind an old man's lack of manners.

Lucious Christopher said, gesturing to the bench in front of them,

–Young lady, have a seat.

And, then, a light tap on her shoulder.

–Ah, beg your pardon there, er, you don't mind me saying, but you a little *old* for swimming on the block there, Miss Grayson. You should go on down to the beach.

Lucious Christopher and Lee Williams looked at each other with the all-knowing, we-best-watch-this-one look on their faces. Ndiya's face heated up as she ignored them. She had a spinning-dizzy feeling like she was a ball of string that was being very quickly unspooled.

And then Lee Williams:

–Grayson! Yes, Lonnie and Lucky, old Clem and them—but that's all I can get back, it's been a long time.

Lucious Christopher:

–Is that right? I knew a Lonnie and a few Luckys, can't recollect they last names, but now you mention it, years back, didn't one of them Grayson ni—well, *brothers*—take up with a fine young woman who got herself one of them new apartments off in The Grave? Then, remember there was that crazy thing with—

Lee Williams cut him short:

–Don't know. Like I said, they was Greenville ni—I mean, *brothers*—when I knew them. Now, hush while I sight-guide Nesta's brick on toward the hoop in such a way that it don't do a "Chocolate Thunder" on Junior's backboard.

Ndiya sat, stunned, thinking, this is *not* happening. Melvin immediately climbed into her lap to wait for the shot to go in or not. While helping Melvin change out of his boots, she welcomed her thought: "This might not be happening, but it's certainly going to impede the dreaded conclusion of my evaluation of date number two."

Wrong again. As they watched the ball gain speed on its way down the slope toward the front of the rim, Ndiya heard the faint sound of a piano from above the court. The music sounded like it curled around itself in circles of differing speeds and radiuses. In wide, slow sweeps cut by faster, tighter arcs, the first note of each phrase was loud and clearly audible. The notes that followed faded until they almost weren't there at all when a new phrase began somewhere else, loud at first and fading as if it curved away. It sounded like the piano rode the curve out of ear-shot. Then, there it was, come around again. It sounded to her like wheels inside wheels.

From time to time, the phrase would start with a note sung by someone and once in a while a few notes would be sung inside the phrases. She'd just noticed it, but Ndiya guessed that the music must have been there all the time because, now that she did hear it, the players' movements seemed to follow the phrases. They didn't all follow each phrase, though, nor did they move for the complete audible length of the brief, arc-like tunes. Nonetheless, now that she'd noticed it, the music provided a cadence that held the scene together. Up close, it all seemed less like the baseball diamond inside ripe nighttime and more like she was watching through the thick glass of an aquarium. Movements behind that aquarium glass had always made Ndiya slightly nauseous so she closed her eyes to steady herself. This was a very bad idea.

Upon closing her eyes, Ndiya felt like she'd been lowered headfirst into the music coming from a window above the alley. Instantly, the whole of date number two flashed through her body and behind her eyes as if it had all happened in about twenty seconds. It didn't move like *her* memory; the fluid thing washed over her body in one piece like if you watch a wave pass overhead from beneath the surface of the water. She felt the pull of its weight draw over her and move through her at the same time. She saw herself standing immobilized at the Violet Hour window watching the SnapB/l/acklist folks toasting Maurice at a large table to the right of the bar. Maybe it was the way that window framed the scene? Or being home in Chicago? She didn't know. In that window she'd seen clearly for the first time the vast distance between herself and these youngerish, blackified, professionalized peers. The distance had always been there, she'd insisted and depended upon it. But she'd never opened her eyes and stared at it like this. "Hope it works," she whispered, either to them or to herself. She had been leaning toward the window. Her face was close enough to the glass that her breath clouded the surface. Suddenly a cement-like certainty seized her. There was no way she could get through that door. At least it seemed like they hadn't seen her, she thought. But she knew that she didn't care what they'd seen. She didn't know what to do.

A new note sounded a new phrase from above the alley. Ndiya saw herself turn away from Maurice's birthday party and enter the bar next door. She'd leave the bar after half of an Elton John song and two drinks. "Two Blue Labels, please, neat," she heard herself say.

She'd said it immediately upon reaching the bar, without knowing why or waiting for the barman to approach. She didn't realize that she'd repeated verbatim what Shame said seconds after the thing with Malik's house-arrest bracelet. So, we could say she called him up. In the space of about thirty seconds, she downed the brown contents of both tiny glasses, thinking the liquor was too soft to be considered liquid. Then she looked in disbelief at the bill, eighty dollars? Without a pause she placed five new twenty-dollar bills in the black leather folder and left. The price of "whatever the hell Blue Label was" echoed around. It contended with what little she'd assumed she'd known about Shame. International laborer in some local 269 or something? Joycelan Steel-something-something? What *was* that?

Then she thought, "And here I am soaking wet, sitting on this bench with a little boy in my lap and Shame's whole block's high? My whole life's high?"

Before she could turn toward the southbound bus stop in her memory, the music faded away and a new note punched through the air over the alley. The note brought the scene from date number two to her eyes like the whole thing was a movie on a screen in the alley playing for everyone to see. It wasn't really in her eyes, of course. It was worse—the physical scene was on the loose in her body:

Shame on his cycle pulling up to the opposite curb. He waves and takes off his helmet, staring at her. She sees herself nod. His U-turn through traffic. The ride. Helmet smell. Sun on scalp. The drinks in her arms and pools of heat in both heels. Song by a long-lost, one-hit group, Surface, in her head. "Happy." Shame's toe popping the bike into higher pitches around corners and the pop into a low growl when the road was straight. *Oh, you coming right over? Beautiful, baby.* Diagonal park. Worn boot heel. Kickstand down exactly onto a small square of wood nailed into the gutter.

Then stoop.

Inside, steps.

The sound of twilight joins the memory wave to the present. Shame's back on the piano stool. Drowning.

This music. The same music she's hearing now.

Phrases, broken circles. Splices. Zoom lens. Her fingers strum Shame's ribs beneath his extended arms while he plays. Four up, four down. A scar-notch in his skin, two fingers wide on left rib number three. Shame plays. The Surface song in her head, *Only you can make me. . . .* The voice in her head, just then, going under, Ndiya has left the building . . . far below the surface. The stool spins. He turns around but the music continues. Shame's hand Shame's hand on Shame's hand on her back. Up under her shirt. Her sudden panic that he'll touch the scars. That he'll stop. That he won't. That he'll ask. That he won't.

How he both does and doesn't. The music doesn't pause, moves from the past to the present and back. Notes fall and stick to her like an April blizzard blown through a fire escape. Her head turns toward the ceiling. The open Y of his thighs narrows against her legs. Her body overhead. The room in her mouth with a voice of its own.

She woke up on the floor. Midway to the bathroom, she paused on tiptoes and turned back to look. Shame laid out immobile on the rug like a crime scene. After she nearly stepped on it barefoot and a stack of books tumbled over, she slammed a thick hardback volume down on a huge, glossy, black spider. The spider hadn't tried to run. Ndiya had a moment's sense that it may have turned toward her just before the book smashed to the floor. She stood up and read the title of the weapon from above: *Milestones: The Music and Times of Miles Davis*. She left the thick tome there on the floor, covering the murder.

■

Ndiya forced her eyes open as the shot hit the net and bright rain sparkled out from the tinsel and sequins. Melvin raised both hands and said,

–Boo-ya!

Lucious Christopher:

–Lee Williams, the ever-if-only-from-time-to-time-sermon-iferous, I say that'll be legal tender the equivalent of one American quarter, or do I put it on your tab?

And Lee Williams stood up and stretched his back:

–Let it ride.

The players chanted "On and on and on and on." The ones against the wall raised up their hands and called out, "Like a—say what?!" And the chant repeated. They all began to move toward the other end of the alley. The three against the wall got up and joined them as they walked south toward Sixty-Fourth Street. Ndiya saw that it was the young woman's arm they had been staring at on the side of the court. As they walked away, the woman held it out in front of her and each player bowed and kissed the underside of her forearm. Ndiya noticed that the extended arm was multiple shades lighter than the woman's other arm.

At least that's what it looked like to her and, "At this point, why not?" she thought. Melvin looked up at Ndiya:

–Could you take me back to Nana, now?

Tingling in the music, Ndiya realized that most of her was still back on date number two. She shook her head to get Shame's fingers off her spine and replied,

–Ah, yes, let's go.

Though she had no idea where to go. She stood up to go somewhere. Lucious Christopher said,

–If you can't find Mrs. Clara, just take Melvin up to Shame's with you, Ndiya Grayson. We'll tell the old bird to come get him when we see her but she'll probably check there first herself.

Ndiya, minding, nodded in silent disbelief.

As she stood up with Melvin's hand in hers, she felt like she'd been off the bus and on that bench for hours if not days, maybe years. But she knew it hadn't been long because her shoes and skirt were still soaked. And it was still twilight. She knew very well that all of this was crazy: "Dripping wet, the whole damned neighborhood's high, Melvin, Mrs. Clara, Lucious Christopher, and Lee Williams who seemed to know where I am going, to say nothing of where I've been, better than I do?" She knew it was crazy somewhere, but it didn't feel crazy here which, she knew, too, made it all the crazier. Melvin looked up to her and said,

–I'll take you to Shame's house.

With a security wall of hard-won tricks and tactical anger beginning to fail and leaving a person she barely knew exposed, Ndiya walked with Melvin toward 6329. If nothing else, she knew it was within easy earshot, whatever that meant. At the very least, she thought, it meant Shame lived nearby.

■

When she turned toward whatever was nearby, Ndiya encountered a memory that had been following her around for days. On the morning one week after the house-arrest night, she sat alone at her sublet's drop-leaf kitchen table with a bowl of oatmeal. She replayed the triangle of Shame's reaction to Malik's busted bracelet. And before that, there they were in the street outside the party on the Fourth:

–Where do you want to meet?

–I don't know, neutral corners? OK?

–Fair enough; I know just the place.

She sat at the kitchen table, crossed her legs, and felt herself slip as she corralled the last pool of melted butter and brown sugar into her final lump of oatmeal.

She couldn't decide. So she paused with the bowl in her left hand, elbow on the table, the spoon held in her right. She uncrossed and reverse-crossed her legs and felt herself, again, as her legs moved over each other into the new position. As if she'd snuck around the back of her self and looked in the window through the split in the curtain, she thought, "Ndiya, my girl, that's different." Fear followed the pleasure. "That was a date all right," Ndiya thought, and looked at herself in the window. She nodded in the moment and planned to deny everything later.

She balanced Shame in her memory like the spoon in her right hand. Sugar melted into the tiny veins in each swollen grain of oatmeal. The final bite was light brown, sweet and perfectly hot. She thought, "Last bite in the bowl, perfectly hot *and* the first bite hadn't burned my mouth. Is that possible?" She glimpsed 9:15 on the clock as she figured the possibles or not of a perfectly hot, honey brown, *last* bite of oatmeal in the bowl. "Improbable, at best," she thought. Fifteen minutes to get dressed and get on the 9:30 bus to work. "But possible?" she weighed the one thing against the other.

Her eyes narrowed, she stared at her reflection in the window. Her bedroom door ajar, its reflection hovered like a dare above the street behind her reflected face. "Yes, OK, it's *possible*. It's also possible that I'll get the 10:30 bus and Ms. Yvette Simmons"—she'd just begun to think about Yvette-at-work's actual name—"can do like this," she said to her double. A thin blade of anger flashed. She knew it was her fault, not Yvette's. She decided not to care, took a deep breath and puffed her cheeks into her best Dizzy Gillespie in the window until a laugh burst out and fogged the glass. She turned and, in a bright rain of descending minor thirds, Evelyn King chimed her brain. She left the bowl where it was on the table, sing-whispered, *All the way down*, and walked back to her room. Just then a heavy pendulum swung suspended from a long wire and for a slow moment Ndiya's body came near, then closer, almost within her reach.

■

Fifty yards from Shame's door, Ndiya said to herself, "Just get it over with." She held Melvin by the hand while they walked. An instant from the first date at Earlie's hung in her mind like a portrait. For the rest of that evening they'd talked. They did all the things that couldn't be avoided. Ndiya watched herself listen while Shame talked around things, trying as she did, to fill space but reveal nothing. The kind of things people say when they first talk. Granted that those conversations don't usually begin with a ruptured house-arrest bracelet plummeting its way through the sugar bowl and toothpick box and into your date's lap. But still, that was the kind of conversation they'd had. She hoped it was anyway, because she couldn't remember a word of it. The first time, then: a bassline like a thumb in her mouth and down her spine, Malik's damned bracelet, an open triangle in Shame's face, and that one phrase, "Bic lighter." All of that and "maybe I am" hadn't come near the place. Then the fucking battle of Jericho, date number two when her tongue found a notch in the skin over Shame's third rib and she felt music smooth as a heavy stream of mercury poured over her waist and down her legs. Afterward, she nearly stepped on a seemingly self-sacrificing spider, which she'd murdered with a huge, hardback biography of Miles. Her thought echoed from when she'd first met Shame, when they first shook hands on the porch outside Renée's party. Her first thought had been, "Whose hand is *this?*"

Then, at home, the email she sent to Yvette-at-work. Ndiya wrote: "Didn't make Maurice's party, regrets. Ran into Shame. Went home with him. Ran *into* Shame, girl. Never been anywhere like that. Where *have* I been? Where am I *now? Please* advise." She thought about ending the note there but continued: "Told him: it felt like he'd waited his whole life to touch me. When he dropped me back home, he smiled looking down at the ground and said, 'That was a risky thing to say to me, Ndiya Grayson.' I didn't know *what* to say, I could barely hear him over the vibrations in my legs. Don't know why I'm telling you? What now, Yvette? *What* now?" Send.

Ndiya stared at the screen. She could still taste Shame Luther's salt when she suddenly regretted writing anything to Yvette. Open confession wasn't her style at all. It seemed so strange to confide things to someone before she'd really confided them to herself. She was just about to click the screen to reread her sent message again and ease her mind when a new message appeared. There was the sender's name in her box. She thought, "Even Yvette can't be *this* quick." The new message wasn't from Yvette. For an instant she looked at the words in the inbox and it was if she knew no one by that name. She blinked hard and looked again at the sender's name: Ndiya Grayson.

The message Ndiya had replied to had been sent by Yvette to the SnapB/l/acklist, not to her. So, her reply had been to—there it was. Date number one might have been a hot, sweet, last bite of oatmeal. No one knew. Date number two wasn't supposed to be a date at all, turned out hotter and sweeter than number one. And now *everyone* knew. Ndiya's forehead touched down on the keys. "When a fever breaks," she thought, "it's like being hit with a bucket from a cool mountain stream. Forget 'maybe I am' and the ABP. *Here* she is everyone: Ndiya Grayson has come back home."

■

Ndiya and Melvin stood on the steps. This was, indeed, date number three, which everyone *but* her seemed to know about. Sixty-three twenty-nine in chipped, cursive gold script painted across the top of the glass double doors. She looked at her reflection, soaked skirt, foaming pumps and all. As she reached for the bell she whispered to the window,

–No there or maybe about it, here I am, both of us.

She smiled at Melvin with his goggles on his forehead. He held her hand and pulled it in front of his face. She thought they looked like they'd been playing together in the deep, hydrant-puddle of twilight. Ndiya whispered to the glass,

–Tsunami it is. But he's going to have to tell me his real name.

She pushed the doorbell with her index finger and they heard nothing. After a moment Melvin said,

–It's never locked. I think we should go on up.

BOOK
TWO:
STOLEN
HANDS

One day you'll realize we're not strangers.
—CHAKA KHAN

He had work and plenty of it. By some measure, at least two jobs. Probably four and maybe more than that. Work was about all he had and that's how he'd wanted it. And money, he'd saved ten years of wages. Good wages. By the summer we're talking about, the summer that had waited almost until it was over to begin, when he met a woman named Ndiya Grayson, Shame Luther had steady work during the day around Chicago. The small construction company he worked for as a laborer had found a way to downsize its scale and insinuate its specialty into a wide range of factories and mills in Chicago's rapidly changing—meaning quickly evaporating—industrial sector. So he had that. That particular summer, the job repairing the acid tanks at Joycelan Steel looked like at least a few months' worth. Steady, if irregular, work. The mill was operating at as near as possible to full capacity during the repair. So the schedule fluctuated from week to week: four days on, three days off; seven days on, no days off; three and four; five and two; and so on. This was the way it was in the twenty-first century. The days of long jobs on newly constructed factories were, as far as he'd seen, over in Chicago. He'd spent ten years of his life chasing that kind of work through the South and Southwest until it crossed the border and disappeared into Mexico, the Philippines, Vietnam, or elsewhere. Ten years living on out-of-town expense checks, banking his wages. He'd worked out of his twenties and into his thirties: ten years in orbit. Then back to Chicago to work as he would or wouldn't in the city. So, that was one job, which he'd decided would be a rhythm around Chicago, or nothing. That was all he wanted, all it made any sense to want.

He had a job as house piano to the alley cats in "the green zone" behind 6329. An hour of twilight, a few nights per week. That paid whatever rent he'd otherwise have owed Junior. That wasn't exactly true, but that's all he knew at the time. He had the deal with neighborhood parents, that is, the mothers, to cook dinner weekdays for an ever-fluctuating rack of kids. That didn't *pay* anything in cash or otherwise, a fact that the mothers were still trying to figure out. In fact, far from charging, Shame regularly loaned the mothers and their families money. Then, after he'd taken the dare, he had the new job at the Cat Eye across from Earlie's Café on North Broadway. He played Wednesday nights, one hundred dollars for three twenty-minute sets. He'd insisted only that it be Wednesday. The piano a job? Work? Not hardly and, he thought, it wouldn't last whatever it was. It didn't matter. He didn't need the hundred dollars. He did it for the simple dare of it. And that wasn't exactly true either.

Soon he found another reason to play at the Cat Eye. After the first two weeks, he decided he should sit down at 6329 and plan out three sets' worth of music. Not a play list—he didn't play "songs"—but at least a set of chords or basic motifs to concentrate on during each of the twenty-minute windows. He couldn't read or write music but he could, so he thought, at least make a plan. The time went by in a flash. It was over almost before he'd started. Planning a few things out seemed simple enough. He couldn't do it. When he tried to keep conscious track of the music all hell broke loose: ideas spiraled from the chords and chords from the ideas until he was paralyzed and dizzy. More than that, he found he couldn't remember anything at all about the previous six sets' worth of music he'd been told that he had played at the club. The sets were empty windows in his memory.

He remembered the surroundings and conversations going on around him and a few loosely involving him between sets. He remembered people telling him that they liked the music. He remembered that there were more people there on week two than the first week. But the time at the keys was perfectly—almost too perfectly—*gone*. At this particular time in his life, recently returned to the city, the city that for him had been rebuilt around the one grave in his life, *my* grave, he'd have *paid* a hundred dollars for a blank hour, an hour beyond biography and its endless ventriloquisms. Of course, that hour was far from blank, but he didn't know that either.

So those were the jobs: Joycelan Steel, the alley music, the kids, and the Cat Eye. When, rarely, he thought about it, it seemed like a lot. It seemed like he should be a busy man. He wasn't. Or maybe he was, but he never felt like what he heard people call busy at all. He never felt like he was in a hurry. Mostly, he felt like something he couldn't see was watching him take apart and reassemble his life.

■

South Rhodes Avenue. The building is three floors, two apartments on each floor. Red brick. Shame lived on the third floor next to a retired man called Luther B. People in Chicago know the neighborhood as Woodlawn. People in Woodlawn know it as the Washington Park Subdivision, which is where the old Washington Park Race Track once stood. People in Washington Park know the first three of the five buildings (6309, 6319, 6329, 6339, and 6349) south of Sixty-Third Street and before the vacant lot on the west side (yes, on your right walking toward Sixty-Fourth Street) of Rhodes Avenue as Juniorville. Sixty-three twenty-nine had been built in the 1950s when that particular piece of the ghetto had been razed and rebuilt to house old black people who weren't allowed into the new subsidized and segregated "retirement" housing in nearby Hyde Park. The building had an elevator which quickly went out of service if it ever, in reality, made it into service. When the neighborhood hit its low point in the mid-1980s, the hydraulics, the stainless post, even the elevator carriage itself had been either sold, stolen, or both. It didn't matter much to the old folks. Most had either died or otherwise left the building and or the block. All had vacated the top floor that was dangerously inconvenient most of the year and deadly in the summer heat.

A market abhors a vacuum. Ad hoc drug trade moved in and made a bad thing worse. In the late 1980s, Junior came up the ranks in the Black Swoosh Syndicate that replaced the demise of Jeff Fort's El Rukn empire. The BSS sold franchises. Junior took a lease on the north part of the block. He gutted and rebuilt the buildings. Then, inexplicably, he moved other aged residents back into the buildings. Many of these people were retired police. Among other things, he'd decided to move the oldest residents into first-floor apartments and give up on the idea of an elevator altogether. He closed off the shaft and left the space empty. Instead of security cameras, payments to the police, and bars on the windows, Junior and his minions circulated an invitation to any thief who thought he could rob residents or burglarize residences in Junior's three buildings and live to fence the proceeds. As a kind of punctuation in the warning, the locks had been conspicuously removed from the front doors of his buildings.

Junior didn't pay the police because he thought he didn't have to and so did the police. A series of half-truths spliced with incontrovertible facts no one could figure out how he knew signaled that something was up. Finally, by a few key bold and imaginative leaps, which had to be real because they made *no* sense, he'd convinced everyone in Cook County Detention that he knew and could prove valuable things about powerful people. The formal precision and logic of Junior's mix of information and isolation alone could have provoked serious doubt but the people he needed to convince were very narrow-minded realists; they didn't give a shit about form. Their language was a grammar of powerful and powerless, the visible and the invisible. Junior's brain contained a portfolio of documented relationships between very visible, officially powerful people (police commissioners, district attorneys, members of the Mayor's office) and other very powerful, officially invisible ones. He had a clear chart of how the visible power of the official ones offered an official invisibility to the interests and operations of the others.

When he came out of Detention, Junior became a charter member of the latter group at an opportune time. Which brings up two reasons that I'm the one telling this story: 1) my family was at the center of the officially invisible web of power on the South Side; 2) the worker-piano player now known as Shame Luther was my best friend. We were best friends, that is, until the day I died and he split and stayed split. I'd say he split town, left Chicago, but the split was far deeper than geography. I died a week before my twenty-fifth birthday. Shame was actually in Los Angeles on a job, the last day of a job to be precise. We'd had very specific plans for my birthday and thereafter.

So all the splitting started there. The point is he never came back to Chicago. Because we'd been inseparable for years, Shame's prolonged absence raised a few invisibly powerful eyebrows. About ten years later, when Junior heard that Shame had come back to Chicago, the gears of our present story had locked teeth. All they needed was one of those everyday accidents in life—the kind often blamed on form or on the logic of fiction—to set it in motion. Meanwhile, Shame had returned to the city all but consciously guarded against knowing anything about the gears or the story. He'd returned as he had from an isolation that masked his outrage about being alive at all. So, in other words, he was an accident waiting—maybe begging—to happen.

During his first weeks living there, Shame had extended the bedroom in his apartment. He'd taken out the wall and added joists, subfloor, and flooring to make an alcove where the elevator shaft had been. It was a perfect place to put the bed. He'd added what he called a wall of light in the wall facing the street across the vacant lot to the south. This was useful in walls that couldn't support a real window of any meaningful size. Instead of a window, he rebuilt one alcove wall using frosted glass blocks to allow light in without taking down the building and without putting his bed on display to everyone in the street. He added a pattern of clear glass block in the wall as well. This became Shame's wall of light on the third floor of 6329. The clear blocks were perfectly transparent but telescoped objects indirectly in the viewer's sightline by several orders of magnitude. The effect was startling, and Shame thought the volatile but precise optics had to be an accident incidental to the rigor of the clear glass blocks' integrity as weight-bearing building material. In other words, the view was weird and it wasn't the point. In ways similar to Junior but to drastically different effect, Shame had a knack for fixating on details others passed by. Junior used this to accrue power over people's blindnesses and fears. Shame did the opposite. He rode those fixations; often this made him oblivious to his own blindnesses and fears.

Nonetheless, in this case the effect of the glass blocks turned out to be crucial for Shame. In whatever direction he looked, focused by one of the clear blocks, the thing just to the top right of his focus was enlarged as if seen through a telescope while everything else appeared to slide down a convex dome out of sight. When the angle of vision shifted, the dome revolved. Images from the street in front of the building slid upward toward and downward away from the point of intended focus as if the world rode on an off-center carousel. So Shame thought he had the best view in the city from his bed facing east across Rhodes Avenue.

■

Another thing Shame had at 6329 was a roommate that he was unsure about. The roommate made him self-conscious about guests, especially ones who threatened to invite themselves to stay the night. In late April, he began to wake up with spots on his ankles. One, maybe two per month. He'd moved in and immediately used steel wool, excess expansion rope he took from the job, and a dozen tubes of construction foam and caulk to close cracks along walls and inside closets. The roommate situation wasn't about mice or rats, that he knew. The first spot on his ankle was thick in the center, almost as if a tiny marble had been placed under his skin. It itched and stung a little when he sprayed Benadryl onto it. Over the next week, the thick dot disappeared as a halo or a kind of atoll appeared around it. The marble had become an island on his skin an inch or an inch and a half in diameter. Shame decided that he had a large spider living with him who visited him in the night. Over the summer the bites moved up his body.

For ten years he'd lived on the road with the company's traveling crew. He'd lived *intensely* alone, worked at least six days a week, studied after work and on his half-day off in his endless series of cheap motel rooms. On his half-days off he almost never talked to anyone. Ten years. Then, upon his return to the city, his first company had been a spider he'd never seen.

He'd come off the road last year and taken up Junior on his offer. He didn't know how Junior knew he'd come back or why he'd offer him a place to stay in exchange for "services to be named later." Upon returning to Chicago, Shame had found that, without his noticing, all of his senses had begun to work basically like the glass blocks he'd installed in the bedroom wall. Maybe it was only like this in Chicago? He didn't know. He'd had enough of the road and didn't plan on leaving town again. He didn't know what his life would be about. He meant to figure that out here. As soon as he'd returned, he noticed things and, even more, people would approach into magnified focus and bend out of range in a rhythm that changed constantly but didn't seem to alter in response to anything he could determine or control. On the job, no problem. Everthing fit in place. Off the job, things slipped and slid. Since moving into Junior's building, the intensity of his perceptual exile was easing up bit by bit at Earlie's.

The first step had been Earlie's Café all the way up on North Broadway. He'd heard an interview with the manager who'd said they opened the place "because we love music." Shame thought that was a place to start. He'd begun to go there after getting off work and cleaning himself up. Shame was clearheaded at work. But everything else he looked at appeared to him as if it was behind thick aquarium glass. He'd allowed people—he guessed they were people—to talk to him at the bar: Lester, Than-ha, JiLisa, Wayne, Reg, Karmen, the four Kims, and maybe a few others. He trained himself to sit still and listen while their faces slid in and around folding over on themselves. For weeks he watched people talk.

After a few weeks, he'd begun to sit at a table in a corner of windows near the garden and read. He'd intended to keep on studying as he'd done on the road. For years he'd traced the music of what he considered the great voices in American jazz: Miles Davis, John Coltrane, Billie Holiday, Charles Mingus, Wynton Kelly, Lester Young. He didn't exactly know why he was doing it. It struck him that the music he studied (phrase by phrase, song by song, year by year, each artist one at a time) was older than he was. Sometimes twice his age or more. It also struck him that the music was much closer to the age of the old men he worked with. Maybe that's why he'd done it. He didn't know. He'd grown to love the music. It never felt old to him. Note by note, gliss by gliss, it felt like it'd become flesh of his flesh, as if his body bore the old-time music into the contemporary world. He'd become a kind of time warp. He wondered if this alone had caused his senses to bend and smear in the gap between the music he'd slow-poured into his brain like warm honey and the manic, info-flow world he found around him in Chicago during the first years of the twenty-first century.

As far as his studies went, he thought it wouldn't matter that he was back in Chicago. It mattered. As soon as he arrived, he found it impossible to concentrate on the music as he had. In retrospect, the next part looked like a cheap setup. Maybe it was. When he arrived on the third floor of 6329, there'd been an old upright piano in the hallway. It sat on oversized, hard rubber studio rollers. On the back of the piano was well-stenciled script: Mount Carmel High School for Boys. He didn't ask and he didn't know why. He rolled it into his apartment mainly because he didn't have much furniture. He'd never sat at the keys of a real piano before. When he did he loved the feel of the mechanism connecting his fingers to the felt-covered hammers he found hidden inside. From the time he rolled that piano into his apartment, it had seemed as if he didn't hear recorded music anymore. He'd assembled a vintage stereo system before he found that listening had changed. He loved it, still, for the way it filled space around him with electrified warmth. He could listen, of course, but he didn't hear it like he had on the road when it seemed like he could step inside the music and watch the world as if through a window in a song. On the road, he'd felt like he could grab hold of the sound, like it was made of physical components. At 6329 he always had music playing. But he didn't really listen because he really didn't hear it any more than a fish feels the water that surrounds. Maybe what Shame had begun to do with music had more in common with breathing than it did with listening. Or maybe more with drowning.

When Shame sat at the piano and touched the keys, he felt the notes made by the hammers before he heard them. It was as if the hammers were inside his body somehow. And he could feel the mechanism between the keys and hammers as if they were joined to his tendons and muscles.

He began to suspect that the piano listened to the recorded music he played more than he did. Even if he couldn't play anything, he began to hear music when he played the piano much more than when he listened to recordings. He didn't hear what he played. It was coming from somewhere else. So he decided to leave music playing for the piano to listen to when he was out of the apartment. He turned it off when he came back. Then he'd play the keys and listen to what appeared in the distance. Because he did all of this, whatever it was, alone, Shame had no gauge for the intensity of what was happening to him.

There were the recurring dreams of being trapped in narrow alleys by collapsed buildings. His hands buried in brick, he tried to cut them off at the wrist but couldn't cut through thick piano wires in his arms. The dream of showing up to work with keys instead of hands, pedals instead of feet. As he'd learn later, he could hear music performed live as well. But for six solid months, other than work, sleep, and log two hours a few evenings a week standing on the bank or wading ankle deep into conversations at Earlie's Café, Shame had done nothing in his house but listen to what happened elsewhere as the living tendons of that old piano moved the hammers in his body.

During the first months, a few of the people he'd talked to at Earlie's had worked their way up to inviting themselves to his place. They were all women. By then he had come up with the afternoon-chef job with the kids and so he'd clean up from the first shift—more on that to come—in the kitchen and cook dinner for the visitors from Earlie's.

He kept it cool. He'd play the guests music that he couldn't hear anymore on the stereo. Visitors were more interested in the glowing tubes of the amplifier than any music that happened to be playing. In contrast to the dice-roll of kids he'd host on the first shift, he enjoyed the adult company, the presence of a fully grown body in the room with him. Human stillness. He wasn't studying anymore. He didn't know what he was doing. It felt like he was skating. What he was skating on and what was below that, he didn't know. People were there but it felt to him like no one really came to visit. No one stayed the night. And no one ever came twice which, at the time, was a good thing.

No one, that is, except Colleen, who turned out to be a very crucial presence, a real person and a friend. After a half dozen of these other dinner visits, he figured out what they felt like. He and his guest were ventriloquists' dummies. They talked but in ways that, somehow, weren't theirs to say. For years after I was dead, Shame hadn't talked to anyone effectively. The ventriloquist thing with those first visitors didn't bother him too much. He didn't mind the feeling. But he didn't recognize it and he didn't trust it. Everyone was still cool at Earlie's as far as he could tell, but none ever mentioned coming back to 6329. The closest he'd come to his visitors, in fact, was when he'd fall on his bed and watch them leave out the front. He'd watch them warp down the street as the scene poured up through the clear glass bricks in his bedroom wall. That was enough for a while.

■

He knew it was ridiculous. But he thought of the spider as his first overnight guest since he'd quit traveling full time with the construction crew. He'd had no overnight guests on the road, either, only music. If there was sex, that usually took place in the company-owned Ford F-250 he drove. He looked. There were no webs in the room. The boards in the floor were warped enough to allow easy transit to untold worlds of tiny, flexible beings like spiders. Not roaches. He'd caulked and puttied and steel-wooled and foamed those openings. He'd spent enough years on the road in efficiency motel rooms where he had to stomp his feet on the way to the bathroom at night and shake the cereal box before pouring it into the bowl in the morning. He wasn't going back to *that*. He'd rather go back to planet college. Well, OK, maybe not that. If the spider wanted to come from out of the old elevator shaft through whatever crack she found and slip up next to him in the night, as long as she left nothing more than one of these small hickey-like bites or so per week, he could live with it. With her. Again, he knew this was strange, which, he told himself, was half the battle.

So he made a quiet deal with his silent roommate. As long as she could slip in and out of bed with him and he didn't wake up and she was gone by morning, she was more than welcome. It was a pact with silence and a truce with its consequences, a kind of embroidery of fear and, maybe, an experiment with trust.

The bites traveled up his body. Another appeared on the inside of his upper arm. This one was the same as the others. A marble on days one and two that diffused into a poison reef and atoll by the end of the week. The barrier faded and went away by day seven. The spider's visits made him notice spiders. He read that, in fact, westerners in temperate climates are never more than five feet from a spider. He made a small series of transactions with his roommate during the first six months he lived at 6329, apartment 3B. Spiders aren't silent, they're silence. During the years working on the road, he'd come to understand himself as a repository of silence in a mad-loud world. The hemorrhaged world bled noise. He didn't participate. Less and less. On some jobs he ran a diamond-blade brick saw, cutting very dense, ceramic brick. A small hose sprayed water on the blade. This meant specialized cuts, expensive brick, no mistakes, and a diamond blade spinning at 4500 rpm an inch from his right thumb.

The blare from the blade was beyond deafening. Earplugs did nothing. The sound waved its way past skin and flesh directly into the bones. It rode the marrow, bypassed the ears, and opened into the mass of the skull. Floating in an amplifier, his brain itself translated the vibrations into sound. In fact, he'd come to believe that, like water, bone marrow transmitted sound better than air and so he had given up on the earplugs altogether. But it wasn't just the saw. It was the world gone agog on blather. The saw was, however, good training for this world. He'd imagine that he was a set of inverted waves that canceled out the noise of the saw. Same amid conversations and in front of all manner of media. TVs had proliferated in public spaces. When he'd stopped watching altogether, it became obvious to him that TVs watch people, not the other way around. And he could see clearly that TV had turned many people into things that didn't need to be watched. In fact, TVs worked much like spider webs. Those caught ended up like the dried husks of bugs one finds in a web. It was only a matter of time before the screens had sucked all the juice from people's homes and would then need to reduce their size and find a way to follow people out into the world and into every waking moment. At that point the only unwatched piece of life would be sleep; Shame doubted that wall would hold. Screens would be invented that could watch people in their dreams too.

Noise and him. That's where the name "Shame Luther" came from. He invented it on the road. It was a name for Allen Sardonovic's pose in a guerilla war against noise. Actually, it was more a psychological operation than a guerilla war, but either way. Shame Luther began life as a psyop. He thought of himself as fighting a battle behind the lines of his own brain. Denied territory. In ways he didn't understand, it was also a desperate attempt to not let a terrible grief turn into despair. Following an intuition covered by impenetrable waves of pain, he named the silent border between grief and despair Shame, which strikes me as accurate enough. It was a way to survive, which, I can tell you, doesn't exactly mean it was a way to live. But he did survive.

So the first transaction was the silence. Shame decided to leave little Ms. Nasty the spider in charge of a few tiny points of silence in the room. He could immediately feel the decline in his responsibility. He was shocked that those tiny points of silence could make such a difference in the battle against massive and pervasive sounds. The conflict was asymmetrical. He thought it must be like the difference between duration of a dream in dreamworld and its span in minutes on the clock. Maybe silence is a volume. He imagined a bucket full of silence would be as heavy as the matter that physicists described at the core of collapsed stars. Maybe heavier. He wondered if there was five gallons' worth of silence in the universe. Or maybe it was infinitely collapsible. *Could* you fill something with silence? If it worked in his room, in the alcove of the converted elevator shaft, then he'd deputize other spiders in the operation. If it was, indeed, true that we're never more than five feet from a spider, Shame reasoned, there was always at least a tiny teaspoon (which seemed to mean a trainload) of pure silence nearby. It was available if we'd only use it, not run from it or hide away in it. And not scream, flinch, and kill it, he thought. He decided to try.

If he lost faith in transaction number one for a moment, he'd sit and concentrate and attempt to come up with one way that a spider could make a sound, not cause one, mind you, *make* one. Jungles and deserts maybe. Spiders the size of rodents. He'd read about a spider in the suburbs of Bangalore who'd been caught killing chickens. OK, even though he'd no evidence that they'd made (rather than caused) any actual sounds, he left them out of it. But these city spiders in Chicago, they check out every time. So, they could take the pressure off Shame at the silent border and allow him to focus on a few sounds of his own.

The second transaction was an accident. Shame had

noticed the similarity between the view through the glass blocks in his bedroom wall and the way his convex personality slid through the world. Who knew how much trouble it had spared him? Who knew how much despair? A little shame was a small price. Still, he didn't consider it an end in itself. After the first few of Ms. Nasty's visits, he decided not to spray the ointment on the bite. He traced the itch; he knew it was the action of the poison tempting him to scratch and help it along. He didn't. He attended passively as the sensations moved outward from the center, circled clockwise down the dome of the wound. As the dome dissipated, he found less traffic and a slower, deeper itching sensation. Once in a while, just to check, he drew two fingers across the wound on either side of the center and the itch would flame, the clockwise pattern appear. He'd count his pulse and allow it to go away. After five days, the dome was gone and the convex patterns in and around the wound would ease away altogether.

Beginning the day after each of Ms. Nasty's night visits, Shame matched his slippery self to the pulse and static that crossed between his skin and the wound. "The world and the wound," he thought. He found he could put up with people at Earlie's, for instance, to the tune of his dissipating spider bites. After a while at it, by day two or three, he found he could actually enjoy a person's company. He could actually talk to someone without having to watch from above in horror at the same time. He didn't know how it would play out, but that's the way it went. He followed along the border between grief and despair. He began to suspect that despair wasn't the only possibility beyond grief. And, by degrees, Shame became just a name and not a way to be in the world.

The final transaction was a simple matter of scale. Shame decided to imagine it from her perspective. A cold, intricate structure in a revolving abyss of space. Sunlight from the cracks in the roof travel the abandoned shaft under the floor. She catches light on her invisible legs. If he looked he wouldn't see her legs at all. He'd see blackness and points of light where the sunlight collects at her joints. He'd never see her in the dark, a constellation of elegant needle-tip joints. Think of a hollow tube that's too thin to see. Think of the tiny transit such a tube is designed to convey. Think of a being who strings up a vast nervous system outside of herself. A silken, spinal world hitched to cracked brick and rusted springs. Listen to that for a while.

Her silence is held open by the limitless, asymmetrical power of accuracy. Architect of silent wounds, she'll commit no scar in sound. This fact requires no withholding. She's here to make poise a verb. Because nothing is withheld, because there's only nothing *to* withhold, it's not a pose. If there was something to withhold, to hold back, that silence—like most—would curdle and spoil; it would become a vanity, a simple disguise. But accuracy is never vanity. Real pride was never false. That's why the webs are beautiful. Ms. Nasty in her spinal net. She poises there a leg for each major cable in the web. Webs aren't discarded when torn. Most spider webs are never torn. They're discarded when they dry. A note in the spine runs fluid in the weave. She designed poise, an invisible system of fluid.

Poise the verb: to take a position where you are; and as a noun: a way to know where that is, a method. And, at a rhythm, when the arc of light leaves the shaft she migrates through an eye in the floor. Climbs whatever post or wall and, via another, single, fluid cord of spine, she descends.

■

She descends to me. By our bargain with each other, I feel nothing. She's a fact in this silent dimension of poise. If I hear her there's nothing. And she walks me, along me at the yawn of shade and shadow between my skin and the folds of cloth. For her, I'm a living landmass, a geography. An unbound cloud of violent rhythm, a source of gravity across which she strings her fluid spine that she leaves weekly to make the migration to the source of sound and dream and back through the open eye in the sleeping floor. Even asleep, my body thunders under her touch. There are spiders who attach bulbs of air to risk transit to their underwater sources. She carries only the cold, quiet of her lightness, which is mostly made of darkness. For her, even small feathers from the pillow are cruel iron blades. Dust a roaring machine. She knows I'm asleep beneath dreams by the even rhythms of all the pulses in the bed. At bottom, if it comes to that, she knows all she has to do to disappear is be herself.

From there we can see that the noun form of the verb "to poise" is: poison.

■

When Shame Luther thought of Ms. Nasty in this way, he almost craved her. No matter how close, he was able, in her silent, poisoned company, to flatten out his own web of cravings a bit. Undulations remained, always, of course. There were no level fields or clean slates. But with her, in the rhythm of her visits and the patterned traffic of her poison, he began to rebuild his senses around a sixth sense: a structure of proportions between sound and silence, grief and despair, need and want in the world. Shame built a conscious sense of how to poise himself. The poison in him had become an island of "want and don't need" surrounded by oceans, abandoned webs of "want and can't have." His skin became a reef between the two—self the surf at the reef. Shame.

After my death, what Shame never knew was that everything he did and didn't do was a move within an unbounded circumference of grief; there's no word for the surface area of a sphere. Grief says it's unbounded because there's no word for the boundary; but it isn't. The skin of grief is a membrane with no pattern. It's hard to get a grip on the surface inside the sphere of grief. Ms. Nasty had, in effect, given Shame a way to grieve, to attach himself to the smooth, inside skin of the space. If he could grow from that point, he might learn enough to want something else. He might use the surf of himself to impel another seeking. The hammer hits everyone. After it hits many people, all they ever want is to awake and die quickly every day before they open their eyes.

But the dead aren't dead. There is no death. The closest thing to death is the living who refuse to live. To allow the dead to live in one's life has to be the end of grief; grief is the price the living pay for the presence of the dead in their lives. Despair is the failure to accept that price. That's why despair is a living death. Shame knew none of this. For him it was an invisible maze. But everything he did and didn't do was measured by something that moved quite on its own in this maze, in the world. Though there were no words in the maze, something down there spoke nonetheless. It told Shame that the only way to reach the end of grief was to swallow all of it, to bring the dead back to living. And the dead have no names; that's why there's no word to mark the boundary in grief. Pulled under by the death of someone they love, the grieving mark the line when—if?—they struggle back to the world of the living. One learns the location of a border, a line, any line, only by crossing it. Borders are never where they appear to be and they don't stay where they are. We could almost say that they don't stay *what* they are. In a way that had no name, Shame had measured everything he did as a course through this invisible maze.

Shame woke up at exactly five thirty no matter what happened the night or morning before. He never drank coffee before work. It was not that kind of job. The body kept the brain alert. Juices of all kinds and, no matter what, he had to eat. He forced himself to eat. It was the most difficult part of the job, really. He was never hungry before work. But if he didn't eat, he'd be starving after the first few loads of brick or a few glassy black pours of tar. It nearly made him sick to think of food this early and he was chronically cold in the mornings even in the summer. He ate anyway, to avoid struggling, empty and dizzy, the whole morning. At times, syrup and fruit and sweet rolls did the trick. At others, hot salsa and fried eggs on toast. He built a four-foot-by-four-foot closet, floor to ceiling, for work clothes, boots, and the few tools he needed. It was next to the front door in his apartment.

By five thirty, the clothes were already awake. Work clothes waited for him with the distinct smell of whatever job was going on at the moment. The graphite powder and resin in the acid-proof mortar he mixed combined with the smell of whatever plant: sour malt from the breweries, burnt hair and flesh from the slaughterhouses, boiled sugar from Tootsie Roll, vinegar from Peer Foods. His bricklayer father's mantra was: "Smells like money to me." All the old men on the job agreed. These were men who argued, when the big boss showed up driving a

Honda, "The man used to drive a Jaguar. Some of you bastards must not be working hard enough. Speak for yourself!" Shame watched this. He'd think about it later. The smells that summer were sweet acid and matte dust from Joycelan Steel, a wire mill on Thirty-Eighth and Morgan Streets. Summertime, and the living was twenty minutes on the cycle to the job.

He woke up and got out of bed. Half the apartment in Junior's building wasn't Shame's in the morning. He walked to the kitchen as if it was a torture chamber. Opened the old, round-edge fridge. He squinted against the glow. If he felt the cold fall onto the feet on the floor, they were someone else's feet. The half-open table was his in the morning. Before work, none of the books he left stacked around the place were his. He'd come back to them later. He didn't open the piano before work. He didn't see it, knew no one who played it. He treated it like the rest of his non-working life in the morning; it wasn't there or, at least, it wasn't *his*. He didn't always do this. At first, as a teenager, he wondered about how "he" could do this work and then go off into the rest of his life afterward. He wondered about borders. He asked one of his fellow laborers, Jay Brown, about it. Jay Brown told him not to worry, the rest of his life would disappear before too long. Now almost twenty years ago, Jay Brown had said,

–Boy, one of these soon days you're gone wake up and be what they call weaned. You'll be what they call a man. Grown. Questions like that will burn away like fog in the morning.

Jay Brown's big hands. His high-pitched laugh.

Shame used to stand on the loading dock watching the world outside go by. One image still hurt like the missing limb war vets talk about. He was working in LA on a new Kraft plant. The place was spotless. They were pouring the bed of tar for the floor. Ninety-six degrees in the shade. Three hundred fifty degrees in the tar. His body was a hollow needle somewhere in between. At lunch he stood there in long sleeves, sweat running down his arms. He could taste the tar smoke caught in the sweat on his face.

He heard a fast bike, a Ninja or a Hurricane, pulling through the sport gears on the boulevard outside the fence. He looked up to see the rider with a woman crouched behind him on the bike. They swooped into view, signaled. He saw the helmet move, a quick jog into the blind spot, down and to the left at the entrance to the 405 and then the heel twitch and the engine whirred up and out of Shame's hearing. He watched the woman's black braids, the Y-shaped lines of her brown back against the tight, white muscle shirt. He closed his eyes as the sound trailed off and then—he could still see this with his eyes closed—another heel twitch, and the sound trailed off again. He knew they were gone. It felt like it always felt to watch the world from inside the job. It felt like his guts had been tied to the bike, like he'd been broken by horses running in different directions. Like "he" was impossible. He was right. So was Jay Brown.

When that lucky couple on the bike disappeared, Shame noticed that he'd bitten through his lip. He could taste the salt and the blood mix with the smoke-taste of the tar. All at once, he felt it in his boots and his stance.

"Here I am," he said. He could taste it in the blood-smoke in this mouth: "You can't miss *them*, man, *they* were never here. This is where you are. They ain't you. *This* is you: boots, sweat, that full feeling in your shoulders, this vibration in your hands, these gloves in your pocket, and, most of all, those pallets of brick and material out back behind that loading dock. You exist in the money that trades places as you work, putting those materials where they need to go. They need to go exactly where you're paid to put them. Labor: you're it. That's the real you, the historical you. What happens to that person really happens. Accept it." And he did. And, then, he worked with it, in it. That was my friend. Couldn't fuck with him.

Six years after that I died and the roof fell in.

More than a decade after *that*, after knowing Ms. Nasty, Shame had begun to understand what all that was all about. It was poise: tangent instant on the inside skin of grief, a stance in the wind of one's own history, a still shot of experience, a sip of poison.

Shame's before-work place was stripped down to bed, fridge, the first forced meal of the day, the painted pine closet full of worksmell, bodysmell, chemical-scented clothes hanging in there. The feel of worn cotton. Cotton was his one working extravagance. It was expensive and it wore out fast. But he wouldn't wear the polyester work clothes that the old men wore. Wouldn't do it. When he put his work clothes on, it was as if they already knew what to do. He felt like he hovered around in the dim morning light. His hands, the ones that existed, stayed in the gloves he hung on a nail in the closet. He didn't have feet. His real feet waited for him in the boots. He never wore them in the place; the last thing he did on his way out was lace up the feet. Morning light on his face. "I'll try sweet today," he thought, "thick biscuits and jelly. Four of them should hold till lunch."

There were four loose boards in the floor. Three made creaks. The one at the foot of his bed squawked into the hollow shaft beneath the plywood of the subfloor. One in the bedroom, one in the short hall on the way to the bathroom, one in the middle of the living room and one attached to the threshold of the kitchen. He knew he was ready for work and everything had been done right if he hit three of those boards twice and one of them once. That meant a squawk and six creaks. No need to think. It was the morning song. He laced up his work feet. If he left by six twenty, and he always did, he knew he was good. That part always was. He'd arrive to that place where being on time meant you were twenty minutes early. Where not being ready to work meant you didn't really exist at all.

■

With a few months here and there as exceptions, Shame Luther worked on jobs like this since he was seventeen. He was never late to work. No one was. Most of the men were there by six thirty; the jobs started at seven. Shame never missed a day. He never left early. It was like clock-work, though: during weeks here and there when the company didn't have a job lined up, he got sick then. He turned his ankle on a brick in the alley. The flu. Knocked his head on a limb, hit sand over an oil patch in a corner and put his bike down. He thought to himself, "If I didn't have to work, I'd be dead by now!" At the job, everything but work went behind his brain and he aimed himself at the next immediate thing. Was that himself? It didn't matter; at work he was the thing he aimed at the next task at hand. The whole world collapsed into a few physical tasks. Everything plunged through and bottlenecked into the present-tense weight and balance in that body. Most of it came in through his hands.

It wasn't like that for everyone. He knew that. He'd seen distracted men injured on jobs. He'd seen fingers lost, ankles broken, spines ruined. Men stepped off scaffolds as if they were hopping a curb and broke ribs. They were elsewhere when it happened, until it happened. He'd been on jobs where lives had ended. At least by the chance of their endings, those lives were exactly like his. But not Shame. Others moved precisely and vividly through their other lives while they worked. Wives floated in the air, politicians burned, children's futures pulsed in the rhythms of the job. Not Shame. At work, his mind went perfectly blank. He became brick, wax, leverage, scrape, mortar, breath, tar, mix, carry, sweat, heat, stance, sweat, heat, heat.

It wasn't thought. He knew that much. Wherever the brain was, it lived in objects. Work made things appear in the rhythm of connections between objects. Beyond that needs took care of themselves. He could watch the job, the plant, even the world, even the motorcycle with the girl. It all disappeared into his body through his hands. Work made him a mirror to what happened, to what he did. Objects concentrated; he never forced himself to pay attention. It surprised and frightened him, at first, the way things he thought were important vanished when he stepped across the line into the work area. It was just like Jay Brown had said, or almost; people vanished too. He learned to let them go, to relax, to expect it, the way the pain and sweat of a job enclosed him and, exactly then, he sensed a place of peace almost within reach. Never here, always just off beyond his reach, *there*. Shame heard about the loss of jobs, vanishing work. The old men talked about it. He knew it meant exile from poise. What would he do without poison? Maybe if one knew it well enough, it could be found elsewhere? He didn't know about that.

Four bricklayers worked on the job repairing tanks at Joycelan Steel. The mill made wire of various gauges, the whole process: forge, pull, wash, wrap, ship. The job was in the acid-wash part of the plant: open tanks filled with different kinds of acid for use as finishing cleansers. There were six tanks, fifty feet long, twenty feet wide, twelve feet deep. The tanks were placed horizontally across the main area. A crane rode rails at the ceiling. Wire was dropped off at one end after being wrapped into coils ten feet in diameter. About three to six tons, depending, Shame was told. The crane picked each coil up, soaked it in a series of tanks, and placed it at the open, opposite end of the space on a pallet for the forklifts to deal with.

The job was to reline each tank with new brick while the plant kept the others full and the crane in operation. The tanks were made of concrete and lined with sixteen-pound block. Not concrete block, now. These are four-by-four-by-eight-inch ceramic brick. Each would fit in your hand, sixteen pounds apiece. For the laborers, that meant a workout and a new pair of leather gloves every week. Hands numb by 9:00 a.m. During the first few weeks of a tank job, his body ached, morning stiffness felt like a cast on the limbs. It wore off during the first hour on the clock as if the minutes kept track of the body coming back to life. Putting brick in was the easy part, at least for the laborers. The hard part was getting the old ones out. And there were no electric hammers on this job. No power tools were allowed into the acid-wash wing of the plant. That meant a six-foot, eighty-pound iron post sharpened into a wedge at the end, brick hammers, shovels, and five buckets with rope tied to the handles. Shame saved almost all the empty resin cans from each job. He kept them in the supply yard down on Ninety-Ninth street.

■

I first knew Shame in the summer of 1989. I called him AS at the time. It was his initials, plus it was our all-time favorite song. I never could call him Allen. When we met he was on a job like the one I'm telling you about now. He'd say it was nothing like this. He spent his days busting out a floor in the Tootsie Roll factory out near Midway Airport. Look, all those jobs were the same to *me*. It was another summer. I was new money, still had a year to go in college. I usually ran "errands" for my old man in the mornings and then played volleyball at the beach. I remember Shame wanted to put the cycle he had at that time in the shop and he wondered if I'd pick him up after work.

—Man, that's Cicero!

—Can I get a ride or not?

I remember getting my hair cut on Oak Street. Ernest was an artist with his portfolio of combs and his alphabet of tiny scissors. Ernest hated clippers. "Child, this *ain't* the Marines," he'd say. He insisted on the intimacy of scissors and straight razors. So, hair *laid*, fresh lined, I left the beach at three and went to get AS in my old man's 928. Much as I'd have preferred to go incognito, I had to take it. My grandmama said I wasn't taking *her* Benz anywhere *near* Cicero. So I drove up and there was my man AS. Looked like he was singing *Swing low* . . . on the corner of Sixty-Sixth Street with his boots wrapped up and an old bedsheet to put over the seat. He looked like a coal miner or something.

—Thought you might not think to bring something to cover the seat with.

—Think? Damn, *look* at you, don't they air-condition those steel mills?

Shame looked at me like I just said some shit to him in Swedish.

—It's a candy factory. And no, they don't *air-condition* them.

—Whatever. Get in. I'll push and you can tell me all about the value of a hard-earned dollar. We're going to Rocky's, I'm buying "the endangered American worker" a pound of fried shrimp and a *cerveza mas fina*.

Look, a little background. As I've mentioned, I came from the kind of family that dealt in cash. Call it unregistered money; your grandmama gives you a thousand dollars to fill her car with gas. That kind of thing. Straight face, a clip of hundreds and:

–Here, baby, make sure you fill it up all the way.

I have to admit, I loved to see the look on those old men's faces when they watched me pick AS up in my daddy's new black Porsche. He dug it too. Don't let him fool you with his whole "man of the people" routine. We were young. And, hell, that money we spent *was* the people. Anyway, Shame started this job as the youngest person in the company. By the summer we're looking at, he was still the youngest person working there. No one got replaced. The old bricklayers hung it up and then died and the old laborers died and then hung it up. The company shrank. But there it was back then. Shame worked with some real avant-garde types: Duffy, Big Jock, and Shame's pops who had long given up on his only son and tried in any way he could to pretend he was not working on the job. When Shame's old man couldn't deny Shame was on the job altogether, he'd fall back on denying that he was his son. He just couldn't forgive him for leaving college after six weeks. I understood that much. Shame didn't care.

I met Shame's pops just once after work on some job. I think it was at Oscar Mayer right across from Cabrini. I remember I smiled. I remember he didn't.

–How's it going there, Mr. Sardonovic?

And he didn't even look up from putting his tools away behind the cab of his pickup truck:

–Gotta go.

I laughed. He didn't. Instead, he got in the truck,

hiked up his work pants so his calves and the tops of his boots showed, and slammed the door. Then, still without ever looking up at us, he said,

—So long.

And he drove off. Just like that. Man, I could feel the wind playing in and out of my wide-open mouth. Look, I knew about the "Chicago worker." I read *The Jungle* at the Latin School, thank you very much. But I'd never seen one up close, like in the wild.

—Damn.

—Yeah, that's him.

—You all working in there together? I mean, you're filthy and his work clothes look like they just came from the cleaners?

—Yeah—well, I wouldn't say we work *together*. The laborers work *for*, not with, the bricklayers. And then there's him, he pretty much works all by himself no matter where he is. If he says something, it's usually something like, "We're not here to homestead this fucking slab of concrete," or, "How about we keep our goddamned mouths shut and our joints even for a change?" That kind of thing.

—Joints?

—It's the space between the brick.

—Oh, OK. What's he all mad at?

And Shame, brows all down. Actually, for once, he sounded a little like his old man:

—Man, how the hell would I know?

After that I'd call Shame's pops Gotta Go and laugh. Shame didn't laugh.

■

August at Joycelan Steel was hotter than July. By mid-month they were about a third of the way through the job, working on the second of six tanks. It would have been one thing to break all the brick out, line each tank with tar, fabric, more tar, and then put in the brick one tank after another. Hard and hot, but it would have been simple. That, however, would have required shutting down the plant. The only time they got a shot at that kind of systematic work was when they built a new factory. That didn't happen anymore in Chicago. If they did, they avoided acid-proof brick altogether. It was impossible to pack up on flatbeds overnight and ship to the Philippines. So they repaired working operations. It had been like that for years.

The first step was the worst. The tanks had been drained. But a thick layer of acid sludge and grease remained. That needed to be shoveled out and carried away. As he shoveled, Shame noticed his arms began to itch. It wasn't like a poison spider itch. It wasn't local and it didn't hurt. It was just there. He asked about it. Cutting the question short and without looking up, the foreman said, "Don't worry about it." Shame shoveled up the sludge and loose brick into buckets. Jay Brown pulled the buckets up by a rope tied to their handles and took them off to dump. There would be about a week of this per tank. Layers of heat in Shame Luther's days: the heat outside; the heat from the blast furnaces next door; heat from the sweat under the work clothes. Then there was the heat of the anger on a job. Anger was the currency of this kind of labor. Anger and its cousin, physical violence. Work was dead in the water without them. They *had* to be there and they had to be focused, contained. And then there was a new heat itching Shame from whatever film covered his exposed arms.

On his way to lunch he noticed a small tear in his white T-shirt. The shirt was only a week old. He wore old clothes to work, but never torn. The union allowed no torn clothing. Even the flagrant extravagance of this cotton shirt wasn't old enough to be garbage yet. He sat with Jay Brown and ate his sandwich and didn't, as usual, say much. His mind surveyed the new heat itching at his skin.

One way to gauge a job was to compare the work on whatever plant he was in to whatever work went on *in* the plant. At times, the construction crews looked pretty bad. Budweiser, for instance, in St. Louis, Houston, New Hampshire, or in LA. It made you feel like shit. The brewery employees whistled tunes and tugged hoses around the tank rooms. Three breaks per day. Regular raises. They went home every night. Word was they had to cap wages and overtime in the brewery so that the wages of senior plant workers didn't surpass the salaries of bottom management. God forbid. It looked pretty great to Shame. Welch's and Kraft were like that. Tropicana, not quite.

Then there were places where the construction crews looked pretty good. Places like Tootsie Roll in Cicero, a hateful, dirty, slimy place with workers to match. One day Shame asked someone to use the water hose and got cussed out six ways from Sunday. Even years later, if Shame saw someone about to eat a Tootsie Roll:

—I wouldn't do that!

And he remembered off-the-path places, usually in the South. No unions allowed in the plants, some unions weren't allowed in the state! One plant in Mississippi had a seven-foot corrugated ceiling over the battery line. They made car batteries for Sears. That's what they were told; the batteries weren't labeled. That happened elsewhere. The place had no ventilation that Shame could see. It was so bad the local union steward wouldn't even let visiting construction crews like them carry their lunches through the plant. Shame had looked around in there. There wasn't a full smile in the place. Acid fumes ate the teeth. He had walked through to go to the bathroom a few times during the brief (thank *Christ*) few weeks they worked there. He saw more than one visibly pregnant woman working where the union wouldn't let him carry his sandwich. All that, Shame knew, for at most a third of his Chicago-scale wage. The South. But that South wasn't south enough, apparently, because most of those off-the-path and out-of-the-way plants went elsewhere altogether. The global South—Shame worked there before it was global. He'd watched it go global and he knew why. In a way, he was why.

Shame and his laborer partner Jay Brown watched the Joycelan Steel workers and thought they were doing OK. Shame thought he'd be doing better once the shoveling of acid slop was done. He looked down and there were several new tears in his shirt. By the end of the day, the shirt was ready to come apart thread by thread. There were holes where he'd splashed grease against himself. And there were two round holes near the back of his neck that burned and would thereafter always burn when the sun hit them. These hurt more than the others. He'd tried to keep his eye on it, but a few times the crane had gone overhead unnoticed and dripped the fresh acid-wash on him as it made its way across to rinse a load of wire in whatever solution they had in tank number four. Shame brushed the first off without a thought. When he felt the second drop he paused and looked up. The glare of the glass in the crane's cab blocked his view, but he thought he could see the crane driver looking down at him, smiling. Motherfucker.

Shirt or no shirt, by three, he and Jay had a good quarter of the tank cleaned out, revealing the old brick. Next step was to tear out the old brick, too, then scrape out the tar lining. So that was job number one. On this particular August afternoon, it was 3:45. Shame was on his cycle headed home to get job number two on the table for whatever kids showed up. After that he planned to be home to meet a woman named Ndiya Grayson for date number three at his place. The last part, he thought, "if she showed." He assumed she wouldn't.

Melvin loved puzzles. Shame had a stack of them and Melvin had gone straight to the shelf where they were kept, took two boxes down. Ndiya watched as he dumped out the pieces on the floor and began to pick them up and put them in place without apparent effort or pause as if the pieces were totally interchangeable. She checked, they weren't. The top left corner appeared first, castle spires and a dark sky grew down until the narrow river at the bottom right corner appeared. Melvin stood up, put both hands, palms up, in the small of his back and bulged his belly out. He stood there for a second, stretched his back, then he stepped to the opposite side of the puzzle, now pictorially upside down. He began to place pieces in the bottom left, a mirror of what he'd done before.

Shame came into the room carrying a short stack of clothes, a folded pair of jeans and a white tee shirt with an old leather belt coiled up on top. He handed the stack to Ndiya, staring at her soaked skirt.

–You can't wear *that* all night. These'll be loose but, hey, roll them up and use the belt if you want. I guess the shirt's optional, depending.

–Thanks. I guess I'll give it a try. Umm—

Shame pointed to a closed door to the left.

–Bathroom.

–I think I remember.

The bathroom's floor was wooden, bright grain, and

thickly glazed with a glossy coat of something hard as glass. Someone had tiled the three walls adjoining the shower, in front of which was a clear curtain of plastic. A streetlight glowed outside a window on the fourth wall. Ndiya hung her matching aqua and blue linen-cotton blouse and skirt on brass, two-fingered hooks. After quickly splashing off the gutter water in his shower, she slipped her legs into Shame's jeans. She guessed they were his. She wondered how close in size she and he really were. She hadn't thought about it. She stared at herself in the mirror. A thin gold chain S'd its way along the V-neck cut of the shirt he'd given her to wear. A white knot at her waist tied up the shirt's baggy excess. She'd cinch the top of the jeans with the worn brown belt and roll the bottoms, twice, up past her ankles. Fine belt, she thought. She lifted it to smell the age in the leather and paused when she noticed faint teeth marks along one edge. Pain beach on each eye, she saw the setup and whispered into the mirror,

–What kind of . . . get me in here, dress me up, and in *his* clothes, what's next? Half the living room's a daycare, or is Melvin his kid? Does he have kids? Jesus, what's wrong with me? What am I doing here?

After getting upstairs, Ndiya had told herself that she was more at ease than this, at least. Now another voice was telling her she wasn't.

The impulse to walk out of the bathroom and straight out the front door was familiar. Ndiya walking away—she'd already seen that film. She felt it in the backs of her thighs. She knew the route it traveled up her spine and into her shoulders. And by now, she knew where it led:

Phoenix. In the mirror, the impulse popped into her jaw muscles. Involuntarily, she visualized angles between the three points of her escape: her current position, her purse, and the front door. She knew her shoes were next to the door. Then she heard a different voice:

—Ndiya, sweetness, may we have a quick word?

She half listened to her memory for a knock at the door, almost checked behind the clear shower curtain and then looked around, laughed to herself, and stared back at the question in the mirror:

—Sure, it's *all* Shame-what's-his-name's master plan. You do know, of course, that it was you who got off the bus and decided you needed to wade in the water? That's not beyond you, is it? I know that. So? What's the man supposed to do? Have you sitting wherever you're going to sit wearing clothes soaked in that nasty water? Or maybe you think he should have a rack of replacement clothes for women who decide to go swimming on their way to his place? I get it. Good, you *can* dial it back, right? Plus, if you'd stop playing Phoenix and blowing kisses to your eyelids for a second, the blue scarf doesn't look half bad with the jeans.

Ndiya answered this out loud:

—OK, but do you have anything intelligent to say about the teeth marks in this belt?

—Well, you *do* have your knife, right?

—Perfect.

Now, *that* was a knock on the door:

—Ah, Mrs., *Ah-kneedia*? . . . Ms. I Need The—I mean, when you're done talking to the mirror, ma'am, *I* gotta *go*.

Under her breath:

—Good thing none of this is really happening.

Out loud:

—Yes, sweetie, one second. OK, it's all yours.

Ndiya passed Melvin in the doorway of the bathroom and reentered the living room to find six puzzles finished on the floor, two of them facedown, complete, and blank. And Shame nowhere to be seen. She heard "Gotcha" and water running and thought for a moment she'd left the water on in the sink. Turning, she saw Melvin's sturdy little legs and his tiny butt looking like a couple of eminently spankable baby melons in a brown paper bag. Melvin said, "Direct hit!" His head bowed in concentration and his red shorts accordioned down at his ankles.

She walked past the puzzles and the shelf with games, another shelf of bright, oversized books, boxes of cards, and a big laundry basket of colored wooden blocks. There were six booster seats in primary colors stacked up in the corner. She'd somehow seen none of this on date number two. *None* of it. This was the same place, right? There was a four-foot-tall, blue-tiled wall jutting out halfway into the space that separated all of this from the flat couch, dining table, and a time bomb–looking thing connected to speakers on a low table. Two doors were at the end of the room, one open to the kitchen and one closed to what must be the bedroom.

As she looked back at the old piano pushed up against the dividing wall and near an open window, the "must be the bedroom" phrase in Ndiya's survey of the space sent another spiral of flight-impulse through her body. Silent voices:

–Was that "must be the bedroom" I heard you think, just now? Date number two and you didn't even *get* to the bed? Don't tell me you all did it right here on the living room floor? Least you let the man get up the stairs and down the hallway. Least you *seemed* to know where the bathroom was.

Ndiya felt her face flush. Color photos flipped in front of her eyes. Her index finger and thumb slip behind a silver button on a pair of blue jeans, an upsweep of black hair in a stream out of the denim. An out-of-focus image of an electrical outlet, a few wires, and the legs of a piano bench. A clear photo of her fingers, palm down, grasping the golden fringe of a coarse, kilim-weave floor rug, her hand rolling and wrapped up in the rug. She knew the sounds would come next and so she shook the vision off and headed to the kitchen.

–Hey there.

–Dry? And you used soap?

She frowned and nodded. Shame stood at a worn-looking rectangular butcher block. The top of the block was low, midthigh height. Its top sloped off-center toward the edge and was streaked with white lines. Ndiya slapped the first thought out of her mind. He kneaded a grapefruit-sized ball of dough, an open stainless container of flour to one side, flour on his jeans and white dusted up each wrist. Behind him squatted a cobalt blue stove with several doors on the front and a ventilation hood above. Sausages fried in a pan beneath a screen cover and a large silver pot with a blackened bottom sat in the center of the stove. Above his head on her right, two empty clotheslines were strung from side to side. His eyes fell to the floor and bounced back to her eyes. She looked at the big silver pot.

–Nice jeans. How's Melvin doing?

–Last I saw, his aim's dead on.

She had so many questions loaded up, she could almost see a red squadron of laser dots hovering on Shame's chest and forehead: Is Melvin your child? Do you have kids? Were you ever married? Or: Why not? Hell, are you *still* married? What's with the damned teeth marks on this belt? The booster seats? And, as ever, what's the story with the name? There were other questions, she could feel them, but they moved in an atmosphere she wasn't going to breathe. Not for a while in the "when 'if' means 'ever'" kind of way. With all this stirring, she came up with:

–Is there something I can do?

–Two plates, water glasses, two wine glasses if you'll drink some. One if you won't.

–Where?

Shame palmed the dough with his right hand and gestured with his shoulder and forehead behind him. Ndiya turned and heard three slow knocks on the front door.

–That's Muna.

After nodding at his flour-dusted hands, Shame gestured toward the door with both hands as if he was cuffed at the wrists:

–Could you get that.

It wasn't a question. Ndiya completed the spin and a quarter and exited the kitchen, crossed the rug—"Shame's rug, *that* rug," she thought—behind the piano and proceeded to the door. As she did, Melvin fell in behind her and grabbed hold of the gathered knot of fabric at the bottom of her shirt. Ndiya opened the door and found a short, rail-thin, dark-cinnamon-skinned woman. She wore her hair in a tight, bright-red, smooth wrap around her almond-shaped head. A three-pronged lightning bolt tattoo appeared diagonal behind her right ear, ending just before her jawline; a spark from a diamond chip in her nose searched the left side of her face. She had on a short, beige second-skin of a dress, and brown flats. Red satin dance slippers with wide, black ribbons for laces dangled from her right hand. The woman held the hand of a little boy—maybe he was eight?—with a few dozen newly twisted knots of rust-tinted hair on his head. The boy gazed up at Ndiya as if he knew her and immediately revealed an off-center three-tooth gap in his smile. The woman's eyebrows were line-thin and tinted with a red pencil that matched her hair color. Her left eyebrow was split in two: the two lines abutted into what looked like a cross between a timeout sign and a signal with glowing cones to a taxiing airliner. The effect was that the top left of the woman's face was stuck in an appearance of broken surprise. Her right eye was cut low enough to pass for asleep. Before the door was all the way open into the room, Ndiya was still stepping back and unaware of Melvin stepping back behind her.

–Sha—oh shi—well, hi.

Muna stepped back one pace. She did an up-and-down glance at Ndiya in Shame's rolled-up jeans, and assumed a first-position stance for a theatrical smile. Then, after holding the pose for a beat, she made a perfect dismount from surprise into speech:

–Look, tell Shame I'll be right back, an hour or so, tops. Go on in, Ahrrisse. I'll be back in a little while.

She placed the accent between the syllables of "little" and somehow shrunk the amount of time implied in the phrase. The woman nudged the little boy gently with her hip and let her fingers fall between the knotted twists over the top of his head and down his neck. The way Muna's hand traveled the boy's head stuck in Ndiya's eye. She thought again of what her brothers used to call touch.

Just as Ndiya began to introduce herself, Melvin came from behind and dove on Ahrrisse. The two rolled across the floor in a tumble of *you*s and *be*s and *bet*s and *not*s and *don't*s in various combinations. Immediately it sounded to Ndiya like one of them was laughing and one was crying. Without a thought, she'd grabbed them by the arms and stood them up.

–Boys, boys.

–We just playing.

–Who she?

–Her name "I Need A . . ."

–Ooh, she Mr. Shame's honey-y-y.

Both faces twisted up to look at Ndiya while, somehow, the boys still stared directly at each other. Ndiya swung back around to the open door holding onto both boys' wrists in her right hand.

–You know I'm not really—

Muna cut her off with a wave of her hand. She stared at the boys dangling from Ndiya's grasp.

–Doesn't matter, girl, you sure good at this!

The hallway was empty behind Muna who stood there and smiled. Ndiya thought she heard car tires peel off down in the street and then she heard,

–Her name be "She Need A—" if she don't let go my arm.

–What?

Ndiya's free hand flinched up, ready to—and Shame slid into the room:

–Ahrrisse! Catch. Hey, Muna.

Ndiya saw a pale ball fly through the air across the room. She ducked. Ahrrisse caught the ball with his free hand in front of his face. Shame pivoted back toward the kitchen:

–Give and go. Hit me.

Ahrrisse wound up and threw the ball back to Shame, who made the catch, then released the dough ball. He yelled "Crip!" and slapped the doorjamb with both hands, snatched the ball back out of the air, and disappeared through the door back into the kitchen. Then, in a voice that sounded like it had been turned inside out, she heard Shame say,

–You and Melvin play *in*-side, here. You all *know* that. This time of night, you both know what that means.

Ndiya didn't recognize the voice. And "crip"? What was that? Ahrrisse and Melvin nodded at the changed voice that came from the kitchen. They went back to the corner where the puzzles were. They argued, apparently over the puzzles, in silence via some kind of sign-slash-mime language made mostly of throat-cutting gestures, shoulders jerking forward, and finger pointing. They took two puzzles, mixed all the pieces in a single box top. Each boy then stood up and stepped back. They looked at each other. Ndiya watched the boys shake their hands facing each other. They counted one, two, three fingers before they went down on one knee and began to take pieces out of the box. They examined each piece and then either placed it by their side or tossed it back in the box.

Muna vanished without another word.

Ndiya walked back into the kitchen, staring back at the two boys and the closed door where Muna had stood seconds before. Shame had the ball covered in a dishtowel and he'd turned the sausages off. A small saucepan was out and he was busy skinning two large tomatoes.

—Do you know how to crush garlic and sauté it without making it turn brown?

—I can do that. Shame, ah?

—Yes?

—Does she, you know, Muna, does she come here every night at this time? With, what's that boy's name? I mean—

—Ahrrisse. No. Rarely this time of night.

—Then how did you know it was her?

—Three slow knocks. And then she waited. I knew it was her. She's probably got a quick appointment.

—An appointment.

—Yes. You know, an arrangement. Do you know how to slice fresh ginger?

—No. Are we talking about what I think we're talking about?

—No, we're not. No trick to it, really. *Thin*, though.

–We're not?

–No, we're not. But we will if you want to when we get this meal ready, OK, Ms. Ndiya-no-ginger-slicing-full-of-questions-Grayson.

Shame, with elaborate theatricality, held up a knife with a small triangular blade, nodded at her, and put it on the counter with the handle pointed in her direction. He pointed at the knife.

–Use that. *V-e-r-y*, very thin. This slicing of ginger is very technical, you understand? Precise. Hold it with your fingertips. Mix the slices together awhile with your fingers to release the scent. Leave the ginger slices on the board and then stir the butter and the crushed garlic together in that pan over the flame.

–OK, then what with the ginger?

–Just leave it.

Shrugging off the precision technicalities—he can't be serious—Ndiya looked at the knife on the counter with its handle pointed at her. She thought, "Jesus, 'Never hand a knife to a friend!' How long has *that* been? Who even said that anymore? You'll *cut* the friendship." Then, "So we're *friends*, now." Ndiya frowned her smile down at the ginger surgery she'd been assigned.

She sliced away the pink petals, stirred them up with her fingers like Shame said and set them to the side in a pile. She took two plates and four glasses to the table. Ahrrisse and Melvin were statues of concentration. Each on one knee, only their hands and their heads moved at all. Ahrrisse rose up slowly in a hula-like motion, waved what Ndiya realized was the final piece in his puzzle around his head, kissed it, and placed the piece at the bottom right corner of the completed rectangle. She was just about to say, "Good job," or something like that when Ahrrisse stood up straight. Melvin's puzzle still had a scattered half dozen pieces missing. So, Ahrrisse slapped him on the back of his head. *Pop!* Ndiya winced. Both boys then fell on the floor silencing their laughter into faint squeals. The fit subsided. Immediately, they took out two other puzzles, dissolved them into a box top, repeated the one, two, three with their hands. Ndiya turned away to find Shame at the saucepan adding the garlic, butter, a can of tomato sauce, skinned tomatoes, and several small piles of green flakes to the mix. He closely inspected the small pile of ginger slices. Shame rubbed his hands together in the "now we're getting some-where" motion, nodded, and pointed to the garbage can.

–Would you please stir those again with your fingers and then toss them?

–Something wrong with how I sliced them?

–Nope. Perfect.

Slowly, for emphasis on the absurdity, Ndiya stared at Shame while she stirred and then tossed her pile of technical ginger slices into the trash. After he savored the theater for an instant, Shame poured a glass of wine into the pan and it fizzed up steam. He put his nose into the vapor and whispered,

–Inspissation. Don't you love a word that sounds *exactly* like what it is?

Ndiya was still confused but she was beginning to see a puzzle, a pattern of her own. On top of that pattern, she liked how he moved. She felt a splayed-out tinge of the last-bite-of-oatmeal feeling. To distract herself, she started to ask something but Shame spoke first:

–I'm glad you're here. I'm really glad you're here. Most people, you know, they don't come *back* here.

–Why not?

–I don't know. You could probably tell me better than me telling you.

–A few things come to mind. But I wouldn't want to guess.

–To speculate?

–Correct. Plus, in my book, I didn't come here the first time, you *brought* me here. So I still have a chance.

–That's the second time. You came along.

–First time here. That was an *accident*.

–OK. But the bad kind or the good kind?

Ndiya knew this game. She didn't mind playing for a while. It was fun and he was good at it. But as she stared at her feet, she couldn't fit some piece of his question into the box for the game she knew it belonged in. She looked up at him hovering over the stove, flour still in the hairs on his wrists. It looked like he was dancing without moving. Like he was moving to music but there wasn't any playing. The lack of music struck her. That felt strange. She paused, said nothing. He asked,

–What time is it?

–Almost nine.

–OK, when Mrs. Clara comes for Melvin, I'll send Ahrrisse with them. That'll be very soon. Mrs. Clara's got a Swiss watch where her brain should be. The woman doesn't play.

–I gathered that down the block.

–Oh, right. Exactly how *did* you meet up with Melvin, anyway?

Two minutes to nine on Ndiya's phone, Mrs. Clara knocked once on Shame's door, entered the apartment, and took Melvin by the hand. She blew a kiss at Shame and pointed to her cheek. She took Ahrrisse's hand, and, while Melvin opened the door for the three of them, Mrs. Clara said,

–Thank you for minding Melvin, Miss Anita.

–Oh, that's Ah-ndi—well, you're certainly welcome, ma'am.

Mrs. Clara's chin raised up, she aimed her eyes over Ndiya's shoulder.

–I've got Ahrrisse too. See you tomorrow, Mugga-bugga.

–Right. Sixish.

–You know I don't *do* ish-ness my dear. See you at six. Sharp.

And they were gone. Ndiya put her phone in her pocket and stared down at her wrist.

–Wow. 8:59.

–I know, and that's just a taste. And your wrist is slow.

■

Ndiya sat at Shame's table in a pause. She hadn't been back to her job since the confessional fiasco of her errant email to the SnapB/l/acklist. She took that as an invitation to come back to the scene of the crime. She definitely didn't believe in signs. But still. Yvette had called, left messages, emailed. Her supervisor had called too. Then she emailed to say that, in light of the high quality of Ndiya's work over the summer, they had decided to place her on emergency leave-of-absence without pay and hoped she'd return when she felt better and would she give them ten days' notice before returning? Ndiya had stopped checking all of it. She had enough money saved for six months of life if she concentrated a little and stayed away from Shame's Blue Labels.

She hadn't told Shame any of this. After date number two, when he dropped her at her sublet townhouse in South Commons, they had agreed to see each other "next Friday" and hadn't talked since. The last thing they'd said to each other before she arrived at twilight swayed before her like the loose, frayed end of something. She'd told Shame how it felt with his hands on her and he'd said: "That was a risky thing to say to me, Ndiya Grayson." She knew she was skating on soon-thinning ice, again, but she couldn't place the unfamiliar feeling. When she did pay some attention, she found several feelings turning over like a basket full of snakes or maybe twisted like currents in a mountain stream; maybe it was going somewhere? When this possibility dawned, as if in a chorus of one hundred songs at once, something in her hummed, "Let it go."

She didn't plan to ever go back to that job. She meant she wasn't going back to any of those jobs; they were all the same job. Even thinking about it in Shame's place made her feel sick and dizzy and she didn't know why. She kept feeling a train passing under the building but told herself the train didn't go beneath this block or anywhere near it. It wasn't the El. It was too far away to feel and that wasn't the sensation at all. And in a way that accompanied the train feeling, she felt something like a heavy weight swinging behind her in wide, slow arcs. The dinner was great. She concentrated on finding the trace of absent ginger in the sauce but only succeeded in locating a sharp, electric tingling in her fingertips.

Shame had rolled out the dough flat, rubbed flour on the surface, rolled the sheet up into a tube, and sliced it into discs. Then he unrolled the discs one by one into thin noodles in a bell curve of lengths and hung them up in suspension-bridge arcs on the two clotheslines strung overhead across the length of the galley kitchen. After ten minutes, he walked beneath the lines with his hands between them, gathered the noodles into a bunch, and dropped them in the boiling water. Minutes later they sat across from each other at the kitchen end of Shame's long table and ate the thick noodles, the sauce, and sausages. Shame tore a hunk of bread from a baguette with his teeth and offered her the other end.

Trying to ignore the train-penduluming-in-the-mountain-stream feeling of tastes and tingling fingertips, Ndiya studied a horizontal painting behind Shame. It was unframed, and hung tacked to the wall at four points along the top edge. Across the canvas, one bold line separated ground from sky. The painting was large, about five feet across, about four feet tall. On the ground a three-dimensional outline of a house leaned and twisted under the force of a strong wind. To the left of the structure stood a telephone pole broken a third of the way up. The power lines billowed off to the left and out of view. To the right a huge figure with three intersecting arrows in its head leaned over the house. Lines of breath appeared from where its mouth would be, curled around the roof and joined the power lines exiting off the edge of the canvas to the left. Behind the structures and the figure, a golden, elephant-shaped mass of hot air rode its way up a cold gray dome hugging the ground. As Ndiya stared at the golden mass visible through the lines of the house's roof, she noticed flames blowing from the house. At the bottom, under the ground, were the words: *Oyá en lo Suyo* *.

Ndiya nodded to the painting behind Shame. He looked behind him and then turned back to her.

–Bad weather?

–Depends.

–On what?

–Well, on which arrow's which. Coffee?

–None for me.

–Me neither. I have to be to work early.

–Saturday?

–Only till noon. How about a cognac?

–What do you do at work?

Shame got up, collected the plates and took the wineglasses between his fingers. Ndiya heard the plates slide into the sink. Water sprayed and there was a pause while cupboards opened and closed. Shame came back into the room with two tiny, square glasses of brown liquid. He set one in front of Ndiya and sipped his as he sat down opposite her again.

–We're repairing tanks that they'll fill with acid to wash steel wire. The mill's in operation while we do the repairs so the schedule's a little irregular. All in all, not a bad job. It'd be better if it was in winter because it's hot as all get out in there.

Ndiya watched the house lean in the painting behind Shame's shoulder. She felt the train again and almost heard the weight swoop behind her head, low enough that she ducked slightly and covered it up by bending down to inhale the warm smoke-and-walnut scent coming from the small glass. The scent burned in her nose.

–That's the work you do?

–One part of it.

–Do you want to know what I do?

–What do you do?

More trains, closer. The swinging weight vanished. Ndiya noticed that the figure to the right of the house in the painting behind Shame's shoulder had what appeared to be a bullhorn-shaped breast protruding from its lower chest. The figure hovered about the line of cold gray and seemed to have a crest of some kind sweeping back from its forehead. Thinking about her job, all of her jobs over the years, suddenly made her feel sick.

–Well, I—you know, you don't want to know about that. It's just a job. Who is Muna, Shame?

–Ahrrisse's mother. She has two daughters, as well. She lives two buildings down. She walks—well, she works irregular hours. Most of the women around here work all the time, but sporadically. If something comes up, most evenings, they know they can bring the kids here.

–She *walks* to work?

–One might say that.

–What else might one say?

–About Muna? She kind of walks *as* work. Did you notice the shoes?

Ndiya nodded in disagreement, held Shame's eyes with hers, and turned her face down so her eyebrows obscured everything above his eyes. She focused, trying—and failing—to read the slightly serious smirk he wore. Her face felt like a flock of already answered, unasked questions. Shame continued,

–What's there to say? The woman walks. Far as I know, she got started walking on an old man named Christopher with VA benefits. Word got around, a preacher got involved. Soon as that, she's been at it since.

–A preacher? Involved?

–Well, a sometimes-preacher. But he's not in it as a preacher, really. More like a broker.

–Right, they've got another term for that . . .

–I *know*: Pastor!

–Funny.

Ndiya measured a whiff of the liquid and touched the tip of her tongue to the surface. The low burn on her tongue reminded her of the ginger-feeling at the ends of her fingers.

–It's good. Strong.

–That means a lot coming from you, Ms. *Blue* Label.

–Well, I hope it doesn't cost that much or else I'm going to have to ask you who *you* walking on.

Ndiya laughed and abruptly stopped.

–Does she walk you, Shame?

–Used to, a few times. I paid her twenty dollars, loaned her the rest. *Long*-term loan.

Shame laughed. The weight swung back and seemed to strike a huge, silent bell somewhere back there. Ndiya sat amid the deaf clang, ready. She waited, almost afraid to listen, like when a bright flash of lightning clears the way for a crash of thunder. She didn't want to ask:

–Paid her for?

–Just walking, Ndiya. Nothing more. She offered. I said, "Muna, twenty dollars is twenty dollars, the rest is a *loan*." She took my money with a friendly snatch, said, "Damn skippy," through her smile and never mentioned it again.

Ndiya reverse-whistled a thread of the liquid into her mouth and rolled her tongue through the middle of it. The motion of her tongue seemed to triple the amount of liquid in her mouth. She swallowed and traced the heat down her throat and decided that, no matter the feeling, it couldn't have poured straight down to her feet. She felt warm. And pendulums. And a kind of distance, some-where, maybe an empty space. Then, in an exhale, that space collapsed.

–Shame, what the hell's going on?

–There's a whole lot going on, Ndiya Grayson. But as far as Muna goes, nothing more than a historical walk or two on my back. That woman's got her some talented toes.

–I bet. What? Does she hold weights? She can't be but ninety pounds.

–It's not the weight, it's the action.

–OK. That's enough. It's my fault for asking. And you watch her son when she's walking to work? Is that bubble thing over there a stereo?

–Yes. And yes.

–Does *it* work?

–Yes. It has to work, *it* can't walk.

–Ha. Funny.

Ndiya stood up, keeping a hand on the table just in case. Shame noticed that. She started to walk around the dining table toward a low, smaller table placed underneath a wide window along the wall near the piano. She crouched down near the bubble thing Shame called a stereo and examined a shelf of plastic slips, each containing a CD. Jazz. Jazz. Jazz. Jazz.

Ndiya didn't know anything about jazz by name but had lived constantly within its sound as a child. "Your *father*," her mother would say, turning up the volume. He was "your *father*" to her mother, but he was "Daddy" to her. Thinking of him sounded like funky breath through some horn made mostly of sound filling up a vacant space in their apartment or maybe whistling through a hole in her chest. Memories of that apartment mostly felt like holes in her chest. Just then, while flipping through Shame's CDs, she remembered playing with a friend in the box gardens they'd made at school. So far back she has no image of the little girl who asked her, "What you think it would it be like having one of them all-the-time daddies?" And tears rose up behind Ndiya's eyes as she remembered. She heard herself, hands in the cool dirt: "Then I could be myself *all* the time." She snapped herself away from the memory and back to the present:

–Mind if I play something?

–The power switch is on the back. I'll clear this table.

Ndiya flicked the switch and watched an amber-and-blue glow fill each of the tall glass bubbles. She walked her fingers from CD to CD and stopped on one with a close-up photo of a handsome, middle-aged black man in a small bow tie. Along the edge of the cover she read:

ART
BLAKEY
AND
THE
JAZZ
MES
SEN
GERS
BLUE
NOTE
4003

She turned the slip over and found a photo of the same man caught in a state of rapture. She glanced down at the songs on the album:

1 WARM-UP AND DIALOGUE BETWEEN LEE AND RUDY

2 MOANIN'

3 ARE YOU REAL?

4 ALONG CAME BETTY

5 THE DRUM THUNDER SUITE

6 BLUES MARCH

7 COME RAIN OR COME SHINE

8 MOANIN' (ALTERNATE TAKE)

The names of the players and songs meant nothing to her. She liked the two photos of the man very much. She flipped back and forth between them. The face on the cover was a mask, a portrait: thoughtful, sad. Anger burned behind all that like the paper the photo was printed on. The man's face on the back was open in a totally private way. "Open, that is," she thought, "if you were willing to meet him where he is and on his terms." She wondered why she thought that. Ndiya then inserted the disc. She played song number three. The horns appeared in three notes and she heard Shame laugh over the running water in the kitchen.

–Ah! You've got nerve, Ndiya Grayson. And jokes!

More laughter. She listened to the solos. She knew it wasn't just nerves. She felt a mix of underground trains, distant pendulums, and cautionary mountain streams. Beyond that she wasn't sure what it was. The song was upbeat but not fast. The cymbals galloped. When the song concluded she popped the button back to song number two. She read that the piano player was Bobby Timmons. She thought it sounded more like he was playing the change in his pocket than a piano. During the first piano solo, Ndiya's fingers started to move with the sound. The notes pulsed together, fell like rain blown by a strong, slow wind. She looked back at the painting, touched the tip of her tongue to the surface of her drink, and thought: "Can a strong wind be slow? Can it pause and still be strong? Still be wind?" She heard the image of Muna's fingertips coming off the slope of Ahrrisse's neck. Touch.

While Shame washed the dishes, Ndiya stood still on the kilim rug. She swayed imperceptibly in time to a rhythm much, much slower than the tempo of the song. Her fingertips tingled and burned a little and she felt like she was a weight swinging at the end of a very long wire. While Mr. Timmons played, she said to herself,

–That son of a mother—

Suddenly it was obvious. The sliced ginger had nothing at all to do with the sauce. The ginger was for her. Or, she thought, eyes narrowed, for *him*? Ndiya felt the pendulum behind her back, trains underfoot. She moved her spiced fingers and felt like she could taste the sound of a distant bell.

The song ended and Shame appeared from the kitchen, handed Ndiya a white towel.

–You dry, OK? If you can't find the place for something, just leave it on the stove.

She took the towel from his outstretched hand, walked into the kitchen, and took a plate out of the dish drainer. Wiping it with the towel, she noticed Shame kneeling down at the stereo.

–I guess two can play this game, right?

She kept at the dishes with two fingers wrapped in cloth sweeping inside a wineglass. Shame chanted to himself,

–Six minutes, six minutes . . . uh, uh on—

He raised up and Ndiya, without turning her head, watched his back as he walked the length of the apartment to the bathroom. The back of his head went from shadow to light, back to shadow, and back to light just before he disappeared. He closed the door but left it ajar. She heard the bathroom fan, the slink of curtain rings, and the shower spurted into action. She recognized his "six minutes" foolishness, of course. Everyone their age knew "The Show." But that was a decoy. Then she heard synth-bells float in an empty space of cymbals—

Ndiya's vision immediately began to sweat. Her eyes felt exactly like her gingerized fingertips. And then a voice, *Whis-per-ing-ing in his e-e-ear . . . and that the-ere's nothing too good for us.*

By the time the song's intro ended, tears streamed her face. Ndiya thought, "Like hell two can play." Echoed in how the singer's voice broke the word "there" over different dimensions, Ndiya found herself in three places at once. She was drying dishes with slow-burning, ginger fingers, in tears, standing in Shame's kitchen staring at the steam in the stripe of light next to the bathroom door he left ajar. Her mind blew back to her sublet table with the oatmeal and the meditation on the Bic Lighter phrase. Standing in these two places, she thought to herself, "Shame couldn't *play* a game to save his damned life." He clearly didn't know how to play. She thought, wrongly, that passing up all kind of preliminaries and going straight in for the kill must just come naturally to the man. It wasn't even the kill part. It was the "straight for" of the thing. But straight for what, and for who? And from *where?* The ways Shame arrived at where he came at her from weren't, what? Regular? Predicable? It was beyond that. None of it was natural. His arrivals arose, she thought, from another dimension—

Then all that vanished behind Ndiya, age ten, in bed beneath her eight-hundred-foot-deep blanket, listening to her favorite song. The soft beat and synth chimes leading her into sleep. The voice, wan, slight, was heavier than the blanket pinning her legs to the sheet. The song sang, *I'll only be here for while*, and she wondered what that meant. The singer sang *I just got to be me* and *I just got to be free* until she couldn't tell the two words apart. The song rained portraits of women on her floor: her mother and her mother's sisters, all her aunties, to which of whom she had no idea how or if she was actually related. "Why 'actually'?" suddenly occurred to her. The song rained women listening to the song. Singing along with the rain raining themselves, listening to each other sing, listening to each other rain. That soft rhythm sledgehammer, the light voice that blew out the wall.

By the time she was ten, she'd learned what "free" meant. They'd talked about freedom in her school. She'd heard about it on TV. Freedom was loud men with fists. They died by getting killed. She'd learned about that just like all the other square-box-type stuff in school that no one ever heard of. But this song swung open a secret door, an unknown room in her arms and legs.

It came to her just then, standing on that thin rug in Shame's jeans: "What happened if a woman couldn't tell the difference between the words 'free' and 'me'?"

She remembered lying beneath the immovable weight of her blanket. Freedom was invisible fluid. It vanished into the space of sleep. It rained women who knew what fantasies were and what they were good for. And she knew how the world fell apart on people, in people, women, who were forced to play the near side of the border they'd all been born beyond.

Music like this went where they lived but couldn't never go. Somehow, in a bottomless, electric way that would swallow her if she let it, all that led to where she'd been taken and how everything . . .

Ndiya felt the pendulum swing behind her and wondered all over again how such a light wisp of a song could rain that lead-weighted invisible fluid she'd heard, partially hid from, partially hiding in, as a child. She could see it *now*, standing in Shame's kitchen wearing his clothes. Whoever he was. She glanced at the bathroom door ajar. The swinging weight wasn't in the song at all. It was in the world the song didn't sing about. A world of hard sense and fanatical control the song refused, a room with no room for common mistakes, a room no one owned, a room each person built around herself with no windows and no door. Refusal was the song that this song *didn't* sing. Refusal was her mother's song, which is why her mother loved *this* song. Then the song fell out of that place and swung around like a flashlight dropped deep in Ndiya's underwater life.

The circle of light in the floating song flashed around Shame's place. Ndiya felt surrounded by overlapping waves of frailty and strength, fullness and vacancy, in the voice. She saw four black numerals above a white, battered door: 2337. And she knew it was a house address on Monroe Street. She didn't know how she knew that. The flashlight voice swung and lit up other voices. Her daddy and his brother arguing with her mother. Her daddy didn't come around much. He used to say Ms. Alexander, the building president, had barred him from the premises unless he was willing to work security for her. He wasn't. When he came around anyway, there were always *words*. And he always dropped off money. She remembered thick knots of worn, green bills. And she remembered the way her mother took the money from her daddy while staring over his shoulder at whatever was back there. The song just then sounded exactly like how Ndiya always knew how to stay out the way of her mother's eyes whenever her daddy was there. The words between her parents were always about any little thing. It was obvious to her even then, even more now, that there was always something else going on. She had no idea what.

–Now, Vee, look here—

–Naw, nigga, you look 'cause I already seen what you saying.

This argument was about the cold. It was December.

She knew because her mother kept asking him, "You *do* know it's December?" She must have been three, almost four. The flash of sound curved out of the song on Shame's stereo and blew out of focus like sleet through her body. Her body felt like those warm winter nights when it snows and grass is white and the streets are wet black. The clean, cold black smell in the street. Steam from the manholes. Black and white grains fell together like how an image became itself in a photo or like the way an old-time TV warmed up, the image beginning at the edges of the screen and filling in toward the center. She recognized this scene as one of her two blurry, earliest memories. But it had surfaced this time with a strobe of irregular details she'd never known. It was a feeling behind her eyes. It felt like when her hands went numb in the cold, a blur, imprecise, studded with vivid flashes of feeling.

–You're not going to have *my* child standing out there in this cold, I don't care if Jesus Christ is handing out keys to the Kingdom over there.

–She's going to see *this*, Vera.

–She's seen enough. Gonna see more.

–Which is *why* she's going to see this.

The ceiling was as close as the floor. She wondered what was so special about seeing this cold or not. Ndiya's daddy held her around her thighs so her face was just beneath his. She could smell sweet wine on his breath, the smoke in the woolen arms of his dark blue coat. The smell of distant cigarettes would always make her feel her daddy's arms. That close-up scent of her daddy's distance. He carried her away and stood at the window of their apartment. The freeway and, beyond that, endless rectangles of black-streaked gray out the window. She heard her uncle Lucky's soft voice.

−Look here, Vee. I know there's noise and all. But this—they—we got to—we can't just—why don't you come along? We'll bring blankets.

−Oh, now *you* asking?

−No, you *answering*.

Lucky could always approach the wall of her mother's face when her daddy was there. They paused, eyes broadcasting invisibly to each other. Ndiya saw her daddy was the white grass and watched her mother turn into the warm, black street, her uncle the steam between them. For a minute she sensed a pause in the cold.

Ndiya and her mother sat in the back of Lucky's car. Lucky always had a car. The puffy green, quilted seats warmed up under them, the back windows were fogged. She remembered Lucky had wiped the windshield with his coat sleeve while he drove. The rhythm of the wipers, the rhythm of streetlight bulbs, black against the gray sky, stared straight down at her. She lay on her back, her head in her mother's lap. She fell asleep.

She remembered standing on the sidewalk surrounded by coats. Fur coats. Wool coats. The smell of leather from long, quilted coats. The fringe-ends of scarves tingling her head like the heavy-dancing flop-things she'd seen at the car wash. Black. Brown. Crème. Coats. The sound of gloved hands slapping each other, the deep thick sound of gloves hitting the backs of men's coats. Clouds of breath. And smoke. And gloves. It was a waist-high world of leather breath and fur touch. A man stood in front of them, his right glove at exactly her eye level. It had a small V cut at the back where a tuft of fur came out.

The crowd stood close to each other. No one spoke. At one point, Ndiya leaned forward and the fur from inside the man's glove touched her nose. She thought it was as soft as nothing-at-all must be soft. The glove was brown; it had three tracks, like the tread on a car tire, on the outside. Each track pointed toward a knuckle on the back of the man's hand. No one talked. She remembered the sound of people's shoes and boots on the cold sidewalk. What she remembered most is the strange sound, a sound she'd never heard before. She stood there wondering what it was. Cars passed. A jet plane flew overhead in the clouds. Sirens, a city bus. Nothing strange about them. Then she knew what it was: it was the sound of all those people at once, the sound of no one talking.

Her daddy must have picked her up on his shoulders, because she remembers looking back behind them and seeing the long line of people they were in. This from above. Then she looked up ahead. And nobody talking. She knew it was cold but she couldn't feel it. She woke up inside a house with everything tumbled down. Her daddy held her in one arm, held her mother's shoulder with his other arm. The house was *all* thrown down. Chairs broken, flipped. Posters torn and hanging off the walls and papers all across the floor. No one talked except now one loud, loud man who pointed to holes in the front door. Each hole had a thin, straight stick coming out of it. They pointed into the house. She remembered the man's voice. Loud.

−Don't touch nothing, don't move nothing. Don't touch nothing. Don't move nothing.

She remembered:

−Brother . . . Chairman . . . Sister . . . Pigs . . .

Her daddy said,

−It's murder, Vera. Stone-cold murder.

Her mother nodded. She said nothing. That was odd. Ndiya wondered if the nothing her mother said just then was the same nothing everybody else was saying. Her daddy's eyes were underwater. But he didn't cry. And he didn't say it loud but somehow she could feel that word in her chest when he said it. Murder. It felt like a breath so deep it hurt her lungs and when she tried to breathe out it wouldn't go out. In a low voice, her daddy said it again and again. "It's murder. Murder." And that deep, too-full, can't-breathe feeling stayed in her chest. They walked through the first room and into the hallway. Records and a mattress up against the wall and something spilled all over the floor, papers stuck together in the spill. Everyone stepped over the spill. From across the room it looked black, when they stepped across she could tell it was deep red.

There was another room but her daddy, Lucky, and her mother each held her in the hall when one of them went in that room. Ndiya has a major key, melody-clear memory of asking,

−Is there more-dear in there too, Daddy?

−Yes. It's murder in there too, Ndiya. A beautiful young brother was murdered there.

Ndiya had begun to ask why but she saw the red

water in her daddy's eyes deepen. She hugged his neck and he carried her out the back of the house, back into the cold, and down around the back to the street. Ndiya looked back over her daddy's shoulder has he carried her. Then she knew that *more-dear* meant red water. She still couldn't feel the cold.

They passed a tiny old woman who had three little boys in front of her. She had on a long coat with a fur collar and a matching fur hat. Each boy wore one of those Sherlock Holmes–type hats with earflaps. Ndiya heard the old woman. She told those boys hard questions:

–He always said he wasn't going to die slipping on no piece of ice, *didn't* he?

She took one of the boys under his chin with her hand and bent his face up to hers. Ndiya thought she was treating those boys rough. The old woman told the boy, loud,

–Now, I say, didn't he?

–Yes, Mum Mum. He dee-id.

Then she looked at the other two. Ndiya wondered if they were twins.

–Now, you tell me. What he'd say?

And the little boys answered back one at a time and then in unison. The first:

–*Said* he wasn't gonna die off a trippin' off a no piece a ice.

And the next:

–Said he wasn't gonna catch no heart attack.

And the woman:

–What did he say?

Then all three:

—Said he was gonna die high on the people, Mum
Mum.

And the old woman:

—That's right. Now, come on.

■

In the cold, early December mist, on the night before
the day conjured by Deniece Williams in Ndiya's memory, a sixteen-year-old singer and student at Kenwood
High School in Hyde Park, Chicago, still stunned by the
hammer of the news of the murder, walked alone into
Washington Park. There she took out a snub-nosed .38
from the sleeve of her mock-fur coat and took a long look
at the dead glint of the metal in the ambient light, the
city reflected off the snow. Fender Rhodes light. The light
looked as if it had emerged out of the ground. Still light.
The gun had been given to her the night she'd been renamed in the way of the Revolution. Since she'd carried it,
by exactly what luck she now numbly wondered, it hadn't
been fired.

Watched over by a lake-blown, slate sky and a pan-
theon of newly anonymous gods, she threw the pistol as
far out as she could over the dragon-shaped Washington
Park lagoon. A sudden wind rose, then, as she turned. It
covered the sound of the splash in her ears. She promised
the gods that, if they'd reveal their real names to her, she'd
go about the Revolution in her own way, in a different
way. And she walked out of the park over the trampled
snow. Reaching the west edge of the park, she left the path

and stood at Fifty-Eighth Street and Martin Luther King Drive, a street that had been renamed just over a year or so earlier to project Chicago's forward-looking image.

She thought how she and the street now both had new names. She thought that the street had certainly been renamed too late; just then, she wondered if she'd been renamed too soon.

The sixteen-year-old Ms. Khan crossed the one-year-old King Drive and walked west, as if following the sun that, that night, seemed to have left her behind and gone down for good, taking the names of the black gods she'd learned with it. The diviner-priest who'd named her had repeated a phrase: he said it proved that black gods went home by going into the ground. Said black gods never flew away up into the sky. She didn't know where to go. Back off inside her, in an unswept corner beyond words, in a place no one gets decisions about, she decided to lead with her voice and follow that.

Shame came back into the kitchen just as the song was fading out. Ndiya stood with her two fingers wrapped in the dishtowel, still inside the first wineglass. Her mind was a score of the little boy's voice in the alley of her memory. Over and over she heard him: "He wasn't gonna die off a trippin' off a no piece a ice. Off a trippin' off a . . . off a trippin' off a no . . . he wasn't gonna die off a trippin' off a no piece a ice . . . no piece a ice. He wasn't gonna die off a trippin' off a no piece a ice." Then she heard again how Niecy's song made it so you couldn't tell the difference between the word "me" and the word "free."

Just then it struck her with a new shock that her favorite song had absolutely nothing to do with what it *said* it was singing about, that songs never *sing* what they *say*. If they did we wouldn't need songs. And singers wouldn't exist.

Niecy's song, like all songs, was simply a way of making a certain sound. And in that sound Ndiya heard things that were at once singular and anonymous. It was both curse and blessing, prayer and oath. The song was a thin veil of words dropped in front of a speechless howl. But which was which? Was the curse anonymous, or did it have a name? And the blessing? The prayer? The howl? The song was over and Ndiya heard the boy's voice from her memory like it had been etched in bone on the inside of her skull. "My skull?" she thought. Curse or blessing?

"Thought?" "Who the hell put that sound in that boy's head? What brought about that voice? What happened to the anonymous perfection of *his* sound? Where are those boys now?" She heard Niecy's song again:

–And that there-ere's nothing too good for us . . .

She felt Shame behind her. Ndiya, trains in her arms, bullets for eyes, pendulum in her pulse, stuttered,

–That's an *old* song.

–I heard it again a few days ago and it reminded me of you. I don't listen to music in here much anymore. I can't really hear it right.

Ndiya felt like someone was wringing out a soaked rag inside her belly.

–What if I want to go?

–I'll shoot you home like before. No troubles. Just say so.

She winced, invisibly. Shame left the room. The music changed. Instrumental music. A drummer, a violin, and a string instrument Ndiya didn't really recognize. It wasn't a guitar, wasn't American. She knew that. She allowed herself until Shame came back in the kitchen to decide whether to go or stay. Which is it, she thought, "free" or "me"? She turned around to put up the glass and heard him step back into the room behind her.

■

They fell on his bed about eleven. Music playing in the next room. Music he couldn't really hear. Music she said she didn't know. They brushed the books off the bed onto the floor. The books hit the wood and sounded like a waterfall applauding itself with heavy gloves on. His hands lost songs on her skin. Under her shirt. His shirt. And a light tug and her body a rising S of movement and then no shirt. The cursive M of her shoulders leans into his view, cuts the room. His left hand an eight-fingered chord on keys in the other room. Keys he can't name. His right hand almost still. She stares past him. He holds on to his jeans with a finger in the belt loop and she slips up out of them, invisible, leg-by-leg appearing back under his hand.

And as she arches up, to the side, his touch runs down the way gravity wants. Touch like beads of the heaviest liquid collects at the low spot of her. She breathes even and long, her breath an invisible glove on his hand.

The streetlight broken by the pattern of glass blocks in the wall. The blanket thrown back, the shadow of an unmade chessboard covers them both. The empty elevator shaft beneath the floor. An ambulance passes in the street followed by a police car. The red flash from eye to eye, a blue riot along her neck, over her hip and across the floor.

–Tell me your name, Shame.

–You just said it.

–You know what I mean.

Her belly a downward curve and his right hand on along—

–Remember you said I'd waited my life for this?

–I never said that.

–You know what I mean.

By measures that don't exist, his fingers disappear and her voice changes back into breath on his hand. Her voice moves like smoke through his fingers. He feels her thumb pause into a question on two smooth scars high on his shoulder. One finger back and forth between, circles in the two pools, one twice the size of the other, where the acid had dripped on his neck. Each touch makes the numb pools boil. It's as if the liquid escapes the pools. Pain runs down his arms into his hands. Acid in her fingers, and a trace of fresh ginger.

–Your breath tastes like smoke.

–It's the tar.

–Your skin tastes like dust and salt.

–It's the mill in my sweat.

–You showered.

–It's in there beneath the skin.

A sharp sound. A loud crack shoots through the room. Ndiya tenses up and draws back.

–Shhh. Easy. It's Luther B next door, teeing off.

–On who?

–He golfs in there. It's a late start, probably won't be more than three holes.

She laughs and Shame pushes himself until their hips meet. She feels a swell lift her, the wave moves and passes her off down its back. Another, and as she rises she grips his neck tight, her fingers press into Shame's acid wounds on the way down. He winces at the touch, sucking breath through his teeth with his mouth closed. She thinks it's pleasure. Three more quick cracks next door.

–That's the wedge. First hole, par three.

–What?

–Luther B. Tee shot probably landed between the cushions in the couch. The bunker.

They both laugh.

He pulls back and rises up. She closes in front of him. He stays there, tangent.

–You winking at me?

–Oh, shhhh-it—

Her hand to his thigh, pulls him. Their hips back together and she holds on, eyes shut. He tries to draw back but she holds him down inside her eyes. Her eyes are already shut, but he watches her try to shut them more. Then more. Shut eyes shut again. Her other arm pulls him down and her face vanishes from his view. Someone's shaking and at first he can't tell who it is. There's a loud crack and *he* almost ducks; Luther B's second tee shot.

And the tremor rises. Ndiya holds him by the thigh and around his back. He's so still she can feel the bed swing at the end of a long wire. She feels the ceiling holding back the sky. Something heavy arcs past just above his back. The shaking leaves the surface and he feels a vibration in his chest. Neither of them move but he feels the tremor in the subtle, double grip and give of her pulse. Grip-grip, give. A bottle breaks, a lamp or something tips over and they hear Luther B next door:

–Sit, dammit. Sit!

No one moves, no one pause. The vibration continues. They're beyond where they were. Shame begins to feel that this is not intimate, isn't about them. He wonders if it involves him at all. Or her. He can feel her move again but when he draws up she's there. She's still. Eyes closed, chin up and to the side. He moves in that underwater weight, that strong slowness that people can suddenly, without warning, become to each other. That brief, focused endless-ness. He sees her through a dark, liquid clarity where pres-sure closes vision down into a focus that's also blindness. She feels to him like a current has flashed into motion, like still water he'd waded into come alive. A slow, strong wind. Somehow he knows it's not private; they're not alone. This is nothing intimate. They're barely here at all. He feels the tremor pass beneath their bodies and he knows it's her, not hers as much as something she belongs to.

He feels Ndiya Grayson shaking inside. She moves without moving beneath him, around him. And she's else-where. Anywhere. She's anywhere and he's everywhere else. There's a sudden, universal slowness. The river of passion Shame has put his body near grows wider, wide enough that the narrow channel of pleasure disappears. Then a risen depth announces its pain. Ndiya's pores open. The room turns cold and he knows that this is pain, this body beneath him, whatever swings above him, an anguish nowhere near him. A vein of something that's nowhere near anyone. It's right beneath the palm of his hand. This is something you can't get near and can't see from a dis-tance. Yes, you. If you come close to this, he feels, you're in danger. Back away and you're lost.

–Jesus.

–Shsssssshss.

–Come on, girl.

No one moves, no one pauses. Her pulse shifts his vision toward her. He can feel himself approach and hears the quick upsweep of her voice—

–Don't.   Don't.

–OK.

Then nothing. He tries to move away and catch her eyes, and her arms close down on his back. Sweat floods the bed, more like a cold bucket of water than sweat. A broken fever. And more. He doesn't move; neither does she. The sweat pours between them, runs down his arm onto the sheet. He tastes it from behind her ear and tastes it again to make sure it's sweat not water. Not fire. Or blood. It's sweat. Ndiya, mouth closed, begins to hum *m*'s into his neck. Holding on. No one move. The tremor doesn't stop. It dives again beyond them both. He can feel her pulse around him, a half beat behind her heart. Grip-give, give. Then she begins to move again. She says,

–Shame, I'm not leaving.

–Yes, you should stay.

–I mean I'm not leaving.

–Stay. OK. Don't go.

–Shssshs. Not going. Not leaving.

–So come on.

They're both over. Ndiya looks at him and it's like when you drive up a mountain and then look back, down on the impossible ribbon of road, the route you'd come. There's always a thin thread of a stream headed some-where, on its way elsewhere. A vein of something clear and cold that never noticed you at all. He leans over and she leans along with him. They lie on their sides, her leg draws up into the number 4 laid down on its back with his. Under his ear, she whispers,

–God, I love this song.

A song she doesn't know. A song he can't hear.

BOOK
THREE:
INFLATION

Shine like diamond ice.

—JOYCE SIMS

5 41 East Sixty-Third Street. Inflation was a lounge, one of dozens on the South Side. Lounge meant fifty customers in two and a half shifts. Inflation opened at noon and closed at 2:00 a.m. when the back room, along with its card table, opened. There were eight stools along the bar on the right of the lounge. Three tables for two placed in the middle and six booths for four, maybe five, on the left. A hall at the end of the bar led to restrooms, a storeroom, and a back door to the alley behind the building. Relic from a bygone age, an upright piano, set diagonal to make room for a jukebox, sat at the back wall along the left.

That's where Junior Keith was headed Saturday night at nine o'clock when he left his two-bedroom condo at Seventy-Third Street and South Shore Drive. He blew a glow-blue kiss goodbye to Lexi, logged out of the chat room, and grabbed his coat. He glanced back before the screen blinked to aquarium gold and angelfish began to float through the room. Alexis hadn't moved. She stood behind the chair in a floor-length emerald robe as if Junior was still seated there. The screen beamed with the familiar colors of the Erotic Neighbor log-in page.

Member Name: _____
Password: _____

Junior closed the front door, texted P. W., who was surely circling nearby, and doubled back to the rear of the building to wait for P. W. to show up and for the Lexi buzz to wear off.

Lexi was Junior's online girl. As far as he knew, she lived in Miami. He considered her the perfect woman. They'd never met. She was bisexual, confident, outspoken, and all about business. He texted a message to Alexis and Valerie upstairs: he would be back about two. The snow had begun to fall. It quieted the night. He heard the *briii-ing* of his text light up Val's phone upstairs.

The debate this evening in the EN chatroom had been as to whether, no matter what, by its nature, sexual desire was androgynous. And so, argued Junior, when you're hot enough, you're not really either a man or a woman. You became pure person in a way so you could feel the fork in the road between the sexes. Junior concluded that eroticism was really a matter of how far you could go back on the single road before the fork, that is, how long one could stand it, the road upward, until you pass over the top and return to the present, half person that we'd all been condemned to be in the world of the sleepwalking. Junior hit submit and waited. He thought his post would get a few woke and up out the woodpile. Right he was.

Strictly Soul: Not man or a woman? You best stay in your lane. When I'm ready to go, the kid's ALL MAN. Bet that.

Juniphyre: Touchy touchy now, S. S. Come to tell me that you never felt a woman's shimmy-shimmy staring at a man, another man in your brain. You must know that you're never alone when you're loving the one you're with. Never. Otherwise, you'd never know you were there.

Strictly Soul: Man, what?

Junior had thought to himself, "This is too easy." He typed: Well, then. Do you like sex?

Strictly Soul: I gets mine.

Juniphyre: And it feels good to you?

Strictly Soul: All night long.

Juniphyre: And so you want more for yourself?

Strictly Soul: Can't stop, won't stop.

Juniphyre: By what you're saying, then, S. S., you're, as you wrote, "ALL MAN," and you want more of what you feel when you're with a woman. So think about this. You don't just want her, you want you with her. So you, in fact, at least in part—which is the closest part—want a man. Yourself. The experience of yourself; 'cause that's what you feel. You never really feel *her* at all. If you think about it, all you really feel is a man, you, feeling her. You are the one you love when you love the one you're with. And if you can't be with that—

Strictly Soul: You must be crazy.

No Man's Hand broke in: Strictly Soul. I think he's got you here. Take a moment to think about it. What do you have to lose? Intellectual virginity? Emotional adolescence? Love thyself, brotherman. For only then can you live—

Juniphyre: I suggest you reread what I wrote above. Maybe reread it twice. And then continue here: So if you like sex, and you are a man (and exactly to the degree that you think you're "ALL MAN") the *only* way to stay heterosexual at all is to become, at least, part woman when you feel your own pleasure. Because, if you stay all-man while feeling yourself, a man, I don't care how many women you conjure up and try to put between you and yourself, well, I think you can see where this leads. In fact, the only way to retain *any* contact with the false myth of the strictly "heterosexual" is to accept the basic androgyny of your desire.

No Man's Hand: I think what J's getting at is that you can't be with anyone else as long as you're repelled by yourself. May I ask how you feel when you see another man nude?

Strictly Soul: You better hope I don't see you in life, in the world.

Juniphyre: No Man's Hand doesn't mean any harm, S. S. Easy, now. Such words? May I ask, then, simply, seriously, what are the odds that out of all the men in the world, you, Mssr. S. S., are the only man you're not repelled by? Long odds. Long odds, wild repressions, and threats made in words. *Not* what our people died for! Think about it. Singing off. In sister-brotherhood.

Junior rehearsed the checkmate paradox in his evening's discussion with the EN community. He heard the Range Rover enter the alley over the snow bank. During the winter, he paid the city's plow driver to keep a deep snow bank at both entrances to the alley to minimize traffic behind his building. It was still early, but the plows had already been out.

Text from Valerie: wait up. am dressed. coming w/ you.

Junior Keith had two older sisters and one younger brother. His sisters were in prison for assault and armed robbery. His little brother was in college in Evanston. He himself was in business: pharmaceutical heroin out of the UK, sent through Nigeria. The tabs came wrapped in plaster casts and splints: arms, wrists, an occasional ankle. A full leg cast could be laced with enough doses to supply Junior's clients for six months. Junior employed a set of wayward but functional, clean-cut, suburban addicts as couriers to bring the magic home.

Junior called them import specialists and marketing associates.

P. W. pulled through the untouched carpet of new snow in the alley, leaving two ruts behind the Range Rover. Before the car reached the back steps of the building, Junior could hear the bass and a long-held, high note from a woman's voice. He opened the door and Joyce Sims's *Come into my life, I've got . . .* spilled out into a triangle of light on the snow below the door. With a thumb on the left side of the wheel, P. W. turned the volume down. He knew all about Junior's objections to loud music. Junior climbed into the passenger seat.

–Hold up, Val said she's coming.

–What've you been into?

–The usual—enlightening the masses. Taking it to them.

–Show you right.

–How about you?

–Same as you, a discussion with our neighbors to the south, Bliss 70s. No pressure. I assured them that that wasn't our work in the dumpster over on Cottage Grove. I told them if it *was* our work, they wouldn't have to ask.

–That's right. "Don't *ever* wonder." And our line in the sand?

–Good for another day.

Without turning his head, Junior watched P. W.'s wide, freckled face under his crushed suede driver's cap. A light from the building's rooftop poured through the windshield and sunroof. The music was low enough so the men tracked the intermittent pace of the wipers and the way the flakes dissolved into granular liquid spots when they hit the warmth of the glass. Each flake fell on the glass and boiled itself clear. Junior watched P. W. watch the liquid from the separate flakes find each other. Just when there was enough for a pool of drops to run like a rumor down the glass, the shadow of the wiper swept across P. W.'s face. Ms. Sims's song faded out, the iPod shuffled and a snare drum and guitar were followed into the air by an organ. Junior leaned back in his seat as a voice sang, *When I give my love, this time,* and Valerie came down the steps in black jeans, high brown boots and an open silver lynx coat almost long enough to touch the deepening snow she stepped into. Valerie opened the back door. She got in where she normally sat, in back of the driver.

–Where—Ohh, this my song. Where we going?

P. W. and Junior together:

–Inflation.

–That old place? What for? And why so close to the block?

Junior turned to her in the back seat. As always, her hair was pulled back tightly into a ponytail. Snowflakes in her hair glowed in the light from the sunroof as they disappeared into the warm, leather-scented air. Looking past him at her reflection in the rearview mirror, Valerie did that beautiful, getting-ready-to-go-near-my-eye-without-disturbing-mascara thing with her mouth. She removed a large, single flake from her eyelid with her left ring finger and looked back into Junior's eyes. Her smile flipped her face open like a freshly polished pocket watch.

Junior: Word is, the place is changed.

Valerie: How so?

P. W.: That's what we're going to find out.

Junior: A little recon.

Valerie nodded to her reflection in the side window, the distant star of a nickel .38 steady in each eye.

■

Ndiya stood at the window with her coat on. She felt the cold air on her fingertips as they tapped the wooden sill. She watched the street beneath the swirl of snow going past the streetlight. A snowless, black Range Rover rolled by, the only car that passed in the minutes she'd been standing there. A glimpse of a woman's hair, something silver shining as if under a spotlight, flashed up to her through the sunroof as the car passed below. A blizzard in November? She twisted the bracket and lifted the window. She leaned and blew a deep breath out the window. The cloud blew back past her face and disappeared into Shame's living room. The cold fit like a custom mask of clear ice, the snow zazzled in the street. The warmth from her breath felt like the features of her face vanishing into the open collar of her shirt.

The phone buzzed in her coat pocket. She held it up. It was Cass.

–Hey, Cass.

–He coming?

–I'm coming down there right now. He said he'd be there by nine.

–Set starts at eight thirty.

– . . . You know he says it's not a set. That people shouldn't be there for a "show."

–Right, whatever. He's coming though?

– . . .

–Well, where is he now?

–He took a walk. You *know* this isn't my job, Cass.

–Well, you set it up. Now, all kind of people showing up down here. Don't know most of them. Doesn't even look like my place!

–Well, you don't have a problem making money, do you?

–Look, there's money and then there's money, you know?

–I'll see you in a few.

■

Junior sat in the passenger seat. Ms. Hyman's voice threaded needles through the speakers. P. W. guided the Rover through the heavy snow. The ruts deepened. The streets narrowed to one set of tracks. The parked cars were soon to be snowbound. It was the beginning of an early winter. Bikes chained to signposts would disappear into snowbanks and reappear in April, bent into hieroglyphs. Bodies recovered along the train tracks or mummified in abandoned basements and rooftops. Snow provided cover for all kinds of invisible action.

Junior's life was a capsule. He was an accident that forced ever more purposeful behavior, which caused what many people thought were mystical results. He was nine when he was sent away from his grandmother for the first of his crimes. To Junior's mind the first one was the *only* crime. He considered nothing he'd done, or even seen, since his years in detention illegal. In fact, he'd almost done away with the category altogether. "Illegal," he thought, the word described a realm of behavior where one did things like stop at an intersection because a light said to do so. If illegal didn't mean that, it didn't mean anything. Not to him. He thought his one and only crime involved only looking. The crime was that he'd really *done* nothing, he'd just seen. Only that. He hadn't even been seen.

He could still feel his childhood, criminal attention crawl in him. The way what he'd seen had found a crack in him and blew through it like some kind of winter wind tunnel. That narrow passage flayed open under his skin. He'd been immobilized by what he'd seen. He returned for three nights to watch, frozen still, on fire, perfectly still except for the motion of what he witnessed being done to that girl. He knew now that that kind of attention to anything was criminal. One had to move, had to make anything seen see you back. As long as what you watched watched you back, no crime was really possible. He thought this through slowly, used his whole body. Curving his arms into commas, parentheses, slashing a karate hand for dashes. *That* was his crime, only seeing. That was his *only* crime. The only other crime possible after that would be to say anything about what he knew to anyone. So it was. One crime: he'd *only* seen, watched only with his eyes. Doing that, he thought, meant he'd already been in prison.

Since detention Junior had a concrete awareness of the sky of accidents called "on purpose," and the certified deliveries often mistaken for accidents. "Unbelievable," he heard people say. Criminal behavior, he'd learned, is about following rules; following rules inevitably made a person imprecise. After he had been made imprecise by *rules*, the rest might as well *be* fate. So what people called unbelievable was to him inevitable. What he'd seen done to that girl, not much older than he was at the time, in the abandoned elevator of The Grave had blinded him to the operation of any single force. There was the force holding the elevator between floors in the dead wing of the building. There was the pull of the weight straight down the shaft to the center of the Earth. He watched from above through the crack between the doors from the eleventh floor. There was the blurry pine scent of smoke and the tight laughter of needles scattered on the floor. There was the stained chair the girl was tied to. He remembered the metal wind in his brain and slow-motion lightning in his arms and legs when he watched from above what the boys did with her. As always, Junior felt a pulse of that storm in his body tonight as the wipers plowed the snow into a perfectly straight reef at the bottom of the windshield. As always, he kept that pulse locked up, closely guarded in the hole. At his side, his fingers drummed a rhythm of real accidents on the smooth brown leather of the seat.

At the hearing that put them all away, he'd observed the city lawyers split things into single pieces. Lies. They took all those forces apart and handed the boys their "individual" lives according to what he'd heard called "purposeful behavior," "malice," and "forethought." It was Greek to him then; it was clear to him now. Plural lines to singular effect, or vice versa. That lie *was* the law. It was the only law. He didn't care what all those people said around him. He knew that his crime was stillness, a detached attention. He'd been invisible to motion, moved by what he saw without moving, seen without being seen. He knew *he* didn't have any forethought or malice. But he knew that was wrong. If anything, he thought, now, "malice" had seen him coming from a long way off. In fact, *plenty* 'fore-had-thought of him long before *he* was born. At the time what the lawyers said happened had happened, he was nine years old.

Far as he knew, the girl lived. He forgot the name. She was shipped out of the city by sponsors and private schools. Some said she was lost, others said she'd been saved. Years later, there'd been a story about the girl, grown, on her way to Harvard. All this, he imagined now, after she'd survived a razor-spiral of detox and who knows what else. Back then it was a high-profile case. The publicity brought calls that the buildings be emptied and demolished. There was a series of spectacular cases over the years, all according to the law: babies in the trash incinerator, bodies thrown from rooftops, police shot by teenage snipers. Below all that proceeded the slow grind of anonymous destruction. And, every election, ten thousand votes delivered to the Democrats' safe. None of these crimes brought about the closing of the buildings. Meanwhile, Junior knew, the real crimes were continual and all of them were legal. Everyone was guilty. Finally, when it did happen, when those buildings *did* come down, it seemed like there wasn't a reason anymore to do it at all. The law had its reason.

Junior's business was small and secure. He knew better. But P. W. and his young corporals went ahead anyway as if tomorrow was on homemade ice. Diamond ice. Junior figured it was no different from how he'd read that Columbus had lied to his crew about the basic facts of their journey. Junior had studied captains: Ahab, Kirk, Columbus. He saw their mistakes. Ahab got caught up. It was too personal for Kirk. Columbus believed. Junior's aim was to keep things simple so that the law could be used precisely by him. The law must be *led*; only a fool followed the law. He'd learned that much in court, in a pre-trial hearing for a trial that never happened, when he was ten years old. He believed in clear poverty, and clean dope sold to people, and sold by people, by people who were loved by people, who had a *lot* to lose. Somehow an invisible weight swinging from the necks of people with things to lose made their behavior easy to predict; it was as if no matter what random way they might decide to go, the weight swung them in a direction of its own. They couldn't help it; that meant Junior could use it. Junior's life was remarkably simple and he aimed to keep it that way for as long as the law, his law, would allow. After that, he'd bounce. He loved his people, good music, and bad money. He hated racism, suburbs, sexual stupidity, and hip-hop.

■

The whole Inflation thing had been Ndiya's idea. The old, half-empty lounge was there just down the street from Shame's place. The piano was in the back already. It seemed obvious to her. But it wasn't to him.

—I only do that, OK, I only *play*, at the Cat Eye because someone at Earlie's dared me and, really, no one listens anyway. People come there as an excuse to hear themselves talk, to look at themselves in the mirror. They're not there to see and listen to each other. All that's just cover. So they're sure not listening to me. It was a goof. That's all.

—Was, yes. And what is it now?

—Nothing, really.

—Well, sir Shame, I've listened. And I've *watched*. I know what nothing looks like . . . and what you're doing ain't it. And anyway, why all the long-ass way up on North Broadway? If it's nothing, there's a piano right around the corner.

—*Please.*

—Please, yourself.

That was six weeks and four shows at Inflation ago. Shame said they weren't "shows." Ndiya felt the deepening snow collapse beneath her boots as she walked up Rhodes

Avenue toward Sixty-Third Street. A maze of yellow flakes dazzled the street lamp. What she knew of the sky was blackness. What she saw in the sky then was the glow of city lights. What she felt on her upturned face were pieces of a broken maze melted by body heat that pushed through her skin. She was a pressure alive under a blizzard of details. Without that heat, she thought, like the cars parked on both sides of the street, she'd be covered already. She thought back to their argument.

—And, FYI, people up there have *started* listening, I've watched that too.

—Exactly. But they can listen to me all they want and still only hear themselves.

—So what's the difference?

—Exactly, again. So "what" *is* the difference. Folks down at Inflation are already hearing a bunch of shit they trying not to listen to. And it ain't themselves!

—And again, I say so what?

—Well, adding me to the mix of shit they trying not to hear can only cause trouble. That's what's so . . .

—Trouble for you or them?

—Neither, trouble for *everybody*. And most of all for *us*.

Ndiya wouldn't be surprised if Shame just didn't show up one of these nights. Maybe tonight. It was obvious by now that more than one person lived in his skin. She'd watched him move in the mornings before work. Back and forth from room to room. Nothing about him suggested he knew the person he'd been the night before, or who he might be later that afternoon. No radio. No music. One morning during the first week she was staying with him, she wrapped herself in a sheet and stood there in the middle of the living room waiting to tell him goodbye. He passed her three times, then finally on the way to the closet near the door. It wasn't simply that he acted like she wasn't there that prevented her from saying anything. It was the heavy weight in his pace. Apart from his face, masked in a surgeon's neutrality, she didn't recognize the way he moved at all. She decided there was no reason to stand there, so she went back to bed, wondering if that might snap him out of it. She said, "Bye," when she heard him lacing up his boots at the door. The door closed and the place was quiet until she heard the motor jump to life and disappear down the street. 6:22 a.m. on her phone. She heard herself, arguing with Shame:

–Well, according to the Gospel of Shame Luther himself, trouble's what everyone's got anyway, so—

–What? Listen, we're all better off with songs. Songs no one listens to because they've all been tunneled under like border fences. People listen to radio and plug jukeboxes for the same reason they pay a toll on a bypass to go around a traffic jam.

–What people? Most of those Inflation folks don't look like tollway types to me.

–Woman, how can someone who is always right get everything so *wrong*?

Ndiya stopped walking. She tried to remember how exactly Shame had changed his mind, if he had. Or how he had relented, if he had. She couldn't. She doubted that he'd done either. All she could remember was:

–What about the alley cats?

–That's eavesdropping, unofficial, bootlegging. It has to stay that way.

But he'd begun to play that piano at Inflation. He played music unlike anything she'd heard him play before. She didn't know what they heard. But people listened. Still, something in Shame's blank, before-work face kept her from gloating about being right; she held back.

The temperature was supposed to drop overnight. At this point, it hovered around freezing. The snow carpeted the dead parts of the street. Ndiya's eyes scraped along the rooftops to her right on the east side of Rhodes Avenue. Each flake that hit her face made her blink. She pretended that her face was a clear, glass bowl of water. She remembered the first time she heard Shame play the piano. She was upset. The cover-up and cul-de-sac of her life wouldn't be denied any longer. She was also buzzed from the shots of Scotch she'd slammed uptown and a little dizzy from the ride on the cycle along the lake. This was the infamous date number two. She stood behind and above him as he played. He wandered toward a melody that never seemed to actually happen. She watched the delta of veins on the back of his wrists and hands. No watch. No rings. Dark crescents under his tar- and mortar-stained fingernails. Those hands. That was when she'd caught a brief, first moment of his scent, a distant whiff that made her think of her father.

–Shame, do you smoke?

–No, my life does.

She put her hands on his sides, his ribs opening slightly with each breath. She hadn't noticed it at first, but with her hands on him, she felt how the tempo of the notes breathed when he did. She had never thought of a piano as a wind instrument; in a way it was. She didn't realize that her breaths had fallen into the opening and closing rhythm of Shame's song too.

She couldn't tell where the song was headed. Each right-hand phrase popped into motion like a sleeping dog falls into stillness, over some dream-reef into nameless sleep. "How do you do it?" she asked. He said he didn't know. They weren't songs. He knew that. They weren't his and neither was the piano. He knew that too.

–When I started to play, I thought of it as a kind of drumming, really. I found I was full of rhythms, and certain keys made them possible. It felt like anonymous precision. It felt like self-defense.

–Defense from what?

–From names, naming, namelessness.

–And from what else?

–From questions!

That first night, they'd half stripped and fucked on the rug. One arm still in her sweater, neither of them had meant it; they just didn't know what else to do. Shame's touch seemed to come from somewhere far away, too far to be so close, so fast. A cloud of static, and heat. Their ankles knocked against the legs of the piano bench. There they where. She remembers the feeling like just before a plane takes off and the sense that the ground speed is lethal, the only thing left to do is look up and let go. Shame cursed under his breath when he came and bit her shoulder. She felt the seam of skin close into a slip of heat when she pulled him down on top of her with both hands. He rode her home on his cycle and she cursed herself silently, vowing not to see him again, ever. Her precisely anonymous self-defense failed. Since the first, her time with Shame felt like a question faced off with itself in the mirror.

■

All of it, no matter. Junior's romantic criminality made it possible. Sentimental psychopath. P. W. too. They'd met in the Cook County Juvenile Detention Center. Jaded social workers and racist family lawyers in Chicago called it the Chocolate Factory. It was a city of children, mostly brown. They'd lived there together for eight years, until they were eighteen and could no longer be tried, back then, for the crimes of ten-year-olds. Junior had attempted to play the piano in the recreation room their teacher, Miss Lisa, had set up in the Center. P. W. sang abstractedly to the radio. The piano never took with Junior. Now, as adults, P. W. was as much a DJ as he was a driver, as much confidant and metaphysician as he was a killer. And he was all of that. P. W.: rare groove aficionado. Junior: connoisseur. Junior was the steel sight in front of P. W.'s trained eye.

The two men found spots on the lake where they went to park and strategize. Their arguments about business strategy were always masked conversations about lyrics in certain songs. If Vice had them on a wire, it better have a few champions from *Soul Train*'s Scramble Board on retainer. P. W.'s choices of tunes were a kind of divination chart. They smoked American Spirits and P. W. played the grooves on the custom system he'd had installed in the Range Rover. Junior remembered P. W.'s observation on one of those nights: "You know, Jazzy and Fresh Prince's 'Summertime' is really a remake of Gershwin, think about it. 'Give me a soft subtle mix.'" And Junior: "'And if it ain't broke.'" P. W.: "That whole 'living is easy' thing . . . it just hit me today."

– . . . You know?

–Nigga, you right. You should write a book!

They'd both missed the social part of the music as boys. Underwater in their lives, in detention, the songs were beamed in from space. Communiqués to a gone bathysphere. Back then, they'd debated the success of lyrical choices. Abstract meant they were prisoners of genocidal economic choices made by people they'd never see. People who would never look at them and who used their image every day. Junior and P. W. used the music Ms. Lisa allowed onto the radio in the Center like a series of mirrors. The mirrors stared back. As all prisoners do, they romanticized and exaggerated the freedom of the lyricists and singers who were really fellow prisoners. A falsetto voice chimed in: *When you're short on cash, I've got your length.* Junior thought that the metaphor was too literal, too gratuitous, and didn't make sense. The metaphor strangled the line. Junior: "That's that Verne Gagne shit."

–What?

–It's "the sleeper hold."

–Oh, OK, got you.

–You know he taught it to his son, right?

–Which son?

–Greg, I think.

The next line in the song, countered P. W., paid back for excess in the first one. Remember, these boys are, like, fifteen at the time. They're prisoners. P. W.:

–When you're weak, I'll be your strength. When you're cold. That's us, man. None of it even makes a song unless both "length" and "strength" rhyme with, say, how Ms. Lisa says what comes after "ninth."

–Tenth?

–See. And everyone in here says you're slow.

–So I'll *be* slow. I'll be so slow till I'm gone. I'll be the invisible *g*.

Like all prisoners, they never really left. They still did that. Though, on the outside, P. W. played the songs as if they were part of a riddle: riddle me this. And part divination: roll the shells. It was also a corner hustle for whoever might have been listening: Where's the pea? The bassline of Anita Baker's version of "You Belong to Me":

–Why'd you tell me this? Were you looking for my reaction?

Junior:

–That's why I didn't even flinch. No nod. Watch. They won't do shit.

Further back, Loose Ends:

–Baby, I feel it too, what am I supposed to do?

And Junior:

–You think it's that deep? I think it's a bluff.

The lines and lyrics wound out of the rhythm that was wound out of how the world moved, how it didn't spin at the same speed in the same place for very long. Lines that were all about how one listened or didn't. Usually, when the relevant line went by, the men didn't need to say anything. Their eyes met and there was a nod between them that, were you watching closely, you wouldn't have seen happen. One song bloomed out of another until the decades and voices merged into one song. Trussel: *Rock is in the pocket, Rock is in the love socket.* Janice McClain: *Give it up, give it up, give it on up.* Change: *Reach for the sky, I'll be nearby.* Man Friday: *Didn't I show you love, show you love.* . . . And if you were watching with binoculars you wouldn't see a thing. Joyce Sims: *What price must I pay, to make you see things my-y way-ay,* and the lines scat out of view. Paris: *I choose you.* Floetry: *All you got to do is say yes.*

The revolutions were kaleidoscopes. Police could try to follow on the wire if they wanted, record everything. But the code couldn't be broken—it could only be lived. No one came and went from it, no one was free to leave. Since they were boy prisoners, they'd turned phrases from brain to brain, from eye to eye. In the Center, they did it for as long as Ms. Lisa would allow it. Now, they did it for as long as they wanted, as long as it took. *Nothing can come, nothing can come, nothing can come between us.* Sade always had the last word. Junior sang along: *I'll wash the sand of the shore.*

P. W. hits pause on the steering wheel.

—You know it's "off the shore," right? "I'll wash the sand off the shore."

—"Off the shore" makes the line ordinary. If it's "I'll wash the sand of the shore," it opens the line into forever.

—What, grain by grain?

–Nigga-naw. Sand washed *of* the *shore* . . . the border gone, limitlessness . . . then you decide the shape, the shift.

–Shape of what?

–Naw-nigga, not what, the shape of "if" . . . which is always the shape of a shift. You know, like when "if" is a fist.

–Oh, that's *old* school. Next you'll be talking about back in the day when Gimme got shot!

Somewhere a detective ran a check on a 187, victim's name: Gimme. So they worked around to the subject at hand. Junior leaned forward and hit play. . . . *blow you right through my door.*

–See. Same as shore-washed sand . . . door with no way . . .

–Shame, ain't it?

Junior stared at his own face in the tint of the passenger side window. He nodded.

■

In detention, Junior had lived within the prison of formal control. What he hated most was performance of any kind, the neon exaggerations in them, the formulae. He and P. W. had been surgeons on the inside. They'd bounced songs back and forth between each other. Spent days in secret concert with a chorus waiting for it to leap out of itself. It'd become a spontaneous grammar between them, precise and open-ended. By the time they were released, after nine years inside, they could sniff the lie of plot, the consolations of momentum, of

cause, from across town. They'd both stand up after fifteen or twenty minutes in a movie and walk out down
separate aisles when the story arrived to guillotine the
actor's subtleties into the performance of the plot. Fuck
you. Having been the boys they'd had to be, neither man
could stand the sulfur whiff of "behavior." It attacked
the eyes like an allergy. Junior's favorite saying—he
never said it out loud: "In jail everything is obvious."
He remembered reading that in a book in Miss Lisa's
room. He tore out the page and kept it. He isolated that
sentence and swallowed it.

At the movies, one waited for the other outside in the
parking lot of Evergreen Plaza. Never more than a few
minutes.

−I wondered how long you'd be in there.

−I figured you'd already be out here.

Junior was a committed sensualist and militant mor-
alist, militant against any limits set on the preliminary
ambiguities of action. Intuition was close but there was no
system, that elevator was no longer possible. Someone who
never existed might call him a radical noninferentialist.

Alexis almost never left Junior's condo on the lake, off
Seventy-Third Street. She wore a housecoat and Gucci slippers. Rose water, blue powder, and epics painted on her toe-
nails. Her open robe, belly and nipples dusted as if they'd
been loved by moths. Valerie was Junior's shadow. She was
never more than around the corner. These were Junior's people, his clutch. And P. W., no performer either—he was the
sandman's hook and the heavy sweep of the curtain itself. His
job was to cut any plot before it had the thought to begin.

Junior survived by moving in directions no one expected. By violating whatever people seemed to think the song of the day was about. More often than not, this meant moving exactly in a way so as not to move at all. Learning how to stay still in a hall of revolving mirrors amounted to inventing an invisible kind of arrest. When a killing opened up a building to his south, he wouldn't even glance. Low-cost, high-yield concoction came up the Ike from St. Louis. Not a sniff. He'd fallen into immunity through a misperception he didn't understand. This envelope turned his pharmaceutical connection into a perpetual motion machine. He used the combination to keep himself exactly where he was as the ground moved beneath his feet. He'd say, "I'm either the day before yesterday or the day after tomorrow. People think I'm the clear space in between but that's just their mirror, that's their confession."

All those around him saw this as his unpredictability. Junior didn't know exactly what the envelope of his immunity contained, who sealed it, who had sent it to whose attention. He knew there'd been a pact sworn over the dead son of a made man. An underground tremor. It didn't involve the mayor, DA, or police as much as it involved those who owned influence in those offices. Word was that the only person present at the pact was the best friend of the dead son, the dead heir himself. The friend wasn't in the game at all and neither was the son. It didn't matter. Word was that whoever touched the dead heir's best friend would bring down the whole house of cards. So Junior had decided to look but not touch. For now.

Word just was. And that's just what word was. There were all kinds of words. And Junior didn't have it exactly right, but he was close enough. The friend of the dead son had left town just before his death, true enough. This is my death we're talking about. So I've looked closely. Word was that the friend's leaving was part of the pact and maybe it was. All the words were likely wrong, of course. Everyone knew *that* for sure. But no one knew *which* words were right and which were wrong and so word stayed word. When Jeff Fort's Temple went off, spoiled meat, it happened that the few blocks claimed by Junior in the franchise auction were covered by the mythic pact, which is exactly why everyone stood back and let him have it. No one expected him to actually take it; no one knew he already had. No one said anything about it. The only proof Junior had that the mythic word held any water at all boiled down to the fact of his daily life. The fact that, each morning when his eyes broke open, he had a daily life.

As anyone could see, only a serious fool or an un-touchable person would have accepted an offer from Junior to be put up in 6329 in return for no one knew exactly what. Junior had known plenty of fools. They were all performers, predictable. Shame didn't resemble any of them. For instance, when Junior mentioned it, Shame hadn't asked even one question. There was no negotiation, no poker face, no hesitation. No "What's the catch?" No "What's in it for me? For you?" Shame just nodded and said he'd go over there after work. He moved his stuff into the space the following day. All anyone really heard after that was hammers and saws and that piano that no one had ever heard before. If there was anything or anyone to the word, Junior figured it, or they, would do something just like that. In other words, like him, they'd do as close to nothing as possible. Junior didn't know what to think. So he decided to not think and to simply keep the safety off and deal with Shame as little as possible, which turned out to be not at all. Then he'd wait till Shame showed his hand. Shame didn't. And Junior's safety stayed off.

■

Shame stood on the breakwater and watched the blizzard disappear in waves. He'd walked all the way down Sixty-Third Street through Jackson Park and crossed under the Drive to the lakeshore. The Joycelan Steel job was coming to its beautiful end. All the jobs ended this way. The bricklayers left to wherever they went next. He'd find out soon enough. The last of the courses would go in by Friday. The scaffolds at the bottom of the final tank would come down and they would hoist them out. They'd load them on the truck and take them back to the yard. Then he and Jay Brown would bring in the steam washer. The acid-wash wing of the mill would be closed down for however long it took to wash down the end of the job. It would be just them.

These were waxed brick. That meant one face of each brick was covered in a thin sheet of wax. On small jobs, he and Jay Brown arrived early and waxed each brick themselves. They set them each on their sides to dry. The equipment was low-tech: a paint roller rigged on an axle drilled into a tin cake pan. They melted the wax in the pan with the torch, then set the rig over candles to keep it liquid. Each brick drawn back and forth over the roller. This happened over and over in an unending coma, a rhythm. They added squares of wax to keep the bottom of the roller in the liquid. The first brick was almost weightless. By 80 or so, Shame could barely lift his arm, couldn't hold it steady. Time to switch. Jay could wax 400 brick without a pause. But he stopped after 150 or so. In this way, Shame and Jay, wordlessly, could wax a few thousand brick in a day. The quiet of their work made Shame feel like a monk. They never talked, as if it was some kind of sin to talk while waxing brick. The candles burned down beneath the pan and were replaced one by one. The bottom of the pan turned black. Smoke spilled up. Their wrists banded black from the smoke that curled around the edges of the pan. Any more than a few days' worth of that, it was cheaper for the company to buy the brick waxed at the factory.

For big jobs like Joycelan Steel, 25,000 brick per tank, six tanks, the brick were factory waxed. The wax protected the brick in transit and during the job's progress. A dropped hammer might chip the face. Even one crack could compromise the seal. Engineers came to the job after the final wash and placed dimes on the joints. Any edge exposed more than the width of a dime would be marked for removal. The bricklayers had to come back and the mistakes were relaid. The foreman said it was in the contracts. So they'd leave each job clean and smooth enough for the dime test.

What mattered to Shame was a pure beauty and rhythm at the end of the job. They washed all the spit and sweat and curses away until all that was left was clean, smooth pain. Standing at the lakefront, he watched the blizzard come over the Drive. Behind him, wind gusts accelerated the snow, which gave the traffic the appearance of slow motion. In front of him breathed the undulating border between the black waves and the white lung of chaos. The lake gulped the blizzard's spray, drew it down. At the job, the hose's nozzle disappeared in steam. They moved the spray back and forth in three-inch swipes, thirty seconds per brick. Concentration in a stance, his mind was his wrists. Behind the jet of steam lay a newborn brick. Another few appeared each minute, pristine, as if they had never been touched.

The wand wanted to blast off and cavort space. He aimed the white spray between his boots. Thirty minutes was enough, his wrists gone mind-numb. It was time to switch. He watched Jay Brown aim the gun and disappear into the steam. Shame marked the urge to strip off the goggles, hard hat, coveralls and stand nude in the flame-white clouds. He stood at the drain and swept the waves of water and wax back on themselves. The streams and waves met, crested, and dropped the wax into the beginnings of reefs. This must be done on angles so that the water dropped the wax and then washed past down the drain. The reefs of wax cooled and turned gray. Shame shoveled them into empty resin buckets from the mortar materials. The foreman said it was in the contracts: no unattached materials left at the job site and that included wax in the factory drains. "We carry it in, put it in place, or we carry it out," said the foreman. It was elegant, expensive work. It was opera. And it was doomed.

Shame watched the steam gather in flashes, light through the cloud became a prehistoric monster. He wanted to scream, "Cut," to turn off the lights. He feared that if the steam dispersed, bodies would lie strewn in their final stages of agony. Jay Brown's back hunched like a bear in the steam bath; the broom held itself down in Shame's hands, the weight of the handle was all that held his feet to the floor. A quick touch, a wrist-twitch caused a new ridge to begin in the wax-wash. Minutes later they'd switch again and the violence of the nozzle would be gone silent, again, trying to blast out of his hands. The pressure was a clean, blind spot, a white inch from the peeled face of a newborn brick. The broom perfectly owned its weight in space. Jay Brown held the jet. The pressure stripped the surface back down to the pain that put it there. Shame felt like he was in orbit, in slow motion. He watched Jay Brown hold down the ancestor of all light, the obliteration of sight.

This was an early dinner, the second, after he'd been living in Junior's building and was still wondering why. How? They hadn't yet agreed on what he'd do in return for not paying rent. Colleen had invited herself to Shame's place which, turned out, she had wrongly assumed must have been somewhere near Earlie's. Shame's life was a distant planet. At that time, Shame's job was relining tanks at Peer Foods at Thirty-Fifth and the river. Peer Foods made pickled pigs' feet. Everyone who worked there spoke Polish, from the young woman in the security uniform at the back gate to the old men with shrunken-apple faces who pushed stainless vats of pig hoofs through the plant. It was a good job. At lunch there'd be a platter of ham hocks and the old men brought loaves of Italian bread, onions and peppers and mustard. Colleen had been charmed by the shimmering irreality of all of this while Shame told her about it at Earlie's. His eyes were bent in his first attempts to talk to an actual person and the room curved forward and away from him behind her open face. She could only approach what he said aesthetically. She laughed out loud at the alliterative:

—Right now, I'm working at Peer Foods, a Polish pickled pig's feet plant in Bridgeport.

They'd talked a half dozen times over a few weeks. She was from Minnesota, a river town called Winona. She'd been visibly incredulous when he told her that he knew the town, that he'd worked there years ago. He couldn't remember but thought it was a factory that made chains. Colleen laughed and said she didn't know but that sounded exactly right. Shame remembered that from the loading dock at the back of the plant he could look over the bluffs across the Mississippi. It looked like three or four rivers snaking between low islands and sandbars in the morning fog. She said he made the place sound much better than it was. And he said that was probably because he was only working there, not trying to live. He didn't say that that was before he'd begun trying *not* to live.

Colleen said she spoke five languages, had been a romance languages and art history major at Oberlin. Shame thought he had heard of Oberlin but couldn't be sure, gathered it was a college or a university. As Colleen went on Shame began to rely heavily on the reassuring pattern of pain streaming from a recent, formidable welt given to him by his roommate. He spent most of their first two or three conversations discretely brushing the marble-sized spider bite on the inside of his bicep and concentrating on the radius of pain that stretched down his arm and, it seemed, up from his hip at the same time.

Colleen had the impression that he attended her self-disclosures with a rare, singular attention and, in a way, she was right. Shame did enjoy the birdlike motion of her Oberlin, romance language–inflected hands when she spoke. The way her brown hair broke over her shoulders and the way her eyes must have been what "open" really meant. Whenever she spoke about herself, as if in the third person, she found an object at the bar or on the table to fix her eyes upon. Her eyes swallowed what they saw. Unlike anyone he'd met from the college clan, her voice always ended sentences with its tone turned down and curled back toward itself. He thought she had a healthy air of remorse about her. Soon after they'd met, Shame had decided to trust that about Colleen.

Shame hadn't talked to Junior about it, yet. But he'd been playing that piano he'd found in the hallway night and day. While he played he noticed that his left hand wanted his right to curl notes downward and toward itself in a way that asked to be followed. At one point, in response to a surge of pain in his arm and a moment of overconfidence in his mouth, he interrupted her description of the way to fold egg whites into a meringue and how one should never attempt a meringue on a rainy day. "A meringue needs light, bright air," she'd said. Shame interrupted, asking about her form on the harp.

–Harp?

–Yes, do you play the harp?

There was a pause, how long he didn't know. Colleen was still. She stared at the table. After a moment, shaking his head in apology, Shame said,

–Sorry, go ahead—

–Oh, forget meringue. How did you know I played the harp?

By the evening of the dinner at his place, Shame knew that Colleen worked at an art gallery in a loft off of Madison and Halsted. He swallowed the urge to share that he'd known a DJ who had overdosed on the rooftop of one of those warehouses and lay there buried under snow until late spring. He let her continue. Colleen beamed with pride over the glossy-grungy profile of the gallery. An old-time freight elevator still opened its oversized, clanging metal door directly into the space, she said. Shame didn't say he rode one exactly like it, usually accompanied by an old Polish man and five thousand pig hoofs, about ten times a day and six days per week. He suspected that she thought his job was what he'd heard people at Earlie's call "alternative." He never could quite figure out exactly what such things were alternative to. Nor did he know how he was supposed to feel about that.

He listened, though. He loved to watch Colleen glow with what a city could mean to someone who could live in a misty bluff town with a beautiful name and still need to imagine Romania or wherever to make her hands move when she spoke. She seemed to switch between voices as she named the international list of artists whose work they showed. "Lisboa, that's in Portugal. Bogotá . . ." He loved it. Here and there, he asked, slowly, as softly as he could,

–Would you say that again?

Colleen thought Shame was a riot. He wasn't sure how to feel about her reactions to what he said. She laughed out loud when he confided, "When I worked at a brewery, I knew a painter for a week in Houston, in the Fifth Ward." When he didn't join her laughing, she swallowed the laugh and replaced it with a look that seemed to contest the position of English as a romance language. One night at Earlie's Shame had excused himself to the men's room and returned to find Colleen still laughing at his mistaken impression that R.E.M. was "some English dude?" At that time Shame thought, wrongly, that Colleen was searching for an alternative to the alternative.

Colleen persisted her way down to Shame's place and, give her credit, up the stairs and to his door. The place was almost empty at the time. Tubes of caulk, tools laid out on the floor; he'd agreed to store a vintage cigarette machine for Luther B, so that was turned with its back to the room on the wall facing the front door. The piano was directly opposite. Duct tape marked the space in the floor where his work closet would go. Most of the rest, not much, still sat in boxes in the living room along with dozens of glass blocks that would, Shame told her, go into the bedroom wall. Planks of plywood angled to the wall, no floor in half the bedroom. Shame said he was extending the room into the space of an old elevator shaft.

Colleen tried to look calm. She dropped the bottle of wine out of the bottom of the paper bag and darted to the floor to pick it up. Shame couldn't tell if she'd caught it in the air or not. In her manic speed and the oblique way her motion almost swept up the sound of the bottle hitting the floor (if it had) along with the bottle itself, Shame caught a slow glimpse of what his situation must look like from the outside. Soon he found himself trying to act calm.

"The poor child was panic-stricken," Shame thought. But Colleen wasn't paralyzed. The bottle survived, a good sign. The bag had come apart, soaked by the unconscious electricity and sweat of Colleen's grip. She bolted up straight, smiled widely, and handed him the bottle as if it had never fallen. The torn bag disappeared into the pocket of her coat. All that happened in one motion. Shame thought she should work for one of those magicians who disappear the Eiffel Tower, the Brooklyn Bridge. Or maybe a pickpocket? The woman *had* something. Give her that.

On the wall behind the bare wooden table, Shame had tacked up a painting he'd won at a Cuban cultural raffle in Miami. He'd gone with Felipé Moreno, a local laborer with whom he worked years ago when he was first on the road to stay. Shame was still in shock from my death. He was new to looking at the world as if everything was far away. Felipé's mother, explained the laborer, as he gunned his Toyota Celica down I-95, was actually Puerto Rican, but that didn't prevent him from hating Castro and American Democrats with a fascist abandon glowing in his eyes. Call it passing.

The Miami job was at a Tropicana subsidiary. Shame had a great time at the Cuban cultural festival. Cloudy drinks made his hands feel as far away as everything felt, and he was surrounded by women who wore mint in their eyes. Plates of seasoned meat pounded flat and grilled, black beans, yellow rice, and syrupy plantain. Unlike the men who dealt with politics through exceptional hair coiffing, the Cuban women Shame saw around him seemed to carry their fascism in their matching jaw and calf muscles. The calves for dancing, he understood. But he caught himself wondering what produced those protruding jaw muscles. Years later, a doctor told him that one could measure the latent anger people carried in their sleep by asking them to clench their teeth and flex jaw muscles.

Shame loved the flowery fabrics and the spectrum of light brown brows circulating around him. His raffle ticket, number 4104, was still taped to the backside of the canvas he'd won, to his embarrassment, at the end of the evening. They'd given him the painting rolled up with a personal note, also stuck to the back of the canvas, from the artist who had been there at the event as well. All night people had spoken to Shame in Spanish while he stood next to Felipé and smiled. They looked down at his black dress pants and work boots and asked, "¿Eres un artista?" Shame: "Sí," feigning the beguiling silence he imagined must accompany all creative people.

The evening with Colleen pivoted wildly away from the tension created by her repressed nervousness and the underwater-shaped contours of Shame's alienation when she sat down at his table and noticed the painting tacked up on the wall. She came to life in the most genuine, beautiful way. Shame hadn't ever really thought of it as a piece of "art" and, stupidly, hadn't connected it in the remotest of ways to what Colleen had described as her passion and her job at the gallery. Shame made sure his passion—so close to rage, cover for despair that it had been—for his own work radiated inward, never outward, on or off the job. When she saw the painting tacked to the wall behind him, Colleen's face seemed to accordion in on itself fourfold and pop back open with each panel in a different position. New eyes where her mouth was, a new voice in her eyes.

–Is that an early Bedia?

Still surprised by the changed face of Colleen's voice, Shame had to turn around to see what she was pointing her fork at.

–That? No. I won that in a raffle where I was working years ago.

–A raffle? At work?

–No, at a festival a laborer took me to.

–Cuban?

–No, well, you could say he was a Puerto Rican posing as Cuban. Like I said, it doesn't matter, this was years ago, in Miami.

And Colleen's fork hit the floor. Her voice called all the way back to Winona, Romania.

–Mi-ami?

■

Colleen ate dinner facing Shame, determined to pretend the painting behind him wasn't there. Her concentrated distraction distracted him. Her focus had closed down. She drilled his face while her glass of wine magically rose to her lips and back to its place at ten o'clock above her plate. Then she turned, flicked her chin at the piano, and smiled. Her eyes relaxed.

–Do you play?

–A little. You could say I don't do much else, work and that. At least that's the way it feels to me lately.

–That's "a little"? I mean, I *know* you play. I've heard you playing that piano on the back wall at Earlie's.

–Oh, that. That's not even me, forget about that.

–Where did you learn? Did you study?

Colleen thought he was playing with her. People at Earlie's often assumed Shame was joking when he wasn't. It seemed to him that they laughed at the strangest times. Shame shook his head at Colleen in that way one shakes one's head and it's clear that the disagreement or mystery isn't anywhere nearby. It was a perfectly reasonable question. She'd just asked it on the wrong planet.

–I think I learn in my sleep, more or less.

–Your *sleep*? Like one of those tapes for learning a language?

–No. No. I try and can't play and try and can't play. Then I go to sleep, go to work, come back and try again and the way I can't play has changed. I still can't play, but all of a sudden, here and there, things appear that I *can* play. Then I try *that* and can't, and so forth. I guess. That's how it feels to me. But it's all stupid. I don't know what I'm doing. Or even why.

Colleen held her fork midway to her mouth. The tail of a very fine, gold-link bracelet joined at a clasp dangled down. It wavered between a lower-case *q* and a small *j* in Shame's eye. He followed the chain upward and saw that her hand trembled slightly. The bite of noodles hovered before her lips. He thought her eyes had narrowed again.

–Would you play for me?

Shame looked down and said very softly in an attempt to be more gentle than he knew how to be,

–I said I can't play.

Colleen looked at him through a slight squint in her vision. She decided he either wasn't angry or it didn't show.

He wouldn't play for her. But, she decided, he wasn't play-ing *with* her either. He wasn't being coy. She could also see him underestimating her. She'd become used to that in her dealings with the male species. Then again, maybe he *was* putting her on—he probably went to Berklee. She'd known a dozen musicians at Oberlin. They often slept in practice rooms but, she sensed, that wasn't what Shame was describing. She decided on a little test to see if he'd give her a better clue.

–Shame, would you mind if I took your painting up to the gallery sometime?

–Take it when you go, if you like. Why?

–Not tonight. Sometime. I'd like to see where it comes from.

–You mean other than Miami?

Utterly no clue there, she thought. Colleen's laugh-ter just then was really at herself; it covered what Shame thought he saw in flight behind her eyes.

–Yes. Other than Miami. Is it signed?

–Maybe on the back? I forget.

–These noodles are fantastic. They're meaty but not stiff at all. Where did you get them?

Shame tipped his head to the kitchen.

–In there.

–You made them? From scratch?

–No. From eggs and flour. And a little crushed caraway and cardamom. You'll be glad to know I *bought* the sausages, however, from a Polish butcher an old man at work told me about.

Colleen traced arrows of wind and power lines blown

cursive on the canvas over Shame's shoulder. The noise of the wind was almost visible between them.

◼

Their forks and knives were in their plates. Wine glasses empty. A bottle of Scotch and a bowl of ice sat on the table. Colleen and Shame had slid back in their chairs. Their reclined positions made the conversation seem long-distance, possible. Shame's feet propped up on the edge of the table.

–You asked where I learned to play piano before.

Shame had said that he learned to play in his sleep and he meant it. He'd rehearsed in his sleep for years, maybe all of his life, before he'd ever touched a piano. Maybe everyone did? He didn't know. When he wheeled the piano out of the hallway into his apartment a month or so before Colleen's visit, he'd pulled up a chair. He didn't know why. To fill space maybe. Then he put three fingers of his left hand down into the keys. The sound that leapt back at him felt like it leapt directly out of him.

Most of the brick he handled at the jobs was floor brick, two and a quarter inches thick, ceramic tiles. They were dense, smooth, and deep red in color with wax on the top and sixteen quarter-inch grooves on the bottom side. Shame was right-handed. To carry brick, he picked them up with his left hand and stacked them in his right arm. He picked them up mostly two at a time. Together they were about five inches in width. In a hurry he could pick up three brick with his left hand but it didn't pay to hurry. Why hurry on someone else's time? Especially when there was nowhere to get to by hurrying, just more brick, as the old men he worked with put it, "down in that other town." And anyway, the foreman was militant about chipped brick: "We're not building garden walls in this goddamn mill. The man's not paying us for 'rustic.' You break a brick in a fool's rush, you pay for it."

The first thing Shame learned about the piano was spaces. A musician would call them intervals. Oscillations of spaces made a rhythm with a distinct pattern of tones, two intertwined stories. Shame could feel the stories, the tone and the rhythm, pull apart and tangle toward each other in his arms, in his legs. It was like waves at the breakwater or wind in the trees. Headlights through the curves in Washington Park made trees dance with their shadows. Fish broke from the place where a stone hit a pond. Birds in a flock lay down in a field like a deep breath. Something spun backward into his hips pressed into the high-blare of the brick saw. The lateral, painful pull of blood in his veins at a glimpse of the free world from inside the fence of the job: a thin brown girl disappearing on the back of a motorcycle in LA that still felt like the molten core and sum of his broken life. Three little girls' voices boomeranged and tarantella'd their way around an open fire hydrant in the summer sun. The way lean, stick-thin boys fell in to defend a fast break on a basketball court. The flung-loose weight of the dead alive in the love of the living. A keen and material, almost mineral, agility that sprung into action in the moment of helplessness. Smoke in the eyes of a woman who talked him to sleep with her hands.

Shame put his left hand on the keys and the sound of stories X-ray-visioned his body. It was as if scenes from the world had fallen into him and then resided there. They then went on their way, as if somewhere beyond him, intact within him, a mirror image in profile, someone beyond him. Facts. One brick, two, three, one white one black, two black, two white. "So it all goes in, and it goes in whole, almost without us," he remembered thinking, after his first moments touching the keys. "It goes in whole and then we can only pull it out in pieces. Even with a light touch, it's broken. Ruined."

His middle finger worked on its own. And he remembered panic and that slip-silver pain that appeared behind his eyes and in his hands. He'd play something twenty times and he'd have to physically shake the pain from his hands. The pain wasn't from the playing. It was the touching and the breaking, the piecing and retrieving. It was the ruin. Pain? It wasn't like the pain, real pain, *his* pain on the job. The pain the company bought with his time. Truth was, with this piano-pain, he really couldn't tell if it hurt or not. At work, if it was *his* pain, that meant someone else owned it. He knew who, he knew how much they paid him for his pain. Now he wondered who owned this pain he was playing around with on the piano. And who paid for it? If he didn't know that, how could he tell it *was* pain and not something else?

Within a few days he began to see how to do what musicians would call diminish and augment. This controlled color in the stories. If he slipped a finger up a key he tilted the color of the story east, toward the lake, toward morning. Slipped one down and dimmed the shade to the west, sunset. As if from another life, Shame remembered listening to Nat Cole use his left hand as a synonym for effortlessness. No monstrous stride rhythm, no bravado, no hundred-dollar diamond chip in a front tooth, no bravura. Left hand wasn't nothing but loose change thrown on a tabletop. That was the act, and it wasn't nothing. He remembered wishing that Nat Cole had refused to sing, just talked back to the effortlessness, the lie of ease, happening over there in his left hand, over to the west. And to the east, hot feet on thin ice. Nat Cole threw his hands like a magician threw his voice across a room, found something you'd lost a year ago, and took it out from behind your ear.

Shame could taste the rhythms. Then people appeared. And he'd pick up brick with his left hand on the keys and follow them down the street, into their kitchens; he'd follow the shadows and white crests of folds in a sheet wrapped around someone's ankle. The number-four-on-its-back shape made by one leg drawn up into a beam of sunlight, the shadow of heat from a radiator on a worn wooden floor. Taste of coffee-skin, whiskey-skin, a whiff of fresh nicotine in the breath behind a kiss. He played with his right eye closed, left-handed stories. One rhythm swallowing, one two-timing in his chest, a vein-twitch in his right thumb, the way a hard blink cut the story back two frames. Lives spliced. Taste this. A spoon held out across a counter, steam from a stainless pot on the stove. The economics of opening your eyes, the search for who owned you. The modern mystery. How we stole ourselves off and sold ourselves back. Price high enough meant free?

How everything, always, insisted on itself and something else. Everyone consisted in themselves and someone else, the way a glimpse of a stranger could tilt the world and spill you down the street. A human geography. Hours of tilted and tipped spaces east, west, stretched skin over shoulders, up the back of thighs. Sun in the room. Trouble in mind. Repetitions, hours, go and go and nothing, ever, happened *twice*. Repetition on its way out of sight and into sound nearer to the old-time delta of the newfound darkness than the eyes ever got.

After a few weeks the rule appeared to him. He'd lived it at work, for years, from just surviving labor, but the thought came to him on the piano: the definition of insanity was doing the same thing again and again and expecting the same result.

■

Then, the right hand began, literally, index and middle finger, straight out of the old yellow pages ad. Two fingers, walking. Hurdling black keys or crossing a white stream on upraised stones. A roar of the falls fallen somewhere upstream beyond the range of human hearing. The current pulled away from there down into the range beneath human feeling. The remaining fingers raised up in the air. Two fingers, a visitor, émigré to the left-handed planet. The right hand callused from the mixing paddle, gloved by its own skin. The left hand wore its glove of breath. For Shame it was like watching himself writing his autobiography at the age of two, when words still tangled with their tones in a battle over what they would become. When meaning fought with pure sense for sense, a prehensile mind pulling against the limb of solid body.

Thumb as a kickstand. Right pinky and ring finger, a stunt double who waited in the trailer. Late night, still playing, the shadow of his right hand sprawled across the wall.

The right fingers walked and the left hand two-bricked, three-bricked the sound, tilted it upward, downward. It immediately sounded good or bad. Then, after a while, that certainty failed into goodbad, badgood. Everything began to depend upon the traveler to the east, a plot that threatened the story. Shame drank the endless repetitions, his mind spooled in his arms. His foot worked the pedal like a high-hat cymbal, popped it off like a clutch on the steep ramp from Madison Street onto the Dan Ryan headed south, 85 mph all the way to the merge at Ninety-Fifth. Repetitions until the last phrase didn't recognize itself in the mirror of the first.

The sham of repetition unmasked became a way to learn from himself, to learn what he knew without knowing, had known, hadn't learned. Aristotle's gravity: the heavier an object, the faster it falls. Turned out it was only true for people who fell through space inside other people. It was like taking a spoon in a dream and tasting someone else from a bowl of what you are. It made him think of how, at the job, he'd taught himself that any word repeated ten times, twenty, anyone's name said over and over, became unrecognizable. Shame's hands wondered. The ache traveled up his wrists, across his shoulders. He learned that the title of every song is: "Who Owns This?" He'd tacked a white tarp to the ceiling. It dropped behind him when he played: the false curtain, a temporary illusion, privacy. Shame himself became a shadow on the other side: three points made a plane, one sheet made a wall, one wall made a room. Any three consecutive steps vanished the route left behind.

Rule: there was never a route left behind.

Repetitions. And, at first, the thirtieth word was always "pain." The fifty-first repeated word was "fear." And he'd forced himself to deliver fifty more as if the foreman was pounding the mortar board and demanding the brick be placed where he could swipe them up without taking a step. Then the pain and fear were lost and even Shame wouldn't believe any of it. None of it. None of it until he found another path across the street and it began all over again, the keys mined with mind, body trapped. Felt-covered hammers touching tensile steel wires, low to high, might spring loose a wheel of anger from inside. His nose brushed over the backs of his hands. Thighs off the cliff of the chair. The whole machine drew him away from the falls downstream. The pull, a momentum gathered beneath him. The push, the way one looked at the edge of the roof and heard, "Come a little closer, I dare you." The pull, a stranger who walked behind you in the street. That Aristotle thing pulling someone else over the ledge inside your chest and into a space unmapped by any sound. An abandoned wing, an empty shaft.

And power. Enough, he thought, to make two handfuls of red dust out of a still-banded full pallet of ceramic block headed his way on the back of a flatbed truck. Jobim's *sound of a gun in the dead of the night.* Enough to make strangers of his family, to make family of strangers. Enough so it seemed that he could watch his roommate crawl along the inside of his arm, pause, and pierce him there to put her poison. Poise in mind drowned in the fluid need that lured hips to touch. Touch tangent to the mirror; the complexity of fingers, an infinite sensuality; a human freedom to search for terror along the rim at the eclipse of control. And then how long one could hold one's breath in and what lay beyond that, in the mute iron weight of any shadow cast, as if by grotesque incongruity, as if by choice. Choice? Flakes of it. Dead skin on an onion. Try it, he thought. Then try again until you were out of agains, try to follow it around in the dark. There was no route. Nothing was ever empty.

Enough so he could lose himself in a room of people he'd never met, enough so that he could approach each of them from behind, a felt hammer tap on the shoulder and waited for them to turn around. Then Shame would play. He'd walk them toward the edge of the roof in his chest. Everyone a riff, every phrase meant, "Just a little closer, I dare you."

■

Take anything into the mind. Let it travel with the hands. A boxcar full of scrap rebar. The tune of a lunch wagon, ice cream truck. A soft swipe of red chalk across the sidewalk. All of it could be taken apart, flipped by a sudden pulse from the sea floor. When the mind be hands on your back, when the bet be fingers under your belt. A whole system of city lights twirled on the point of a pin, dark come feline come around a corner, the torque of stretched skin, almond slope, the cornea-color of love. An engine. Take lust. Something with silent wings contours the air just above an up-twisted belly; a tongue tastes furnace dust from its career across your shoulder.

The present was a rushing stream of absent water. The past was the shadow of a yellow-pages man who taught himself to walk in Shame's sleep. The future was listening.

The temperature had fallen fast throughout the evening. Cass saw Junior, P. W., and Valerie walk into Inflation out of the snowstorm that had become a real blizzard. To Cass, they looked like three years of raised rent. He met them casually at the door, as if they were regulars.

–Gentlemen. Madame. Please keep all firearms outside.

–What? You know it's illegal to carry a firearm in the city of Chicago.

–Right, I know. But in here we have what I call the in-balance of power. Only gun in here is mine. That keeps everything in balance.

Cass nodded toward the bar. Angie S., exaggerating a pause while she wiped out a glass, looked the other way. Then, under her voice:

–Except for mine.

P. W. nodded—"Fair enough"—and exited back out of the front door. Junior and Valerie went through the room and slid into place perfectly, new pennies in an old slot. They took the open booth, last on the left. Valerie and Junior faced the piano at the back. After returning a few minutes later, and feeling almost weapon-naked, stripped all the way down to the G43 in his boot, P. W. sat facing them and watched the door. The place was a cloud of talk. Valerie handed her coat to P. W., who took it to the bar and ordered a round of drinks. Whiskey, a double with ginger ale and cherry juice, for Valerie; ginger ale, neat, for Junior and for himself. P. W. sat down again, booths full of people and others standing in front of him. The piano sat diagonally behind him, empty stool pushed in.

■

Word moved from place to place like dust around Juniorville. One spot swept clean, the nonsense blew off somewhere nearby to settle in. Cass hadn't asked. He never did. Had never needed to learn to ask. He knew that whatever he needed to know would show up and become visible all by itself. And he knew that whatever he learned by asking was, at best, beside the point.

He was in the back room changing the sour line when Shame came in looking like a polar explorer. He shook the snow off his coat and hung it up on a tangle of deer antlers screwed into the wall near the door. Cass made an intricate maneuver of pulling back his sleeve, flicking his wrist down, and checking his watch. Then he went back to twisting the valve in place on the neck of a silver cylinder.

–Don't know who's drinking all this. I don't serve college kids. Feels like I ain't bent down to the rail all night.

–Did you ask?

Shame knew the answer. If you asked Cass anything the truth was in your question. And, in truth, Shame wasn't even really asking. Cass knew that too; he answered by pausing with the valve for the space of a breath, and then finishing off the remaining twists.

–Place full?

–Wouldn't say that, now.

Then, in a tone of voice suited to interrogating a prisoner of war or pressing a suspect into a false confession, Cass asked,

–Do you know what the fuck an apple martini is?

–You know this wasn't my idea.

–You'd know. Should I put a jar up on the piano, piano man?

Shame paused for a breath of his own, bent down to knock the snow off his boots and out of the cuffs of his jeans. He turned and walked into the hall. Angie S., Cass's longtime ex-wife, set a drink at the end of the bar. Shame pushed the swing door out and walked into the room. Low in the corner of his eye he saw that a thin, woven rug had been placed under the piano, both still set diagonally to the room. The top of the upright was propped open. But Shame didn't see that. He plucked the drink from the end of the bar and it felt like he'd stepped on a frayed corner of why Cass and Angie S. had been so long divorced and had stayed together, now, far longer than they'd been married.

Angie stepped behind him at the end of the bar.

–That you?

–You asking?

–Oh, *that* you. *Ex-cuse* me.

–Man, you both all incessant tonight. Have you *looked* outside?

–I ain't 'cessant-nothing. Why bother looking out? Look to me like it's *all* coming in here tonight. What?

Don't tell me you had some trouble with the commute, piano man?

He didn't need to turn around. Angie always had an old-time, Southern anvil swinging behind her eyes when she looked at you. Whether she was playing or not, it was the same. He didn't need to look but he almost ducked. He could feel her eyes sweep over his shoulder into the crowded room when she'd pronounced "all" with her neck like he knew she had. She knew he knew. They'd known each other a few weeks, had been finishing each other's sentences since the first moment, sentences they both knew didn't mean what they said they said. So this was trust, or it was close enough.

–You know, that reporter from the *Reader* was back here earlier asking questions, "following up" about the "construction-laborer-slash-piano-player."

Shame nodded his head to the side toward the piano.

–And who put that rug under there, Snow White?

–Oh, I see, you want me to come around the bar and commence to *being* 'cessant?

Fighting back a smile and narrowing down his focus to a pinpoint, Shame turned back to the right and walked to the piano without looking any further into the room than the near end of the bar. He didn't want to know. He told himself he didn't care who was there and who wasn't. He sat down with his back diagonal to the room, facing the corner. He took a long, thin sip from his drink. A slice of ice slipped into his mouth and back into the glass. "Exactly like that," he thought. "That's how this would go." He didn't want to see the room that had Cass and Angie's snitches in such playful, taunting stitches. He could feel Angie's smile warm on his back and he knew she wasn't smiling anymore. He thought, "What a pair, a short chain made of two missing links." He could almost hear Angie: "Oh, right, now you want to talk about pairs."

■

Shame had played low on the keys all week. And Pearlie's nine-year-old twins had been at his place. She'd been cleaning two houses, one for a wedding and one for a funeral. Both way north, past Evanston some place. Shame's playing hadn't been east of middle C since the twins had been there. La-Tessa and Va-Nessa. The girls said that they wanted to be a tag team of magician-beauticians. They resolutely ignored all of Ndiya's attempts at communication and spent their time braiding each other's hair while they rolled pennies and dimes back and forth across the tops of their fingers with their eyes closed.

To an increasingly eerie effect, they almost always spoke in perfect unison. After almost three full days of the silent treatment, on Wednesday afternoon, the ice broke for an instant. They asked Ndiya if she had any eyeliner and blue mascara. Ndiya gave it to them and then the ice froze back shut. They painted open eyes, bright cobalt-blue eyes, on each other's eyelids. Then, blue-eyed and unblinking, they'd resumed their no-look training with the coins and the braids. While shut, their eyes beamed precisely the same color as Shame's stove.

On Thursday, Ndiya asked what they planned to

do with their truly unique and finely honed skills. She thought she saw one eye blink brown as if to check if they were being patronized. Seemed not. Open eyes closed, in blue-eyed unison:

—We 'bout to get real good at this trick and then we 'bout to get to disappearing all kind of stuff.

Ndiya thought she heard one of them said "stuff" and the other said "shit" but she wasn't sure. She figured it was Tessa who said "shit" because one of her eyes blinked brown for an instant before it shut back to wide-open blue.

Each day, when Shame arrived at home that week, Ndiya had gone out, said she needed some air. But the weather was turning cold and she'd begun to stop into Inflation to warm up. Listening to Cass and Angie talk, with that upright piano in the corner of her eye, and at least less than sure about what she was doing in her life, Ndiya had come up with the idea of Shame playing music on Fridays and Saturdays. Cass and Angie's response was that they didn't much care who did what with that piano. It was Angie's father's piano. Stone Simpson hadn't ever made a public name, but everyone with ears—that is, as it was said, everyone who had *eyes*—around the scene knew him; he had played stride piano all around Chicago at places like the Pershing and El Grotto, just a few blocks from Inflation. As it was said, the man could *blow*. When he died, they didn't have room for his piano in their apartment and didn't quite have the heart to give it away. When Stone Simpson died, Angie learned that her father had had a second career as a Cook County inspector. Cass had known that all along; he played it off.

Shame had disappeared from the Cat Eye and Earlie's and people seemed to notice not hearing what they hadn't been listening to before. As a result, the migrations began setting off a soft subtle breeze on smoldering coals, a soft fix on something that didn't need to be mixed.

■

Before she went into Inflation, Ndiya stood and listened to the piano from outside the front door. The front windows were blacked out up to seven or eight feet. The glass on the door was fogged over. She could tell the fog was freezing into filigree clinging to the inside of the glass. The storm had all but ceased traffic in the street under the El tracks. The block was nearly silent.

The sound of the piano came and went. Notes and phrases advanced at an angle and evaporated into mirage. Ndiya remembered a stranger she'd met while at college in Cambridge, an old black man in a blue-and-red beret, who'd asked her in a quiet voice if *she* knew why it was always less lonely near a mirage. She'd asked him, playfully, if that was also true near the cryptic whisper of a stranger? He was a big man. Maybe sixty? He'd laughed deep, one hand in the pocket of his overcoat:

–We're not strangers, little girl.

And he'd walked away with his briefcase. It might have been the snow, but when Shame's sound evaporated into the near-silent space behind her, into the snow beneath the tracks, it seemed to leave an exile from sound. It wasn't like silence at all. The effect so different, she thought, from Shame in person, in private. At home he played distance in a way that, when he left, say, for work, his presence surrounded her like a hot bath. It was like sound in her bloodstream, in the marrow, as if her lungs breathed the sound out of the air like a fish's gills took oxygen from water. She stood in the street as if in a dim valley between the conical chaos of snow lit by two street-lights. The space between each of Shame's phrases felt like cotton in her ears. She put her hand on the door handle and stopped. She stared down at the snow drifting in the doorway and walked away.

Whatever was going on in there, she thought, she'd come up on it through the back door. At least brush off the snow, clear her ears, and hang up her coat.

Over the years, the alley behind Inflation had been widened into a grand boulevard by the absence of two buildings that burned and whose remains were razed. Cars in the alley were disappearing beneath the surf of snow. There were no tracks back there at all. The snow reached the fur-rimmed tops of her boots. When she entered through the back door the air inside felt like warm fluid against her face.

She reached the back room door on her right. A piece of paper was tacked to the door, written on the paper in wide, red marker:

STOP! THIS IS NOT THE RESTROOM.

THE RESTROOM IS BEHIND YOU.

Cass must be on edge, she thought. She entered. There he crouched, changing the sour line. Again. The three tabletops from the front leaned against the wall, a dozen table legs placed next to them. Six chairs stacked up to the side. Cass didn't check to see who'd opened the door.

–This is the *last* bottle of sour. After this the hip kids can get on down to Greensboro for milkshakes or they'll take their whiskey neat.

Cass looked back and nodded openly, tipped a hat he wasn't wearing.

–You're right on time, Your Royal Ms. Shamefulness.

He turned back to resume his task. Ndiya nodded at his back.

–How's it in there?

–Well, it ain't Ramsey Lewis at the Starlight, but it's mine. Or was. ·

–People come out?

–People? Let's call it gumbo. But hey, they *out*. I'll give 'em that.

The hum of the ice machine canceled the music in the back room. All Ndiya could hear in there, or feel in there, was a slow, walking rhythm of bass chords. Actually she felt it more than heard it. She wondered if Cass had put a mic on the piano. He finished with the nozzle. Ndiya was busy knocking the snow from the rims of her boots and putting the cuffs of her jeans back inside when Cass bowed in exaggerated formality.

–Come on, let me show you to your seat, m'lady of Shame.

–I'll stand by the bar.

–Not tonight, no room. There's a perfect seat open, though. Come on.

They stepped beyond the drone of the ice machine and into the sound of triplets over a minor chord. Each phrase repeated with shifts in the accent that altered the tone in the air. It sounded like someone trying to spray-paint wind. There'd be five cycles of triplets, a pause, a new chord answered with a first inversion of its mirror. The mirror then broke into arpeggios, another right-hand color wheel of variations. Ndiya stood still a moment thinking, if you could spray-paint the air a rainbow of colors, and then you swung an old hammer through the painted space, that'd be about it: the look of that hammer after its path through the cloud of color. They both stood still for a minute in the hallway. Cass stared at Ndiya's profile. Ndiya faced the door to the front.

–Could you wait here, Shame-bolina? I better wash my hands.

–OK, Cass. And could you rest the Ms. Shame-shit?

–Fair enough.

Cass turned to the door.

–Shame-o-nisha.

Ndiya felt a strange lace of hope that she was joking with Cass. It blew through her, she noticed, and she was surprised. This was new. He liked to mess with her, of course, and, somewhere, she knew she enjoyed it. She knew he did too. But tonight it felt different. One of them was clearly enjoying this more than the other. Was it in what he said? Or was it in what she heard? She didn't know. There was a new edge somewhere in this hallway. Or maybe a new space with no edge?

Something was changed. She felt heat collecting in

and around her waist and around the back of her neck under her scarf. Something was thick and sculptural in the voice of the air. Maybe it didn't have to do with either of them. Maybe it was just the crowd. She told herself this, but she knew she didn't believe it. It felt heavy. Then she recognized a weight, an exile, that she'd felt just before, when she was standing outside in the street. Cass came back, motioned "this way." Ndiya followed him into the empty weight of the near future. How easy to step into the future; how impossible to step back once it has become the present.

On Monday, at about ten in the morning, a few hours after Pearlie had dropped off her twins, an unfamiliar knock interrupted Ndiya's twin discoveries that, one, Va-Nessa and La-Tessa didn't appreciate diminutives.

–Um, Ms. Grayson, we feature our real names—

–Well, certainly, ladies. Excuse me.

–You're excused.

–Ah. OK, but don't push it.

–Yes, ma'am.

And two, the twins made it clear that they would attend to the pre-algebra workbook in the fullness of time. They had their own work to concentrate on. To *feature*, no doubt, Ndiya thought. She was right.

While the twins dealt with unambiguous directions, ones addressed to their real names, that they complete lessons one and two before turning to their *own* work, a decidedly forthright knock broke the eye-rolling, tongue-swishing, lip-pursing silence of a nascent compromise. Debating with herself about calling this "progress" with the twins, Ndiya heard a voice from out in the hallway.

–Ndiya?

–Yes?

–Um, is that Ndiya?

–It is.

–Yes, OK, Shame said you'd be here. I'm here to

take his painting to the gallery for authentication and appraisal.

–Painting? OK.

Ndiya opened the door to find a brightly smiling woman with her hair pulled tightly back into a pony-tail, black and gold sunglasses riding like a crown atop her head. She wore a loose coat, open, and a scarf over an army-green work shirt. She had on tights and a pair of certifiably liberal flats on her feet. In her right arm she held a very large plastic tube.

–Hi. I'm Colleen. *So* nice to meet you.

–Likewise. I'm Ndiya, which you already know. Come in, meet the girls.

–La-Tessa and Va-Nessa, meet . . . sorry, what's your name?

–Oh, hi girls, I'm Col—

–No, sorry, your name.

–Name? Oh, Morgan, Colleen Morgan.

–Girls, say hi to Ms. Morgan.

Colleen felt something mildly abrasive in the formal-ity. La-Tessa and Va-Nessa, both, without looking up, in the voice of rote recitation:

–Hel-lo, Ms. Mor-gan.

Colleen looked at Ndiya with a twist of "and that works?" and "good luck with that" in her face. Ndiya caught this and felt the impulse to close up the shop of her face and slam down the gate. She thought, "Please don't come up in here with that 'we in this together' mess." But she didn't do that. Instead, she glanced back openly, her eyebrows up in the nothing-from-nothing setting, and smiled. Ndiya felt salt collecting in the glands of her throat. She knew what to expect. "Just see what she wants, or what *else* she wants, and get rid of the white trick," she thought.

Without saying anything or making a gesture, she turned and they walked across the room. Ndiya stopped at the far end of the table near the painting and paused before turning around. She'd been on this walk before. She knew the woman would either be lost back there by the door, not knowing what to do, as if the path forward led atop the heads of crocodiles, or she'd be all up on her heels, in Shaggy and Scooby position, like the room was full of ghosts.

Instead, Colleen had stopped at the near end of the table. When Ndiya turned, Colleen shifted her gaze from the painting to Ndiya's face. Ndiya noticed a warmth. It felt like the sun had come from behind a cloud.

–I think it's a great piece. It might be an important piece.

Ndiya was shocked to find a real neutrality in Colleen's voice and in the way she stood midway in the room, in her *own* space. But it wasn't neutral. It was focused. Colleen wasn't worried about crocodiles and ghosts. She'd been on that walk before, herself.

–I like it, yes. But what do you mean by important?

–Oh, an early piece by a now-famous painter. Balanced but without strict symmetry, playful but laced with something ominous. It's an early piece, but it's not an apprentice piece at all. Possibly the first mature work by this painter . . . so that'd be important. And it's also totally unknown. So . . .

–I see.

Ndiya could now feel very clearly that Ms. Morgan wasn't going to deliver her expectations, at least not right away. Like allergies, Ndiya noticed that her expectations of white folks could sometimes be a little late in arriving to new locations. Still, she hinted to herself that the woman of her expectations likely wouldn't knock on *this* door at all. A voice whispered in her ear—"She ain't no Jehovah's Witness." Nonetheless, Ndiya wasn't going to fall for whatever it was all at once. For all she knew, after she had no more magic stunts up her sleeve, she'd be on about the Art Institute and don't you just *love* Chicago? She probably lives "up near Wrigley Field!" Ndiya held her ground. With no ground to hold, she knew, *she'd* be the patronizing one.

Ndiya turned to face Colleen across the length of the table.

–So, now.

–Well, a few weeks ago, I ran into—

–Ran?

–You know, it was a Saturday, I think, and I bumped into—

–You bumped?

–Ah, *oh-kay*, well . . . and I saw Shame standing on the corner up near where I live. I think I was coming home from the gym. And I had stopped at the Jewel . . . yes, that's right.

–Oh, so you saw—

–Right, Shame said you were in a store around the corner and he was waiting for you.

–Right. Now, I remember. So that was *you* . . . an "old friend" he'd seen while I was inside. I see. And you didn't wait? In a hurry?

–Well, I had groceries, I was a mess from the gym, and, if you remember, it was cold and looked like it might rain that night. So I was really *on* my way home.

Ndiya couldn't tell if she really meant these little barbed midterm exams she was spinning like tops down the length of the table at Colleen. She did admit to herself how much she admired Colleen's way of not dealing with them by not dealing with them. But somehow still dealing. The woman was precise, give her that, and she seemed to be standing where she was standing. Still, Ndiya had known a few good test takers. Colleen continued,

–I guess he remembered my interest—

Dealing without dealing, Colleen paused just a half beat to almost acknowledge Ndiya's opportunity to interject something, and then went on,

–in this painting. He said I should come *back* by his place and take it to the gallery. I work at a gallery west of the Loop. Halsted and Madison. The first time I came over here, I was shocked to see it and I suggested that he have it verified.

–Authenticated.

–*Pre-cisely.*

As if she'd been reading Ndiya's mind, Colleen pronounced "precisely" with a kaleidoscopic twirling in it, recently threaded eyebrows up in the "something we share" position. She'd also mentioned, *twice*, being here before.

–That means having its origins confirmed. Checked against technique, biography, etc. He told me he'd won it in a raffle—of all things—in Miami years ago.

Ndiya said nothing. She held her face aggressively neutral and thought, "Let's see what she'll do with this much rope." After the frozen pause, Colleen allowed,

–Look, I know . . . I'd have called but Shame has no—

–Shame?

–Well, OK, but he also has no phone.

Aces. Colleen Morgan was either a great test taker or a natural-born something else. Or, maybe she's a person? It didn't matter. Ndiya liked her; there was no point in denying it. And she resolved to cease with the midterm exam routine, presently.

–Did you ever take the LSAT?

–Me? No. Why?

–Never mind. How do you plan to transpo—

Colleen held up the tube.

–I'll roll it up. It's safe. I can write you a—

–No need. Just give me the phone number to the gallery. I *have* a phone. And I imagine you must have a card?

–Sure.

Colleen opened up the tube, walked around the table, and handed Ndiya her card. Ndiya nodded in the direction of the painting and, just for symmetry, decided on one more quiz. It was a little in your face, but what the hell? She reached for her phone and dialed.

–Yes, may I please speak with Colleen Morgan? Oh,

I see. Do you know when she'll be back? OK. No, that's fine. I'll call back. Thank you.

She turned back to the painting expecting Colleen to be either staring at her (ghosts) or ignoring her (crocodiles), thinking, "Either one and I'm going to call, 'Pencils up.'"

But Colleen was not behind her. Ndiya turned right and found Colleen standing behind the girls. Her face looked like an open quotation mark in search of something to say—

–Tell Ms. Morgan what you're doing, ladies.

–We going to be twin magician-beauticians. We're going to call our act Fame Us.

–Well, I'd say you're getting there.

Colleen walked over to the wall.

–May I?

Ndiya nodded.

–It's an important piece. The earliest Bedia, from when Bedia had become Bedia, that is, that I've seen. With the signature and the little statement and even with the story about how it was acquired, yes, it's an important piece.

–Important?

–Well, collectible, salable. If it is what it says it is, and I'm pretty sure it is. It's too strange not to be true. You know?

–Ah, as a matter of fact, I do. But salable to, collected by, who exactly?

–Anyone, really. Any gallery who deals at all with diasporic, Caribbean . . . our gallery, for instance, would buy the piece with an option to show and, at the right time, to sell it at auction. That's why it should be authenticated. But I'm sure it's real. Shame should enter more raffles.

–You're telling me—

Colleen laughed. And turned back to untacking the painting, carefully, from the wall.

–Look, when you're done packing that up. Do you have time for a cup of coffee or something?

Now, it was Colleen's turn.

–Coffee, sure. Something? Now that depends.

–Good, I'll make a few cups . . . of something.

–Lovely.

Colleen sat at the table and looked at the blank space where the painting had been. She didn't remember much about her first time at Shame's place, but she most certainly didn't remember this. She wondered how much owed to him, to time, how much to Ndiya's presence here. She recalled the former ramshackle barrenness of the place. In her memory, "former" twisted into "formal." Without the painting on the wall to orient the table, she'd have been unable to recognize the place at all, unable to connect it to the apartment she'd visited, nervously, sixteen months ago. Back then, she couldn't help viewing the whole apartment like it was a kind of exhibit, an installation. Ndiya entered with a tray.

–I didn't know if you—

–No, black is great. Thanks.

Ndiya paused for a reaction. Nothing. A shadow appeared in her head and she wondered into it, why the exam questions still? Then Colleen dove.

–Look, this is probably breaking the rules, but—I met Shame when he used to go up to Earlie's. He'd play the piano sometimes, way in the back, by himself. This was before anyone began to listen. He'd just be over there by himself, as if he was at home, or so I thought. How wrong I was! I was pretty new to town. New at the gallery. Lonely. I'd had a good six months of the "girl alone in the world" thing, you know, the solitary, uptown, urban-vibrator thing. You know? Enough! I'd had enough.

Ndiya narrowly avoided choking on a sip of coffee. She put down the cup, glanced back at the twins. They appeared oblivious, which wasn't true, of course. Ndiya wiped her chin, and, at a loss, came up with:

–Hasn't everybody?

–Well, back then Shame was, um, he didn't talk much, his eyes didn't toggle all over the room when he listened like most men's eyes do, and so I kind of insinuated my way into an invitation to come over here for dinner. Apart from the fact that I didn't know this part of town down here even existed, when I got upstairs, he'd barely look at me. He was a totally different person than I'd known, or thought I'd known at Earlie's. It was as if, when I walked in the room, we both realized immediately that something indecent had happened. No one belonged in this place at that time, not even him. I'd trespassed a place . . . not a place, a kind of labor, an attempt . . . it was like . . .

–Indecent? How?

–No. *It* wasn't indecent. *I* was. Or not even me. I

was a catalyst, really. It was just not a place for anyone to be. Maybe just him, but I think even that came later. Or maybe me being there made it possible for him to see it and then maybe he *was* there. But one thing was certain and we both felt it immediately, much as we tried to ignore it. There was nowhere for *me* to be in that room. No air to breathe, if you know what I mean?

—Go on.

—I mean I could have handled private. I expected it. I thought he played at the back of Earlie's, and even later at the Cat Eye, like he was at *home*. Everyone thought that. Like he wasn't performing, you know, like he was *alone*. As if privacy was informal, casual. I had it *all* wrong. And I knew it as soon as I stepped in here. I can't explain it, standing in this place back then, with him, it felt like no one in the world had ever been, or could ever be, alone. Anywhere. Being by yourself doesn't make you alone . . .

—OK, you lost me. Back up?

But Colleen didn't circle back to explain, she went ahead. Her eyes drilled into the top of her cup. Ndiya thought, "OK, touché." So now, she followed.

—I'd never seen privacy laid out like a diorama. I'd seen *that* attempt. It always came off like the opposite of privacy, like a peep show, like a window you look at but not through.

—It wasn't like that here at all. The place was set up for no one to be in. Until . . . I mean there were tools piled in a corner. I remember the smell of raw wood. The piano was there. I remember asking him if he played and he stared at the table and said it was kind of all he did but that, no, he *didn't* play. He said what he did at Earlie's wasn't him at all.

–He still says that.

–Well, it was true *then*.

–It might still be true.

–Hm. Well, I don't know. I was expecting electricity. Sex, you know, or at least the threat of it, the rush of water under the ice. Something. Instead, I found myself loving what I saw like a . . .

–Like a friend, perhaps, or like a sister?

–No, well, of course, that's what I told myself at the time. There was something very strong I could feel, but there was nothing like arousal. Nothing I recognized as sexual—

Colleen tipped her head at the twins and made an "is this OK?" face. Ndiya nodded, *please*, and waved her hand.

–The truth is I felt blasphemous and was trying to cover it up with fake guilt. I told myself that I felt the "failed to love it" kind of way like when I first spent time with Van Gogh's peasants, or Caillebotte's floor planers. But it wasn't that.

Ndiya stared at Colleen over the rim of her raised cup. She felt like she was hiding behind it.

–I felt kind of sick—a dread at having been looking for "fun" or "art" or something "interesting." You know? And then, I walked in here and ran into a glass wall.

–A wall?

–I mean, I don't know. It was an unnamed—what's the word? . . . an *endeavor*. A *life* was trying to happen.

It needed space. But that space didn't exist. I won't say it was desperate, even that might be too self-conscious. But it was intense. That scared me.

At the phrase "a life was trying to happen," something clicked. Ndiya noticed that she'd been nodding without meaning to. It had happened on its own. She was leaning into what Colleen was saying, trying to follow but also pulling her forward. She thought she understood. She thought she disagreed. But she believed Colleen. She'd think about it. And then she thought, she believed Colleen *had* thought about it. Ndiya then, possibly, suspected that she *did* know what Colleen meant by incongruity, that thing about "endeavor." And she thought she had glimpsed a small piece, likely involuntarily revealed, of Colleen's endeavor. This conversation, or story, felt strange to Ndiya; it felt like something that might bend without breaking. Suddenly, she felt tears behind her eyes.

She laughed to herself, thinking, "Damn, is this what trust feels like when it begins?" She'd never felt this kind of thing begin. She'd walk through plate glass for Shame. But she hadn't felt *that* begin. She fell into that like stepping backward off a cliff. Even now, when she thought about it, it wasn't him she trusted; it *was* something else, something he moved in that she'd committed herself to, that had changed the way she breathed. Ndiya had nodded because this Colleen was close. She'd shined her light in a way that had shown into Ndiya's past with Shame. But not quite. A life wasn't *trying* to happen here. Shame's life had been *dying* to happen here. And here she was. Then Colleen:

–What about you? Are you from here?

Colleen's question struck Ndiya back from her thoughts. In fact, she didn't know who'd asked whom. Colleen took a sip of coffee like one does preparing to listen, so Ndiya thought she knew. Now, it was Ndiya's turn at indecency. She lied and salted the lie with the truth.

–Yeah. South Side, Chatham. Same old story. Whitney Young. College. Then I moved around a lot from here to there. Jobs. Mostly temp jobs. Paralegal-type work. I tell people, "You know what a nurse does for doctors, or the hygienist for a dentist? I did that for lawyers." In other words, damn near everything. It paid pretty well. I found it easy. Finally, I took a job at a firm in Chicago. I came back.

Colleen gave a doubting look. It *was* Monday morning.

–Do you still work there?

–No. I quit. What about you?

–From here? No. I'm from Minnesota. Went to Oberlin to study music but ended up studying languages and art history. The rest is much closer to history than it is to art, believe me.

Ndiya enjoyed Colleen's laugh. It seemed to collect and clean the air like a windless spring rain. The woman seemed at home in herself and openly at odds with herself at the same time. But there was a comfort in it. She'd always instantly resented this, what she considered a privilege, in people, in white people mostly and in white women especially. It wasn't like the Maurice Thomases of the world who'd made a grim, possibly heroic, discipline of being at ease. Nor was it like Yvette, who, with an equal heroine-ism, had made ease an over-the-top, in-your-face kind of thing. And white people's ease mostly felt like it was stepping on your face in a way no one noticed but you.

Ndiya felt none of that here. And she felt herself *not* feeling it. Maybe she was feeling *for* it. Years ago, a friend had told her she thought it was impossible to have an interesting conversation without some kind of sex in the air. Ndiya thought of that, now, about a feeling she could feel she *didn't* have, and about what that felt like. And what did that mean, "some kind of sex"—a sense, a real sense of the person one talked to? Did that have to be an attraction? Desire? Or was the simple sense of it enough? Ndiya thought maybe it was the latter. Involuntarily, she slipped off her shoe and extended her foot under the table, subliminally expecting her toes to feel the edge of a cliff.

Colleen sipped her coffee, admiring the way Ndiya, discreetly but noticeably, absented herself into faraway thought-lands during conversations with people she'd just met. She wondered if Ndiya had any idea what her comings and goings felt like to be around. What she looked like? It was like standing to the side and trying to talk to someone who was riding a huge carousel. She found it pleasant enough. She was curious just where Ndiya went off to. Of course, she wasn't going to ask.

–How did you meet him?

Ndiya wondered where to go now. Her extension of Colleen's sense of what she called Shame's endeavor was still on her mind; a life was dying to happen. She had felt it immediately. So the usual shortcuts were out. And so was the truth, which even she didn't quite believe yet: Oh,

253

how did we meet? Thirty-three lightning bolts and a bum email? Come on. Quit my job and moved in? What else? Shared destiny and simultaneous orgasms? Soul mates? It was all she had. And it didn't fly. The rest was off-limits even to her: clouds of static, pendulums, invisible trains—

–Oh, you know, we met by chance. Some party. Then, after that, one day we ran int—

–Wait—you *ran*?

They both laughed.

–I know. I deserved that. So, we met again by another chance. Finally, you know, the truth is that I really met him down here and I never left. It's been about six months. Five months? Feels a lot shorter and a *lot* longer than that. Both. Now, I'm here. These twins' mother, and a few other mothers in the neighborhood, they used to drop their kids off at Shame's in the evenings—

–They stayed with him? Are some of them his kids?

–No, though that crossed my mind too. But no. Well, now, some drop off kids during the days, as you can see. I handle all that.

–They pay?

–No, no. It's not about that. For now, that's what I do. That's really all I can say—

–No, that's enough. That's plenty.

Without another word, Colleen and Ndiya both moved to get up at the same time, which made them both smile and shake their heads. They walked past the twins and to the door—

–Ndiya, it's been so nice to talk. *So* lovely to meet you. I better get back to work. Tell Shame I'll tell him what I find out about his Bedia . . . or maybe I should take *your* number, I mean, since you didn't leave me a message at the gallery? Or at least, the message didn't have your number in it, did it?

–No, you and Shame can deal with his painting. But take my number too. Call me sometime, we'll continue our—whatever it is.

–I know, I'd like to continue our—as well.

–*Our* endeavor.

Laughing again.

–OK. Lovely to meet you. Bye, girls.

–OK, bye.

– . . . Ms. Morgan.

–Ms. Morgan.

–No. Bye, Ms. Morgan.

–Bye, Ms. Morgan.

–OK. Talk to you later.

Ndiya closed the door and turned around, feeling like if she leaned back against it she'd fall free into the hallway.

C ass emerged from the washroom, clicked a penlight in his right hand and, in his best attempt at an usher's instruction, murmured a low,

–This way.

Ndiya followed. When she came through the doorway, a dim red light was spilling out of the ceiling fixtures. It fell around her neck like a collar of ermine. She put a hand on Cass's shoulder, drew him back, and whispered,

–Nice touch, Cass. The lights.

–That's right.

Cass smiled, then winked.

–No shame in that, right?

– . . .

–Come on.

She was shocked, she had to admit, at the human density in the room. It was a divided density. All the seats occupied by black folks. Some she knew, like Lee Williams and Lucious Christopher, were seated in booths, others at the bar. She may have glimpsed Muna's red crest of hair in a booth along the right side of the room. The white people stood in the capital T of standing room. The stem of the T led between the booths and the bar and was crossed in the space at the end of the room against the blacked-out windows and the fogged-over front door. The place was packed.

She didn't look, she said she wouldn't, but she heard Shame's chord change. The sound was still deepened as if amplified. Possibly, she thought, the crowd of people caused it: Just less air in the room? Human acoustics? Shame's right hand shuffled a deck of quadruplets now, three sets each, each with the forth note bent in a different direction. As she followed Cass, who made the way, she could see it: the left-hand chord was the crowded room, thick; the right hand was finding its way through. She could feel it bumping into folks, into things, a stool, and pausing to keep it upright. Keep it civil. She heard Shame's right hand step on someone's shoe and apologize. And some echo down low in the left hand. No, it was below that, the low echo said, "Alright, it's alright." She listened again, something happening below Shame's left hand was saying, "Whatever happens is alright." This was *certainly* a new sound for Shame.

Her hand on Cass's thick shoulder as they moved through the edge of the crowd, she pulled Cass back again and whispered,

–Is this possible?

–No. It's not.

Cass had answered too loudly, and on purpose.

–Cass, shhh.

So, then, even louder:

–Girl, please, this is my place!

And then, like a diagonal flick of a wrist:

–Your seat, saved, just for you—

And facing up to her, face closed, Ndiya saw a bald, dark-skinned man in a black, open-necked shirt and a woman with short-cropped hair and silver earrings dangling. Next to an open space on the facing seat sat a big honey-brown man with a shadow of a beard along his jaw, steady staring through the crowd standing between him and his view of the front door.

Ndiya took her seat, mouthed a mocking "Thank you" to Cass and smiled while mouthing "Evening" to the table. The two across from her nodded blankly. Ndiya thought, "Oh, great." Cass's profile descended, exaggeratedly, into her view as if he was about to kiss the tabletop.

–A drink, m'lady?

–A double.

–Very good. Jah Reeve.

And then, almost tenderly, with a gesture across the room, as if waving over an extensive estate:

–Could be a while.

–See what you can do.

Cass was off. Ndiya leaned back into the seat. She faced the front door from the back booth that, she knew, wasn't ten feet from the piano in the corner. "Back to back," she thought. She didn't watch Shame play in public, though she could stare at him effortlessly when he played at home. She knew he hadn't prepared anything formal. She thought, just then, that she knew that the family of a tightrope walker never watched the wire. She knew you didn't watch the wire when the ones you love were on the wire. The wire couldn't hold someone you love; it could only betray them. The wire could only convey something *else*, something it wasn't, to the other end. She glanced beyond her booth into the crowd that stood there staring at the piano and the man behind her. "No net," she thought. She felt a sting like smoke in her eyes, so she stopped. She didn't really listen, either, but she loved to be in the sound. She decided to be *there*.

By now Shame had talked to her a little, just a little, about playing. She heard the little something he had said as if he repeated it behind her,

–If you fuck up and say more than you know, you're trapped in what you said. This old piano taught me that. And it's true. Then I learned that if you hold back, and say less than you know, you're trapped in what you *didn't* say. You can't think about playing when you play. Too many things happening all at once, if you think about them, you paralyze yourself; you're trapped outside. But if your mind wanders onto something else, anything else, you make mistakes. Or nothing happens in what you're doing, no door opens. Trapped again, this time inside. So the discipline is to keep the mind open and sit right next to it and play only what comes in and out of the door. When it steps in, play that. When it steps out, you let it go.

The way he said this scared her. Ndiya's life maintained a constant vigilance against exactly those kinds of comings and goings. After he'd said it, though, she'd found the same was true for her listening. She didn't listen to the music; she didn't listen to anything else either. The open door of the ear, she learned not to aim it. If she sat next to the open ear, she felt within reach. What it meant to be "in-touch." Not touched, not untouched; in-touch. In that place she found an action, a physical action, part memory, part vision—or hallucination—unlike anything she'd known. She felt the fear at what might appear, of what might touch her, like going to sleep within arm's reach of a barred window on the fire escape. She remembered nights with Arturo in Alphabet City. They prayed for a breeze through the small window, measured the possibility of cool air against the chance of someone coming up the fire escape and reaching in through the bars while they slept. She heard it: dreams of a cool breeze on an open throat. Unconsciously, she held the root of this need, this vigilance, at a distance.

Another part of her wondered if the whole open ear-door thing was just an erotic illusion, something *only* private, like the way desire closed down the field of vision, slowed time, amplified feeling into echoes in a way that made a person blind and numb to everything else. She wondered if it was real at all, or just between them. If she was honest, part of the motivation for these nights at Inflation was about that. She'd needed to test it, to see if it existed, even for her, beyond them when they were alone. She wondered if she'd forced Shame into a similar confrontation. Ndiya had no way to know how the stakes of confrontation could deepen, how its scope was uncharted, beyond reckoning.

She realized she had her eyes shut. When she opened them she found a double shot of bourbon and a small glass of ice with a spoon next to it. The ice glowed red in the low light. She spooned in an ice sliver, stirred it gently. She thought she could feel the eyes of the man across from her on the motion of her index finger stirring the ice. She threw the thought off to the left, took the ice out of the drink and, absently, put it in her mouth, rolling it around until the heat of the bourbon disappeared. She

let the ice diminish in her mouth, cooling her tongue until it was gone. She thought and whispered it to herself:
"Exactly like that." She'd sit by the door like that. "If this
trapdoor-eyed Negro across the table was watching," she
thought, "let him watch." Then she took a double sip of
her drink.

Almost reluctantly, she drew her eyes up. The woman
with the earrings had her eyes closed too. One hand on
the table, every few seconds her middle finger and thumb
feigned a snap like her fingers were dreaming about snap-
ping. Ndiya's eyes panned to her left and the man was
there. Ndiya thought, "Or somewhere." To look at him,
she thought, you might not imagine music existed. His
bald head didn't even move the way something stock-still
still moves. His face wasn't calm or contained, with the
stress and overflow those features always convey despite
themselves. He seemed more sharply focused in her vision than her eyes were capable of, as if seen through an
optical lens of some sort, sharp in the unapproachable way
a dream image was sharp. His skull and face looked like
someone pulled a thin, black silk sack over a black marble
sculpture of a face. She didn't realize she was staring, if she
was, until their eyes met. And he smiled in her direction,
conveying no sensation at all that he'd smiled at her. He
was still neutral except, by some invisible motion, all the
features of his face reflected in his dark eyes. They weren't
trapdoors. "Eyes like tunnels," she thought, "until they
folded into bright, cold candles."

In that moment, the man Ndiya saw wasn't himself
anymore. This wasn't the man she'd sat down in front of a

few minutes ago. The eyes were not candles because there was no glow in the brightness, no motion in them. Surgical light. Or ice. And she heard a distant falsetto, at once a lifetime away and so close it felt like earlier that night:

. . . *shine like diamond ice.*

That was it. And *she* felt cold and wished she hadn't left her coat in the back. She focused beyond him on the fog-frosted windows. She knew it wasn't cold in the room.

The man blinked and his face fell back into its place across the table, as if someone had snatched away the silk sack and flung it into nonexistence. Ndiya nodded imperceptibly and a hand reached out of Shame's sound and tapped her gently on the shoulder. Within reach, intouch. Then another tap, and a whisper:

–Um, miss?

It was the man next to her. She looked his way and he pointed down where space between them would have been if there'd been room.

–My hat?

Just then she felt a lump under her. Reaching down slowly she pulled out a flattened suede driving cap with a pair of thin leather gloves folded in it. She handed it to him, cracking her brow into a silent apology. He wasn't bothered. His mouth tipped a tolerant, as-long-as-you-know-you-were-sitting-on-my-hat "no problem" to her. He put the gloves in his pocket and then reached down and fit the cap over his bent knee under the edge of the table.

Within reach, in-touch. And another tap, this time on the other shoulder. Expecting someone immediately to her left, Ndiya leaned to the right and looked up into an empty space. What she saw wasn't where she expected it to be. Blurry, in the back of her vision, stood a thick black man wearing a small hat, white shirt, and dark jeans rolled up at his ankles. Before her eyes adjusted, she thought, "He's dancing with a maple-skinned mannequin." Then the image focused, "No, he's playing an upright bass." Shame had paused and the man's hand on the strings was making its own way through the crowded room. Now he stood behind the hollow question of his instrument, eyes closed, agreeing with himself. He stared up at the ceiling through his shut eyelids. Unlike Shame, he seemed incapable of playing three notes in a series that didn't imply a melody she wanted to hum along with. She wondered if they'd been rehearsing and Shame hadn't told her. That was impossible. Or was it?

Less lonely "here," she thought, picturing the old man in Cambridge again, because this has *got* to be a mirage. Off to the piano's right, the man with the bass stood at the corner of the rug. They must have nearly brushed shoulders when she'd followed Cass through the back door and into the crowd. How could she have missed it? Him? Then she recalled the amplified feeling of depth she'd felt. So she hadn't missed him; she just hadn't seen him. Either she'd felt him right away, or he wasn't there at all. Mirage or not, she was glad he was— whoever he was—where he appeared to be. The way he played was like taking a handful of here and throwing it over there. But even over there it still felt like it was right here. It sounded like a kind of presence that had nothing to do with the question of distance.

■

Before the set, the man had been standing beside his instrument, wiping it down, when Shame came out from the back. Shame walked in, took his drink, and sat down on a round stool at the piano. Shame hadn't ignored him as much as he'd taken no notice to ignore. The talk in the room had stopped when Shame walked in, so he sat there with his legs wide apart, waiting for the talk to resume and, he figured, for the stranger with the bass to pack up and leave. In a few moments, a thin steam of talk began to sift from the ceiling and drape over the room. It filled in the space between the bodies. Shame looked over at the bassist, now done tuning, who was looking back at him. Shame's first thought was "No way he's an American."

–So. Forgive me, are you the opening act or something? What am I missing?

–My brother, I came to *play*. With you. My name is Kima. I came to sit in.

–Well, I'm afraid you're fifty years too late for a "sit in."

–I know! I get it. Ha! Seriously, I heard you play with yourself.

–That's *by* myself.

–Right. At the Cat's Eye. They told me there that you'd begun to play down here. Last week, I saw a short article about you in the *Reader*.

–The *Reader*?

–Yes, a good article. So, I came down here to find you.

–Oh, I *see*.

Shame's impossible tone flew past unnoticed.

–Yes. If I may. I've studied this music.

–You know I don't play "music," no lead sheets or whatever . . .

–I'll follow you. I've heard you. It's like Rotary Perception.

–Like wha—

–Rotary Perception, Mingus and his drummer, their theory of playing together like an expanding conversation. It goes around and around, wherever it likes, but always finds its way back to where it began.

–I don't know about that.

–Ah, yes you *do-oo*. Look, it doesn't matter. I'll follow you.

–Me? Well, stay out of sight.

–I'll stay out of sight. Like acoustics . . .

–Acoustics, OK, whatever. Um, your voice. Where are you from?

–Kenya. The coast. Mombasa. Have you been? To Africa?

–No. Actually, I almost went for a job a few years ago. It was supposed to be six months, maybe a year. I had my passport, work visa. A whole rack of shots.

–A construction job?

–How did you know that?

–The *Reader*.

–Right, of course. It was in southern Tanzania, near Uganda. Then there was trouble in Uganda, rebels in the north. I don't remember the details. It got postponed.

After a year or so the boss went there to sound it out. The foundation of the plant, a brewery, was still visible but he said the site had gone back to bush. The materials and equipment had been shipped. Two containers. The equipment was gone. The material was in mounds going back to earth. The shipping containers had been moved down near a stream about a mile away. Families were living in them.

Kima stared at Shame for an instant, wondering if he should correct his geography. Then he tossed his head.

–Of course, it's Naipaul!

–Nepal?

–Never mind. You should go to Kenya. To the coast, though. Don't mess with those upcountry people. I should know, my family is in Nairobi.

–Right. Maybe I should leave now and then *you* can play with yourself in here tonight? "Live at Inflation . . ." What was your name again?

–Kima. The name's Kimani.

Shame reached out his hand in acceptance.

–Well, Kima Kimani—

–No, Kimani's the surname. My given name is Merlin. People call me Kima.

Shame wasn't exactly sure what a "sir name" was. He decided it meant a last name.

–OK, Kima. Got it. I don't know how you're going to follow me when I don't know where I'm going. But it's nice to meet you, man.

Kimani bounced his gaze in reply and smiled. He shook Shame's hand, surprised. Despite whatever it said in the *Reader*, Kima was still shocked to be shaking the hand of a farmer in America. In Chicago.

–You've got a villager's hands.

–Yeah, well, we don't have villages here.

And Shame turned around to the keys. Kimani waited with his eyes closed. After a few minutes, during a chance moment's rise in the volume of conversations, Shame found a few brick to pick up with his farmer's left hand. He answered with his right at the very top of the keyboard. A few moments later, he noticed Kima back there, way back down the street. He'd never played with company. It felt like the bass pressed firmly into the small of his back. He felt like he could lean back off the stool onto Kima's sound and not fall. He thought, "OK, I've got a villager's hands, and you, sir Kima, have the hands of a masseur."

∎

Sitting there with her back turned, Ndiya didn't see it. The music didn't end. Shame snatched his fingers from the piano with a gesture that made it sound like he'd hit the last two keys by accident, the way a man might not quite accidentally knock a fork off the table. It felt like he'd put his hands on her shoulders. He would soon; he hadn't yet. Shame turned to his right on the stool, sat sidesaddle and waited for Kima to complete his thought, or catch up from where he'd been following, or maybe just notice that no music was coming from the piano. Kima kept on, looking up, his hands moving like he was climbing a rope to the ceiling.

Still waiting for Kima to come around, Shame stood up and, for the first time, looked out at the room between the bar and the booths. A few people started to clap but Shame's vision was frozen so he didn't see them move. There was a sound at the bar like a drawer slamming shut. His eyes veered left and saw nothing capable of such a sound. At the end of the bar to his left, however, he recognized Colleen, who did move. She smiled, and waved. He may have smiled thinly, he may not have. But as soon as Colleen waved he heard, as if catching it midway, a loud applause and could now see people moving. A young man in a white coonskin hat whistled. And he looked right and saw that Ndiya had been sitting behind him, in a booth with Junior's trio.

He hadn't seen Junior in months. His appearance tonight, in a room that looked like this room, greeted Shame like a whiff of smoke. It was a warning. When he saw Junior, the sound of applause morphed into the cracking-sticks sound of a fire. Underneath his thoughts, and in the copper taste in his mouth, was Shame's knowledge that, in the worst fires, people didn't die from burns or smoke, they simply lost the contest for air to the flames and so suffocated, often quite peacefully, while asleep. They exhaled in a dream and then just didn't inhale again in life. Then that dream didn't end.

When the applause ceased, with the certain feeling of invisible hands still massaging her shoulders, Ndiya opened her eyes and smiled diagonally across at Valerie. She reached out.

–Hi, I'm Ndiya.

–Val. Nice to meet you.

And Valerie, taking over:

–To your right, P. W. P. W., say hello to the lady.

–Nice to meet you, End-iya. Am I saying that right?

And Ndiya:

–Close. Áh-ndiya.

–Áh-ndiya.

–Perfect.

Junior didn't wait for Valerie to continue. He reached over his empty glass of ginger ale.

–I'm Junior. How do you do?

Ndiya blinked quizzically. Junior's greeting sounded like a real question. She didn't know what to say. Then she thought of his name.

–*The* Junior?

In a mock-search of himself, Junior looked down at his chest and surveyed his extended arms.

–I think so.

–Owns-the-building-Shame-lives-in Junior?

–That Junior. Yes.

–A pleasure.

–It's mine. All mine.

Junior caught himself and waved at the table. An iced light danced behind his face.

–My bad. I mean the pleasure is ours.

In Junior's world there was always something wrong. Maybe most things, all the time. He paid very little attention to trivia. He viewed the world as if the lights were dimmed, at an angle that canceled out degrees of gray and minutia. He loved the taste and scent of all the clashing details in and around his life. He just never looked

269

at them, never stopped to consider them. He knew they never really were what they presented themselves to be, knew that by the time one noticed such details they were already something else anyway. Life was a fully saturated solution. So he'd say to himself, "How do you solve a solution?" He treated things like a bowl of soup brought to him each morning made from the leftovers of the previous day. There'd be a spoon somewhere. He'd ask for bread.

The trouble at Inflation was obvious, and he didn't appreciate the taste of it. He could handle that. But after sitting across from her as he had, keeping her just off the center of his vision, he found he was aware, conscious in a way that sliced him somehow, that another trouble was about. This was no detail. And then, something else had begun to crawl in him when she'd spoken her first words to Valerie. It wasn't about what she'd said. He knew that. It was something *in* what she said. He was used to things not being what they appeared to be. He slurped spoons from that bowl every day. This was different. Something had fallen off a tree into the palm of his hand; something that was *exactly* what it was. Something had stayed impossibly still; it was still what it had always been. But what? He couldn't tell just yet.

After a pause, Junior continued,

—So where are you from, Ndiya?

—Oh, same old boring story. Chatham girl. Whitney Young. My father was a bus driver. I went to college near Boston. Jumped between jobs, nothing serious. Then I came back to town late last spring. How about you?

Junior waved off the question and leaned forward across the table:

–Don't sound boring to *me*. How does it feel to be back?

–I'd been gone a while, many years. The city has changed a lot. At times I have to check to see if this is really Chicago. What about you?

–Me? I haven't noticed much change. Until lately. Have you all?

Valerie and P. W. knew better than to answer. Their silence bluntly nudged Ndiya in the ribs; she wondered if it was a signal to her. Still, this wasn't the usual script. P. W. and Valerie were shocked at Junior's interest in this woman's life. He *never* asked people about themselves. They knew he couldn't be interested in anything she said. They knew if he really wanted to know something about someone, he'd say nothing. He'd watch and listen while they talked to someone else, or he'd watch what they did with their hands, or eyes, while no one was talking. They were shocked at each of Junior's questions and by his steady focus on what she *said*. Something was up. Meanwhile, he ignored everything else. They knew Junior: "*Puh-leeze*, fuck what niggas say, man, I *eat* what niggas say. Now, what? I got to *hear* it too?" At each of Junior's questions, they stole glances at each other. Junior saw this too. He was proud of them for noticing.

While Junior's question twisted in the air above the table like a perfectly balanced mobile high in a museum foyer, Shame wheeled the stool from the piano up to the end of the table near Ndiya. He stood behind her with his hands on her shoulders. Shame noticed a pause in the conversation, a shift in the weather over the table. He decided to ignore it, everything.

–Evening, people. Val. P. W. What's going on, Junior?

–Man, you know what. You what's going on, right?

–Please? This? Has anyone checked the snow outside?

–Naw, we've been in *here*. I've been checking out all the snow that blew up *in-side*.

–What about you, P. W.?

–"Mystery."

–No doubt.

P. W. nodded knowingly. Junior caught his reference. Ndiya looked at Shame who was watching a slice of Junior's reflection in the side of her glass. Breaking the silence, Shame observed,

–Well, word gets around, I guess.

And Shame saw six slices of Junior's face turn toward Valerie. His profile refracted like successive phases of the moon.

–Around? Oh. So *that*'s where word's been getting itself to.

Junior looked back to face Ndiya. In a fake down-home accent, smiling:

–I've been plum a-wondering where word done got itself off to.

And Shame:

–Word ain't going nowhere.

–I don't know, cousin, I wouldn't—

And Kima arrived carrying a chair from the back room over his head through the crowd. He placed it down next to Shame's stool. Kima sat. Shame remained standing behind Ndiya.

–Everyone. This is Kima, sorry, Merlin Kimani. He

plays bass, as you know. Kima, meet Valerie, P. W., Junior, and Ndiya. Kima's from Kenya.

–Hello *everybode-ey*.

Shame began to sit down but stopped when Junior moved to stand. Junior rose up and took Kima's outstretched hand.

–Good to meet you, brah.

–Likewise, Junior. A pleasure, man.

In a voice like a wave coming ashore, Junior said to Shame,

–Word ain't the point. But some word done brought a whole *lot-ta* baby seals into the water. And you know what comes after the baby seals?

As Junior turned from the table, he caught a glimpse of Ndiya's face from above. She was looking down at her hands on the table. At first she looked too small, as if she was ten feet below him, as if he was looking down from a ladder, or from the top of a stairway. He wasn't. That effect focused his attention. In the dim red light, amid the blizzard blown into the room, Junior felt a sharp pulse of white light go through him like a heavy blade. He wasn't high up at all. The woman he was looking at wasn't a woman. She was a little girl, a twelve-year-old little girl—

If you've ever been hit in the face hard enough, you know you don't feel the blow in your face. You know you don't feel it at all. It takes you like a scythe at the knees. Junior's knees felt the blow of light but he made his turn and walked away confident, not a hitch. No one had noticed that he'd almost fallen to the floor. Junior could take a punch. He moved through the crowd toward the rest-room, thinking:

–Chatham. Whitney Young . . . and I'm Bozo-the-*fuck*-the-no-no in the Grand Prize Game.

Junior knew the rest but couldn't even say it to himself.

While Junior was absent, the conversation was inter-rupted by a commotion up near the front door. Someone tried to leave and couldn't get the door open. A nervous friction spilled back from the front of the room. Ndiya felt P. W.'s body fall loose sitting beside her like he'd been poured out of a pitcher. He leaned his right shoulder down like he'd dropped something on the floor. Cass told everyone to calm down, went out the back with his shovel, cleared the space. A minute later he opened the door.

–No need to fret. Everyone's free to go when they wish. Ain't like we got a big cook pot out back—

Junior came back and the conversation turned toward inevitable questions of geography, prompted by Kima's voice. The pressure had eased. Shame watched as if sitting in a thunderstorm while listening to the radio report a clear, sunny sky. After another round of ginger ale and Valerie's cocktail, the three were set to leave. P. W. and Valerie went to bring the car around. And Junior stayed behind. Leaning back, looking at the ceiling:

–To go back to your question, Ndiya, where I'm from is gone. They tore down the buildings and razed the houses surrounding them. I'm sure you heard about that. Anyway. Good thing, the houses weren't worth it, the old folks had mostly died. And those buildings . . . tall buildings, you know?

–Yes. I know.

–The place was shit. Those stairwells were deadly. And the elevators, well, they were *worse*. And there's a cube of space still floating out there a hundred feet up in the air, floating in *my* life, Ndiya, and couldn't nothing tear *that* down. You know why?

–No.

–Well, it can't come down because it's not really there, is it?

Junior could feel his pores open up, so he pulled himself back, turned his head up, and sat still. He was blank again. Ndiya had been looking directly at him while he spoke. He smiled brightly, still staring at the ceiling. Then, with his smile broke and slammed shut, he looked down and their eyes met directly. She saw the cold light in the tunnels behind Junior's eyes collapse into one flame. In the back of her mind, she heard the song again, *Together we're one not two, shine like diamond ice*, and she felt sweat on her face. Then Junior's look broadened, as he sat there for a moment, his face changed like a flipped coin, and he smiled a smile that made him look like a perfectly preserved body in a buried ruin, a boy emperor. After a second, Junior stood up to walk to the door.

–You all have yourselves a good night.

In a glance toward Ndiya:

–Good luck with the word, Shame.

And with a glance tossed across the room and back to Ndiya:

–And with the snow. Because, baby, do it drift.

They pulled up to the back of Junior's building. Standing at the window, Alexis watched the car below. She could see the amber flare from a lighter through the tint in the sunroof. She saw Valerie get out of the seat behind P. W., hike up her coat, and tiptoe through the deepening snow around the car to the back door. Now she heard her stomping up the steps. Alexis twisted the blinds shut and sat down in a chair at the table. She looked at the computer. 2:05 a.m.

Junior smoked his cigarette with the window cracked. He didn't need to exhale. Suction created by the heat inside and the swirling winds in the alley removed the cloud from his mouth in thin tornadoes. He asked,

–What time you got?

–"Sweet Love."

–That time already?

–Yep. Do you feel that?

–Nope.

–Me either. None of it.

Silence. Junior nodded in response, touched his gloved fist gently to P. W.'s big hand on the gear shift and exited the vehicle, which disappeared down the alley before he could trace Valerie's steps all the way to the door. To his right, he wasn't sure if he heard what remained of the opening drums and cymbals. P. W. had turned up the volume. In the chaos of snow and wind, he saw the red

glow from the taillights gather at the corner and slip off
to the left like a long neon tail following a cat caught in
the night vision of another cat. Junior's body was tired
and tense. His arms and legs hummed with needles. He
felt like he was floating above himself, like he was staring
at all this from high above the alley. He opened the back
door and headed up the stairs humming *Hear me calling
out your name. . . .*

■

After the shock of recognition, Junior felt almost impossibly high. He hovered above himself, as if trapped in an
invisible elevator. His note to the Erotic Neighbors had
touched a nerve; when he checked on his phone between
Shame's sets, or whatever they're called, there were 620
responses. He didn't read them, but he could see that most
of the comments were shouting down Strictly Soul. When
it came to his writing, Junior only cared about numbers.
He didn't read reviews. On Val's phone: 2:32 a.m.

He stood in his living room, two feet from the window, in full view of the black lake across the terrace and
the Drive. The blizzard flashed through the headlights and
streetlamps and hurled itself into the waves. Sixteen inches
and counting, reports were it could be thirty-six by sunrise.
The wind hit the glass in front of his face and the air in the
room fell down his legs and over his feet. The sill at his knee
and the heat vent he, nude, stood above created a squall
around his thighs and in the space between his thin legs.
He was high off the Erotic Neighbor numbers, the music

(or whatever it was called) that propelled his doubts about Shame and, above all, about the company he kept.

–Who is she?

Valerie asked, as if from ten miles away, behind him. Her hands on his shoulders, she knelt so her arms reached straight up. Her face fit the curve at the small of Junior's back. Valerie stood up and Junior reached back with his left hand. He felt the harness around her waist and her slippery fingers.

–Who is she, Junior?

Alexis's voice bent in his ear as she moved between Junior and the window. She faced out into the weather, both palms open. She felt the wind push against her hands on the glass. Junior was high, and, minute by minute, was losing track of exactly why. He added up and subtracted what to do from the storm of air underneath the tent of legs, the smell of himself and the women who surrounded him. Whatever happened would be decided here. Alexis's open hand left a print of steam on the window when she reached behind herself to collect him. The touch of ice, the crystals spidered in the hand-cloud left on the pane. Valerie's face reflected in front of him, Alexis reflected behind, Valerie behind him, Alexis in front of him. His back reflected back to him, his shadow's strobe in a landscape of shoulders. He watched their faces with his eyes closed, lost track of who was who and who was high and waited for such sounds as appeared to take the air in the room. Junior knew these things didn't happen one at a time. Nothing did. Whatever was most important had already happened, that couldn't unhappen. But an envelope had been slid under his door, a cause that was older than his only crime, a kind of molten wound that lived beneath the scars he'd molded his life into.

■

Things emptied themselves and other things entered the space they left open. Junior knew that. Knew the goal of the equation is zero. Behind his knees, which had almost failed him earlier, and up his legs, tiny follicles twitched alive on the back of his thighs. Everything happened instantly. And an instant was the time it took a bent mirror of the time it took to take it. Alexis sat on the windowsill and faced Junior's waist. She aimed her mouth, left him wet, and blew on the spot. Heat from the vent cast off the last mask from his face, an invisible silk face fell back into the air it was made from. Both Junior's hands covered the frozen, eel-skin prints Alexis left on the glass. He reached one hand down and everything froze. Alexis:

–Ah. Don't touch my hair.

–OK. OK.

Empty things resumed. Alive between breaths, Junior's body felt like it had been lowered into a clear, heavy solution from an airless chamber, a riddle of pride. The solution pressed his body from all sides as if it was the center of a gravity field, which it was. As if he bent time, which he did. He felt formal, controlled. He was an open instant in closed quotes, a silver thimble full of venom. He saw a spigot pour a twist of sunlight into spring water in a stone basin. It was a trick, a flick of a wrist at best. It was a strip with no tease, a discarding down to a disguise more real than his actual face. Junior knew his fate was vanity, and he wore his last disguise to cheat that fate, the mask left after the final mask fell as well. Junior knew that the last petal was loves-me-not. Desire and the illusion of precision, this was target practice. More than to cheat fate, the disguise was there to starve his fate of what it needed. All vanity required a series of disguises; he knew that too. Vanity required a crew to switch out sets behind the actors. Junior avoided all the stages. But damned if disguises didn't keep turning up in new ways, on new faces.

Valerie's left hand on the curve of his belly, he caught his breath when his knuckles accidentally grazed a sweep of Alexis's permanent hair. Valerie's right fingers spread wide, slowly'ing their slowness on the curve of his back. Junior arched back, opened back into her hips. Junior felt his skin beneath the tip of Alexis's upturned tongue. His mind unspooled. He thought, "This is how a snake climbs a tree." Thought if he'd ever recovered even an inch from the twin disasters that had become of his sisters, he'd never have stood even the fool's chance of a flame-swallowed moth. Junior felt beads of sweat on his wrists and ankles. He wondered if his hands had frozen to the window. Imagined pulling his hands back and the blizzard blowing bits of glass straight through him. Sparkles of snow and glass, diamond ice in Alexis's hair. Junior heard a hollow-tipped voice, a falsetto howl that could take his glass hands apart and be on its way.

He came down from his high the only way he knew how, immersed in one of people's deepest needs: the need to feel taken apart.

BOOK
FOUR:
ARCHIPELAGO

Swim me no ocean, long, deep, and wide.
—CHAKA KHAN

Each morning Shame awoke with no idea where he was. Each night he fell into sleep not exactly sure where he'd been. His life—if it could be called his—at this point confronted him with a very strange and very real fact: exile doesn't happen all at once. You don't just pick up and leave somebody. You can't pick up and leave a city like easy as *A*, *B*, *C*. Shame arrived where he'd gone before he left where he'd been; so here he was, in pieces. Whatever it meant to be here was something he'd have to find out in pieces, pieces of his past that had, in effect, vaulted into the future. So we'll encounter them there as he did. He landed in a next place and then, somehow, still needed to tear himself out of the former; we'll get to that. As he encountered it, exile didn't operate according to the mechanics of clocks and calendars. It broke clocks and burned darkness into daylight. Shame found that exile was a little like playing chess on a calendar. The present leapt over days, even weeks. Then time could draw back, veer diagonally, turn corners. Due to this fact of exile as he experienced it, we'll trace the rest of the story in the exact sequence of events as they happened to Shame Luther, an achronological chronology. What Shame's experience of exile proved can—in a way, must—be as challenging to us as it was to him: often enough, in order for events to take place in the present, things in their future must have already occurred.

Properly speaking, Shame thought he knew the distinction but found he couldn't figure the difference. But that was while he slept. He knew there were dreams caused by isolation, and he'd learned there were others caused by solitude. Awake, he found, again, that he knew the difference between these conditions, but he couldn't touch the distinction. Awakened each morning, Shame opened his eyes into a dim light that bore the texture of spiced, roasted meat. Each morning he woke with the impression he was in prison. The difference between being in prison, as he imagined it, and being where he was, as he found it, came into focus with the scent coming through the bars on his window. The distinction orbited him all day, refusing to come within reach.

Next door, or actually across the alleyway, lived another migrant, a Hausa from a village in northeastern Nigeria. Like many of the alleys in Lamu Town, this one was narrow enough that neighbors could almost touch fingers by leaning out their windows. Shame's neighbor began to prepare a signature barbeque before dawn. He called it *suya*. All the Hausa and almost everybody else in Nigeria knew *suya*. But according to him, here it was exotic, a valuable feather in his cap, the finger on his side of the scale in trade. His name, Shame found, was Muhammad, like about half the other men here. He cooked atop a tiny iron grill he had placed on a six-by-eight-foot piece of concrete, the roof outside his window. The roof was so close to Shame's window he could hear Muhammad's morning prayers beneath the amplified, guttural call of the muezzin on the other side of his building.

Muhammad sold *suya* and hot tea from a cart at the waterfront. The dry meat traveled well when wrapped in newspaper and was a favorite of the men who worked on the boats, as well as those who worked unloading them by hand. Muhammad kept a chart of the tides tacked to his wall as a guide. His schedule fluctuated during the months as it followed the moon around the clock. "My monthly cycle!" he'd announced to Shame, explaining it when they'd first talked between their windows. He also hired out to captains who took visitors and various cargoes between the islands to the north, sometimes as far north as Ras Kamboni. On the boats, and with the visitors, Muhammad used another name, Timex.

Shame had arrived three days ago to this town everyone had assured him was poised at the edge of the beyond. He'd spent most of his time feeling drugged and recalling splices of dreams. In his life, Shame rarely remembered dreams. Now he walked around summoned by dreams such as one related somehow to Ndiya's shyness about a tattoo: symmetrical tracts of text on both her breasts. The passages tapered off toward her shoulders like wings of words. She wouldn't admit it, but she was sorry she'd done it. Shame was too, and he wouldn't admit it either. The dream was a cloud of unadmitted regret. He didn't know what the texts stated, but he had a close-up flash of two or three of the gray-beige sentences that clashed with Ndiya's new-suede skin tone, making it look like they'd been written in dried mud. They read like the institutional prose of warning labels and machine-gun disclaimers that ride the tail end of late-night pharmaceutical commercials. In a kind of stupidity that took root in Shame's gorge, the sentences counseled against the wisdom of tattoos in general and their illegality for minors.

The dream was nonsense but its tone haunted Shame for days. There were no streets per se in this town. Out his east-facing window and across another alley was a midsized madrassa. Twenty paces from the door to his building, the neighborhood well was at the corner. He could watch from his third-floor window as small children played around its rim all day. The students at the madrassa were all young children—preschool to elementary age, Shame thought. During the day, the school was full. It hummed in the neighborhood like beehives embedded in the thick stone walls of the buildings. It was audible, or at least the rhythm of its sound was tangible, everywhere he went. At midday the children all prayed on woven mats on the flat, concrete roof of the school's large second floor.

As he watched the children out his window, the dread-sense of the tattoo dream felt like a carpet on which he lay. The mat wasn't as easy as regret. It wasn't a search for self; it wasn't remorse. The obvious connection didn't correspond to his sense of the dream at all. He stood watching the children touch their heads to the patches of fabric checkering the smooth, clean-swept surface of the madrassa's concrete roof. He focused upon the fabric mats themselves. Thousands of threads had accepted the dye that colored their strands, soaked into the texture of each fiber. Before his eyes appeared the physical logic of touching one's forehead to mats that bore witness to the intricate structure of the intimate. The singular nature of thirst, a thread's thirst for color, or was it the color's search for structure? He guessed both were necessary to the action of acceptance and the scene of the children across the alley spun into an emotional focus, a mirror.

In another dream he was eating a long meal with Muna and her man. There was a carefree feeling that hovered over a flame somewhere. It felt like a celebration. After the sensation of hours, Muna took her man's hand, and said,

–Well, that's the best we can do having lost our babies . . .

In the dream, Shame, lacerated by the news, came around the table and held onto them both and, in a blurry spasm, he'd wept stupidly. With his convulsions he felt sentimental. He felt he'd disgraced the physical tone of Muna and her man's grief, the way their restraint hadn't held them back, the way their control had allowed them to move through a depth in what they said while Shame flailed and splashed like a drowning man in the shallows of sadness, of self-indulgence.

In another dream, he'd kissed Ndiya goodbye after a playful and buoyant time together doing something he couldn't recall. The buoy sensation was all he could feel. In the dream he knew they'd be back together later that day. Ndiya smiled and walked away, the frayed tassels on a loose, blue cord she wore as a belt dangled at her knees and danced as she moved her legs. He watched her back, the slow roll of her wide hips. The edges of her orange, sleeveless top fit her shoulders like open parentheses or pieces of an hourglass. Shortly, in the dream, he was thirsty, so he took a seat at a café, outdoors, next to a man in a blue suit. The man's phone then rang. On the other end of the call, clearly audible to Shame, was the frantic and desperate voice of a woman describing her impossible love for a man named Tony something. She was inconsolable, screamed at the top of her lungs. This went on and on. Irritated and increasingly thirsty, Shame waited for his dream-drink to appear. Fighting the impulse to tell the man that the world wasn't a phone booth, Shame heard the man say,

–He'll come around, Ndiya, that's just how Tony is. You *knew* that when you got involved.

The man's voice was the sun rising in the west.

The man rudely dismissed the desperate woman, saying that she'd simply have to handle it. Immediately his phone rang again. Shame watched the man lift up the phone, switch off the ringer, and set it down on the table. Shame:

–Excuse me, was that Ndiya Grayson you were talking to?

–Yeah, crazy as she wanna be. Do you know her?

Carrying these dreams through the waking world left Shame's hands feeling as if he was holding onto an electrified fence.

■

The first step was simple enough. Shame's mind was the exact physical situation of his room, concurrent with chipped tile surfaces. "Here I am again," he thought. The single mattress was raised on a concrete platform in the corner under a high, paneless window. The mosquito net dropped from a ring strung to a bolt in the ceiling. A window across from the door faced the madrassa. To the left, another window faced the waterfront about half a kilometer's walk down through a labyrinth of alleys. There was a gas burner on a wooden shelf and a shower area in the corner with a drain in the floor and a shower-head in the ceiling. In the corner near the window facing Muhammad's rooftop was a small, round coffee table and a low-slung wooden lounge chair strung with twisted cords of fraying rope.

Shame stared at the shapes in the room, moved his vision between them. He closed down his focus and traced the shapes, their relationship to each other. Everything was surface. The light fell through the window onto the coffee table with no reflection at all. The mosquito net caught the tail of a breeze, turned slowly in the wind over the bed. If he struck a match to the gas burner at night, an instant became an outward gasp of yellow light. Then his mind became a cool ring of blue flame. Until he recovered the ability to take a deep breath without feeling washed away in a whitewater of chaos, until he could find a place to put his feet and his breath, the future of each wooden match in the box next to the burner and the moving net of a breeze over the bed would have to serve as enough of the invisible world to depend upon.

A flash caught Shame's eye in the rearview mirror of his truck. He was driving north on King Drive toward Washington Park. He was told the job was in a bottling plant out near Midway Airport. It turned out to be a run-down brick building without any external suggestion of work going on. Inside, McDonald's insignia lay everywhere. He was told the plant mixed the concentrate for McDonald's-brand orange drink. It closed down at night. It was a small repair job. A section of floor had buckled. The hours were eleven to seven, a week's worth of nights. There'd been a pause in winter, fifty degrees at 10:30 p.m. The streets steamed with melting snow. Pools of black water patterned the surface of the road. Potholes full of the dirty water reflected the streetlights and looked like wide-open mouths with gold teeth.

Another dim flash. Until he saw the second flash he'd forgotten the first, if he'd seen it at all. Then, at the red light, from the car on his bumper, the flash strobed again and again. Two black men in the front. Shame couldn't see the back seat. The flash kept on. It pulsed through the windshield of the car following him. When the light changed, he decided to go through the intersection and pull over. If anything happened and the driver stayed behind the wheel, he planned to take off.

The flash continued, the light turned green. Shame drove through the intersection and pulled over in front of a small crowd waiting for the bus. One eye in each mirror. The car behind him pulled over too. The two men bounced out of the car, left the doors open, and approached. Shame saw they wore baseball hats and jeans, which was all he had time to notice. He was partly amazed and partly in disbelief—pulled over with a flashlight? Robbed on the way to work? One man stopped at the back of the truck. The other paused just behind the driver's window and knocked on the glass with the flashlight.

—Get out of the truck.

—What? Who are you?

The man stepped in front of the window, reached down and pulled up his coat, revealing a gold badge fixed to his belt buckle.

—Five-O, motherfucker, get out of the truck!

For about five seconds, Shame very consciously didn't move his hands from their position on the top of the steering wheel. Slowly, he checked the rear to the left. The second man—were they really police?—had his weapon drawn. Shame opened the door, slowly, and began to step down. Midway to the ground, the man grabbed his coat behind his neck and led him to the front of the truck where he was cuffed and placed leaning over the hood with his legs spread. The left side of his face pressed into the hot metal. He faced north into the headlights of southbound traffic. The officer, if that's what he was, made sure to pop Shame's head when he let go, punching his mouth into the hood. This made Shame confident that they really were cops. He tasted a slow trickle of blood in his mouth. The inside of his lip was cut, or possibly he bit his tongue. Then he heard the first man's voice:

–If you raise your face up off of the hood, it will constitute an aggressive act by the criminal code. That means he will shoot you. Am I clear?

–Yes.

–What?

–Yes!

–OK, check the cab.

–Mind telling me what I did?

–Sport, we don't give a *fuck* what you did.

The left side of Shame's face burned, but the hood was cooling. He felt clicks from the engine block in his teeth. His head faced away from what was going on. He thought he was bleeding from at least one of his wrists. He couldn't tell which one. Warm liquid dripped off his fingers. "It might be sweat," he thought. The cuffs pinched his hands. Tingles feathered up his arms. His hands would soon be numb. He heard the truck door open. Someone at the bus stop behind him said,

–Is all that called for?

–What? Oh, you want some too? Someone, *please*, have some more shit to say.

Shame heard the contents of the cab being thrown on the ground. Something solid hit the curb—a boot? Something plastic broke and slid across the sidewalk. The searching officer:

–CDs, some tools, pants, boots, pair of drawers, a few books . . .

Most of these nouns matched the sound they made when thrown in the street. Shame heard an open book flip and flutter across the concrete. A few things listed hadn't made any noise. He figured they were stuck in the snow bank, or they were being stolen. The engine clicks in his teeth slowed down. His cheek measured the falling temperature of the hood while he waited to hear the name of the thing that *wasn't* his. The thing that wasn't in the cab of the truck would bring all this into focus. He thought about how strange this felt, how used to it he'd been years ago. It was as if someone he used to be had been pulled out of limbo and reattached to his body in the present. Still, something here felt different. Shame wondered if it was just time.

One of the police kicked his feet further apart and his face dragged back across the hood. He felt like he might fall backward. A hand pressed against his back kept him upright while another hand slid down his legs, around his waist, and up under each arm. His wallet flopped on the hood like a fallen bird. It lay unopened next to his face. The pat down paused at his crotch. A thigh pushed up between his legs from behind.

–Ever done time? You going to see your other woman or your boyfriend, champ?

–Going to work.

–Where?

–Bottling plant over near Midway.

–What's it called?

–Don't have a name. They do work for McDonald's but I'm told there's no sign or name on the place . . .

–Well, you better get going. You going to be *late*.

Shame thought, "I'm already late." But he said nothing. He didn't move. An open hand popped against the back of his head. His face hit the hood. He wondered again if his wrist was bleeding. His hands came free of the cuffs. He heard:

–Champ, you bleeding, baby. You should get that looked at. But don't move until we're gone.

Shame attended any and all available rhythms. A cross-rhythm of headlights came at him. He didn't move or speak. He knew most of this was an attempt to provoke him into doing something the police could respond to. He concentrated on the metal cooling against his face. He heard car doors close; tires spun. He thought, "A U-turn. They went back south." This kind of thing used to be so common it felt, just then, like it used to happen to someone else, a different life. He thought the timing was suspicious. He also knew that warnings came in threes, or twos, really, the third time not being a warning anymore. He wondered if *that* was true.

Less than forty-eight hours after Junior's sudden appearance at Inflation and his strange behavior, the timing was troubling. It was intentional trouble. Shame listened to the clicks of the cooling engine, the warmth of the hood almost totally gone. He let the streetlights pour themselves out onto his back. It felt like the light collected there, as if it would all roll off into the street if he stood up. There was no weight on his back, but he felt a pressure as if time had boiled down into a physical substance deposited by light. But what time? The short time he'd been facedown on the hood of his truck? Or the collapsed time since the last time this had happened to him? No, the pressure signaled another time. He could almost hear a stopwatch engage and begin to tick. He was aware of faint sweepings and swoopings, but he didn't listen to that. He didn't know how long he'd been there—five minutes? Two days? He stood up, his back stiff under the pressure. Two young men appeared to his side. They each carried one of his duffel bags.

–Here's your stuff. They didn't take nothing.

–Don't stress it, brah. They just doing what they do.

Shame nodded in thanks. Then he was driving to work. Late. Lip swollen. A clotted cut on his wrist. One side of his face felt creased like the metal of the hood, the other side felt scraped by the streetlights as he drove. He knew where he was headed. But that didn't feel at all like where he was going. It felt like a swift tide going out. It felt like if a body was immersed in cold water and the blood left the limbs; the blood called in to keep the body warm, to keep the core alive.

Maybe it was loneliness, that old friend, or solitude, that rather recent acquaintance. Shame watched the alleys of Lamu Town, this medieval trading port just off the northern coast of Kenya, the place Kima told him to go when he'd said he needed to leave. Kima described Lamu as a town poised at the threshold between the beyond and what lay beyond the beyond.

Shame wandered, thoroughly lost, in the narrow alleys of the town, which led up and across the hill from the water. As the breezy morning warmth condensed up into a thick blanket of equatorial heat, he'd situate Ndiya, Junior, Muna, Cass, Colleen, and them in his vision. He wondered: Who was doing what? And then he'd turned each vision on himself. Finally, he imagined how the people he knew looked at each other. He kept coming back to Ndiya and Junior, the night at Inflation. Something at that table had been as thick and hot as this dry-season coastal weather; Shame felt it hover above him now in this unthinkably heavy sky.

Shame had never "traveled." He'd gone from job to job, town to town, for ten years; there was always a focus for him, a sun for his life to orbit no matter where he'd gone. It didn't really matter where he'd gone as long as there was a job to sell his body to for eight or ten hours. He'd lived in workingmen's motels, paid the weekly rent with the meager expense checks the company dispensed.

That covered his body during the hours it was on loan back to him. Here he was, thirty-six years old and, for the first time, in a totally foreign place: foreign mostly meant that he was without a buyer for his time. No job owned his body. For the first time that he could remember, he walked through a place without a reason to be there that he could consider real.

So he had no idea where he *actually* was. He felt as though he'd lost his sense of his body's extent. Everything felt inexact. Maybe his arm was too short to scratch his knee; maybe he could reach down the street and around the corner? All the stone alleys looked mostly the same to him. There were no cars. None of the passageways were wide enough. In fact, there were no motorized vehicles on the island at all. Planes of bad plaster covered the walls. That pattern was broken, here and there, by a pristine, newly renovated building. The old walls bowed out and almost visibly swayed under the weight of the time—centuries, Shame imagined—gathered in structures. A shallow gutter for rain and wash-water cut down the middle of most alleys. Donkeys roamed free in the streets until indentured into work carrying supplies through town. Children were everywhere: boys in robes and em-broidered caps. He'd learn that the caps were called *bar-ghashia*. Girls, in gowns he'd learn to call *leso*, wore scarves. Most of the children ran barefoot. Older girls and women, covered in full *buibui*, with just their eyes visible, appeared across an uncanny impression of vast distance. Their eyes tracked him. He felt exposed and on display. He thought he'd been walking generally downhill for some time and, all at once, found himself on the main street that led along the water, one block in from the docks.

In a way that amplified his disorientation, Shame felt the whole scene was also very familiar. It was a street that didn't just let anyone pass through anonymously. After a few trips up and down a street like this, it knew your name. Familiar or not, he suspected he'd better be careful about the food. He walked down the street past barbers, tailors, food stalls, carpenters, jewelers in silver, a black-smith. He paused every fifty feet and pressed his back into a doorway to allow a caravan of donkeys to pass by. Donkeys trafficked the streets wearing two-sided baskets across their backs. They carried stone bricks, grain, bags of sand, doors, fruit, chickens, fish, a thick snake, anything that needed transport through town. All at once, Shame felt intensely hungry.

He passed a relatively upscale-looking African art gallery with two brilliantly dressed Swahili women sitting inside the door. Next to the gallery was a sign: Echoes Café. These two places stood out. The café advertised cap-puccinos and smoothies on a chalkboard that stood in the street. It was a good sign, he thought. He decided to go in and give it a try. A second caravan of donkeys passed, followed by a tiny barefoot boy wearing a hat and white robes. The boy cut the thick, smoky air of the street with a thin stick and prodded the last donkey forward. Every third slice of the air ended in a crisp snap, at the boy's eye-level, on the rear donkey's ass.

Upon entering Echoes Café Shame passed through a narrow room with tables to his right and a case full of pastries to his left. Behind the case was a small kitchen setup and a bright red espresso machine that looked like a vintage Ferrari double-parked on the counter. At the end of the room was a set of shelves packed haphazardly with books and magazines. Shame waved hello to the young man behind the counter, who wore thick glasses. He paused at the shelves and randomly picked up a small, gray paperback book. Continuing out the back door, he entered a courtyard with high walls at the back. There were several tables, all, it seemed, full of foreigners. "My people," Shame thought wryly. Large umbrellas and two palm trees did their best to make shade. In addition to the high coral stone walls at the far end, the courtyard bordered upon a set of French doors leading to the back of the art gallery he'd passed in the street.

Taking a seat, he encountered the changed reality of shade. He noticed that his body sought it, leaned into it. He also noticed that it didn't feel any cooler in the shade than it did in the sun. The sun created a lightness that made him conscious of breathing. That was different too. It wasn't hard to breath in the sun but it made the space around him feel weightless, like a vacuum. In the shade, there was a sense of being surrounded, almost suspended, much like being immersed in water. In the shade, he breathed without effort. That seemed the only difference. As he breathed deeply, he felt the pressure build. He sat there savoring effortless shades in the pressure of breath. It wasn't static pressure, this shade. It felt like being submerged in a turbulent complex of currents.

There he sat. He opened his eyes and turned the

pages of the book not reading as much as verifying that the script was in English. It was. He saw the name Marco Polo flip past. He remembered knowing that Polo, usually known as a Venetian, was actually born on Korcula, an island in the Southern Adriatic. This meant, he thought, that his name likely wasn't "Marco Polo."

That made him think about names and how they stuck to people, or didn't. How they were given, taken, hidden, and how, at times, they evaporated off a person. Three days earlier, when he met Muhammad on his rooftop, he said people called him Shame.

–Shaheem?

–No. Shame.

–As in ashamed Shame?

–Yeah, as in ashamed Shame.

Muhammad made a series of clicks somewhere in his throat and shook his head.

–Never tell people here to call you that.

–OK, Mr. Timex. What should I tell people to call me? Rolex?

–No. That's taken-o.

–I was joking.

–Tell that to Azir.

Shame didn't know what to say to that. He certainly didn't know Azir, so he asked again,

–Anyway, so what?

"You Americans," and when Muhammad said that it sounded like *Amay-dee-khans*. "Who taught you lot to assume you need only two or three names?" More clicks erupted from Muhammad's throat, this time with a slight melody that sounded to Shame like air in a radiator when a furnace starts up.

–Well, when I was younger, people called me AS.

–Oz? Like the Wizard?

–No, that's where the wizard lives. AS.

–Yeah, Oz, like the Wizard?

–AS. Spelled A-S.

–OK, right. Oz.

Shame shook his head and gave up. He ventured,

–Well, what do you think?

–Shame is *not* an option. Shaheem is a little too much. Maybe Shahid. Are you Muslim? Clearly not with people calling you Shame.

–Shahid.

–Yes. It's the name for a person who's "dying to live." I mean, what does it really matter, I'm not really much of a Muslim and my name's Muhammad!

Muhammad laughed and his eyes sparkled. Shame heard Muhammad say that Shahid means "a person dying to *leave*." He thought that was so close to perfectly backward it fit.

–That's close enough. But *you* can still just call me Shame, right?

–Of course. Oz you like, Mr. Wheeze-hahd.

Interrupting Shame's shade-dream about names, the young man from behind the counter appeared. He wore dark shades and handed Shame a menu. The man stood still and stared at Shame. He ordered scrambled eggs and sausages, coffee and a juice. Across the patio, the two women he'd seen in the gallery sat at a table. Their brilliantly colored scarves loose over their heads. The scarves were sheer, so thin they floated when even a slight breeze made its way through the courtyard. The women talked quietly. Their hands moved constantly, as if subliminally, to adjust the flow of shade and scarf around their heads in the breeze. Shame caught himself staring, which must have been obvious.

It didn't matter, because the women took utterly no notice. He felt as if he'd be hypnotized if he didn't look away from the calligraphy of shade, scarves, breeze, and hands. A sound like a jet taking off emerged from the interior room. He flipped a few more pages until the young man passed him carrying a tray with two clear glass flutes filled with an electrically bright yellow substance. He placed the flutes in front of the women. The yellow beamed. It seemed to displace the shade and cast a golden glow onto their faces. Then the man handed them two long-handled spoons. The women added the spoons to their choreography and, when the man passed by, Shame asked him what they were eating. Fresh mango sorbet, he was told. Shame filed that away for later. The young man left the courtyard.

An actual breeze scaled the walls and came through the pressure of the shade like an invisible wing. Anticipating the choreography of scarves and spoons to his left, but conscious not to stare, Shame forced himself to focus on the book in front of him. He let the breeze flip a few pages and placed down his thumb on a page titled "Cities & Desire 2." His eyes fell to the bottom of the page and he forced himself to begin reading wherever his focus came to rest:

Such is the power, sometimes called malignant, sometimes benign, that Anastasia, the treacherous city, possesses; if for eight hours a day you work as a cutter of agate, onyx, chrysoprase, your labor which gives form to desire takes from desire its form, and you believe you are enjoying Anastasia wholly when you are only its slave.

The passage carried an almost ceramic symmetry that reminded him of work, words arranged like a complex of brick cut precisely to fit around a drain. He looked back: "Your labor which gives form to desire takes from desire its form"—he read the strangely off-balanced fragment again and again. The image of work blurred into music. It reminded him of a phrase he might run back and forth on the piano. The playful passage of "form" to "from" and back to "form," the myth of return. The naïve trust, the faux balance, between "gives" and "takes." These were the conceits of the city. *Any* city. Shame could feel the lure search the stream of his eye, he could taste the steel hook hidden in its pretty feathers. He closed his eyes and repeated the phrase, "Labor that gives form to desire takes from desire its form." The twin appearance of the word "desire" stared back at him like a set of eyes in the line. He thought about aces up sleeves, about Leonardo da Vinci winning drinks from barkeeps by drawing flawless circles in one freehand sweep of soft lead on the bar.

Then he went back and read the whole passage over and over, then the whole page for the first time and again. It was a mirror of where he'd been. A canal connecting work, music, and theft. He turned the book over and looked at the cover for the first time. It was black. The pastel-textured letters of the title formed the shape of a skyline at the bottom: *Invisible Cities*. High in the slate sky, over the city, rode what Shame took to be the author's name: Vintage Calvino.

The food arrived on three plates: eggs, sausages, fruit. The juice and coffee followed immediately. Shame ate his first heavy meal since he'd been away. The eggs in a light oil were the color of fresh orange juice. The juice was the color of an autumn sunset. Placed in the pressure of shade and surrounded by a riot of sunshine, the meal looked permanent, a still life. An old blonde woman in a huge, floppy black hat and thick eyeliner exited the gallery, greeted the women warmly and walked toward his table. When she reached his side she paused. She looked at the book, and then looked at Shame.

–Are you a writer?

–No, I'm a . . . well, a traveler.

–Ah. Passing through?

–Well, I thought I'd stay for at least a while.

–At least a while, hmm. I know *that* calendar, the one where the reasons you're here haven't happened yet, the one according to which things keep happening to you in places you've already left.

Shame didn't know what to say to this. He stared at the woman whose eyes searched to meet his gaze. She looked around the courtyard and turned back to Shame.

–"At least for a while," that's the phrase I had in my bags when I arrived here. I came from Australia. I sat down not far from where you're sitting now, if that's where you are? That was forty-two years ago. I'm Kate.

She raised the brim of her hat with one hand and with the other gestured at the café and the three-story building of windows that rose above the ground floor.

–This is my place.

–It's great.

Kate smiled, again, in tolerance for things people say that they know nothing about. Then she looked back at the book and smiled a totally different smile.

–You know, most people think of Calvino as an Italian, which I suppose he was, of course. But I think about his being born in Cuba, about all the things that happened to him there *after* he'd moved away. I mostly think of him as a genius. That's enough for me. Genius. It's certainly no one's nationality, is it? And it's its own kind of island, I suppose.

Shame nodded and looked down at his hands.

–Sure. I picked this off the shelf inside. I hope that's OK? It's great you have books in here.

–Yes, well. Possibly one of these days we could have a proper chat?

–I'd like that.

–Very well then. *Until* then . . . I didn't get your name.

–People call me Sh—they call me Shahid.

–Ah, I see. What a shame. OK. Until then, Shahid.

Shame felt a little dizzy. Kate squinted her eyes and then they widened just past open. She walked off. Shame turned to look at the first pages of the book. Vintage was the name of the publisher's series. Vintage Classics. Italo Calvino was the name of the author. Indeed, Shame found, born in Cuba, 1923. Died in 1985. Shame thought about 1985. He wondered what he'd been doing then. He wondered what right he'd had to be anywhere, doing anything, while a genius was busy dying.

Shame leaned back in his chair to let the slight breeze blow down his shirt. Vines bloomed and grew out of pauses in the red stone of the walls at the back of the courtyard. His eyes crawled the porous surfaces, looking for places to hold on to. Concrete had been applied at the top of the rear wall of the courtyard. Before it dried, clear splices of broken glass had been fixed in the cement. He caught himself looking very carefully at the jagged ridge atop the wall. His eyes moved slowly as if he could slip in his looking and slice his vision. Above the rock edge of the wall, the sky shot off between the lazy dry-season clouds like a huge blue rocket. He shut his eyes and felt as if he could almost ride along as the sky blasted, peacefully, universally, into that distance that was its vastness, that rimless vastness that was itself. He thought, again, abstractly, how "sky" was that element whose center existed only in the periphery of itself; it was invisible in itself, blue only in its being. And that, being itself, was always far from itself. He imagined a solid core made of endless opening. This was in the word itself, appearance in vanishing. He looked up toward the sun and spelled it out against the flamethrower splashes he watched with his eyes closed:

SKY

The oil and salt, the sweet juice cut by the coffee roiled

in his mouth. He cast a thought back to Chicago but he couldn't get it free of the taste in his mouth and the seductive sphinx of Calvino's passage in his eyes. Then another phrase occurred to him. He wondered if it was in the book:

— . . . of sky, we'd now consider the relative velocity of stillness.

And Shame's vision flipped like a coin. To think about it, he noticed, felt like rubbing his finger on the soft, serrated edge of a thin silver dime. He turned back to the page.

> Your labor which gives form to desire takes from desire its form, and you believe you are enjoying Anastasia wholly when you are only its slave.

He felt a shadow pass across him but he knew he was already in the shade. Kate's phrase appeared again: "Where you're sitting, now, if that's where you are." No, it wasn't that phrase, it was the way her eyes went squint and just slightly past open and made him feel that her walking away was her way of sitting down at his table. The way "at least a little while" became forty-two years; the way her "until then" felt like this, felt like right now.

SKY

Four days after the incident with the police and the flashlight on King Drive, Shame and Ndiya met Colleen at the gallery to discuss what she'd found out about the painting. As she'd suspected, the piece was authentic, one of Bedia's earliest privately owned pieces, an early instance of his interest in the African dimensions of Cuban/Caribbean consciousness. Oyá, Colleen explained, was a feminine spirit of linear force in the belief of Yorùbá people in West Africa, Nigeria, Togo, and Benin, as well as in places like Haiti, Brazil, Cuba, Panama, and elsewhere. In Africa, this spirit was represented by the surging waters of the river Niger. In the West, believers found her in the winds of hurricanes and thunderstorms. The Yorùbá god Shàngó, basically the Zeus figure in that cosmos, was found in thunder itself. Oyá was Shàngó's wife, or one of them. This explained the violent weather depicted in the painting, as well as the vectors or arrows in the head of the looming godlike figure.

And, also as she suspected, the painting was valuable. If he was interested, the gallery could offer him thirty thousand dollars for the piece and a contract for 50 percent of its value above thirty thousand dollars if and when the gallery might decide to auction it. The auction would likely take place through an affiliated gallery in New York City or, possibly, Miami. The thought of the piece as it had been, pinned to a wall in an unlocked building on Rhodes Avenue, made Ndiya shake her head. She said,

–Well, I won't suggest what I think you should do, baby. But I will say that I don't think it's a good idea to bring the piece back home. Oyá or no Oyá.

Shame had been increasingly irritated by the blank spot left on the wall in the absence of the painting which, when it had hung there, he hadn't ever looked at. For years, he'd carried it around behind the seat of a company truck in the tube they'd given him when he won it. Strangely, he thought now, upon returning to Chicago he'd put it up immediately, even before he'd wheeled the piano in from the hallway. He hadn't opened a box. In his mind, the painting was part of the wall, a mural, a window.

Something was turning over in Shame's belly. He felt obscurely surrounded. Ndiya and Colleen asked if he was hungry. He said he didn't feel hungry. They decided to get something to eat after this business at the gallery. Maybe one of the Greek places just to the south down Halsted Street? Maybe the Ohrida Lake? Maybe. But Shame knew the stirring wasn't hunger. It had begun after the flashlight night with the police, and he'd been on a steady diet of Tums ever since. He felt sick, as if it was always early in the morning before work when he had to force himself to eat.

He hadn't said anything about it to Ndiya, not wanting to lend it more reality than it deserved. Or so he'd hoped and his doubts were now snowballing. Sooner or later—he guessed sooner—some invisible thread was going to snap and things would go from zero to impossible before he sensed any motion at all. That's how it worked; he knew that. Any reactions that mattered had already happened, they'd play out in the future almost without him. It wasn't just the flashlights and the abuse by police. That'd been there like rain, or like constant minor tremors, as long as he could remember. The strange part had been the almost two-year calm since he'd been back. Why? He'd grown up? I was dead? Junior really had the kind of pull he acted like he had? Like juggling oranges, he'd tossed these ideas around in various combinations. Until the flashlight thing, he hadn't really cared. He'd had a deep hole to dig his personality up out of. Dying to live: Shame. Grief and despair, all of that. And he had the kids, the place, the jobs, and the piano. Then he looked at Ndiya's profile as she chatted with Colleen.

There was this unexpected person who appeared a few times like a moth and then walked through his door soaking wet and never left. Sooner or later, he thought. His belly churned. And he thought about an invisible strand in a web he'd sensed between Ndiya and Junior. The web had no name. He knew that for certain. No question about it, it would be sooner or *never*. Either that or he was getting paranoid. And before that he'd have to talk to this unexpected person. He had his doubts.

Shame also sensed what he had to say would lead quickly to things he had to ask. Junior didn't show his cards willingly, or knowingly. And Junior had been calmly irate about the publicity at Inflation, about the *blizzard* during the blizzard. The weather that night, Shame thought, had been a sick joke. Junior thought he could control the alley cats he had. But those others out there all with eyes and ears and—who knows?—habits of their own? It was too much. And the press? It did seem paranoid. Maybe it was? Shame really didn't want to know.

But Junior's tone had been about more than *that* crowd. That was also clear. And it had something to do with Ndiya Grayson. Or maybe not her. But it had to do with something Junior had seized upon in her image, in her place in the room, across from him at that table.

The live wire, Shame sensed, however, in all of this, didn't really have to do with just Junior, either. The shock in the wire was that, when Junior pivoted around and left the table, Ndiya Grayson all but audibly sizzled. Shame felt the hairs on *his* arms stand up. He put his hand on her back and he felt her sweat through her blouse. He trusted *her*. But as he sensed often enough with Ndiya Grayson, he felt this was beyond her. And the prospect of a conversation about something he felt but couldn't think or talk about scared him. He could feel that too. Whatever was going on with those police flashlights—if they were police—had to do with her in some kind of way that left *her* out of it. How? He had no idea.

Ndiya and Colleen discussed the dinner possibilities. At once, all of this poured out of his mouth like a drink knocked across the table:

–I think we should sell the piece. I'll take the $30K. And we can see what the gallery does when the auction or whatever comes around. I'm not worried about that. I imagine the money can stay here? In a gallery account of some sort?

Colleen nodded and tilted her head as a cloud of concern built behind her eyes. Seated beside her, Shame looked again at Ndiya's profile. He remembered that she called what she did with her eyelids "pain beach." She'd told him that. She'd been embarrassed. He'd been surprised by his impression that that was really all *she* knew about it. He hadn't asked: Why the beach? What's offshore? Now, for an instant, when she curled up her lips, one at a time, and scraped them with her teeth, he thought he glimpsed a flash of the "beyond-her" that had Oyá or whatever it was blowing on this house of cards. In an instant he felt the impulse to pull back from her and whatever *all* was offshore beyond her and, in that instant, he knew that pulling back *was* the trap. So he plunged in, instead, in the only way he had at hand:

–And I want the account and the money in her name.

Ndiya stared at Colleen. Colleen stared at Shame. Shame's eyes moved back and forth between them.

–I don't know. That painting is yours. You've had it for years.

–I know. But that's the deal. If you don't want the money, and something happens so we can't share it like we're doing anyway—

–Like what "if something happens"?

–It doesn't matter what—if something, anything— well, you just give it back to me then, if you want.

–I still don't know.

–Well, you don't know till you know. *I* know. That's the deal—

He could feel a calm pressure behind his face. His words felt full. They pulsed like veins in your hand if you hold your wrist tight for a minute. Shame shook his head faintly and shrugged. It looked to Colleen like a gesture of certainty. It was. He was absolutely certain that he was forcing himself on Ndiya, that he was thereby, somehow, forcing her into whatever was there beyond her. And he was forcing his trust for her, and his doubt, on himself in a way that would, likely sooner than later, press this tangled situation beyond them both and into view. Once they could see it, he thought, they could deal with it.

It wasn't the money. But money had a magnetic kind of force that acted on all kinds of invisible things. As soon as he'd said what he'd said, he knew he didn't care about the painting, or anything else in that apartment. The money was money. Lost in grief, on the road for a decade, trying blindly to dodge despair, he'd unknowingly ordered his life so that he had enough money and almost nothing else. Then he'd forgotten the money, because "nothing" had been his goal—

The electrical network that had begun to reveal itself, the circuit wired invisibly between pieces of his world, he feared, was life and death. But out of this sense, he knew one thing: the death part was behind him. There was no going back to "dying to live."

Shame kept it together and they agreed to leave it at that. The two women seemed alert, concerned but not alarmed. Colleen would have the official papers for Ndiya to sign in the morning. They decided to forgo Ohrida Lake and go up to Earlie's. Shame hadn't been there in months. It wasn't far from Colleen's place off Fullerton. The dinner was good. It felt good to be in there again. Most of all, it felt good to sit silently while Colleen and Ndiya talked. He knew they'd been talking, had met up a few times. He hadn't known they'd become real friends. He knew now. In ways he couldn't account for, this made him feel good, almost safe, which was insane, he knew, but there it was. Being near their conversation, it felt like being on a beach, near a coolness he didn't need to enter. Maybe these two were *his* pain beach, he thought. The breeze was enough. The pleasure of the sun reflected off the sand. He ordered three Black Labels and a glass of ice. When the drinks arrived, he proposed a toast: "To Bedia, to Oyá, and"—looking back and forth between the women, and then dropping his eyes to look at the table—"to friends."

■

–Who's the blonde?

These were the first words the police said when he reached Shame's window. Here they were, having dropped Colleen off on their way back home after dinner at Earlie's. Shame felt like the truck was floating away, like he could watch it all happen from above. About a mile from Colleen's, back on Halsted headed south, police lights appeared and a voice in a speaker told them to pull over. The officer's first words to Shame announced a change.

There are times when a city moves, time becomes a rhythm you catch on to, and you move along with it. There are other times when you seem to move independent of each other. A city goes its way, you go yours. And then there are those times, moments really, or lifetimes, when it seems like no time exists. The urban polyrhythm: a pin bent over a flame until it snaps, gears break each other's teeth, the spring wheel sprung loose from its axle hovers, mad, whirring at eye-level. A squall line between these time zones, or pressure systems, severs the living air from a sky that's dead.

This was one of those moments. It had actually been a series of them. Shame felt nailed to a board. Meanwhile, some part of him floated away. The city jeered and danced its dance of indifference. Traffic of faces turned toward or away, the way, in traffic, it doesn't matter which way is which. The no-time kind of time when all arrivals are made of departures. And the you you knew a minute ago? Turns out, it never existed. A city is real; you're not. And power appears as if out of nowhere—though it's been there all along—to check IDs at the crossing between who exists and who doesn't.

It isn't like the movies. That severing of living from dying, the separating who exists from who doesn't, mostly doesn't happen in precinct basements, under bridges, and aboard cavernous cargo ships along foggy, abandoned docks. It goes on every day, all day, in crowded streets with hundreds of witnesses who never see a thing. Of course, this is the whole point.

So, here they were aloft, nailed to the board. One police took his stand at Shame's window, the other sat still in the driver's seat of the unmarked squad car. Blue and red lights moved in the grill. Shame knew that the driver in the driver's seat was a very bad sign. Shame realized that he hadn't answered the question only when the police near his window repeated it.

–I said, "Who's the blonde?"

–Blonde? I don't know.

–Two blocks back. You stopped at the light, the blonde walked up, you rolled down your window. She leaned in, kissed you on your mouth, took something from her purse, and reached into the vehicle.

Of course, none of this had happened, which was also the whole point. Shame stared blankly, or tried to. But his stare wasn't blank. He was scared. He turned to Ndiya.

–Did you see any of that?

The police craned his neck to watch her answer. Ndiya shook her head. From her silence Shame immediately realized that asking her was a serious mistake. The very best she could do at this moment was to cease being there at all.

–No.

The officer's eyes drilled Shame's face. He asked for no ID. He took no further notice of Ndiya. That was a bad sign and also a very good sign. The sky closed its eyes. The night was an empty black room. Shame felt like a wooden match that had just been struck awake.

–OK, listen up. Do *not* drive away. Do nothing until you're told to do something, then do exactly what I tell you to do. I'm not giving instructions. I'm describing results. Clear?

Shame nodded.

–I'm going back to the car. Leave your window down. We'll tell you what to do. You do *exactly* what we say.

Shame stared straight ahead. Nodded again at the steering wheel.

–What's that?

Shame, in his best effort at neutrality, failed.

–Yes. Officer.

Ndiya could hear Shame's voice shake. When she was afraid, Ndiya got very calm, very impersonal.

–Just do what they say.

–OK.

–OK?

–OK. But you're not here.

–What's going on, Shame?

–I don't know. But you're not here. Understand?

–No—What's going on?

–I don't know. I love you.

–I lov—

–Listen to me. If—wherever they take us, when we stop. When they tell me to get out, you get out. Don't pause, don't look back, just get out and walk away, whichever direction is away, go that way. Then, when you're out of sight, go back to Colleen's. If it's too far, go to a business street and hail a cab. But go back to Colleen's.

–Shame, I'm not—

–Listen. Go there and wait. Sleep, whatever. But don't leave her place and don't call anyone. Don't say anything about this and make sure she doesn't call anyone about it, either. OK? And, listen, if you two are real friends, lie to her. Tell her anything you want, but do not tell her about this.

They stared at each other. Ndiya didn't move. She agreed with her eyes. The blue and red from behind them flashed into her hair. Shame stared forward with both hands on the wheel. She reached her arm toward him—

–Ah. You're not here. I love you. Don't do anything they can see. Don't give them any ideas. Just sit. Wait. When we stop, you *go*. I'll get in touch. I love you.

A voice from behind them:

–Drive.

Shame signaled left, pulled out into traffic. The squad car appeared behind him, the lights in the grill disappeared. He knew they were trying to make him panic so he'd do something overt. He suddenly realized that he had no idea what the speed limit actually was. It had never crossed his mind. He tried to relax and not think about driving, though he knew they weren't waiting for him to make some kind of traffic error. There were waiting for a big mistake. He was being dared to remember when he was alive. Under his breath, as if they could hear him talk, as if his words would make them notice her, he said,

–Try to pay attention to where we're going, so you'll know.

She didn't move. She didn't speak. For the next hour Shame drove, the police followed. Every so often, an instruction: turn right, pull over, drive, turn right, change lanes. Maybe they were going in circles, maybe not. He wasn't paying attention. He was following the car behind him. He was beginning to understand.

It was the "you-don't-exist" parade. It was a tour of the world, the familiar world, that familiar world *without* him in it. It was a tour of decisions he thought were his. Nothing he saw on the parade applied, or referred, to him. The message was: if he thought what he saw meant anything to him, he had been wrong. It was only traffic, the world could only watch or turn away. Nothing that looked at him could touch what it saw. People he knew, the person next to him, his brother, a wife, a mother; none of them have anything to do with him. They never did. That was the message of the parade.

Shame felt it working. Small waves of panic rippled in his fingers, up his arms. If it got worse, if he began to fear his fear, he might have lost control of the truck, or himself. He *might* have made a run for it no matter what he *meant* to do. Shame had heard of this happening. He'd heard it called suicide by police. He'd always doubted the term, but just then he felt its gears engage. He heard its mechanism as if it had been wound up and set on his shoulder. It bore many rhythms at once. Shame tasted danger. If the fear of fear took over he'd be liable to do anything. He thought of an article about suicide by police he'd read. The officer had said, "As soon as we arrived, I knew we were going to have to kill him." As if that time folded backward and became his past, or as if this time vaulted forward and became his future, he felt his arms begin to shake. Ndiya saw that too. She didn't move.

Shame remembered those first rooms on the road after I died, that technique. Ndiya rode along. Afraid to look at Shame, afraid the police would see her seeing what she saw, she kept track of where they were. She thought she could smell Shame sweat. She smelled distant smoke. Her brain whirled. She thought of her father, his distance, dead stars in his eyes. She remembered Shame's sunspot eyes. They seemed light-years away. She knew she had always been afraid to really look at her brothers' eyes. She stopped that train of thought and resumed keeping track of the route: turns, stops, starts. The police told Shame to turn right from the left lane, across traffic; they instructed him to drive through a red light.

The instructions to break traffic rules signaled the second part of the parade: the laws don't apply to the law. Shame understood this very clearly and he no longer gave a fuck. In his mind, Ndiya was already at Colleen's. In his mind, I was dead and he was in those first rooms on the road, alone, a kid, really, forcing himself to be identical with what was around him. So just then his mind was steering wheel, dash, turn indicator. The word was terminus, an end: a finite list of discrete objects at hand. The mind. Objects separated from him. Objects he identified himself to; objects he separated from each other. He'd known people who'd been on this parade and never came back. Many others who *had* come back and still never came back.

He knew, somewhere, his brain was at the movies. Films of encounters with police. Some he'd heard about, some witnessed, others in the first person. He refused to watch. He wouldn't even look. He knew that nothing he knew made any difference. The next instruction told him to turn right the wrong way down a one-way side street, both sides lined with parked cars. He drove down the center of the street. Up ahead to the right, the curb was open. He was told to pull over and park. He parked nose to nose with a black Nissan Altima that faced the right way up the street. Without looking, he said, "OK," to Ndiya. He heard her door open and she got out. He guessed she closed the door but he didn't hear anything. He guessed she walked away but he didn't see that either.

He sat there. He was told to turn off the vehicle and to leave the keys. He was told: "Leave. The. *Win-dow.* Down." Then a voice sounded from right behind his left ear:

–Get out.

Parade part three: meet the new "*not* you." He was cuffed. A hand gripped his left bicep and led him forward.

–Not bad. You lift?

–No, I work.

–Me too, motherfucker, me too.

They paused on the steps of the precinct. He was led through an open space, amid barbed and blurry voices. He saw no faces but knew there were faces. He was blind. Movies screened in his head and he wouldn't look. He was not booked. No prints. No photos. This was more bad news. They already had all that or had no use for any of it. He was not there. His sight came back when a police cuffed him to a metal chair in a yellow, paneled room and left him alone. Another police entered, removed Shame's wallet from his pocket and dropped it, unopened, on the table. He left. Shame was left alone again. He started to feel cold and felt himself shaking on the inside. The air was humid and warm on his skin. But he was freezing inside.

He knew the shaking was fear, the cold was panic. But he couldn't feel that. He felt his brain screen visions.

He didn't look but he knew someone in him watched. He began to fear the fear again and realized that his mind was still in the cab of the truck. He needed to be the room. He couldn't afford to let his eyes reel. The room: steel table, yellow air, chair, cuffs. The wound from King Drive opened again on his wrist. It was clockwork, punctuation. Drops of blood from his wrist. Maybe it was sweat? Now he couldn't remember which wrist was cut. A clock dropped through his body. That's all it was. It wasn't even time. He thought, "Let it fall like snow."

The door opened and two men entered. They removed guns from their holsters and put them on the table. That particular sound, dead metal, like when slow-crushed teeth finally gave. Something collapsed into an instant like powder poured into the mold of the moment. Man One sat down. Man Two stood. Shame felt like he was dangling from a balcony, in his mind. The movie screened far off in the distance. Man One said,

–Who's the blonde?

Man Two laughed at the back of the room.

–Oh shit, this?

–I don't know.

–She walked up. You rolled down the window. She leaned in, kissed you on the mouth, took something from her purse, and reached into the vehicle.

–Maybe she was helping him roll down the window?

It sounded as if Man One read from a script, but he held no paper.

–You didn't know her?

–No.

−Ah. So, you didn't know *her*.

−No. There was no one.

−You said you didn't know her.

−No. You said that. I said, "There was no one." What you describe, I didn't see any of that happen.

−What happened then? That you *did* see? Tell us.

−Nothing. I was driving, I was pulled over by police.

−When has *nothing* ever happened? You said *you* didn't know her. What if *we* know her?

That wasn't a question. It was a threat. So Shame didn't answer. They sat for a minute. That minute autopsied the sound in the room. Man One stood. Man Two picked up his gun and they left Man One's pistol on the table. The gun stared directly at Shame. The wound on his wrist had clotted again. The door opened and both men reentered. Maybe it wasn't the same men. Shame wasn't sure. He didn't care. He put his mind back in the truck: wheel, dash, shift.

One police sat down, he held a sheet of paper. It stole all the white from the light in the room. The air dimmed from dirty yellow to stained amber. The page glowed brighter. Man Two leaned against the wall, lighted a cigarette. Man One placed his hand on his gun and stared at Shame. Man One to Man Two:

−You can't smoke in here.

−Fuck you.

Neither man reacted to the other. Man One placed the sheet of paper on the table. This called Shame's mind back from the truck. The paper was either facedown, blank, or the intensity of its whiteness obscured the print. Blank or not, a piece of paper was yet another bad sign.

Lying flat on the table, it was the door to a storm cellar, a pressure chamber. Man One sat in front of him.

–Now, soliciting. That's probable cause.

–Nothing happened.

–Got any witnesses? We do, don't we?

–You want to bet we do?

Shame didn't move, he stared at the blaring whiteness of the page on the tabletop. Then Man One:

–What it's going to be, slick? A blank page or an open book? What did *we* find in the truck?

–I don't know. A bag. Work clothes. A few tools in a case . . .

–What else? Probable cause, my man. What did we *probably* find? Think about it.

–It's better if you tell us, believe me.

–Or maybe you want a lawyer?

Both men laughed at this.

Shame shook his head. Paranoid movies rose like floodwater behind his eyes. He refused to look. Someone else watched. Someone he hated, who hated him. The police knew all about this. They didn't hate the men they destroyed. By the time they were on this detail, it was mechanical. It was like "Wet mop in aisle three."

–We searched the truck. What did we find?

–I told you all I remember being in there. Tire jack . . . nothing.

–I'm almost through fucking around, you know? We *searched* the truck. Tell us what we found in the truck or you're going away for ten years. Do not make *me* tell *you* what we found in the truck. *You* tell *me* what we found.

Shame was afraid to close his eyes. He tried not to blink. He held his eyes open, tried to focus on something a hundred miles away. If he shut his eyes, even for an instant, vision screened the movie in his brain. He tried to see how close he could get to seeing nothing with his eyes open. The men left. Man One placed his gun back on the table. The gun didn't blink either. The white page glowed like an escape hatch. That was bait in the trap. Shame didn't look. The room dimmed. Maybe he fell asleep with his eyes open. The sheet on the table became the screen for the movie behind his eyes. His eyes reeled the table on which the screen shone. The two men came back in the room. Man One slapped a pen down diagonally across the sheet of paper, walked behind Shame, and uncuffed his right hand. Then he came around and punched Shame in the face. Shame thought the gun *had* blinked. Maybe he grabbed the gun and Man Two shot him? He couldn't breathe. Man One picked up the pen. He slashed a quick blue line near the bottom of the blank page.

—Sign on the line. Then, we'll type up what we found in the truck. The witness already signed one just like this one. Want to see it?

Man Two:

—So did the blonde.

—Sign. Then you can go. Otherwise, we're going to put you away.

Shame caught a breath and then had to force himself to swallow a laugh. That scared him fully awake because he knew the laugh was panic. He felt nothing. That was the point of parade part three: force all the people you're not into view. Evidence collects on what people aren't like the structure of rime, the undoing we come from, the power of the city, the movie reeling on the brain's screen, the power of a face down page, the unblinking Glock on the table. That page was *always* face down, and it was *never* blank. That was its power.

–I told you what was in the truck.

Man One snatched the sheet and sprang to his feet. The back of his knees kicked his chair violently across the room. The chair slid into the wall. Shame expected the room to go black. His eyes reeled nothing. Nothing happened.

–Man, fuck this sad-sack motherfucker. Let's go.

Shame's right arm was cuffed back to the chair. Both men left. They returned immediately, before the door could fully close. They stopped just inside the door. Man One:

–And what about your friend?

– . . .

–Friend, trick, whatever. What about her?

– . . .

–I thought so. Man, fuck him. Let's send his ass up.

Man One left. Man Two, on his way out, smiled. But his smile didn't smile. As if from somewhere very far away, the undoing that Man Two came from appeared in his smile. Then, in a whisper:

–Your elevator girl.

Shame had no idea what that comment was about but he felt exactly what it meant. It was a threat. It was meant to divide and, as far as the police could know, it would have to work. And Man Two closed the door. Shame felt a bead of sweat inch down the groove of his spine. A thread-thin path of pain unwound from his wrist up his arm. His mind split and followed the thread of pain and the bead of sweat; if they met, somewhere down below his shoulder blades, they'd produce some noxious reaction, a kind of gaseous acid. "The crosshairs body," Shame thought. This was the hateful thing that wasn't him, that watched him from a distance. This was the evidence, the undoing that hated him, and this was exactly how all that could become him. This was parade part three.

If you travel, you go nowhere until something won't work. Then something breaks and when you try to fix it, you move. When you travel, you meet no one till something gets lost. When you look to find it, you arrive. It doesn't matter if you ever find it; all arrivals are found while searching for something else, something lost. And people appear. People appear who could never have been searched for. If you arrive where you set out to go, you've traveled nowhere.

Kima, the magician, put Shame up his sleeve. On the plane, in that spaceless tube, all he could think was that Kima should work with Pearlie's twins. All beautician-magicians needed a bass player, everyone knew that. He certainly knew people went to beauticians when they really needed magicians. He thought Ahrrisse could have dealt with the smashed puzzle of his life; he knew, from watching that prodigy of reassembly, half the trick was not to look at the whole of any one piece; whole shapes were always illusions. Things were made, and moved, by aligning pieces of pieces: a corresponding edge, a shared blur of mixed color or quick texture across a border. Ahrrisse had taught him that. And Melvin.

Shame and Kima sat at a corner table in Earlie's. Kima texted his sister in Kenya who called him back—as Kima informed, "It's nearly free!"—He chatted brightly for a few minutes, then a scowling thirty-minute argument

ensued. Something about their mother and sister—Kima
punctuated his Kiswahili with English words, a thread
of crumbs Shame followed, a controversy about fees and
his nephew's placement in boarding school. Something-
something in Kiswahili and then, in English, "No one
gives a fuck about internet porn, he's fifteen! He's just
massively horny. It's not fatal." Kima made big, can-
you-believe-this eyes at Shame. This went on and on and
on. Then, at the end of the call, he set up Shame's transit
in less than a minute, kissed the phone, and hung up. Still
shaking his head and laughing about his nephew, Kima
jotted two phone numbers on a business card and handed
it to Shame.

—Your itinerary to the edge of beyond. You tell me
your flight. Francis, my sister's driver, will pick you at
NBO. That's the airport, Nairobi.

—OK.

—Sarah will be with him. She's been keen to meet
you, "the piano man." She sends love. They'll have a
phone for you. You pay them $150. The phone will be
charged with enough Ksh to call Jupiter. All set. They'll
take you to the train station. You could fly but two
flights is enough. The train to the coast is a colonial-
era relic. It'll be a proper adventure. You'll love it. You
can lie down, relax. First-class is cheap, a few thousand
bob. When you get off the train in Mombasa, ask for
directions to the Blue Room. Write that down on the
card. The Blue Room. Straight down Selassie from the
station to Turkana. Everyone knows it. You can ask.

Kima sipped his whiskey and pointed to the card.

–Call Su, that's her number, she'll pick you up. You can stay with Su in Nyali till you're unjetlagged, till you've made friends with the heat, then off to the edge of beyond. I say take a boat, or you can fly, the roads north of Malindi aren't a good idea for *mzungus*. Don't worry. It's set. You're good-good. The place will swallow you.

–Mzungu?

Kima looked at Shame and laughed. He put his left hand on Shame's shoulder and twirled his index finger in the air outside his right ear.

–That's you, my brother!

Detainment has its own grammar. In the precinct, Shame heard Man Two laugh outside the door. Then there was silence. He stared at his wallet on the table, untouched. Pieces of his life had come loose inside his body. A drop of sweat ran a wire of pain. A reaction had begun: the city gone centrifugal. Unlike the cinema in his brain blazing away in its shadows, this reaction was no movie. The cinema beckoned. Shame's brain commanded, "Watch me think about it." He refused. He trained his mind: table, chair, cuffs, scab. There was no time here; "when" meant "if." If meant something unwritten on a facedown page. So he sat. He pretended he wasn't spinning in the black sky of the yellow room.

It couldn't have been too long, though it might have been a week. Man Two entered the room by himself. It was the first time he'd come in without his partner. Shame guessed they were partners. He was wrong. Man Two carried a manila envelope. Shame remembered when he was little. He called them vanilla envelopes. He stopped remembering. His mouth felt like it was full of salt water, or sulfur, like swallowing would be fatal. The reaction had begun. Shame knew the rest would happen almost without him. He'd sit this out and watch the movie later.

Shame feared that he'd spit on the man if he leaned close enough. That the hate, dislodged, would act on its own. He'd seen that happen to people, he'd seen people happen to themselves, to each other. His pulse was either racing or his heart had left the building. He couldn't tell. The hate tasted like salt, an adrenaline shot in the heart, a brass hatpin through the tongue. Shame's mind told him that the folder was empty: "Man Two is full of shit. Fuck him."

When Man Two sat down he placed the folder to his far right. During the preceding episodes, he had stood at the back of the room and watched. Shame had thought Man Two was white, like his partner. A breeze blew past behind Shame's eyes, the memory of people saying that to him. Apologies, "Man, my bad, I thought you were *white*." The conversation he didn't need to hear when he got up and left a table: "Do you know, up till just now, I mean at first, I thought *he* was white?" Up close Shame saw that Man Two had eyes haunted by cats. He had sharp, spearmint eyes. His voice was low-pitched with a Southern song lost somewhere in it. He leaned forward on the table.

–I don't know who the fuck you are and I don't know who you're not. Tell you the truth I really don't want to know. But you *real* popular, my brother. The sergeant wants me to show you these . . . these *pho-tos*. They're not from this precinct so I don't know what the fuck they're doing here. And guess what, between us, I don't want to know that either. Same as you, a coincidence. You and me, we just *co-incidents*.

– . . .

–Now, don't talk. I mean don't say shit. Till I ask you something. That's the game. OK?

–OK.

–It's like blackjack. I deal. Do you play cards?

–No.

–Me neither, I hate cards.

Man Two slowly opened the folder with his left hand and slid the top photo onto the open flap. While sliding the photo over, he twisted his arm so his elbow and thumb pointed at Shame and he rotated the photo 180 degrees as he moved it into position. Man Two did this with a deliberate ceremony. The photo was now right-side up, facing Shame.

–One *Pren-tice* Wright. DOA. Now, Mr. Wright must either have been very stupid or real sleepy. Because, do you know, he leaned his head back against the headrest of his Range Rover—nice too, brown leather, Bose system, V-8—while someone had a gun against, you know, right here, against the base of his skull. Dig it.

Now, Man Two covers the first photo with one taken at profile.

–Point blank. One shot. Bullet went through the sun visor mirror and hasn't been recovered. We're guessing it's a special bullet, carbide tip. Forty-six shootings that we know of last weekend. Eight dead. Probably half of them between here and where this happened. And now here *you* are. And now the lieutenant insists I show you pictures of this? I'm going to guess that you're going to say you don't know nothing about all this, which is the fuck fine with me, my man, 'cause, like I said, I don't want to know either. Am I right? OK, that's a question.

Shame paused. He searched for the breath he needed to speak.

–Yes. I've seen him. Don't know him. Didn't know about the killing till now.

–Hey, I believe it! I'd show you the rest of these, but I think you get the point. Did I say his hat didn't even fall off his head? Nice too, brown suede. Driving cap. So, there, you know, like the kids say, "Everythang's Gucci."

Man Two left the room. He left Shame with a new movie to watch. He still refused to look at the screen of his brain. He has no idea how long he sat there refusing to let his eyes reel, mind averted from itself. Then Man One came back in the room and uncuffed Shame. One last dare: Man One strolled slowly the long way around the table leaving his gun within Shame's reach. Shame stared at the gun, he didn't move. Then Man One picked up the pistol and fit it into the Velcro holster under his arm. He took Shame's wallet and walked to the door. Then he turned and threw it at him. The wallet hit the center of Shame's chest and fell like a dead bird in his lap. Man One:

–Get the fuck out of here.

At Echoes in Lamu Town, Shame had told Kate he was a traveler, but he knew that wasn't really true. He'd been a worker and a kind of burrower. This was on his mind during the late afternoon as he walked the inland path over rock and sand, past clumps of trees that twisted their limbs together against the wind. They made near-visible moves, each one attempting to use the shade of the other. Time-lapse footage of such small groves, he imagined, would look like a judo tournament of fakes, blocks, and pivots. Here and there the groves had encased ruins of stone structures, which were held up as they were taken apart by vines and roots.

The immediate problem: What to do with the Danish puzzle box he was carrying in his backpack? The second—illegal—pack of hundreds he'd brought from Chicago. He took it on a hunch, or maybe just to give himself a distraction from the stark fact of his leaving. The second problem: What was he? What was he going to be during this indefinite period of limbo? He had no experience being in places for no reason. With these questions playing in his mind like the contest between trees in the groves for shade, he kept walking. He passed around the back of the Peponi Hotel, a boutique luxury hotel with a conspicuous dose of Italian futurism in its past. In its present, it was half-occupied even though dry season was peak tourist season. Somali militia had stormed the hotel one night the year before and kidnapped three French guests. Stormed? The security guards had been undisturbed, leading to a wave of suspicion and paranoia among the foreigners on the island.

According to Muhammad, word around the suya stand was that an undisclosed ransom of undisclosed origin had been paid via M-Pesa. CNN International had reported a daring, successful commando raid that had freed the hostages and resulted in the unavoidable deaths of the kidnappers. Word was, on a Friday night, a few of those slain Somalis and a few of the US and French security contractors could be found spending their respective loot of undisclosed origin at Bentley's, the only public bar in the all-Muslim town. Shame hadn't been there yet. But he could imagine the Somali "militia" men and their hulky, sun-reddened foes reclined in adjacent lounge areas taking in the night breeze through the open windows. The Americans smoking hookahs and drinking beers, the Somalis drinking juice and chewing khat with sticks of Juicy Fruit, both fencing with the rapaciously friendly female "students" on "vacation" with their short shorts and false eyelashes. The bartender was, as Shame understood it, part Kikuyu, an upcountry Kenyan. He was friendly and well-read, kept a stash of books behind the bar, mostly dog-eared, orange-covered copies from the Heinemann Series. Muhammad had introduced him to Shame at the dock one morning: "Shahid, the Wizard of Oz, meet Satan, the bartender at Bentley's." Shaking his hand, Shame thought,

–I can't call myself Shame but the only bartender in this town is named Satan?

Shame passed by Peponi and walked behind Shela, an upscale resort community populated, amid "rising concerns about security" in the region, mainly by local men paid to live in the mansions until their European owners were brave enough to return. After Shela, the path turned away from the dunes at the south end of the island and bent inland beyond the sea breeze and into the real heat. He walked along the narrowing path, through the thickening brush. Shade began to take on a copious texture of dim, nude flesh. The shadow of a tree could take him in its arms. Occasional stands of coconut palm, tamarind, or bamboo broke the thickening rhythm of brush and deepening heat. With the lowering sun, the flesh-limbs of their shade became longer liquid along the ground. The sand deepened too. There were fewer tracks. Most of them were from donkey caravans carrying water and rice to remote settlements in the island's interior.

After another mile, the path rose along a ridge high enough to afford a view to the east, across the channel to Manda Island and the open ocean beyond that. Shame sat down at the base of a large tree. As the sun set he saw a near-full moon rise to the northeast. He pulled a woven mat out of his pack and unrolled it, took out his water bottle and a trio of samosas wrapped in a napkin. The puzzle box sat, compact, at the bottom of the bag. He ate the samosas slowly, taking small bites. A sip of water diffused the oil and unlocked the residue of spices in his mouth. His tongue tingled over his teeth. There was a tangy flavor he couldn't place. Muhammad had told him that most island recipes included tamarind, which was good for digestion and also offered a mild protection from the evil eye. Shame laughed at the juxtaposition. Muhammad didn't. He'd added tamarind to the mix of peppers he pounded into the thin strips of meat before he grilled them into suya each morning after his dawn prayer. Fusion suya.

Maybe he wasn't fully in the correct time zone yet. Or possibly the hike in the deepening sand and blazing heat had exhausted him. After eating, Shame put his pack behind his head, he lay out on the mat and closed his eyes. Something touched his nose and he woke with a start. He didn't know how long he'd slept. The moon sparkled high in the night sky. The sky was all surface; a sheer cloth of white light had wiped it clean of its sable depth and the usual diamond-milk infinity of stars. Nothing appeared to have actually touched his nose. He sat up and looked around. He'd dreamed but didn't remember much. A little, dark Italian boy. Shame remembered him, and a few details followed. The boy sang. He asked Shame if he knew his sister. Shame said that he'd had a sister once but didn't anymore. The boy nodded like he knew that already. That was all. Shame decided not to look for a place to stash his brick of cash in the dark, even though the moon lighted everything with its bright boneglow.

He packed up his stuff and turned to go back down the hill toward Shela. He noticed an opening in the bush to his left, a path. By daylight that bush had been a solid wall. He'd stared at it blankly while eating his dinner, marveling at its tightly woven density. While he ate, even with his eyes purposefully blurred, there was barely an eye socket's worth of indentation in the wall of branches and leaves and thorns. Now, an opening slashed vertical and jagged, almost in the shape of a question mark. He tilted his head at the novelty that such an opening, in view as plain as day before his eyes now, could have been invisible before. He half smiled. "Plain as night," he thought to himself. He walked over to it and looked into the man-sized keyhole. A narrow path led his eyes ahead. He could only see a few yards because it curved to the right. He leaned into the space and the light changed. There didn't seem to be any light in the path. Things were nonetheless clearly visible, as if they bypassed his eyes and were visible directly to the brain. He took off the pack, a little afraid because he didn't feel afraid. He arched his back, turned sideways, and slipped through the opening. From there he reached back out and brought the pack through. He decided to go far enough to see what was around the bend.

He felt himself breathing on purpose. It felt to him that, if he didn't deliberately expand and contract his lungs, they wouldn't work on their own. The effort at compelling himself to breathe, he knew, meant he was scared. But he couldn't feel that. For a moment, he wondered if he'd been shot or stabbed in his sleep. Maybe there'd been something in his dream about hiding a gun? Was he in shock? Or dead? Thoughts, or just brief electrical pulses, arced his body like swallows and smoke through the dusk air over Lamu Town. He looked at the satin sheen of light on his legs. He wondered if it was still night or if it was now morning. Around the bend didn't happen. The path curved on. He walked wondering how much of what-sized circle he'd completed.

Within his reach coiled vines and entwined branches. The moonlight condensed on vines in the tangle overhead. As he walked, light followed along the vines above him like drops of dew, or like the eyes of paintings that tracked you through a room. The dead-stare kind of way a TV watched people in a room, even if it was turned off. Shame found himself waiting for the light to spring into action.

After fifty yards or so, the path widened and then disappeared into a delta of narrower paths that fanned out and dissolved the way forward. He stopped walking. When he stopped, an intricate system of light appeared. It looked as if he stood before a complexly fractured crystal. Or as if moonlight had frozen into frost designs on a window. He took a step forward and the geometry before him blinked away. He froze midstep and it reappeared. He tried it again and the blinking action repeated. The off-on action of the light echoed a game they'd played at night when he was a kid, Freeze. Then he remembered, in his dream, the little boy held a pin in his mouth like a toothpick. He asked Shame if he'd like to hear a song. Or had he asked the boy to sing a song? Then one asked the other if he knew where to hide a gun. There it was. So there *had* been a gun in the dream. Then the recollection vanished.

The broken crystal of dreamlight drew Shame ahead. He took one step at a time and focused on the first heavy threadbeam in the design that, after a few step-blinks, appeared to be within reach. He thought then of his first roommate in Chicago. His thigh itched under his shorts.

–Is that you?

He was smiling. Up close he saw that the design

was an elaborate cathedral of spider webs. It continued overhead as far up as the light traveled. It seemed strung between paths in the fan of the delta. Shame went further, the design dimming or disappearing altogether as he stepped, appearing when he paused to plot his next move. "The opposite of real life," he thought. "Plain as night," he repeated out loud. A great place to hide. He noticed there were holes honeycombing the ground. "Nests," he thought. "Maybe those had been in the dream too?"

Three strands of silken light glistened at his waist. He ducked under them and stopped. A thigh-thin palm tree appeared like a frozen dancer or an open parenthesis. He hadn't seen it. His nose almost touched it. He took half a step back and the tree disappeared. When he stopped there it was, glowing. He moved closer again and stopped, his breath against it. He leaned back to focus. The tree was wrapped in nearly invisible strands of silk. Almost invisible as well, a gauze of near-microscopic spiders moved between the strands. He backed up a step. The tree blinked away and then resumed its visible existence. From behind the palm tree a torrent of twisting branches funneled into the canopy. He crawled up under the overhang of the torrential bush, around the tusklike curve of the palm. There. In a kind of trance of certainty or dreamlike precision, he wrapped the puzzle box in a plastic shopping bag, rolled it in tape, and buried it in the sand under the bush. He counted thirty steps back out of the delta, along a path that diverged at two o'clock when the crystal appeared. Thirty steps at two o'clock at the mouth of the delta. "There," he said to himself aloud, thinking of Ndiya and Colleen back on that distant planet, "is where here is." He banished the thought.

At the keyhole to the path he paused and put the backpack out first. When he stood up, he paused again. The pack looked like it hadn't been touched, as if he'd left it there when he'd entered. Had he left it? *Had* he entered? He turned sideways, bent backward, and exited. He heard someone say,

–Parenthetical.

He turned but no one was there. The dark-light of the path laughed. Shame picked up the pack and began to walk downhill toward Shela on the main path that now felt to him like a wide avenue. *Wide as Victoria Lake*, he thought to himself, is *that* a crime? He turned around and marked the spot in his vision. Shame turned back and headed down, thinking, "If I'm not a traveler, then what? A spinner? A spider?"

As he approached Shela from behind, he stopped. The sky was black again, its surface had vanished. The moon was gone. In its place starlight fell from the sky like a translucent wing of dust onto the dunes that led down about two miles to the beach. In the distance, in a subtle ink of night, he saw a tiny cluster of stars, seven sisters, first to appear in the sky. The Pleiades. They were his witnesses to all that had been made plain as night. He felt something, maybe possibility, maybe love, move like a crime, like a new dimension of sight, like star-rise, inside his fingers. And, he wondered what—or, really, *if*—it was. He remembered the other planet where "when" meant "if;" now, he thought, here he was where "if" meant "what."

L uther B had left notes for Ndiya at Inflation. After a
week with no response, he traced his way up to Earlie's
and left a note for her there too. He said he wanted to talk
to her. Word traveled from Earlie's and, after delaying for
another week, she met up with him. She'd come to listen. For these weeks she'd stayed clear of 6329. She concentrated on the messages Shame wasn't sending. Shame
had sent no word. She knew he wouldn't. Colleen and a
few others asked if she'd heard from him. She told them
she hadn't, which, as far as they were concerned, was true
enough. She knew different, but there really wasn't anyone
to talk to about that. She knew she'd have to explain. She
knew explaining it to someone meant admitting it to herself. She couldn't do that yet.

Then, on a quiet Thursday evening, she found herself
listening to Luther B tell her things in order to say what
he very clearly wasn't going to say.

–Look, this life, if that's what it is, it's OK with me
just as it is. I'll take it. It's as much or more, or maybe it's
just longer, than anything I ever expected. If I'd known,
or dreamed, I'd be here this long—almost seventy?—I'd
have done a little more work to prepare.

–Prepare?

–For the way time lies down and rolls over on its back,
like a lazy redbone hound in the shade. And there you are
in a stillness, in the quiet, in a long-type, quiet stillness.

When Luther B pronounced that final phrase, he extended his long arms, the sleeves of his plaid flannel shirt neatly cuffed at his thin wrists. All the Southern tones in his voice bloomed open into a bouquet tinged with the Caribbean beneath the American South. Maybe, she thought, she also heard what was beyond the Caribbean and beneath all of it. Luther B looked back in Ndiya's direction, staring over her shoulder, and traced the arc of something, maybe a palm branch, she thought, with his eyes.

–Where'd you find this place? Scratch that. I mean, I know where, or who. Do you know where he is?

–I know where I can find out.

He stared beyond her into the room. She caught a shiver pass over his shoulders, or maybe it was a short run in the piano solo playing through Earlie's speakers. He looked up at her:

–Oh, you heard that too? Different, right? I listened to this song for decades, "Misterioso" from '57. Sonny Rollins on tenor. I listened for years. And right there, when that shiver crossed your shoulders, I used to think, "How did Monk call hisself turning, like on a well-worn dime, into Wynton Kelly?"

She opened her ears past his voice and focused on the sound of the air, its slips and dives. She felt like Luther B was toying with her but if that was it, something was wildly out of place. This conversation certainly wasn't what it said it was, but it still didn't feel like a game.

–You know what I mean? That's *Monk*? I mean he was funky, now, and could roll like he did on "Bags'

Groove," but mostly that was just because he was pissed at Miles and taking it out on the keys so he didn't ring the evil little nigga's neck like a frizzled, Carolina chicken. But even that's not *this*. Not hardly. Two things can be alike, maybe they even one thing, but they still different. You know?

Ndiya listened to him, but she was really hearing the air of the room and the fear, or something like it. Whatever this was about rode in Luther B's voice, in his eyes, behind the curtain of musicology. She listened to the bush he was beating around. He was inviting her to figure out why. Maybe it was a dare?

–Finally, come to find out, and it was Cass who told me when it was playing at his old place before he had Inflation. So we were talking about this and that and the third when *this* song came on. I let it go for a while then asked, "Cass, you ever wonder how Monk changes hats right here and turns into Wynton Kelly?" and I remember I stopped and had to say, "And this drink," I said, "it's got to be the worst tasting-est rum and Coke I ever had." And Cass said, "Well, one, that's because you switched glasses right around the bridge and were sipping out of my Scotch and ice. I was waiting to see how long it'd take your drunk ass to notice." Then, he continued, "And two, it's easy for Monk to 'turn into Wynton Kelly,' you see, when Horace Silver happened to be in the studio that night itching to take a chorus or two—"

Then he turned back to her and Ndiya switched back to the subject she thought they were supposed to be talking about.

–Have you seen any of the kids? Muna? Pearlie?

–Muna's sister brings them up. She stays in Muna's place now.

–And Muna?

–I've heard what they say about those who know— it's OK. Joine, that's Muna's sister, is solid. She's a nurse. A nurse with a habit, but still a nurse. Pearlie drops off the enchanted twins three times a week. Ghettos don't abide vacuums, not when they rent-free.

–OK. Drops them where?

–With me. What? What else I got to do?

–Besides golf?

They both laughed. Luther B's face lighted up like a kicked-open door in a dark hallway. Ndiya, testing:

–Should I come back? For a visit?

Luther stared at her, eyebrows up. He let out a single chuckle and then something in his face darted away. His face turned off for a minute. Door kicked shut, lights off. Luther sipped his drink and stretched. Ndiya asks,

–Are you OK?

–Me? Call it whatever you like—

–You know what I mean?

–Do you know what I did, I mean, before my present *car-rear*?

–You mean before the Tiger Woods routines?

–Shit. Tiger Woods. Forget that little freak . . . I ain't studying his narrow ass. Bet that on Sunday, little girl.

–Uh. Sorry.

Then Luther smiled wide.

–Calvin Peete, now. Now you're talking!

–What?

–I remember when he made it, and reporters had the nerve to asked him that noise about "tradition at the Masters." Do you know what he said?

–Um, no.

–He said, "You might as well ask me how I feel about slavery." Calvin Peete!

Luther shook his head and smiled at something far away.

–I worked in the police motor pool, detectives and vice. Thirty-five years. I never touched a squad car. For the last fifteen years, I only worked on special unit cars. Tactical units, they were called. These were teams with their own funding. Federal and "private." After a while, as far as I knew, they funded themselves. They damned sure funded *me*. Ancient history. I was the only black mechanic in the whole motor pool. And *I* got special units?

Luther sipped his drink again, and then turned his eyes to Ndiya's face. Their eyes met and she saw a glassy surface in his stare, thin red rivers stretched toward the elegant slope of his eyelids. From beneath the watery membrane of his eyes and from a distance, a flame of narrowing focus backlit his face. His stare did like when you focus sunlight in a magnifying glass. Ndiya thought she could feel a spot heat up on her cheek beneath her eye. She touched the spot with her finger in a reflex. Her brothers used to injure ants and moths and then burn them with a magnifying glass on the sidewalk. She remembered watching from above as the twitching insect's body lighted up bright, squirmed in place, until small threads of smoke twirled up and she turned away. Luther B broke the pause:

–You know? I, me, *I* got special units? How do you explain that? Never mind. I did it all. Retreads. Lined trunks. A unit signed out on Friday, come back in Monday with 2500 miles on it. I probably rolled back a million miles off those cars in all those years. I didn't think about it then, rode it out like time was a runaway stallion. Now, here it is, time, a lazy redbone hound. Little girl, there are very few things as beautiful as a redbone hound at sunset. Cass knows. His old place was a deep pool for special unit officers.

–Where was it?

–Just before the tracks on Fifty-Third Street. It's still there. Cass knows.

Luther B paused. He stared into the open space in his speech. Ndiya looked into the frame of his stare. After a few very particular instants, she said,

–I know, "What they say about those who know—"

–Yeah, well, most times—this *not* being one of those times—it's best not to let on you know. You know?

–Naw, I don't believe I do.

Ndiya blanked her eyes and shook her head. Luther smiled with half a chuckle in his throat at something over her shoulder. In that instant he looked twenty-five years younger. He leaned back again, one arm propped up on the chair next to him, the other holding his glass. He tilted his head back and looked up.

–*Love* these old tin ceilings. God damn. *This* song?

–I don't know it.

–Coltrane's "Slow Dance." No song is quite like it.

–I'm not sure I've ever heard it. It's . . . it's *nice*.

–I know the beautiful, crazy motherfucker—pardon my French—who wrote it. Used to be in Chicago. His woman was an actress, a dancer. He was friends with Oscar.

–Oscar?

–Oscar Brown Jr. So, no word from him, I mean, the other him?

–Not yet. I know he's OK. Somehow, I know it. If he wasn't, I'd have heard.

–Well, that's one way to listen. And you? Do you have a good place to stay?

Ndiya knew that question wasn't a question. It was a test.

–Luther, did you ever see a cat at night, and the light shines in its eyes and the eyes glow bright amber?

Luther B smiles, again, and looks back over her shoulder at whatever's back there.

–Do you know what makes that glow?

He shook his head. His smile widened. His face opened as if he was on stage, lighted by an intensifying spotlight. He turned his attention directly to her. Ndiya continued,

–The pupils open so wide that light goes in and bounces off the back of their eyes, the lenses, I think, and comes out the front straight back at you. The short, bright waves are trapped on the way in. Only the long, low waves make it back out. That's the amber glow.

Luther laughed deep and clapped twice before he

stretched his arms out to his sides. He moaned loud enough for half the room to hear. Ndiya felt the moan in her chest. He downed the rest of his drink and chewed the chips of ice in the back of his mouth.

–Ah. Mostly water. Good to see you, little girl. Very good to see *you*.

–It's good to see you too.

–I'm going to the john and I'm going to pay for these drinks on the way out.

He lifted Ndiya's right hand up off the table. He held it in both his hands. His hands were bone dry, smooth, and very warm.

–Be smart. So long.

Ndiya nodded blankly. A chord of fear smoldered somewhere near her like a long fuse. Luther was telling her something with or without saying it. At the same time, she realized that she couldn't trust him. Hell, he was damned near *telling* her that she couldn't trust him. Meanwhile, he was telling her something else by not going anywhere near what he was telling her. He was helping her confirm something that *she* wouldn't say. Her mind turned to Cass and she turned it away from Cass. Luther's railroad spike, "Be smart," while he tenderly held her hand twisted together with her memory of distant smoke and sweet wine on her daddy's breath.

"Fathers," she thought, and watched Luther B's length as he moved between tables, his cap rolled up under his arm, the worn perfection in the drape of flannel hitched up on his wallet. She wondered at the ridge she thought she could see at the center of his back just above his belt. Or was that a shadow? The wonder disappeared as Luther B swung his jacket on before she could decide if the shadow was under his shirt or creased in her eye.

She'd only had a few conversations with him. This had been the longest by far; it felt like the last. She wondered if that feeling, itself, had been the point he was trying to make. She remembered a voice. She couldn't place it—some kind of philosopher, she guessed. Something else, which she dismissed, suggested it was a golfer. Maybe Calvin Peete, whoever *he* was. She heard a detached voice say,

–In one physical model of the universe, the shortest distance between two points is a straight line. In the opposite direction, Danny.

That was the voice. She finished her drink, neat. Luther B paid at the front and exited Earlie's. Ndiya whispered to herself, smiling,

–Who the fuck is Danny?

Shame felt the multiplied weight of gravity caught in the sky-colored feathers of a bird of prey. A symphonic web of muscles and a vascular mathematics of tendril-thin pulses exerted their pressure against the approach of an invisible surface. A convex optics in the lens of an eye canceled reflecting waves of light against each other, and so a speckled trout appeared suspended in vacant space beneath. If it was a bird its approach had been measured against a liquid breeze and the low angle of the sun so that the shadow-double trailed like the certainty of hindsight and the inevitability of regret. If it was a bird there was no regret, no need for certainty and the shadow of the attack followed the event.

But this wasn't a bird. The wheels of the aircraft touched the runway and Shame's eyes opened. A message on a small screen read: ARRIVAL NBO. All the content of his dream evaporated, leaving him with an inexplicable expectation that the engines should reignite, the plane veer back into the sky, pinning the passengers in their seats. The plane morphed in Shame's mind back into the dream-image as it made its ascent with whatever prey dangling from talons of the landing gear.

Most of the people around him instantly flicked open phones and began to morse brief messages to, he suddenly imagined, waiting family members or expectant colleagues. That thought felt like another takeoff. For now, he permitted himself one backward glance.

The last thing he'd said to Ndiya was his instruction to her in the truck at the end of the you-don't-exist parade. At that time, there'd been no way to distinguish concern and fear from paranoia. This was the point of the parade. So, after the night in the precinct, he hadn't contacted her or anyone they knew. Only Kima. Another consequence of nonexistence, this one nearly immediate, was the suspicion, or realization, that he had massively underestimated the capacity of other people. Though this might be more the result of desperation than paranoia. It didn't matter.

Given this chronic and pervasive system of error piled upon error, in a flash of recalibration, the absurdity of which he politely introduced himself to and then banished, he ended his your-one-phone-call's worth of a backward thought with the certainty that Ndiya would find her way to Kima and from Kima to him. Period. The last, most important part, he knew, was too much but he went for it anyway—fuck it. She'd take her time going about it. And he allowed himself to hope she would— "Would what? Scratch that." He avoided the answer by refusing himself the right to ask.

The crowd around him began its flow to the exits. With each step the increasing gravity from their nearing lives diminished the conversation in the aisles. Shame stood. He broke his stiffened knees straight, grabbed his worn-out, black backpack, and told himself he was walking. In his pocket were three Kenyan telephone numbers: Kima's sister, Sarah; Francis, her driver; and a woman in Mombasa named Su. The plane was now regurgitating its passengers into the smudged glass and gloom of an antechamber in Jomo Kenyatta International Airport. Kima had assured him that among those waiting for this crowd would be a man with a sign, SL: PIANO MAN. Kima told him the man would give him a ride and he'd have a cell phone charged with enough credit to call Jupiter. Shame walked through a corridor tinged with the smell of jet fuel and distant cigarettes. He passed two soldiers asleep along the wall cradling old rifles like the spines of ancient lovers. "Jupiter," he kept thinking, "that's good. Apart from these numbers in my pocket, there are as many people I can call on Jupiter as there are here on Earth."

The weatherworn door opened out onto Fifty-Third Street, the main business street of Hyde Park. On the inside of the door, a small bell hung on the neck of a soft, brass knob with a palm-faded lion's face patterned into the blond metal. The sound of the bell wavered throughout the space, announcing his entry. Shame was a periodic customer of the store, The Act Is Natural, a new-age toy store and bookshop that replaced a used record and CD store near the corner of Fifty-Third and Dorchester. The door to the store swung shut and chimed, again, throughout the volume of warm air in the rectangular, high-ceilinged space. Shame's legs felt slightly numb with the vibrations of the previous night's detention and police interrogations. He hadn't slept at all.

He was aware of no decision. He had stopped at his apartment and filled Ndiya's wheeled suitcase with some clothes, passport, random bathroom items, and his empty backpack. He didn't know that he knew that he was not going back there. A severed electrical cord moved, slowly, like a rain-chilled snake in the curve of his skull. Call it thinking. When he closed the door of his apartment it seemed as if he could hear a whistle of air disappearing through the space beneath the door. Some crystal of cold spines was growing in his belly. He closed the door as gently as he possibly could. Nonetheless, the sound of the latch had felt like a cleaver through bone and tendon.

He knew the feeling. The world was trifling with him, again. When he was little he'd always heard pawn, in chess, as "prawn." He'd pictured the bolt-blue eyes and pink body of a large shrimp. He didn't play chess, didn't know the rules. There he was, a simple "prawn" before forces in the world, which bore no regard for the space of his body. It felt like pulling up to a loading dock under a hard, January rain in, say, Florence, Mississippi, or some such place, some unregulated plant, the dock a stump of slime and garbage. Materials out in the rain, brick mildewed. Shame recognized the it's-not-about-you reality, the *job*. This was merely a new kind of work. His first recognition of a job to do appeared in the set of his jaw, all thought collapsed into discrete, repeatable, physical actions, the way the force of a working body springs from assorted triangles of bone, muscle, and tendon. The first thing to do upon the sight of an impossible task or a fearful sight was to face it directly, and imperceptibly nod one's head at something just behind it. A fence post, a freeway, a dumpster, a twisted pine tree, a person: it didn't matter what it was, just invisibly nod at a physical object behind the threat presenting itself. This made it appear that you were leaning toward it. And that looked like confidence to the confident, looked like aggression to the aggressive, and remained invisible to everyone else. Shame shook his head, all that could be sorted out later. He went down the stairs of 6329 and out off into the city which had declared itself impossible.

Shame didn't recognize the young woman with red-streaked dreadlocks behind the counter at The Act Is Natural. He knew the owners who usually worked at the raised counter and in the office at the back of the store. He'd bought a few dozen games and puzzles over the past year or so. They sold sustainable everything, nothing plastic. The toys were imported from factories in Denmark and Sweden, as well as from women's collectives in Peru, Costa Rica, the West Bank, and Mozambique. There was a corner shelf upon which sat vehicles made of twisted wire by children in Kibera, Nairobi. Each piece bore a card stating that all revenue went to school fees. He was here to buy four or five of the 3-D wooden puzzles that came in compact, rectangular boxes almost the size of the brick he was not stacking up at that very hour. He paused to picture the job he hadn't shown up for out near Midway Airport. It was the first day of work he'd ever missed.

He'd seen the puzzles before, never bought them for whatever reason. In his mind he assumed it was a day off, though he'd never had one. He didn't allow the anomaly of buying the toys for himself to cross his mind. Near the rear, behind the imported sandals for toddlers and in front of the shelves of books at the back wall, he found the puzzles. He held the solid weight of the different options and selected five puzzles of the same oblong shape: one blue, two red, two in green. On the back of each box was a plain diagram of the abstract shapes a child could configure using the various interlocking bamboo pieces. Statements on the front of the boxes assured the absence of chemical additives and affirmed the renewability of the ingredients and fair-trade labor practices in the crafting of each puzzle. Each had a small white sticker with a price hand-printed in red ink: *$17*.

Shame brought the stack of boxes to the front of the store. The clerk looked up from her hardback book, *Purple Hibiscus*. The fringed tassel of the bookmark glanced across Shame's wrist and dangled over the edge of the counter made from an old door with a sheet of glass cut to fit its shape. Reluctantly, the clerk put her book aside. On the book's cover, an alien-antenna-looking stem from a blossom reached toward the chin of a young woman. The top of her face was cropped out of view.

–Is this it?

–Yes. I think that'll do it.

Staring at the amputation in the photo, Shame forced the response out. The clerk's eyes brushed over Shame's hands and he wondered if he could feel the tassel again. Looking up, he felt himself nod invisibly at the woven fabric on the wall behind the clerk's head.

–How old are your kids?

–Um, not mine, I work with kids.

–Are you a teacher? There's a discount.

–No, actually, these are gifts.

–OK. Fun.

–Yes.

–Would you like them gift-wrapped?

–OK. Perfect. Could you leave them open at the top, I'll slip in a note.

–Sure.

The clerk walked to the back of the store with the puzzles. Shame moved to the front and stared blankly across the street. People passed by. Cars. A bus. Three old men on their way, he guessed, to Valois, a diner a few blocks east. Kids made their way to the bus stop. Everyone was bundled against the cold wind that had sculpted the grit-blackened snow into prototype-looking aerodynamic shapes. An old woman passed by. Shame guessed she was Jewish, but maybe she wasn't. She wore a fur hat with a matching wrap. The woman pushed a walker with high-tech foam grips and a hand brake on one side. A few feet from the store she stopped abruptly, turned the walker toward the storefronts and set a foot brake. Shame watched as the woman made a deliberate series of movements. As she did this, she switched places with her thinly—and very finely, Shame thought—gloved hands like a slow-motion gymnast. She lifted her handbag from a basket in the front, lowered a cushioned panel over the basket, and sat down slowly on the cushion facing the street.

Shame watched from an angle while the ritualized gestures continued. She removed a small white box from her bag. She then took a thin brown cigarette or possibly a cigar from the packet and placed it back in the bag. After she paused to watch the street, or perhaps to wait for a still moment in the wind, Shame saw a silver lighter appear and soon a white cloud of smoke drifted to the left until the wind caught hold. The previous night with the police alive in his arms and legs, Shame marveled at the scene, the intimacy of deliberate movements, each with an identifiable purpose. Under his breath, Shame heard himself say,

–Could have fooled me—

A voice approached from behind, it had begun its address in some inaudible reach of the room. Shame picked up the speech midway:

–Just tape the end closed. Oh, I'm sorry, did I hear you say something?

–No, I don't think so. Look, thanks.

–You're most certainly welcome. Come see us again.

–Sure. Of course. Thanks again.

Shame heard the bell's tone waver backward as he pushed the door open into a triangular wedge of snow lodged between itself and the wall to the left. He passed the old woman still sitting on her chair. A very, very tall, thin young black man wearing a black-and-gold Pittsburgh Steelers hat had stopped at her side. He bent down at the knees and waist. Shame's peripheral vision caught the extreme angles in the young man's body required by the effort to equalize their heights. Why all the effort? Shame didn't ask. He didn't care. As if leaving him out of it, the erector-set collapse of the boy's body asked Shame's eyes a question. He stood still and let his eyes answer. The young man's head didn't bear the attitude or tilt of a question or the initial sweep of a dialogue. Shame felt his eyes come to the absurd expectation that the two were about to kiss but, no, that wasn't the angle of the chin.

As if watching from behind a glass barrier, Shame remeasured the intricacy and nuance of one moment in the world around him; he knew a million moments such as this happened all over the city all the time. There were dozens of invisible pieces in this one moment his eyes had witnessed. Each moment gave way to what it became. This happened beyond the power of any reigning force or will. This was true. He'd just seen it.

And Shame knew none of it mattered. The world

would tickle your chin with an exotic flower, then it would cut your face in half. Events last night had indelibly marked the irreality of all of it for him. It was an irreality he'd known—or that he'd told himself constantly that he knew—and so now he wondered at the stupidity of his surprise. He wondered if it was all an act, natural, to avoid the pain alive and on the loose in his body, his one fragile, temporary body that dangled by strings with its feet an inch above the trap door in the floor of the stage. He suppressed a tingling, violent urge to lash out at the fabrication surrounding him.

As he turned to walk to the truck he switched the canvas sack full of puzzles to his other arm. A new cloud of smoke appeared in the air. The young man raised back up to more than double the height of the sitting woman's fur hat. Shame saw a quick swivel of light and her gloved hand dipped back into the brown suede purse on her lap. A barely visible pulse of motion had completed the woman's act of lighting the boy's cigarette, which, when Shame looked at it, was thin and brown just like hers. Both acts had been performed right in front of his concentrated attention and he'd hardly seen half of it.

The trunk of the old Peugeot 505 slammed shut. Shame stood waiting for Francis to unlock his door. The space between him and the edge of the parking lot was full of upside-down funnels of amber light that spilled from the top of tall lampposts. The scene was smudged somehow; it felt like he was wearing old safety goggles. The cold surprised him—maybe in the high forties. Beyond the airport's perimeter, space dropped off an edge into a blackness Shame hadn't seen before. He gestured to Francis and pointed out beyond the edge of the parking lot.

–What's over there beyond the fence?

–Over there? Nothing. Bush.

Francis arrived to where Shame stood, to indicate that the right side of the car was the driver's side. Shame headed around the nose of the car. The wind was full of diesel scent and charcoal smoke stirred by the invisible tussle and tumult of international money. Something strange in the air felt alive to Shame's presence and location, maybe even his posture, as if millipedes of sensations tingled and surveyed the surface of his body beneath his shirt and his jeans. The air itself was a body search.

–OK. Off we go. Your first time in Africa?

–Yes.

–Ah ha. It must be very strange, all these black people everywhere, eh?

–Well, not as strange as all that. But different.

–Yes, different. Well. I have some things for yo-u.

Shame had noticed but not remarked that everywhere he'd looked in the airport, almost all the travelers, employees, soldiers, cleaners, porters, were black. But Francis's comment made Shame conscious that he'd remarked but not noticed how strange it was to be in a space with no black people in it. The back of Shame's brain was working on that knot so it took him a few seconds to understand what Francis was saying. Like his image of the United States, Francis thought Shame was white, of course. Even that wasn't all *that* strange. It was another roll of the same dice. What *was* strange was the tingling millipedes on Shame's arms and legs and the countermelody that seemed to pull everything Francis said in two directions. Francis's words wore their sound the same way his legs pulled at his thin, tight slacks that were about two inches too short for his height.

–OK. Sarah?

–Oh. She's at home. We'll go to pick her now. There's a train to Mombasa at midnight.

–Midnight?

–Yes. It's the night train. Arrives in Mombasa in the morning, no telling exactly when, really. But tomorrow, in the morning, probably.

–I see.

–Now, first, here's your phone, full charge should last a few days at least. SIM card, charger, all in the box. Receipt, $70 for the phone itself and $130 for the credit *in* the phone. And in this envelope is your train ticket,

\$45. You have Sarah's number, and mine, and Su's in Mombasa?

–Yes, I do.

–Perfect. You're all sorted. So-o, *you* know Kima?

–Yes, we played music together in Chicago.

–Aha. Chicago.

Thumbs up, Francis pointed both index fingers at Shame.

–Bang, bang.

–Yeah, pretty much.

Francis laughed, turned the ignition and the radio came on.

–Nairobi is the same! Always robbers, from the coast.

A bassline blasted into the air and covered up the sound of the engine and Francis's blanket indictment. He turned the volume down and turned his smiling face into an apology. A deep, assured voice dubbed over a chorus of itself sang, *Girl, I've waited all, all, night for love to find the place* . . . This was Shame's arrival in Kenya, in Africa.

–Wow.

–I know, too loud! Sorry, *pole, pole.*

–No, no. It's just you don't hear *that* song much, ever, in the States. Kashif, damn.

–Really? You know Kashif? Do you know what the name means?

–Yes. But no, I don't know what the name means. I never thought about that.

–Kashif is a name for an explorer, a searcher.

Shame nodded. The car pulled through a parking lot filled with porters coming and going with massive stacks of luggage. Others lounged on their hand trucks. Now, Shame had to agree with Francis, it was strange to hear this song, once so familiar, then missing for twenty years and forgotten. And then here it was, totally familiar again, in Francis's car as they drove through the charcoal-smudged amber air past statues of three camels at the exit of the airport and onto a wide, mostly empty boulevard. The buildings seemed similar to those that sprung up around airports, totally commercial and hardly pretending other-wise. The song handed Shame's memory a clear image of his childhood poster of George Gervin seated on blocks of ice with his thin legs crossed. He wore a sweatsuit. The rim hovered like a silver halo just above his head: ICEMAN.

Even after two decades, Shame found that he knew every instant of this song: the precise inflections that pointed words in sharp angles; when the keyboard trills and guitar riffs would arrive; the choruses of Kashif that echoed key words in the verses; the other chorus of women, *Pretty baby, give it to me baby*. A totally forgotten, invisible, and intimate familiarity made for a strange sense of arrival, no question about it. It was as if a forgotten part of his past, almost a part of his own body, had been waiting for him here. He thought about Kima and his love of the music. Shame felt like he'd shown up to Kenya and found it floating in his world when he was sixteen. The unfamiliarity of the surroundings pulled Shame's eyes in one direction. The intimate closeness of the music pulled the rest of his body in another. All around him were black people who bore no resonance his body recognized. One such person sat beside him. Meanwhile something in the air searched his skin and an inaudible howl in the distance called to him like his own disappeared flesh.

As Shame watched the scene scroll past Francis's Peugeot, he noticed space slipping into shapes and vice versa. Between the buildings, an emptiness moved with something visually whistling into or out of it. "What does a visible whistle look like?" he wondered. But it wasn't visible, nor was it audible. That whistle was spatial, a black vastness. Why did he call it a whistle? It was the same, different blackness he'd noticed beyond the lights at the airport boundary in the parking lot. When he asked, Francis had said it was nothing. Bush.

When the song ended the whistling vanished from those spaces. "Kashif!" Francis pounded his fist down on the dashboard, smiled at Shame.

–In this country, that man is loved!

■

Shame slept in the back seat of Francis's 505. A thin dark-skinned woman with a gold nose ring and very short, red, natural hair woke him.

–So, Mr. Shame, when we cross this road we'll roll up our windows. Nairobi has its robbers and thieves. I'm sure you've heard. So sorry you'll go tonight. Kima says you have a very, very urgent need to relax in the most complete fashion. I've texted him to say that we've received you and now *he* can relax.

They crossed some border out of vacant, yawning streets of a downtown-type area pillared with 1970s-style office buildings. Shame heard Sarah say something about Tom Mboya Street and cell phones and watches. Half-awake, he wondered which half of him was asleep. They inched through a crowded market lined with small shanty shops filled with an impossible variety of goods. They passed racks of neon backpacks, tomatoes, CDs and DVDs, kitchen supplies; one store had a welder, one electronics, and one mini storefront was stacked with old coffee cans filled with charcoal. The items rolled across Shame's half alertness. It wasn't the smallness of the shops or the variety of the goods. Those features of the scene blurred on his half attention. What struck him was an absolutely coherent clash between the unthinkable variety of products. Shame felt millipedes of air search his skin. His eyes told him it was random, but everything else he sensed disagreed. Francis said that they were almost to the station as Shame drifted away into sleep again.

Somewhere underwater a phone rang. Shame couldn't hear the voice but Sarah's reassurances made it clear she was talking to Kima. Then she relayed news of an official who'd come to River Road Market a few days ago. She told Kima that the man had ridden in his car speaking from a bullhorn. He'd informed the merchants that they'd "henceforth and hereby" be required to have permits, and shoppers that their purchases would be subject to an official value-added tax. There had been confusion at first. An uproar followed; the official and two escorts were dragged from the vehicle and beaten to death by a group of men armed, apparently, with steel rods and tire irons. As Sarah narrated this to her brother, Shame felt himself veer upward toward the surface of sleep. He kept hearing echoes of Francis proclaiming Kenya's national love for Kashif. Shame didn't fully wake up. Some force or weight kept pulling him down, as if by his ankles, away from the surface of his brain.

Before he actually realized what was happening, Shame found himself hugging Sarah, who had approached him around the car walking with no indication that her feet touched the ground. Francis came around and Shame heard the trunk croak open, then slam. Now awake, or at least maybe awake, Shame stared at Sarah. It was clear to him, now that she was standing still, that she was not in fact in physical contact with the ground. Sarah was afloat. And then as she stood beyond arm's reach after their embrace, Shame swore there was no space at all between them. The space either wasn't there or the distance was made of a substance Shame failed to perceive. His feet felt like they'd been permanently installed in the pavement like piles for a foundation. Francis shook Shame's hand abruptly and rehearsed:

–So, phone in the box. You have the numbers.

–Oh, right. The phone. The ride, how much can I pay you?

Sarah laughed and Shame felt her arms around him. She hadn't moved. Shame thought to himself that Kima should have warned him about his sister. But how? And about what? Or, then again, maybe he had.

–Let's say $250 US.

–OK. Let's see.

Francis counted the money.

–You can change currency inside, if you like. Or, of course, there are ATMs. When you get to Mombasa station ask anyone how to get to the Blue Room. Then call Su, who will come pick you from there.

Suddenly, Francis whistled, jerked his head, and scowled. A bone-thin, tiny young man, very dark, with his hair dyed blond, appeared. He wore sandals, shorts, and a lime-green T-shirt: SAFARI.COM. Francis motioned toward Shame's bags and said something in what Shame guessed was French, and then to Sarah in another language—Kiswahili, Shame assumed. Sarah answered him and laughed. Shame interrupted to say that he didn't need help with the bags. Francis waved away Shame's interruption and pointed a few more scowling phrases at the tiny man.

Francis shook Shame's hand again, and walked back around to the driver's side of the Peugeot and got in. Sarah turned to him:

–OK. Mr. Shame, piano man. If I come to the coast, I'll expect to hear some music from you. I might need to relax too. There must be at least one piano at the edge of the beyond.

She stepped up to Shame and embraced him again. She kissed him on his ear with some lightness in the touch of her lips. He heard a high-toned bell ring in the distance. The sound of the bell came out of the nowhere-millipedes, the body search, and the inaudible whistle careening from invisible bush of black spaces and shapes. Shame thought it was the exact sound that the taste of a plum would make. Sarah stepped back and whatever plum-bell-flavored, glossy substance that surrounded her flowed back between them. Shame saw her step back but still couldn't sense any space between them.

—Oh, I almost forgot. Take these. Kima insisted that I give them to you.

She handed him an orange packet of cigarettes. As he simultaneously attempted and gave up attempting to refuse the gift, Shame took the box from her hand and noticed a white circle with a brown horse's head in it. The box read: Sportsman. Shame objected,

—You've done enough, really.

Sarah handed him a yellow box that read: KUBWA / RHINO.

—Matches.

—OK, why not. But I don't smoke.

—Well, you never know.

Shame shook his head again but protested no further. He placed the pack and the box of matches in the top pouch of his backpack, looked back to Sarah and nodded, brows down. He felt electrically awake now, solid, like an oil of seriousness had been rubbed on his skin where the millipedes were a few moments before. Sarah smiled.

—You're not cold?

—No, I was before. I'm warm now.

Sarah almost mentioned that he was trembling but decided against it. Instead, she smiled again. Another distant bell rang in Shame's ear. He looked off to his left as if in the direction of the bell sound. A train was leaving the station. Shame could see the outlines of people in the lighted windows. Others were reclined, and some lay flat on their backs on the roof of the train, legs dangled over the edge. Sarah waved and bent down to get into the car with Francis.

–Be well, Mr. Shame. Su will help you. No worry no.

Shame waved. He watched the car pull around the circle and out into the empty street beyond the parking lot. He turned to see the red lights on the caboose of the train trail off into the space beyond the curve described by the pounded silver surface of the tracks. The distant-bell sound of plum, he thought, the curved-silver taste of steel. The *new* nowhere.

■

The gray metal door slid shut. The latch was turned so that the red DO NOT DISTURB tag appeared in the dial. The window wouldn't close; a few mosquitoes had arranged themselves in manic orbits around the yellow bulb over the door. Shame lay on his back with the small Nokia phone in the palm of his hand. He stared at the bottom of Ndiya's bag on the luggage rack above the bunk. The rack's leather straps triangled their way back to the near wall casting shadows opposite. The shadows traversed the outside wall and disappeared into the space of the open window.

Kima had been right. The train from Nairobi to Mombasa was a relic. A steel-rasping sound began as the train jolted, and jolted again, and again, before it achieved forward motion. The station slid from view. As the speed of the train increased, the rasp became a scrape and that turned into a spinning, continuous tone that hovered high, Shame imagined, in the human range of hearing. Soon a maraca scratch and something that sounded like a thick spring thrown down a flight of stone steps, dragged back up, and thrown down again joined in. Shame lay still, amazed at the cacophony. He tried to match vibrations in the thin mattress to punctuations in the sounds. He failed to connect the vibrations and the rhythm of the sounds. He imagined that the train's speed had leveled off, though it appeared that they were not traveling much faster than a casual speed on a bicycle. Finally, as if to announce the cruising speed, a peal that sounded like a bassoon crawled through the thicket of sounds and settled into a low growl.

The phone box also contained a pair of earbuds. He took them out and inserted them in his ears. He plugged in the phone. A cold wind played into the cabin from the window and spiraled up the leg of his jeans. Shame wondered if he should call Sarah. Despite the rigor of his concentration, he knew he had no bearings for where he was and knew he was headed toward even less familiar surroundings. Then he thought about the distant bell, the space with no distance, the hovering when Sarah should have been walking, the fluidlike substance that enclosed him when she kissed his ear. He decided that calling Sarah certainly wasn't the cure for his lack of bearing. Then, like putting a coat over a puddle and calling it a bridge, he decided that, one, he didn't want to impose and, two, that he couldn't afford to admit that his reasoning was a cover-up. He decided that he'd treat himself as if he were looking in a mirror, knowing that the image wasn't closed on the back. He would let this chaos of new nothings do whatever it wanted on the backside of his mirror.

He'd played this game before. Then he looked down at the face of the phone and switched it on. An image of the phone began as a point of light and spun into view, the image increased in size until the phone vibrated and NOKIA flashed up, found its way to the corner of the screen, and the home page of the phone appeared icon by icon. A twirling in the corner revealed Kenya Orange, four bars of signal. At the opposite side an icon indicated full battery. He'd been told that people depended on these devices. He'd never owned one. In the early days of his time going to Earlie's someone had asked him for his cell number. He had just arrived back in the city. The phrase stuck out in a way that made the whole situation obvious to him.

–My *cell* number! No, there's at least one thing I've been able to avoid.

And at the time, he regarded anything that he couldn't have afforded on his weekly expense check from the road as simply off-limits. It wasn't for him. In ten years on the road he'd learned that income wasn't to be spent. At times, soon after returning to the city, he wondered if his warped perceptions of his surroundings in Chicago weren't simply the result of one simple fact: he had no debts.

Amid the vibrations of the train, the word "debt" echoed. He also knew that money wasn't the only kind of debt. He knew he owed Colleen, for instance. He didn't know what, exactly. Muna, Pearlie, and them all owed *him* money, but that was hardly the whole story. Then the thought of calling Colleen crossed his mind. He knew he wondered, or, really, hoped, that Ndiya had decided to stay with Colleen. He knew calling was impossible so he let the thought cross over to the back of the mirror and keep on going. Kima? As he exiled all thoughts of calling Chicago he took out the card with the three numbers. Now, minus Sarah, there were *two* he could call.

He had to admit that there was something comforting about holding this device in his hand. It bent people's presence, brought distance nearby. It wasn't like Sarah's plum-bells or the body-search air in Nairobi. But Shame noticed it, whatever it was. The possibility of calling someone pushed against the rhythms of the train massaging his back. It would have to be Su. He calculated the impression calling this late would make, as if manners were his worry. Just then the screen twirled, the phone icon spun backward diminishing in size until it disappeared into a point of light and the phone went dark.

■

As if watching from beneath as they were poured into a clear glass bowl, Shame remembered his worries about the broken window and the cold wind when the train reached full speed. They were beyond the city and the soot-yellow sprawl of its sky. As he reclined on his backpack, he watched the night sky. Its crayon-scribbled darkness changed frames, a horizonless blackness. He remembered Kima's line, "Don't worry, the place will swallow you." In a long, irregular loop of repetition, the train jerked back and forth like a spastic rocking chair, a movement that gave way to an easy lope as if the rails led across diagonal waves in the tracks. These slow spasms were structural, he thought. They left and returned and left again with their own sense of rise and fall; he wondered if they traveled the length of the train the way dynamics of a chord coursed the wires in a concert grand piano. Below that was the rhythm of the track itself, which was constant, and beneath that the percussive symposium in polyrhythm that was the train's mechanical works. Amid it all he sensed that the slow-jog speed of the train was what it was going to be.

Shame felt heavy in the bunk. He measured the train's attempts to move in many different directions at once against the strength of the rails, which kept it all from coming apart, kept it all falling forward.

■

He woke hovering above the percussion that just then felt as if all of it was trapped in and trying to tear its way out of the thin mattress beneath him. The train rocked back and forth on its loping way. It was almost 4:00 a.m. He'd slept three hours. He stood holding the rail of the luggage rack against the manic compulsions of the compartment. Something was missing. A wave of panic washed across but the bags, his shoes, everything was where it had been. Looking out the window he could now see low hills in the distance, everything doused in an amber fluid. The rhythm of the train made another attempt to vault from the rails. The motion passed through Shame's body.

Shame heard Kima walking behind him on the bass when they'd played together at Inflation. His hands ached for something to do. He thought of Sarah and those distant bells and wondered if he'd really heard them or not. And plums? He began to wonder where in the hell he was going. As if through black mortar with a clean silver trowel, his mind cut the thought. A huge moon had risen over the sloping horizon. It hung hardly an inch above the low hills. Distance collapsed into a substance illuminated by the moon's hazy light. His mind unspooled as if on a reel with one end caught on the spiked plants that appeared to be cultivated in this region of Kenya. Sisal, he'd learn. He noticed that he didn't really need to hold on to the rail anymore. His body anticipated the timing and direction of the train's lurch and stammer. He stood still and closed his eyes, bent his knees, and surfed the trembling floor.

Then he felt what was missing. The breeze was gone. No, he confirmed, the wind still spiraled into the cabin. But it had lost its brittle, upcountry chill. This breeze was soft against his face, around his neck. It felt full and warm, nearly liquid. With his eyes closed he couldn't determine the exact extent of the space his body contained. The breeze changed shape as it passed across his body. But he couldn't mark where the breeze began and his body ended.

■

Shame never smoked but just then, in that boxlike compartment, a-clang in the train to Mombasa, he thought it might be the time to try. He unzipped his pack and took out the Sportsman packet Sarah had passed to him. There was no wrapper. He pulled open the top and discovered two rows of neatly twisted cylinders. With his nose close to the opening, he recognized the pine-needle scent.

He lighted one end of the twisted paper and pulled in a moment of smoke. After a few lurches, he breathed out a stream of smoke that clouded around him, gathered and flowed out the window. He repeated the action. He'd witnessed this here and there when it seemed the smokers acted ridiculous, as if passing a joint between them was some occult and sacred ritual. Shame had never thought he had the option. As far as he'd thought about his aversion to drugs of all kinds, he'd decided that it was a kind of pact with what he wasn't, a fidelity to the other side of the mirror, the blank part of the page.

He blew another stream-cloud out the window and tossed the joint out after it. Noticing a faint burning in his throat and chest, he lay back down on the bunk feeling nothing special but maybe, an impression that his body was now far too long to fit where he'd been reclined most of the night. All at once the space embraced him, the breeze opened itself, again, even warmer than it had been. The wind's skin became an even more viscous fluid with a twin inside his body. Unbuttoning his shirt, he felt very private as the thickening fluid filled the compartment and moved slowly as if it was being stirred with a long stick. He propped his foot on the outside wall next to the window. As the moon rose diagonally into the frame, its light grew sharper and brighter. He closed his eyes, imagining the bone-colored wash on the fields, the sparkle of stars being flooded from view by the moon.

The border between his body and the world arched its back, sloped into his mind. A wave approached in silence. It rose through him and broke into a surf of nearly audible vibrations in his chest and arms. His body felt like a soft turbulence inside his name. A river moved through his clothes. He felt like some plasma-like jellyfish in a loose tide, a torn plastic shopping bag caught on a wire fence or tree branch. He wasn't dead in Chicago; the rest would catch up. OK. He was headed down to the coast, the Indian Ocean. OK. One arm behind his head in a triangle, he found sleep came along like a tongue across the seal on an envelope.

His initial weeks in Lamu proved that Shame knew nothing about idle time. As he knew he would, he needed work. As far as he could remember, he always had. Rare, however, had been periods where he didn't have overlapping jobs, so this need was a foreign feeling much more than a familiar texture in his muscles, in his voice, in his dreams. Maybe it was the shape of the lens in his memory pointing back? He recalled a dim kitchen table, a window looking out on a snowy courtyard in the middle of the building. The scene floated behind his eyes. His father's voice, 6:00 a.m. on a Saturday, "Rise and shine, daylight in the swamp," or, "Chicago, the city that *works*." The floor of his father's pickup truck was a thick silver layer of cement dust and cigar ash.

–Oh yeah, well, what would you do if a *T. rex* came up to *you*?

–What would I do?

–Yeah, what would you do?

–I'd spit in his eye.

Further back, another dim table, elsewhere, when his father was away on a job, his tiny big sister leading them in prayer before a meal, "Our father, who works in heaven—"

Shame asked Muhammad, who asked around. There were always boats to unload. Muhammad said he didn't know the pay. Shame said he didn't care. The first day he went to the dock and waited until noon. Boats arrived

381

across the sound from the airport on Manda Island. Private crafts from the hotels came and went. Every other man who walked by asked him, "You go to Shela? To beach? Smoke, smoke?" He shook his head. No boat arrived with anything he thought needed unloading. No one seemed to be there waiting for work, either. The sun came up and the dense dry-season sky rolled over, revealing its luminous silver back. A young man wearing a wrap around his waist and thong sandals strode past wheeling a smoky, sky-colored shark draped over a black bicycle. Shame stilled his vision and watched the shark pour across the frame of his sight. Its head draped over the handlebars and curved toward the ground. Blood drooled from its open mouth. The shark's eye was diamond black, a hole left unfilled by the world. Shame waited. Nothing continued to happen, Shame thought, in rather spastic actions, so he left.

He went to Echoes for a lime-banana juice and a coffee, walked back to the dock. Still nothing. He walked the dirt road along the water headed out of town. At low tide, scores of boats sat aground and leaned to their sides. The distant boats looked like scattered toys left by children whose attention had suddenly been compelled elsewhere. He noticed a few men huddled in the mud and stones under the shade-side of the boats. Something was wrong about their postures. Shame kept walking. When the third man appeared beneath a blue sailboat—he'd been told these boats were called dhows—Shame was close enough to see that the man wasn't huddled. He was crouched on his haunches, a worker. He moved in the shaded patch, knees totally flexed, wobbling side to side. Something was wrong.

The fourth man solved the puzzle. A boat leaned aground even closer to the road. This man wore torn denim shorts and plastic sandals. No shirt. He held a tiny wooden mallet. It looked like he had several over-sized toothpicks in his mouth. Then he stopped with his forefingers extended. He touched the smooth slime-sheen on the underside of the boat. His fingers moved gently back and forth, moving less and less, as if the hull of the boat was the stretch-curved belly of a lover overhead. He reached out and touched the boat above him as if he was finger painting a cathedral ceiling.

They weren't toothpicks. They were bigger than that. They were shims. The man removed one from his mouth and placed it before the spot where his touch had stopped. He put it back in his mouth and removed a second shim from his mouth and repeated the gesture. Then Shame watched the man pound the thin strip of wood into the crease marked by his fingers. The impact of the hammer seemed to create the space more than replace it. Shame felt the way work resonated in the body of the worker, and the way that resonance radiated into the world. He was thirsty for that.

Shame watched the man work. He saw an unknown, underwater error and a way to bring it up into air, in the shade. It was an error that didn't exist underwater, where the point was for water to reclaim its cousin, the wood. The worker had to bring it out of its element, above the surface, to force the error into being, to force something into being an error. Then fix *that*. Later the water returned, but the error in the wood, now no longer itself, could hold its own against whatever would happen where it had come from. If the man did his job correctly, it wasn't just that the error in the wood wouldn't appear again underwater. Immersed again, the error disappeared into a past in which it had never existed. By working across dimensions, the man found mistakes in the future and then repaired them, in effect, before they happened. Then he and the boat returned to a past in which the mistakes didn't exist. This required the man to feel his way. He was a visionary, working. He was seeing by touch. They all were.

Following the resonance of the work he watched, Shame remembered Francis talking about Kashif, "a searcher . . . in this country, that man is *loved*!" The song, Francis's fist on the dashboard, and the way his voice scowled in French at the porter at the train station tangled together. Shame consciously decided not to add Sarah's floating, space-eclipsing presence to the perplexing mix. Still, Shame couldn't solve the knot of love and contempt. Instead, he blamed his confusion on the heat and sat for a minute beneath a tree. The heat had begun to draw the breeze off the sound that, at low tide, carried the smell of exposed muck more than the coolness of water.

A small, lone donkey wandered near him and stopped with its face headed the way Shame had been walking. This meant the donkey's freakishly large left eye seemed to be staring straight at him. Straight, in the case of a donkey's stare, Shame noticed, described an axis in both directions exactly perpendicular to the direction its nose faced. Was that facing? Shame smiled at the donkey, thinking, "Headed in one direction, facing another." The donkey's implacable expression remained.

Expressionless, perhaps, the donkey, a male, then leaned forward without moving the position of its hooves and peed. As far as Shame could tell, the left eye of the donkey was fixed upon him. The lake of donkey piss found a channel in the dirt road and began to depart toward the water. These donkeys were, Shame was beginning to realize, quite strange and often, he then began to suspect, deeply sardonic creatures. "No work. OK. It could be worse," he thought. "I could be sitting downhill from a pissing donkey."

The donkey seemed to be wearing false eyelashes. The effect of the dramatically oversized lashes multiplied the mocking force, somehow adding an aggressive bent, or depth, to the idiotically neutral surface of the donkey's gaze. Still, Shame wondered, who was the idiot, who was trapped in one dimension? Who was confused about what "straight ahead" meant? Who had arrived in Africa and found a place with no black people in it and another nowhere made of space that moved about in millipedes? Who was feeling around in the silky muck for an error in a past that didn't exist?

To distract himself from these dizzy thoughts, Shame changed the subject. He'd been surprised, in a way startled, to find that, in a so-called conservative Muslim region such as this, so many women wore long, false eyelashes. These women were totally covered but for their hands and a thin, exposed band between the bridge of their noses and eyebrows. Often the rim of the veil, the sheer, black plane of fabric that dropped from the bridge of the nose past the chin, was intricately adorned with silver embroidery or patterns of black glass beads. Shame gathered vaguely that all this was supposed to convey a kind of modesty. But the way these women's exposure to the world had been narrowed, that narrowness, garishly or elegantly adorned, lent a force, even an aggression, to their gaze. The effect of meeting one of these women's eyes was unlike anything he'd experienced. He'd felt obscenely exposed in his T-shirt and shorts, in his stupid American availability, his physical näiveté. "There I am again," he'd thought. Shame. No wonder I'm not supposed to tell anyone that that's my name.

The day after he arrived in Kenya, he remembered, Su had driven him to a drugstore in Mombasa to buy toothpaste. In the aisle that held toothpaste as well as cold beer, DVDs and CDs, and a rainbow array of hair products, he found a woman fully covered in buibui. She was facing the rack of DVDs, swaying beneath the layers of her black robes to Whitney Houston singing "I Wanna Dance with Somebody." She took steps back and forth, dancing in place, to the beat of this song Shame had always hated. At the bottom hem, inches above the dull, worn tiles of the floor, a bright flash of color caught his eye like a glimmer of refracted light in a muddy stream. The color was a flash of a privacy that was very different from its public costume. That made Shame think again for a moment about Whitney Houston. Shame considered the triangle made by that terrible pop song, its singer, and this buibui'd dancer in the DVD and toothpaste aisle in a Mombasa drugstore. It seemed a door to a private room, to many rooms.

He bought a tube of Crest and two pilsners, pushed open the glass door to leave the air-conditioned interior of the store. He looked back at the woman still swaying as if entranced. The weight of the outside air landed on the right side of his face and neck. As he turned toward the car, a glowing tower of clouds began to pour a thick metal sheet of rain into its shadow. The rim of the shadow was just across the street. In a narrow crescent of sunlight beyond the hem of the downpour, another woman had stopped to adjust the cap of her buibui. As she untied and retied the string at the back of her head, a beaded bracelet on her wrist beamed an anthem of sparkles to Shame through the heavy weight of the equatorial rain.

Shame snapped himself back and blinked at the absurd vanity of the donkey. As if he'd mistaken him for someone else, or as if he'd recognized Shame at a distance and had come simply to deliver this lake of piss for his close consideration, the creature turned around and walked back in the direction it had come from. Shame turned away from the donkey and looked further up the shore. A boat had appeared near the waterline. It hadn't been there before. It was very low in the front and leaned radically to one side. At least two feet of the rudder was exposed, the rear third of the boat was above the surface. He could make out a few figures on the boat and a few more up to their armpits in the water near the bow. He decided to go for a closer look.

As Shame approached, he found eight donkeys with

large saddle-like pouches across their backs. Two stood with pouches loaded with rectangular blocks of coral stone, six blocks balanced on each side. Two others had loads of sand on both sides. A glistening spindle of a man came across the rocks at the shore with a sack on his shoulder. He had widely spaced, narrowly opened eyes and, Shame imagined, a somewhat irresolutely resolute expressionless expression on his face. It was as if the man wore a. mask positioned a thousand meters from his actual face. He nodded his mask in Shame's direction, approached another of the donkeys, and emptied half of the sand from the sack into each side of the donkey's pouch. The pouch bulged with the load but it was clear that each side would hold several loads of sand.

In a few paces Shame stepped up onto the rocks at the shore. Two men stood still on the boat. One leaned on a long handle, probably a shovel. A third man used a hand-held scoop to shovel sand from a pile at the end of the boat into bags. When he finished a sack, he set it to the side and one of the four men standing in the water took it from the edge, wrapped a cord around the open end, hoisted it to his shoulder, and turned toward the shore. As he emerged from the water, this man's impossibly thin looking legs appeared with each step until his white-and-blue sandals were visible. He carefully chose his steps, maybe fifty yards from where Shame stood watching. As that man grew near, Shame saw a head and two stone blocks come from the bow of the boat. The shirtless, shimmering body that held them rose step by step out of the water and turned toward him as well.

The rocks Shame stood upon were on shore. The water had receded with the low tide; Shame felt an invisible screen between him and the world where all of this took place. He glanced back at the donkeys standing stock-still, expressionless, holding their loads. The flagrant vanity of the lone donkey he'd encountered earlier, Shame thought just then, was more like an insolent vulgarity, as it stood in his mind between him and this scene. Suddenly it was perfectly obvious that the pissing donkey was insane. Then he thought to himself: "Me, a stevedore?"

The thin man with the torn shirt passed him almost close enough to brush shoulders. It felt like an attempt to refute the fact—if that's what it was—that Shame was standing there. These gestures were familiar enough from Shame's experience in life and at work. The first was usually a question before it became a confrontation; if answered correctly, which really meant if answered at all, in any way, the question usually didn't lead to confrontation. The first question was: Are you where your body says you are or not? Not answering was unequivocal; no answer being the clearest answer. No answer meant "I'm nowhere near where my body is standing." In other words, it meant violence. No answer meant space had been stolen, was being stolen at that moment. There were people Shame had met who asked that question while they were already enduring the consequences of many, many nonanswer-answers given to them by the world they lived in. The world of space thieves worked this way.

There were others who expected, and would at times demand, an answer-answer from space thieves.

Confrontational as it might seem, this insistence was really a kind of obdurate openness—an acutely vulnerable hardheadedness—in the person, which was expertly covered up with a transparent sheen of aggression. No one at home would admit it, of course, but that's what it was. So, when the answer-answer came along with some indignant obliviousness as to why the question had been asked in the first place ("What did *I* do to you?"), offering clear evidence of the person's inability to get anywhere near where their body said they were, the result was predictable. Space thieves are *always* innocent, most often indignant. Such people bear no humility in the world. People, especially the most aggressively hopeful, react to pain in different ways. But very few are graceful about it.

So, having in effect been asked, Shame dove.

–Excuse me, sir? I'm looking for work?

The man didn't even pause on his way back toward the boat. He stepped clear of the rocks and passed the man with the stones who was now approaching the breakwater. The man with the stones was much taller, shirtless. The muscles in his stomach twitched diagonally on the side opposite each stride. The stones couldn't be that heavy, Shame felt, because he took extremely long strides. He wore a thin, wispy goatee which gave his chin a sage effect. He was much younger than the other men but he carried something in his face that might otherwise pass for age. After unloading the stones into the pouch of a waiting donkey, he passed by Shame, stealing a quick glance. Shame was surprised to find that the man was wearing thin, wire-rimmed glasses. The bows bent behind his ears where his loosely curled hair disappeared into a freshly faded haircut. When he passed and after a few steps, Shame dove again. "Work?" The man hesitated and then took another step toward the shore.

–Sir, um, mzee, I'm looking to work?

The man pivoted on his right heel, his face tipped slightly backward to reveal a diagonal eyebrow, bright eyes, and a smirk pitched, Shame thought, loosely between curiosity and disbelief. It was, he assumed, the posture of a person who decides to talk to a stranger who appears harmless but is quite obviously mad. Shame thought, "So this is how you talk to a pissing donkey."

–I'm not the boss, my friend. He's on the boat, you know. Kubwa. You're not British?

–American.

–Ah. And you're looking *to*—

And here the man's left eyebrow straightened and the right one tipped up.

–not *for*, work?

Shame paused to rehearse the distinction the man had drawn and emphasized with the eyebrow gymnastics. The comical twist had put Shame at ease and allowed him time to consider the question. Shame had always much preferred confrontations to passive allegations over stolen space. It was a test that Shame's history working with the verb "to poise" had prepared him well to pass. The man stood stock-still, his face openly awaiting an answer. Finally, Shame smiled.

–OK. Right. Yes, looking to work. That's what I do.

–You look?

–Man, work!

At this they both laughed, and the man's posture un-froze and fell loose from his shoulders to his heels. He extended his hand, two thin silver rings on his index and middle fingers.

–I'm Muhammad.

–I'm Sh—I'm Shahid.

–Oh, I see, that's a shame—I mean, it's a strange name for an American.

Shame shrugged. The man smiled again and looked up at the sun squinting his narrow eyes.

–Shahid. The American who looks *to*—not for—work. Maybe that makes sense after all. You know, me, *I* wonder what exactly we look *to* work *for*?

He tipped his head to the side for Shame to follow.

–The man, *halas*, *to* work *for* is on the boat, my friend. He's Kubwa. This way, mind your step. The stones are sharp.

■

Up close the men on the boat looked as Arab and, un-derneath that, as Indian as they did Kenyan. Their hair had a silky looseness in its curls and a sandy red hue in the sun. They all wore sashes of striped cloth tied around their waists instead of pants or shorts. They said they were brothers. Their boats hauled materials up and down the coast, mostly between the islands, but sometimes as far north as Ras Kamboni or even Kismaayo. He was told that there was no work today, the day was done. He must start in the morning when the work started. No, there was no place to wait. The boats unloaded up and down the coast depending on materials, tides, weather, destination, etc. When there was a delivery in or near Lamu, which was often, word was sent to Matondoni, on the other side of the island. "We're all from Paté. Those men who work for us are from Matondoni. It's a workman's village, weavers and boat makers, lime burners. Lamu is a trader's town. It's for traders, merchants, imams, and their slaves." There was a visceral contempt in the leader's voice. "Did you see those pitiful donkeys?" The brothers laughed, sneering. Standing waist-deep in the water at the side of the boat, Shame asked, "So, you're Kubwa?" The men all laughed looking down at him in the water. The leader put his open hand on his chest, and then gestured to the other two.

–We're all Kubwa!

They all laughed again, looking down at him.

–We're almost done here. Tomorrow at dawn, if you want to work, take the path out of Lamu, just over there, toward Matondoni, three kilometers. You'll reach a place where the paths converge, four of them. Wait there. If there's work, some of these men will be coming from the village. Muhammad is their leader. You met him. He'll lead you to where the work is. Of course, it might be back in Lamu. It might be elsewhere. They might not come at all. You'll see then. It's the only way.

Shame nodded and reached out his hand. Kubwa held his shovel, staring at him blankly.

–The pay is 250 bob per day. We'll try you. OK. Tomorrow.

Kubwa put his hand back on his chest and bowed imperceptibly. The fact was that he was simply interested in whether or not the American looking to work would really show up.

–May I ask what the materials are for?

–These? A garden wall at the Leakey residence. They're English Kenyans. The grandfather was a famous scientist. He found the oldest human remains up-country in the Rift Valley.

Shame didn't know Leakey. "Yes," the man at the back of the boat said, "it proved that we're all Africans!" The three all laughed again. A short, silent man with one arm severed at the elbow leaned in to take a stone onto his shoulder, holding it in place with the stump of his left arm. He moved quickly back toward shore, swaying his hips, almost without disturbing the water as its border fell down his body and off of his legs with each twist of his hips.

Shame said he'd meet them at the path. Or try. He met Muhammad midway across the muck. When he told him that he'd meet them tomorrow morning, Muhammad, with the same how-to-talk-to-a-madman look on his face, pointed to the path.

–Wait where the paths meet. Nzuri.

When Shame reached the shore he found the waiting donkeys almost fully loaded. There was a white man leaning against a tree, smoking. He held a long stick in his other hand and wore his hair in a thin ponytail. He wore a loose short-sleeve shirt, shorts, and leather sandals. The shirt was unbuttoned. The man's pale belly protruded into view. Shame began to nod hello, assuming it was someone from the famous Leakey family. Before he did, however, he noticed that though the man was looking in his direction, he'd made no sign at all that he'd seen him. Shame turned back toward Lamu Town. "250 Ksh per day," he thought. "That's the price of one breakfast sausage at Echoes." A week's wages would almost buy one person breakfast there.

On the boat, one Kubwa said to another, in Kiswahili, "An American who works? I don't think so." "We'll see how he works tomorrow," said the other. "Likely not. He's another agent. Or, maybe he's another broken one who walked away from the base. We'll see which." To which the first Kubwa said: "Or maybe we won't."

BOOK
FIVE:
ANGEL,
UNARMED

Preening and untangling, feathers in her wings . . .
—CHAKA KHAN

Each morning the dry-season sky wedged space between the equatorial clouds. The sun appeared over the high, narrow wall of perfect white plaster. A thick, curvy vine led up like a frayed rope had been thrown over the wall from the noisy alleyway on the other side. As the sun rose higher into the sky, a bright border cut the shadows like a leveled cup of flour, and light sliced into the space below and above the water. The roof, or lip, made by the surface could be invisibly still. The circulation jets in the wall were three feet down, placed opposite each other midway in the narrow length of the space. The propulsion caused no stir at the surface. The water deepened as the floor sloped from the near end and the glass-smooth stone steps toward the wall over which the sun was just then appearing. Bushes and plants grew along the foot-wide border between the water's edge and the outside wall. On the opposite side were three heavy wooden reclining chairs strung with thick jute to make seats and backrests. The space was inside the mansion, half of which—including this room—was roofless and exposed to the elements. The effect of sculptural water and the geometry of the walls cast a vertical shaft of light that disappeared into the clouds.

Ndiya woke up, put on a white cotton caftan that fell to the tops of her feet, and walked through Peter Goodman's house. All the floors were polished concrete.

The interior floors were covered with woven mats; two wings comprised the vacant property. Huge wooden doors opened off the street into a large courtyard open to the sky. Narrow paths divided patches filled with plants and trees that made a thick canopy of shade broken by patches where liquid sunlight fell to the ground through shifting spectrums of fading and accumulating green. If she stood still for a few minutes, tortoises began to move about, visible in the way they disturbed the underbrush.

Inside the front doors, a path to the right led to a ground-level wing entered by a door in a wide wall patterned on the interior side with dozens of symmetrical niches. The niches varied in size according to some rule of proportion. In each niche was placed a bright ceramic object: a cup, a small plate, a broach. There were at least one hundred niches in the wall. As one stood inside the room facing back to the central courtyard, the pattern framed both sides of the door and continued in the space above the doorway.

Saidi kept the house. His father had kept it for the owners before Goodman. Saidi was in his late twenties. He told Ndiya that the wall with niches was a trap for djinns. On her initial tour of the mansion, Saidi pointed and asked her to remove a small orange-glazed saucer from its place. He then suggested that she place her hand inside the opening in the wall and feel its shape. The space sloped up above the opening; it was far bigger on the inside than one would guess. The tallest point was in the middle at the center just inside the arch in the wall. Saidi said, "Is smooth, very smooth, yes?" She'd nodded. He smiled strangely at this. She felt he was watching her from a distance. She also felt a ridge of faint ripples in the center of the small, curved ceiling of the aperture. Saidi said the inside of each space was identical in shape, and smooth. He seemed emphatic about this smoothness. His eyes narrowed. He said the openings were made in the plaster by special (Saidi said "*spee-shall*") workers. Long ago, he said, *towashi* did this work. At this term he frowned and shook his head as if in a mocking regret. He had two wives and, in a tone of frugality and pious self-denial, said he was saving for a third. His younger wife removed each piece and dusted it once each week, sometimes twice during the dry-season months.

Holding the ceramic dish as if it was a poisonous lizard, he explained that djinn were attracted to the shiny objects. Then they were entrapped by the surprising height and confused by the smoothness of the space inside. Saidi handed the saucer back to her and asked if she'd put it back. She noticed he was wiping his fingers with his shirt. She asked, "You can't?" He smiled and shook his head: "No, no, I have *two* wives." When he said that, he brushed his hands back and forth over each other as if freeing them of sand or dust.

When Malik had first brought her here with the idea that she and Shame should move in, he told her about *waungwana*, the patrician merchants of Lamu who'd modeled their mansions after the those of the Gujarat, north of Mumbai. He said the back rooms were where the women would have lived. At the far right was another small open courtyard with one tall date palm curving upward at the very center. A stairway led up to an office-like space with a window looking down into the narrow alley teeming with people and cats and donkeys outside.

Inside the front doors of the mansion, a path to the left led to a stairway. At the top, a landing overlooked the central courtyard and a set of doors into the second-story wing of the property. There was one bedroom with a canopy bed and a green wooden desk. The wall at the foot of the bed was made of panels carved from mahogany. Each panel had rows of octagonal openings about the size of a tennis ball. Each panel could be unlatched and opened like a small door. Through that screen one looked down on a long, narrow swimming pool that looked more like a glass sculpture of a pool than a real one. If you stood in the bedroom and looked down at this moment, midmorning, you'd see Ndiya Grayson, nude, floating on her back across the diagonal line between sun and shade. Outside the bedroom a steep stairway led down to the pool and a hallway on the second floor led along the length of the water. The hallway was open on the left looking down over the pool and on the right stretched a concrete bench covered with pillows and a thin mattress. Windows over the bench looked out over Lamu Town toward the sea. At times the breeze whistled in the screens cut with the same mahogany pattern as the bedroom wall. The hall ended at a large bathroom with several narrow, paneless windows and stone fixtures: sink, toilet, and a large, open shower stall with a green-tinted, copper nozzle for the water.

Each morning Ndiya woke up and walked the full property, entranced by how all the spaces were inside and outside at the same time. The openness was vertical, however; the spaces were all formidably walled off from their surroundings. These Swahili mansions carved spaces that extended up above themselves and into the heavens. After a few days she'd noticed that the pool and second-story wing were actually across one of the neighborhood alleys in a different structure altogether. The landing at the top of the stairway outside the bedroom had seemed strangely elongated. In fact, it was a bridge over the alley. The whole place was as much a sculpture as it was a dwelling. Malik said Peter bought the place and had it totally rebuilt so it would be a work of art. "Unreal," she'd said. And Malik:

–Well, yes. These *waungwana* families hovered over the towns on the coast and islands, held aloft by the men who were traders and the patrician women's contempt for the *washenzi*, the trash, the workers.

Malik's eyes flashed, "Magic," he'd said, laughing. Malik had a beautiful, open laugh full of bristling irony and sparkling contradictions. In fact, he was laughing at the look on Ndiya's face.

–Child, you ain't in Kansas no more! Enjoy it, honey, *you* have *earned* it. This is Lamu, even the donkeys think they're above working. And, you know, whatever these people are pretending to be, at least they're not pretending to be equal to each other. We've *both* been to that rather obstreperous Broadway production, haven't we?

Malik had just about spit the phrase "equal to each other" at the street out in front of Peter's mansion.

■

Now, Ndiya floats silently on her back. Her mind attends subtle cables in the turbulence below. She closes her eyes and knows her position by the geometry of currents across her back and down her legs. The flame surface of her body cools as she crosses the line into the shaded end of the pool. She opens her eyes and lets the sculpted rectangle of endless sky fall on her outstretched arms. "Sky sushi," she thinks. Sun-doused and maybe a little sense-drunk in an English banker's faux-Indian, East African, Modern museum of strictly minimal opulence: "Here I am." As she floats she feels elevated, as if the level of the water lifts her high above the pool, over the mansion, and holds her aloft, alone, above the town.

■

How easily they'd fallen into this stenciled forgery, the precision of their lives lived, if that was the word, in symmetry with each other. It wasn't life nor living, but she'd agreed to let some time unspool in the patterns that fell around them while they were here. "OK, no Shame in that," she'd thought, laughing to herself. She smiled up at the depthless sky. "Me time," that's what she said. And it was a lie. Everyone she'd known, all the men, for sure, had left her alone with their absence when they weren't there. No matter what she told herself, she knew she'd always considered the absence of those men a gift. Not so with Shame. As it had been in Chicago, he got up and left out. The weeks he'd spent with the boats before she'd arrived and now, of course, arranged by her, Shame and Malik and Malik's partner were laying the groundwork for some kind of cooperative plan. Meanwhile, she woke feeling not Shame's absence but a clarity, an almost surgical emptiness, as if the gap he left open was a lens of focus. *My life, my life, my life, my life*, she hummed, *in the sunshine*. "My life as a room with no ceiling," she'd thought, as she drifted across the surface of the silent mirror in the sky. She'd float for a while, swim for twenty minutes, maybe do what she'd happened upon and then go down to Echoes and talk with Kate. Or maybe she'd look around for where Muhammad had parked his stand for the day and talk to him. Muhammad didn't seem to mind. And Ndiya loved to listen.

Sometimes she fucked the pulse of the water circulation jet, midway down the pool's length, before getting out of the water. Most days she'd float on her back until she began to feel as if she were high above the town in an invisible shaft of shadow in the light, a column of shade in the blinding glare. With her eyes closed, she stared up into the vertical space tracing the shaft of shadow-light as it stretched out of sight. Unconsciously at first, Ndiya began to float upward toward a bank of fog and static in her body that she couldn't see through. She'd drift across the surface of the pool until she found herself at the side near the circulation jet. She moved slightly if at all, breathed evenly. Afraid every time the pulse traveled through her. The fog and static appeared in her vision; shadowy figures moved about, came near the edge of her sight, and then returned to the depth of the static. She could feel other figures watching as if from inside her.

In her life she kept a border between herself and all of this, sensed it only as distant trains or heavy pendulums far away from her. She'd only approached the fog and static by accident when pleasure and fear or anger washed together. Shame was the only man who'd ever noticed any of this. And he was the only one who hadn't believed her lies about it. Still, he'd known not to press her about the truth. And then there she was. Aloft on her back, she stared into the shadowy figures who owned her clouded body. She climbed out of the water and reclined in a chair. She watched herself as if she was still up there, floating in an empty shaft high above the house. She remained passive. At least that's what she thought. And she didn't ask questions. And no, thinking certainly wasn't the word. Ndiya tried not to think at all in the pool. It was a place to move empty and weightless. It was a transparent place in which she approached the clouds in the nearing static, where she stirred shadow into light, where she measured the presence of thunder and the promise of lightning.

■

Two candles wavered on a long, blue wooden table. The polished surface of Goodman's concrete floor always looked wet. The shadow of a breeze pushed the light into pools on the paths between overhanging palms and vines. The heavy leaves scraped and bumped in the treetops above the walls. At night, every few minutes they heard what sounded like tablecloths taken up and flapped free of crumbs. Hawk-sized bats with light brown fur and black leather wings careened through the airspace of the main courtyard; they tucked wings and dove in to swoop-drink from the invisible surface of the narrow pool. Almost all of this mansion's rooms flirted with and then defied the idea that interior meant enclosed. Almost comically thick doors and labyrinthine moats of social structure buttressed these open interiors against the disease of danger in the streets. The openness was strictly vertical.

Before he left for the evening, Saidi had chilled a bottle of wine and a pitcher of lime-banana juice on the likely chance that Malik and his partner, a German architect named Norbert, would stop for a visit. Three grilled snappers lay on the concrete kitchen counter under banana leaves. It was Malik who had contacted Peter Goodman about Ndiya and Shame living in his vacant property for a minimal fee to be discussed later. Shame had been skeptical, saying it felt a little too familiar, but he went along.

The fevers and swelling had mostly passed. Shame's left arm stayed in its sling. As the shoreline of the fever receded, the low throb of pain had become a murmur beneath the blurred border between sleep and waking life.

A few weeks before, soon after Ndiya's arrival, Malik and Norbert had explained their renovation and reconstruction of Baytil Ajaib to her while they ate breakfast in an alcove off the towering canal of their mansion's central room. Baytil Ajaib had been a ruin. The two men had restored it into a modernized, traditional Swahili-style home and getaway for the discerning traveler. Norbert explained how they'd learned that modern materials such as plaster endangered the traditional architecture. Modern plaster, for instance, sealed the coral stone walls. They then retained heat and moisture and rapidly dissolved into sand from the inside. Malik said,

–You'd think all this stone makes for a fortress or a castle. But, honey, like everything else here, it may look solid, but it's actually more like gauze than stone. All these rooms are breathing, designed to remain cool in the heat. All around you here, what looks shut up is often wide open and what looks wide open, honey, it's usually slammed shut or half the time it's not there at all.

Malik laughed and leaned back in his chair. Norbert explained that he'd experimented with local lime and sand that needed to be sifted together and aged, effectively fermented, into a dry solution. Plaster made from that mixture preserved the deceptively light and porous coral stone blocks by allowing the changes in pressure and humidity to pass through. Properly arranged and cared for they could last for centuries, as they had. Malik said that he'd come to Lamu to retire. He'd made a good life in banking.

–Long story short—let me not paralyze you with boredom—I came down here to paint. To *enjoy* life.

After all the research and trial and error that went into restoring Baytil Ajaib, they decided on two things:

–One, what good is it to have all this figured out for our place when the rebuilt buildings all around crumble in ten years? And, two, you guessed it, girl, there's money to be made down here. A lot of it. The history here, the climate, the architecture is incredible—it shouldn't be allowed to disappear into the past.

Their trouble was finding, training, and retaining decent workers.

–Well, that's Norbert's trouble. I'm the *bank*, that's trouble enough in a Muslim culture. Hell, in any culture.

Ndiya made the connection immediately.

–So, Malik, how would you feel about an investor that handles the labor issues?

Without glancing at each other, Malik and Norbert leaned forward. Malik held Ndiya's eyes. Somehow he was nodding but his head wasn't moving. Ndiya had that feeling that Malik had been waiting for her, as if she'd just leapt into his outstretched arm. Then a wing passed in back of his eyes. She thought he'd blinked but he hadn't.

–Would you look at us? We can take this trivia up later, when we're all together. Nydia, my child, you know what you and your mister Shame-Shahid need to do?

–What's that?

–Take yourselves a sail. Charter a dhow. Go all the way to Kiwayu, near Somalia—a beautiful, sandy seal on a wide-open envelope. The place is borderless. Isn't that right, Norbert? You can't see where the sea stops and the sky begins. You feel like you don't know if you're lying still or gliding away. You all could use that.

Ndiya leaned back and it felt like she was nose to nose with Malik. She smiled and nodded at him openly, thinking, "That's the *last* thing in the world we need to do—"

The joint worked as a sleep aid if nothing else. It wasn't noise from the ancient train or daybreak that woke Shame. His mouth and throat were so dry it felt like his windpipe had swollen shut. Before he was actually awake, half able to breathe, he found the water bottle Sarah had sent with him and drank what remained. The compartment felt as if it had shrunk. It was the thick heat. After a moment he realized he was still en route to Mombasa. They'd left the high-country highlands with their wide fields and wispy acacias. They were now in the low, coastal region. The heavy sun already heating the roof of the train, he thought he could hear the groans of expanding metal added to the rhythm section of the orchestra under the car.

A porter knocked on his door, announcing breakfast. He thought again about calling Su and the dead phone battery. There was an outlet in the wall of the cabin but when he plugged in the phone nothing happened. He took the phone and charger with him to the dining car. A waiter met him at the entrance and took him to a table where he was seated across from a tall white man who was the only other solitary traveler eating. The man was red-faced and wore a thick shock of graying hair thrown back from his face as if he were riding a speeding motorcycle. When he sat the man greeted him in German, then in Kiswahili. Shame shook his head, "I'm sorry, I only speak English."

–Ah. Well, I knew you weren't a Brit, a KC.

–K-C?

–Kenyan cowboy, a British expat hanging onto whatever's left of his family's stolen land.

–No, I'm not that.

–Well, you're no tourist either.

–No. I'm a traveler.

–OK, traveler. I'm Gunther. Gunther Godar. I'm a painter and an activist.

–Really, an activist?

–Yes. In another life, I founded the Green Party in Germany. Now you could say that I have another agenda.

A wildness in Godar's eyes accompanied the velocity in his hair. His wet, reddened complexion seemed to radiate heat. The unbuttoned white shirt hung open down his chest. A tangle of braided and beaded strings dangled from his neck. He held his coffee in his right hand. A pair of thick silver rings stared across like a second pair of eyes. Shame nodded as Godar explained the crucial importance of his life and his work. He'd lived everywhere: India, California, Sri Lanka, Israel, South Africa. Now, he owned a compound he'd built on land south of Mombasa, in Diani, about two hundred meters from the beach. He was a filmmaker and a painter now. As he sat with his back to the motion of the train, Shame didn't catch everything Godar launched at him. As Godar stressed the intensity and importance of every single thing that crossed his mind, Shame felt like he was hurtling backward in a way the lackadaisical speed of the train couldn't account for. Godar's eyes squinted as he emphasized how backward local traditions treated girls and young women like prisoners. Sculptures and paintings, even independent films, could draw out the imprisoned energies of these women, free them from their bondage in villages and families. His latest revelation involved the infusion of tantric philosophies and practices into technical features of modern painting and sculpture. When Godar said the word "tantric," his eyes flung themselves, as if off a cliff, into the term.

Shame didn't know what "tantric philosophies and practices" were; he didn't really wonder about it. It all came at him too fast. He wondered about this feeling of being propelled backward in front of Godar's zealotry and concluded that "tantric" must have something to do with spiders. He remembered his old roommate and felt like he knew what Godar meant. He smiled and nodded. The waiter brought muffins, poached eggs, jelly, and something he called "upcountry sausages" that Godar recommended very highly.

Looking around for an outlet, he saw only one. Placed on a ledge above the doorway into the car, a phone was already plugged into it. Godar said that they had less than an hour before arriving in Mombasa. He called Mombasa "the island." Shame ate the eggs and sipped coffee that was thinner and cooler than the air that came through the window and caught in Godar's open shirt. He noticed that the upcountry sausages were the same color as Godar's face and neck. He felt slightly nauseated by the impression that the smell of the sausages was actually coming from Godar like some kind of tantric funk.

He rose to leave as Godar's unilateral stream of conversation arrived at the insistence that Shame be his guest at the compound. He got up with Shame and made him come to his compartment so they could exchange addresses or at least phone numbers.

When Shame returned to his berth he tried the outlet again. Nothing. He could feel sweat under his shirt so he took off his shoes and jammed one under the door to keep it from sliding shut. The new airflow made the heat worse, the space felt like a convection oven. He'd have to find an outlet at the station. The train slowed and curved through hills covered with hundreds of shanties and what looked like small mountainsides of trash. People and a few goats were walking the slope nearest the train. All morning barefoot children had run out of huts and rural compounds and sisal fields and down paths to stand near the tracks. As the train passed them by, they'd cease running and stand bolt upright, smiling and waving. Some suddenly froze in place and saluted military style. Now Shame began to smell the charcoal and diesel smells that had greeted him along the airport road in Nairobi. The groups of shanties grew more frequent, much larger. The space between dwellings collapsed until there was no visible pause between the rusted corrugated rooftops. There were lagoons between them. Some of the settlements were on stilts over the water.

Finally, the train slowed to a crawl and passed very close to a huge mass of dwellings amid ground dotted with ponds and puddles. Up ahead, a few dozen children were lined up next to the tracks. Shame watched them grow nearer. They stood in rows by height as if assembled for a class photo. The littlest ones stood in front. One he glimpsed wore a torn plastic shopping bag as a shirt, its handles looped over the sharp curves of his shoulders. They smiled and waved. Shame noticed an older boy near the back. He wore a red top with long sleeves, white stripes down the arms and an insignia of some kind over his heart. He had zipped the warm-up jacket all the way. The collar stood up straight, rising to meet his chin. He smiled and waved too. As the train drew past, the older boy raised his right hand up under his chin and, with thumb extended and still brightly smiling, he nodded and drew his thumb across in the throat-cutting gesture. Then he pointed at the train, nodding his head gently, smiling, and repeated his imitation execution.

A distant flame behind the boy's face collided with Kima's playful voice in Shame's memory: "The train's a colonial relic." The relic bit was obvious enough. But Shame hadn't really considered the colonial part until just now. This thought made the young man's gesture into a forecast, or a confession, more than an imitation. At the table, Shame had decided spontaneously not to tell Godar anything about why he was there and who he was. He thought about that and he thought he could feel his throat swell. Godar's torrential, tantric self-absorption had allowed him little chance and even less call to really introduce himself. But that wasn't all of it.

Ndiya was off-limits in his mind. The distant bells in Sarah's levitating softness were shooting stars, at best. The tall boy's stance, the chilled flame behind his eyes, and the pleasure he took in his calm gesture of vengeance felt like a current in Shame's body. He shivered slightly, and a brassy taste filled his mouth. It wasn't fear. It looked to him like what hope felt like. He felt another chill, though he knew very well he was hot. He thought maybe terror was what it felt like to stare coldly, irretrievably, as one's own eyes stared back from someone else's face. Who, Shame wondered, he or the boy, had been doing that just then?

Ndiya thought she knew all about pain beach. But Kate's approach to eye makeup highlighted another dimension entirely. A thoroughly elegant person, Kate wore a wide-brimmed, floppy black hat and a loose blue caftan, "Adire," she'd said, hand-dyed with Yorùbá indigo by a collective of women outside Oshogbo. She owned Echoes and half of Buraka, the art gallery next door that dealt in imported fine arts from across the continent.

Dusk was falling. Shame hadn't returned from wherever he'd gone to work. Usually, when he did return early he'd eat something and sleep for three hours. She left Shame's room just as Muhammad was unlocking his cart at the front of the neighboring building.

–You off?

–Sha—Shahid, is late. I'm going to walk to Echoes.

–Let me guess, mango sorbet.

–I'm beginning to think it's laced with something, hard stuff.

Ndiya smiled and looked away.

–You want to come?

–No, no. I have to wash off the day's dust. I'll be up very early tomorrow. A large tour group of Italians is due to arrive in Shela. I must be there to offer them authentic coastal barbeque. You know they don't come all the way here to eat linguini.

–You sure?

–Yes. Plus, old Kate gives me the shivers. There was a woman where I lived as a child in Nigeria, a famous artist. They called her Iwinfunke, Adunni Olorisa. Her name was really Wenger. Austrian, I think. The woman was certified . . . well, she was magical. The real thing, an Austrian Yorùbá priestess! She gave me many, many nightmares. She spoke to the red earth. A magic woman whose skin had been peeled off, leaving her the color of worms you find under stones. Kate could be her daughter, or sister. No, no. Too many echoes at Echoes for me, my sister.

–Why did they call her that, Iwinfunke?

–I don't know. We moved from there before my father ceased coming home from work. When the country's highways replaced his rivers. If I see Sh— *Shay-em*—You know I'm not a local, woman, *I* can say the man's name. I'll tell him where you've gone as if he'd have to wonder. And, say, what about *your* name? A white woman with an African name?

Ndiya smiled and looked down at herself. She rubbed her right forearm with two fingers of her left hand.

–I'm not white!

–OK, an *American* woman. *Black* American.

Muhammad considered for a moment, again, Americans and their fanatical insistence on such strange little distinctions between them. So like the British in that way, he thought. He hadn't met many Americans. The few he had met spoke so similarly that he couldn't tell them apart. Ndiya said,

—I don't know. You'd have to ask my parents. I used to think it was because it was the '60s, a fashion.

Muhammad nodded. Ndiya continued,

—Black pride. But now I can imagine. Look, you know, my mother's last name was Monroe. My father's was Grayson.

—Colonial names. Yes, I understand. Many Nigerians have them . . .

—No, Muhammad, not colonial names. Owners' names and that's all they knew. It's all anybody knew. For ten, twelve generations. Think about that. Hell, they were almost brand names.

As obvious as this was, Muhammad considered that he'd never really thought about it. He'd never actually gotten to know a "black American" anyway. To emphasize her point, Ndiya placed her forearm up next to Muhammad's.

—These are also *family* names, Muhammad. So, you know, somewhere in the South, the American South, there are counties full of blonde Jenny-Mae Monroes and Miss Ann Graysons running around. My cousins! Now I can see that names like mine had nothing to do with pride, or maybe it is pride. Either way, I think my parents and that generation simply didn't want us mixed up with them in whatever future they imagined was on its way. *After* the revolution.

—Ha. I see. You, Americans. *All* your names should be *Shay-em*.

Ndiya nodded and smiled. She wasn't going to accept nor contest the point. She'd think about it, maybe. From around the corner came the sound of drums and a crowd of children. Irregular rhythms. The sound was moving fast and getting closer. Then six small children wearing all white ran past. With ropes looped in their hands, they dragged empty, bright plastic water containers behind them on the ground. One little boy stopped, addressed Muhammad as mzee, and announced something else to him in Kiswahili. Muhammad replied, "Nzuri, nzuri sana, sana," and bowed slightly, placing his right hand on his chest. The little boy laughed and darted off to catch up with the receding sound of the water-container drums. Ndiya stepped off the large stone she'd perched on to talk with Muhammad and started down the hill into the maze of passageways that led to the water. She turned and waved to Muhammad who waved back.

"Mzee" was one of the few Kiswahili words she knew. It was the first she'd learned. It meant "sir." And she'd caught it in all manner of exchanges between men and boys. She thought to herself, *there*'s a name for an American. A *girl*. "Nzuri" she'd known. She didn't know exactly what it meant, but she didn't need to know. It was also a brand name for a line of hair products, so she figured she could pretty much guess what it meant.

At Echoes Café, the light failed in the courtyard long before darkness fell outside. The high coral walls and the huge palm that provided shade during the day sifted dark from dusk in the early evening. Kate was distracted by an exhibit of paintings she was installing in a new venue she'd opened up on the waterfront. After a few obligatory questions, she kissed Ndiya's cheeks and exited through a small doorway in the rear wall of the courtyard.

Ndiya's glowing flute of mango sorbet arrived and she took small scoops with a long-handled spoon carved from ebony. There was a large group at the oval glass table over her left shoulder. She'd noticed them when she entered because of the mix of people sitting together. There was an Asian woman—Chinese, Ndiya thought—and a black woman—likely British by way of the Caribbean, she guessed. She took the two men in jackets to be the husbands of the women. The man in matching, all-white kanzu and kofia with red embroidery was obviously local.

The local man didn't sit there like a guide, however, and the group didn't broadcast the manic affect of tourists at all; they talked quietly among themselves, an audible word punctuated here and there, and laughter rose and fell from their table in a regular, unforced rhythm. Something was very attractive about the table behind her. It wasn't the people, exactly, but a slow-swept effortlessness in the pleasure they took from each other. They seemed to be having a great time together but unlike the groups of people she was used to, they weren't advertising it. These people weren't devoting most of their energy to confirming how much fun they were having; this had left some energy, she thought, for actual fun. Ndiya didn't really know why she thought this. Maybe she didn't. But she felt it. She sat searching for a word for the feeling radiating from the table at her back. "Fun" wasn't the word at all.

It was already dark. Now the air cooled into night. Ndiya thought about getting a book from inside and reading before it became too dark. Certain phrases from the conversation felt like a breeze on the back of her neck.

The voices moved like candles. She thought she'd heard an exchange in French but she couldn't tell. Then a clear word punctuated the air, "Dialectics!" followed by a round of laughter. At this she turned around to look. The black woman had made the exasperated proclamation. Her arms were raised. She held her fluted glass of juice high in her right hand. The older, local man in white was laughing openly. His eyes seemed lighted by the voices around him. Just then he caught Ndiya's eyes and nodded, tipping a glowing glass in her direction. Ndiya smiled back and raised her spoon in return. She turned around and went back to concentrating her full attention on the silken texture of the sorbet and the proliferating limitations of her vocabulary while the voices traveled the courtyard like invisible firelight. Maybe the word for what was going on behind her wasn't "fun" but "flame," she thought. Contrasting the occasional cooling phrases, it felt like sitting with her back to a distant fireplace.

Ndiya was reluctantly finishing her beloved mango smoothness, she could feel the what-am-I-doing-here pulse knocking on the door behind her right ear. She wasn't answering. Instead she flipped a coin that kept defying the odds and landing, again and again, on the same side: heads said, "You're exactly where you need to be." She wasn't stressing it. Yet. The game was fixed; tails said, "You're exactly where you've always been." "Be happy to be back," she thought. "Happy?" she wondered, and then, "Back?" "Fun?" "Flame?" None of the words came anywhere near her.

When she walked through the narrow alleys of Lamu

Town she heard loud whispers of women over the cries of babies from inside ground-floor windows. Small squalls of waist-high children blew past her on both sides, separating around her at the last moment like schools of fish. Men in twos and threes sat on the cement benches inside doorways, caps pushed back, talking like men talk. The sky hung down as if something heavy had taken a seat in the apartment above the strained celestial ceiling. She could feel the streams of smoke-scented air moving through the alleys. The air was somehow densely public, she felt, almost heavy enough to swim through. In a certain way, she thought, one *could* easily drown in this air. She thought back to how she'd felt on her soaking walk to Shame's apartment the first time she'd come there by herself, on that singular evening of twilight. That distant planet. "Distant?" Behind that was the elastic familiarity, inside that the family she'd walled herself away from.

Ndiya sat at Echoes with her last bite of sorbet. The radical differences here made it clear that it was all the same to her. She knew it all. She understood nothing she heard; she never had. The opacity of the language around her, here in Lamu, felt familiar rather than strange. It was a strangeness that drew her closer to what she saw, smelled, and felt. She sat there and retraced her route from Shame's room to where she was. "Which room?" she wondered for an instant's dim glow. The amber light at Echoes matched exactly the glow from the strange tubes in Shame's antique stereo. The spaces of her life floated around her: Shame's bed suspended in the defunct elevator shaft at 6329; his nearly empty, cell-like room across from Muhammad's place, just up the hill. It was all one room, in a way. She knew that. And she knew it wasn't. And she knew she didn't. She smiled to herself and rubbed her hands loosely up and down her thighs. Then a surprise:

–*Comment allez-vous, mademoiselle?*

–*Non, désolée,* ah—I mean, sorry, I'm American.

The local man in the white kofia dipped his head and looked at her over his glasses.

–Child, you *are* American, aren't you. Me *too!*

Then, glancing playfully over his shoulder:

–We had a bet. Yvonne said you were American. I said you were French, by way of Cameroon, maybe Gabon, certainly not Senegal! And here you are. Still, we might *both* be right.

He then leaned down and took Ndiya's hand in his, flicking his other wrist as if to erase the space between the obvious and the incredible. Then he put his other hand on top of hers.

–Malik Weaver, né Daytona Beach, Florida, circa nineteen something-we-don't-have-to-talk-about.

He kissed her hand.

–Malik, that's my brother's name. I'm Ndiya Grayson. I'm from Chicago.

–Naturally, Ndiya Grayson. *Naturally.*

Malik laughed, frowning.

–'Vonne honey, you win. This child's from *Chicago.* Well, you must come visit with us at Baytil Ajaib. We're going there now.

–Oh?

–It's where I live. It's also a hotel.

–Oh, no. I have a place—

–Just a visit, Ndiya-Grayson-from-Chicago. Have a drink with, well, with *them* . . .

–I can't tonight. Maybe another time.

–Well, certainly. How long will you be with us in paradise?

–We plan to stay a while . . .

–Ah, "we"? . . . so, you *will* have to visit us. Please do. Here's a card. Just ask for directions to Baytil Ajaib. The name's on the card.

–Ask who?

He looked down at her in mock surprise and theatrical annoyance.

–This is Lamu, child. Ask anybody.

Malik kissed her hand again. Then he reached out and, frowning, he cupped her hand in both his hands.

–No worry no, child. We all got here *some* way; we're all leaving here the *same* way. Unlike our criminally innocent and terminally adolescent confreres and *soeurs* yonder ways back home, folks here have learned that a long, long, long time ago.

He walked over and put his arm around Yvonne's shoulder. Yvonne began to casually walk with Malik out of the courtyard. She reached up to her shoulder and took Malik's hand. She glanced back at Ndiya. Just then Malik said something in French and Yvonne laughed. Her eyes brightened, focused on Ndiya, until the thick beam of the doorframe drew its eclipse across her face.

Muhammad's place was three times the size of Shame's. Three rooms. He used the flat roof outside his window as an outdoor kitchen. A butcher block stood at one end. A small refrigerator hummed low in the corner of his living space, which was furnished with nothing but woven mats, layered one on top of another, and thick pillows. A clear plastic sack filled with water hung from a single strand of fishing line in the center of each window. Like all the windows she'd seen here, none had glass or screens. The oblong shapes spun slowly, waved in the breeze, and cast huge, gauzy shadows on the opposite walls.

Ndiya ran into Muhammad one day on her way, lost, as usual, back up from the waterfront. In Lamu, she'd accepted that getting lost was basically the only way to find anything or get anywhere, there being largely nothing to find and, most often, really, nowhere to go. In order to find something, or someone, she had to find, or to actually get anywhere she really *had* to go, she had to ask. She hadn't met Malik and Yvonne yet. So she hadn't yet glimpsed the magnitude of what such chance encounters could mean. When she did she found that, in Lamu, one's will was interactive, even the most singular happening was a plural thing, if not a cosmos.

As she walked, the sky above the erratic alley she was following had suddenly gone dark. The sound of winds approached and she could smell the fragrant dust of a heavy rain gathering nearby. The alley led waveringly across town, she thought, about halfway up the hill from the waterfront. It jogged upward then downward every fifty meters, taking its course between ruins, vacant lots where roosters and hens picked in the scrub, and buildings strung with laundry. On one line, a row of black robes and sheets of sheer black fabric. On the next, floral dresses and blouses, the likes of which *never* appeared in the streets. She turned, yet again, this time uphill, and found herself face to face with Muhammad wheeling his cart in the opposite direction.

–I left the dock early, the afternoon Fly540 from Nairobi was canceled. Where are you going?

–Ah, home, I think.

–Come. It will rain soon. I'll make you a tea. It's *this* way.

Muhammad led Ndiya back the way she'd come, around the corner and through a low archway. They turned right and she found herself in yet another small, unfamiliar square. There were hundreds of these squares created by the junction of three or more alleys and, at times, by a vacancy created at the site of a ruin. All of these squares were unique, irregular shapes, different colors in the windows and walls, graffiti scrawled or stenciled here or there. Even the smells and sounds were distinct: curry, fresh fish, freshly shaved wood from a shop, dry flame of a welder, dye from cloth drying, the insect buzz of a barber, various attempts at wash water and sewage drainage. The donkeys were a constant. Despite the endless variation, all the different squares looked exactly the same to her. She couldn't tell them apart at all. The fact that they were all different made them identical to her eyes.

The two stopped walking. Ndiya stood staring at Muhammad until he smiled in playful weariness and pointed behind her. When she turned around she was six feet from the dull yellow benches in front of Muhammad's building, fifteen feet from the door to Shame's building where she'd been staying for two weeks. Suddenly she wondered if she *had* recognized the scene, as if she'd already passed by here, maybe several times, looking for this exact spot along one or another of the intersecting alleys. Muhammad parked his cart along the side of the building and chained it to a thick drainpipe coming down from the roof. He looked up at her.

–This may be Lamu, but I'm Nigerian.

He took her hand and led her up the stairs to the third floor. He undid the padlock on his door and locked it on an iron loop beside the latch. Years of motion from locks hanging from that loop had worn the wood away in a deep arc. The door was fastened at the top and bottom in large wooden hinges. It cast open silently and the fresh breeze began to flow into the hallway. Compared to Shame's closed fist of a room, everything about Muhammad's place seemed wide open. He piled three large cushions in a corner of the room beneath a window and gestured welcome.

–I'll wash, pray, and then I'll make the tea. It won't take long.

–I didn't know you practiced, Muhammad.

–To call it practicing is about it, I'm afraid. I go to mosque on Fridays for appearances, for business really. One simply must do that.

–That covers it?

–No, but it has its role. If I want to stay here, I'd have to marry into a family eventually. But the mosque makes me a visible, if not a known, quantity. Otherwise, really, no one sees you at all.

–I see.

–Right. Or you don't. And that vision hasn't really all that much to do with the eyes. That's how it works here. The visible in a losing battle with invisible structures of appearance.

–You're Hausa? That's usually Muslim, right?

–Yes, yes, of course. But my family was mixed. My father was a Fulani. His family were river people. He was a boat captain. My mother was Hausa, but she was a renegade. An American might call her a hippie, how do they say, a flower child. I was too young to understand any of this in the '70s, but the world of rivers and river traffic in the North of Nigeria was changing. Drying up. The mode of a modern nation was to be roads, not rivers. And Islam in the Sahel had been fluid and tolerant. My parents were Muslims, both, but they were unconcerned with dogma. They'd married across race. At the time that wasn't promoted nor was it prevented. Their lives hadn't been defined by Biafra and all that shit as had been the case in the South.

As she listened, Ndiya felt like she was being pulled into a narrowing alleyway. Muhammad went ahead.

–My mother considered herself an artist, beyond tribe. We moved to the Southwest, Yorubaland. My father had found work as a truck driver. The government had gone highway-mad, he said. It was, he said, as if they're paving new rivers every week. We lived in Oshogbo first, on the edge of a revival of traditional arts, sculpture, and painting: a women's movement to reclaim feminine powers and spirituality. My father lived on the asphalt rivers, returning home weekly, at first, then monthly after a year or so, and then not much of ever after that. My older brother was in university in Ibadan when the generals claimed the government, took over the rather low-flying, tenuous national design, or fraud, and crashed it all into the ground.

Ndiya fought the urge to stop him. She followed as the alleyway of Muhammad's story continued to close in on them both.

–In my mind, my brother was killed in the crash of the state. In truth it was a cholera outbreak in his dormitory. The university administration called it an accident, pointing to vengeful gods and even to sorcery and wizardry in the faculty. The students went on strike. But, of course, a strike ultimately depends upon the strength of the opponent. The controlling force must be strong. Otherwise there's nothing to strike against. The universities, like the failing banks, had no force. In fact there was nothing to strike against. The way it turned out, from my teenage perspective, it looked like the students, the living no more than the dead like my brother, weren't necessary parts of a university. Or the nation. One didn't need students, even less citizens. All they needed were bodies and there was an endless supply of those for whom things like cholera, to say nothing of sorcery, were simply facts of life. And death.

Muhammad stood in front of Ndiya who sat along the wall leaning on a huge green pillow embroidered with gold threads and glass beads. He mostly looked out the window, as if he wasn't speaking to her. She noticed, very, very far away, a familiar pendulum swinging in a long arc. It seemed to swing away from her in both directions. She let it be.

Muhammad continued. His voice sprawled over a melody, pushing the beginning and end of each sentence up, the tone of his voice deepening in the middle of phrases. Ndiya felt like kissing him, though the desire wasn't, she felt, sexual in the least. It wasn't him. She felt like kissing his life, the story he was telling her, as much for the texture of the air it created, as he stood before her in this strangely open room, as for whatever he was describing. He wasn't saying much and, at the same time, what he did say—maybe how he said it—felt like it stole them off somewhere together, never to be found again. Since they'd met, Shame was constantly delivering her to people like this. And then, somehow, he'd always be elsewhere while *she* dealt with them. And soon after they appeared, something else came along to subtract *her* from their—or them from her—company. Muhammad continued,

–My brother died when I was fourteen. My mother kept my father alive in my mind by constantly bringing him up and, here and there, by showing me money he sent to her via courier. I remember how she held it up in her hand as if it was a procedural exhibit in an official case of some sort. It looked like a lot but the currency was collapsed, the money wasn't worth anything. I was a kid. It meant nothing to me. My brother was gone. My father's presence had been filmy at best. He'd kept on as a driver but, as far as I could tell, had become a money changer, a business run mostly by Hausas and totally by the small minority of Muslims in the Southwest during that period of national collapse. Maybe my father was passing as his wife's husband, if not her brother. To me, he'd never done much toward passing as my father. And I'd grown up without much sense of needing one.

Ndiya leaned back and looked up through the window at the sky tumbling toward the darkness to her left. Muhammad was right. It would rain soon. Notches of stone showed through in the deep window frame where the plaster had been chipped away. The inverted image of her body floated above her, splayed across the plastic skin of the sack in the window. Muhammad continued talking. She noticed her reflected legs, bent into a mermaid shape. They flipped like a tail underwater when she uncrossed and then re-crossed them. She felt like she was sinking into the padding of mats underneath the cushions. Then she interrupted him.

–This all sounds familiar enough to me, Muhammad. Let me guess: She threw herself into a life in the church? Or did she stay with the women's collective or whatever it was? Very familiar, to me. My experience is that women, especially women with children, who've been through hell, often fall into a cloud of other women who are, often enough, in orbit around a strong but in some way off-limits man of some kind. A preacher . . . or something like a preacher.

Muhammad continued to look out the window. His mouth smiled but the rest of his face didn't move. He tried to picture Ndiya's face without looking back at her. What did the woman who'd just spoken look like? He wondered exactly what kind of pain she'd just fumbled into the lives of women she imagined. He knew there was no question of asking. Ndiya felt cool. A bead of sweat dropped along the underside of the arm that propped her upright. She watched Muhammad's faraway eyes. "He's exactly like everyone else Shame ever met," she thought. "He's always elsewhere." Then Muhammad turned to her, rolled his neck. "Familiar," he whispered, and shook his head. When she looked up at him his eyes were waiting for her. His thumbs rubbed his index and middle fingers in the universal money-motion.

–You didn't hear it from *Shay-em* because I have told him none of these things. Unless my mother published her memoirs, it must *be* familiar. OK. I'll wash, pray, and then tea for two—

When Muhammad said "familiar," Ndiya heard "fa-milia." This made her smile and think of Arturo, all those impossible galaxies away, his wide, open face and the impenetrable dignity of his safely and utterly closed mind. This made her wince and smile. Muhammad walked across the room to a low shelf. Three books lay on the shelf horizontally, next to a pack of incense sticks bound with twine, and a few small, ceramic containers. He crouched down and took out the middle book. Ndiya wondered if it was his Koran. He removed a thin, pink paper pamphlet from the book and put the book back where it was. Rising, he took a small, lidded container from the shelf as well. She watched the mats give under his bare feet as he approached. It seemed just then that he traversed a distance far greater than the room allowed. He bent down, extended both hands and handed her the small jar.

−My mother's mother: this is sand from the Osun riverbank. Taken from the temple my mother helped build before my brother died. It wasn't enough, I guess. When I was fourteen, after his death, we moved to Ibadan to live; as you say, to live with the father my mother had found for my lost brother. Though he wasn't a preacher. He was a guru. Is this familiar?

Ndiya searched Muhammad's face for anger or irony, at least an angle. But she found none of that. He just handed her the pamphlet and walked into the next room. That was actually all he did: these acts were only themselves; they were gestures utterly without affect. Ndiya heard the water tap in the next room open and splash on the floor. Beneath the sound of the water she heard Muhammad's voice, no words. He was humming a song or maybe he was crying? She couldn't tell. She opened the small jar and found coarse grains of sand with green flecks, dried bits of leaves she thought, mixed with the sand. The pink booklet was a song book: "The Divine Song of Creation" by One Love Family. On the cover it read: "For total spiritual liberation and to prevent end-of-century Global De-ecology. To be sung at schools, colleges, universities, and homes in the Holyland, and the universe." She turned the booklet over and, centered on the back, it read:

The Highest Spiritual Center
Of the Universe
KM 10 Ibadan – Lagos Expressway
PO Box 16741, Dugbe
Ibadan, Nigeria
The New Holy Land of the Universe

In the pamphlet she found two folded fliers printed on newsprint paper that was so thin Ndiya worried that the pages would come apart in her hands. The edges were tattered, and tiny insects, she guessed, had made a series of holes in the paper. On the cover of one was an oval portrait of a black man with a thick beard. He wore a look of insistent, somewhat impatient, concern in his eyes; it was the theatrical look a parent uses to say, "You haven't finished your dinner." He also wore a turban and a garland of flowers around his neck. Under the portrait it read:

SATGURU MAHARAJ JI
The Saving Grace Across Year 2000
I am the one who vibrated the whole creation including your very self, taking the nucleus first body, Adam, and changing bodies to save humanity in every age.

Ndiya felt a tenderness toward these thin pages which Muhammad had carefully transported with him. The booklets had been protected but, in a way, not preserved. The partial care hinted at a hope that the power represented by the artifacts, whatever that power was, would be allowed to decay without being betrayed or abandoned. This made her feel as though she had no right to hurry the disintegration, so she took extra care opening the pages. At the same time, she had the sensation of surveying a disaster of some unfathomable depth and scope, a disaster one couldn't escape. One had to let it leave, if it would, on its own. The distant pendulum appeared to her again. She checked her mermaid image hanging from an invisible line in the plastic orb above her head. Suddenly she felt like she was floating in a shaft of shadow and light high above the town. To dispel the feeling, she focused on the pamphlet.

Inside the cover she read a two-page series of exhortations and revelations. They informed that, through the energy of Maharaj Ji, one may:

> Realize yourself, the Grace to re-incarnate and be free from religious manipulation, racism, slavery, tribalism, illness and untimely death. You will become producer instead of consumer.

> It is thus that you will know that all the things you are buying for your comfort like television, radio, cars were originally made here but Satanic forces of Europe stole them, from Africa, forced those geniuses to teach the oyinbos. After teaching them, they destroyed all traces that could link

such high consciousness with the nucleus culture till I came to rescue you.

So, be wise, for a stitch in time saves nine. Many of those who were used by the official Euro-American government-sponsored CIA to mount false propaganda against the people have almost succeeded in ruining the political, economic and social life of this nation and continent judging by the ignorant obsession they have and buffoonery attachment to the scriptures that are part of the colonization of Africa and the world that have denied these blessed people the only chance out of hell.

On the back page of the first flyer it read:

HOW TO USE THE HOLY NAME GURU MAHARAJ JI

To communicate with Maharaj Ji, sit with legs crossed (on lotus), concentrate on your inner self and call Guru Maharaj Ji many times. It has been proved beyond all reasonable doubts that meditating on lotus feet enables one to be taken beyond the forces of darkness.

So next time you have a headache, or any other ailment, call Guru Maharaj Ji seven times into a glass of water and drink it. To kill a witch or dispel any devil from haunting you in sleep, call Maharaj Ji 25 times before going to bed. No one

can block your safety on land, sea and air is 100%
by remembering Maharaj Ji. Try him now. All
it costs you is a discount price of unconditional
Love.

Ndiya looked up from the impossibly thin paper of the
pamphlets. The rain outside had stopped just, it seemed,
when the splashing water in the next room ceased. She
could hear Muhammad humming under his breath. If
he'd been crying, that too had ceased. None of the arched
doorways between the rooms, in fact, had doors. Then she
noticed something different about the air in Muhammad's
place. She thought, at first, it was the rain outside, or perhaps it was the extra rooms that circulated the air. The sun
shone again and the ghostly, oblong shadows of the sacks
in the windows reappeared on the walls. Ndiya couldn't
decide what gave the air in Muhammad's place its strange
quality of openness.

She took out the second newsprint flyer. It seemed
to pick up where the first left off. The cover featured a
cartoon version of the bearded man suspended in an orb
as if he was the sun. From his outstretched hand emerged
lines of energy that fell upon the up-reaching hands of six
beckoning followers. The message read:

By Maharaj Ji's Grace Nigeria is
The New Holy Land Today

At the bottom of the page read the same address
on the Ibadan-Lagos Expressway. Inside, a small tract

explained that all world holy lands were holy only when the spiritual leader, "the source," was "physically there becoming the center or nucleus of the entire universe." The energy emits only from "the God Father Power or the Living Perfect Master of the time and is never a historical matter." Previous holy lands such as "Palestine, Saudi Arabia, Iran-Iraq, Indian, etc." are now "mere historical artifacts, dead monuments . . . instead of receiving real peace of mind, security and the life guarantee, all forms of darkness are found there." Bereft of "the source," "they always resort to arms and other artificial means to maintain their status quo illusively."

Ndiya didn't feel at all ironic about what she was reading. The description was certainly absurd if not insane but at the same time, the prose and graphics and the frailty of the document and Muhammad's brief story of his family and, yes, even the radical insanity of the message itself, it all testified to something that she sensed couldn't be dismissed. It was a disaster. Compared to what? She thought of their mothers, fathers, brothers. Family. She remembered Muhammad telling her: "If you're not part of a family, you're a ghost." Then she thought about listening to "Free," and her maps of the Great Lakes, and felt sweat gathering on her forehead. She remembered that Shame had played the song for her, out of nowhere, before going to the shower on one of those first nights. The sequence of nights was a little blurry in her memory now, but the sound of her life in that song when she heard it in his apartment was very clear to her. Or maybe she was clear to it? She felt a clarity—something that must be called sacred, she thought—absolutely sealed in absurdity floating just above her head.

She closed her eyes and leaned back. She had the sensation someone was sitting behind her. It was a woman behind her. She felt the woman's thin arms reach to embrace her. The woman was weeping in silence. She opened her eyes and the weeping woman vanished. Just then she realized what was missing from Muhammad's room, what was different about the air there. The room had no flies. Flies were everywhere in Lamu. But she'd been sitting there all this time and not one fly had landed on her. The effect was lightness or emptiness, an open stillness that made it seem as if the air was missing a molecule, an irritant.

The rest of the second pamphlet provided "a simple list of tangible advantages Nigerians are graced to enjoy and enjoying first and foremost for those who had already taken a step; so rise up and partake of this manna now also." The "advantages" were enumerated one through eighteen. Ndiya skimmed down the list:

1. You can stop any danger, threat or enemy from your home, office or area without any external support.

2. You can talk or communicate with all the Ascended Masters: Buddah, Ram, Krishna, Laoci, Moses, Orunmila, Elijah, John the Baptist, Mohammad, Jesus the Christ, Oduduwa, Kofi Manu, etc. . . . through the New Holy Name— Satguru Maharaj Ji.

4. You can communicate with your dead ones without fear for a Divine solution to your or theirs when alive that otherwise seemed impossible.

6. You can know the true spirit of your wife, husband, children and relatives and effect a Divine change for them when necessary.

7. You can develop technology without importation and colonial brain drain, using locally sourced materials.

9. You can stop death in your home, on land, sea and air which is 100% guaranteed.

10. You are protected from the predicted cataclysm of Armageddon and Nostradamus.

11. You are shielded from all radioactive fallouts that are plaguing and dehumanizing the current world.

13. You will know that black is not devil but purity, red is love, blue is danger, green is fertility, yellow is wisdom and white is peace.

16. You don't need to achieve your life goals, purpose and your God through tutered monographs, pentagraphs, candles, holy water, sutana, etc. from abroad. Everything is now, direct and immediate.

At the bottom of the back page: "For power against all principalities and the secret to develop science and technology from within you,"

Talk to Satguru Maharaj Ji on the following hotlines:

and a list of eight numbers followed.

A gurgling sound came from the other room. It gained force and then gradually gave way to a rising whistle broken by a dozen or so sharp cracks. After a short pause of silence filled with faint clicks and scrapes of barely audible culinary efficiency, Muhammad entered the room with a board on which he'd arranged two steaming cups and two plates of chopped mango, pineapple, and banana.

–Sorry-o, I have no crisps.

–I didn't know you were doing all this. I'd have helped.

–It's no trouble.

Muhammad gathered a pillow under his knees and sat cross-legged. He wore a long white caftan. Up one sleeve and down the full length of one side were medical insignia and the words IMAGEFIRST MEDICAL WEAR.

–Ah. Spoons. I'll be right back.

Before Ndiya could say no, he was up. As if pulled up like a puppet on a string, Muhammad rose from his cross-legged position without touching his hands to the ground. He passed in front of the window at the far end of the room. The cloth of his robe was thin, almost a fine mesh or gauze. Backlit when he passed by the window, the outline of his wiry body stood forth like a negative of a negative. Across his back was a script in blue. Ndiya focused on the words: ANGELICA HEALTH CARE: RENTED NEVER SOLD. She smiled and shook her head. Thinking that this was when she should wonder where Shame was, she improvised on the code of Muhammad's gown: "Borrowed never begged." Or "Found not stolen." Muhammad returned with spoons and a few wispy coils of grilled meat, which he unwrapped from a grease-spotted twist of newspaper.

–So. What do you think of the Maharaj Ji Village World Headquarters?

–Well, they've certainly covered the bases, haven't they?

She paused, wondering if that was offensive. She could feel a hard edge in her voice. Beyond that edge, she knew, lurked something she and Muhammad shared. The heavy pendulum arced closely behind her. Where she felt the word "shared" she heard the word "danger." She hoped he'd sense the possibility that the distance in her voice was a pose. She hoped he'd leave that possibility alone. "Familia, indeed," she thought.

–The place was perfect for my mother, I think. It made her life, her body, into a vast maze in which she could never be found. We lived there together for almost two years.

–Then what?

–Then I hopped behind a tarp on a delivery truck and set off. I was sixteen. I don't know if I knew, nor if I cared, at that time, whether I was seeking a way out of her impossible maze or a way into my own.

After chewing on a few seemingly indestructible bits of the meat for long enough to wonder whether she'd be able to swallow them, Ndiya felt flushed. Her mouth began to throb. Her nose began to run and she thought she could hear her own pulse clicking behind her right ear.

–It's hot for you? Drink the tea, it will go away-o.

The tea was also spiced and just below boiling. She took a breathy sip and for a prolonged second it felt like her mouth had burst into flame. She couldn't taste the tea and it felt more like blinding light in her mouth than heat. In a flash the bright blast disappeared and the pain was gone. She could still feel the pulse in her tongue.

–Now, have some banana.

After the complex logistics of dealing with two small bits of suya, and while watching as Muhammad chewed thick ribbons of the meat and slurped scalding tea, Ndiya didn't know what to say. The bites of banana were also tasteless but produced a most incredible sensation of low-current electricity in her mouth. It reminded her of putting her tongue on the top of a nine-volt battery she'd taken from her brothers' racing car as a child. There was a smooth texture, which she assumed was the banana, and there was an electric current spreading around her mouth. She suddenly wondered if she could talk.

–Muhammad, what are the bags filled with?

–Those? Just water. But it must be fresh, clear water. I change it weekly.

–What for?

–The clear water in the plastic scares the flies away. They won't pass near them. They see their reflection but enlarged. Imagine. As a fly sees: about sixty huge beasts in every window. Flies don't know what they look like.

–What about at night?

–It works at night too.

–How?

–I don't know.

–Do you think you'll ever go back? I mean to see your mother?

–No. Most likely not.

–Why not?

–She died in the maze. Four years ago.

Ndiya stared at Muhammad. It felt like looking into an open well, dropping a stone and waiting for the tight, vertical sound of a splash. She waited but there was no sound, no splash. Muhammad tore off a riff from a twist of meat with his teeth and held it between his fingers like he was smoking. He slurped his tea. When he looked back up at her she could see his face held back a question he wasn't going to ask.

A new candle's accusations have burned down to shifting accommodations with the dark. The wind rustles the trees and, after a few seconds, circles around the flame. The shadows from moths flurry down Ndiya's arms. After a moment, the shadows flutter across Shame's face. Ndiya has just changed the dressing on his arm. They talk while they wait for Malik to arrive. Blood and fluid slowly seep into the gauze. When the antibiotics do their work, Shame's wound will heal and his fever will fade into the distance. She doesn't know if it is the fever, the wound, or the healing, which seems to have actually begun, but Ndiya feels words, or something like words, change between them. Talk turns supple, maybe swollen, in their mouths. As she listens, she sees words unbutton themselves.

–We're invited to hide. We think we're hiding from each other. It doesn't work that way. I don't have much to say about that version of the world. In a way we talk about nothing else, as long as we imagine words are what we say they are. I wonder, if words could speak, what would they say we are?

Ndiya leans back and smiles. Shame's eyes narrow.

–A life, like a job, like a song, is never won or lost.

–But what if the opposite of lost isn't "won" but "found"?

Shame nods and holds up his bandaged arm. He winces, feels a flock of knives, a pain net. He says,

−And in that world, unless we figure out how to do—not just *say*—otherwise, "found" mostly just means gauzed, bandaged. "There" always points at a scar, and "here" points at a wound. Maybe that's the difference? Maybe that's all we get? Maybe that's enough.

Ndiya sits next to Shame on a bench at the long blue table in the courtyard of Goodman's mansion. She sits forward and leans into his side, rests her cheek on his right shoulder.

−Those doctors humpty-dumpty-ing me when I was a teenager, therapist after therapist. After that elevator, that exile. I mean, I can't see into it, it's like an electric cloud in me. Painful static. Someone must have undergone all of that. And what happened in The Grave did happen to someone, to many, many someones. I'm not sure who. Maybe everyone. And I'm not sure what. Does it really help to call one of them me? Which one? And *why* one? If I really sit and feel it, those questions are absurd, even vile.

Shame doesn't know exactly what she's talking about, but he knows there's no way to ask. He hopes she'll continue. And he's afraid.

−Go on.

−I guess what happened is who we are; nothing can be known about that if we're not willing to be that, and to live. Do we ever know anything about it?

−No. I don't think we do. But is "no" enough?

−Enough to what?

−Enough to live.

−No. I don't think it is, maybe I used to. But if it can't be known, how do we trust it?

Shame notices tears streaming Ndiya's face. Her chest hasn't heaved, her breath is even. Shame feels tears drip off her chin and down his arm.

—Maybe that's how. Anyway, "no" doesn't exist. There's always just what she will—

And Shame cuts her off:

—And, now, there's what we will . . .

—And now there's that, yes. Us. Is that a wound or scar?

She glances up and Shame looks into her eyes. He doesn't nod or shake his head. Ndiya continues,

—We know there's the disease, the danger, which is everywhere. Forever. It's always always always part of what any "here" means. It's the wound in any word, it's what heats the blood in any body. It's life, part of it. And at the same time, everywhere, there's the insanity trying to translate itself into your name. Trying to stow away in your voice, to burrow its way into your words.

—So, if I put my hand on you, do I place it "here" or "there?"

Ndiya nods slowly, nods so slightly Shame wonders if she's nodding.

—That's the question, isn't it . . . and there's no answer, really, because if I know the way to get from your "here" to my "there," then, and *exactly* then, we have no word for what we are.

—Ah. So my wound becomes your scar? Your "there" lives again as a wound I carry? But how do we know if there's no word?

Ndiya shoves him gently with her shoulder.

–Well, you tell me, piano man.

She leans back into his side. Shame reaches out and looks down at his hands in front of them. The shadow of a breeze in the candle crosses the backs of his hands. He turns them so his palms face them. Ndiya continues,

–The first time we touched hands it felt to me like your hands wore gloves of themselves. . . . I put my hands on you and it felt . . . it felt like that's where they were—

Ndiya stretches and her voice softens into a blurry whisper, a gauze of sound:

–Oh, the world will offer us its names; then, we'll know what we know as we deal with that. That's probably all we get. We owe the world that, to live in it—whatever it is. Whatever that means. Whoever that makes us. We owe each other that—

–Well, maybe it's neither here nor there.

As if on cue, a sudden gust of wind almost blows out the candles. Ndiya and Shame hear a light rain begin to fall on the canopy over the courtyard. And then they hear Malik's knock on the front doors.

gratitude and his regret at not having called, while listening and, incredibly, trusting the late-evening tone of Su's morning voice, holding Kima's card in one hand and Godar's phone in the other, Shame had absently walked away from the roller bag, leaving it where it was on the teeming platform. Outside the gate, a hundred yards from the frenzy of the exodus, three motionless soldiers guarded the empty parking lot of the station from under a small stand of shade trees trapped in the center of the buckled and erupted sheet of asphalt.

The soldiers looked relaxed enough, as if they'd been marooned on an island with no hope of rescue. The road at the edge of the parking lot was clogged with vehicles of wildly divergent shapes, sizes, and conditions. Tour buses with neon names like Serena Beach Resort and Spa, Mombasa Beach Hotel, and Nyali Beach Holiday Resort stood triple-parked beyond a wooden barrier. Behind them it looked as if a fleet of taxis had been rolled like a handful of dice into an impossible configuration. Men stood on top of all the buses. Other men handed them luggage that was then stacked and strapped onto metal cages welded into the roofs. Shame looked back at the soldiers. Their image wavered in the heat. The soldiers hadn't moved.

The heat must have been hovering somewhere near him. Shame hadn't felt it since stepping off of the train. Handing Godar's phone back to him with thanks and vague promises to visit the tantric arts compound, Shame's hand swung to his side. His now-phoneless hand reminded him that he wasn't wheeling the suitcase. When he looked back he found the platform perfectly empty and as still as the sea of empty asphalt surrounding the stranded, recumbent soldiers. The heat and sweat arrived in an instant. He didn't know what appeared first, the rivers of sweat or the waves of heat. He thanked Godar again and turned back. The open vacancy of the space that had been dense with chaos a few moments ago felt like a tide pushing and pulsing against his legs as he walked. He could see plainly that the suitcase was no longer standing where it had been but it felt, just then, necessary to stand in the precise position where he'd left it.

The sweat appeared again. Stupidity, he then thought, was all around him, within and without him, was a continuous substance with no regard for the silly membrane of porous tissue that marked the borders of his body. Leaving the bag wasn't a mystical occurrence nor, really, a very important one. He hadn't thought about the hundred hundred-dollar bills he'd stashed in one of the five Danish puzzle boxes in the suitcase. It hadn't crossed his mind. The situation was formal, a discrete and disturbing matter. He hadn't put his hand back on the handle. That was it. Therefore he hadn't pulled the bag along with him while he was talking. This was the second it. Two very simple actions among many hundreds of conscious and unconscious, voluntary and involuntary actions going on at the time, in space and time, one of which *hadn't happened to be* his placing his hand on the handle and so the other *hadn't happened to be, either*, his pulling the bag along.

Neither was this a historical matter; three minutes hadn't passed. The visual residue of the past hadn't completely dispersed. When he looked at the spot, he could almost still see the bag sitting there where he'd left it. Standing in that exact location, he could still almost see the throng of people on the platform. But the bag wasn't there and the platform was now empty. The bag had been a fact. It still was. Somewhere. The difference between where the bag had been and where it was now was also a fact. The sweat running down Shame's back and legs, collecting at his wrists, came from his body's awakening to its unconquerable availability to the effects and consequences of stupidity and to the near-absolute unavailability of simple facts that were, geographically speaking, actually very, very nearby.

Shame's possession of the bag, on the other hand, had *never* been a fact. That was all flimsy theory. Maybe this was part of the heat too. A moment's physical nuance in behavior could instantaneously, possibly irrevocably, alter his relationship to very simple facts surrounding him. Just as quickly as that, the route back to the previous place before the event vanished. The current pushing at him from all directions was fear, but he didn't feel scared. He felt heavy and wet and awake. His pores were open. Something that seemed to replace the sky exploded into being above and all around him. It was like that for exactly the same reason that a fever breaks. A contagion had been overcome: let's call the contagion innocence. In a way that wasn't about planes and trains, he had just then left one place and arrived somewhere else.

■

Shame disturbed what he wrongly perceived as the copious leisure of two uniformed men at the information
and assistance office located on the arrival platform at the
Mombasa station.

−Have a seat. How may we help you?

−I seem to have left my suitcase behind and now it's
lost.

With this, the first man drew himself upright in his
chair and put on his officer's hat. The second finished his
bottle of Coca-Cola and then, deliberately, as if this action
involved a series of intricate decisions, also put on his hat.

−OK. Don't worry. Nothing can get lost in
Mombasa.

Shame smiled and suppressed a laugh. The first officer
pronounced a stern phrase in Kiswahili and the second,
who upon standing up appeared very young and much
too thin for his uniform, went into the small shed and
reappeared with a pen and a form on a clipboard.

−Please fill out this form and we'll look into the
matter at hand.

The younger man then ceremoniously handed Shame
a wrinkled and yellowed form many, many generations of
copies away from the original. The words were blurred and
faded so that they looked like the shadow of words from a
language long extinct.

−Was your passport in the suitcase?

−No, I have it here.

−OK. Put the passport number at the top.

A third man, the size of a child, arrived dressed in a

blue suit jacket and worn slacks. He greeted the two officers and introduced himself to Shame.

–Hello. Su sent me. Is there a problem?

–I lost a suitcase.

–Oh. No worries. Nothing can get lost in Mombasa. I'm Benson Kazungu. Your driver.

Shame looked at the older officer who'd just said those exact words. Nothing on his face registered a coincidence. Benson said something to the officers and they nodded at Shame as if what the driver had told them was obvious. At the bottom of the form was a box to list the contents of a lost bag. The puzzle box now glared up at Shame from the empty space. The faded form made the box in his backpack seem as if it was broadcasting its location. The collision between possibilities that, one, the bag was gone and, two, it would be found and searched, made Shame feel momentarily cold. Then he felt the thin fingers of Benson's tiny, birdlike hand on his shoulder.

–Don't worry. People in Mombasa are honest. Nothing can get lost in Mombasa.

This time the sentence sounded more like a taunt or a curse than a reassurance.

–I'm sure your bag was mistakenly taken by a porter to one of the hotel vans. The porters are very, very good, very efficient. They are *eager* to serve mzungus.

Benson's voice was calm. His English was excellent. Something—Shame thought it was a deliberate quality— made his voice different from the officers', whose English was far more labored. In truth the difference in their voices had nothing to do with English. Still less had it anything to do with their personalities. None of the men had very much in the way of personality in English. In English they dealt with a duty. That was it. Their voices depicted only the nature of the transaction their duty required. Whoever these men were was nowhere near the way their voices came ashore in the historical and political ocean of duties to be endured in English.

Benson had been hired by Su to take Shame to her house in Nyali. Thirty minutes. Now, in his hand, he had a note from the officers on which they'd written the names of hotels whose vans had met the morning train. They were located north of the city, past Nyali, and also to the south, all the way to Diani and beyond. In other words, Benson had just walked into his biggest fare of the week, maybe of the month. *This* was the deliberate care Shame noted in Benson's voice. Had Shame known this he'd have thought Benson was acting and he may have been suspicious. In fact, it wasn't an act at all. It was a very real thing, far more real than the shifty chemistry of any personality. In the US, calibrations in and behind personalities were considered duplicitous by people whose lives were served by them. So the fantasy persisted that economic transactions contained something personal. In the States, where much of this occurred atop an internecine war between idioms within *one* language, maybe they did contain something personal, at least sometimes. Maybe always. Here, as concerned Shame Luther and Benson Kazungu, they did not.

Benson led Shame to a gray hatchback Toyota Tercel. Shame caught himself and went to the left side. When

Benson got in and popped the lock, Shame climbed in the front seat and placed his backpack between his feet on the floor. Shame's black pants collected and stored heat from the air. He was drenched. Benson started the car, washed the windshield, turned off the wipers, and the two drove fifty yards in order to queue in a tangle of cars and Piaggio three-wheeled carts—Benson called them tuk-tuks—inching their way up a wide boulevard. Motionless air and clouds of exhaust in the street replaced the moment of breeze. An almost physical beam of sunlight fell through the window into Shame's lap.

Benson asked how he'd lost his bag. After hearing him out, he suggested that the first thing was to go to the Nokia store and see about Shame's phone. "Always deal with the cause," Benson advised. After a swift U-turn into likewise standstill traffic, Benson turned right into a side route with less traffic. They drove down a district street lined with small shops selling fabrics. Shame thought the proprietors of the small stores were Indian. They stood outside smoking thin cigarettes in short-sleeve dress shirts. Some sat in pairs at low tables set for tea. Benson suggested that Shame might buy some gifts for his family. Shame said he didn't think so.

–Well, if there's anything, anything, you need, you tell *me*. I know Mombasa like my hands. Anything can be bought here.

Benson's eyes popped open slightly each time he said "anything." Shame tried to read his smile but found only a blankness behind Benson's expression, a closed door.

In the Nokia store a young woman in hijab helped

them in friendly and efficient tones. This was yet another idiom of transaction. She opened Shame's phone like an oyster and clicked her tongue against the roof of her mouth.

–You bought this upcountry.

This wasn't a question.

–Someone prepared it for me in Nairobi.

At this she smiled a sneer, leaned back with her eyes on Benson. She either sighed, yawned, or said something to him and he laughed. Someone had installed the wrong battery for this model.

–It's a good phone. You can have email on this. M-Pesa. This takes the 1104 battery.

She opened a drawer to her left and took out a wafer-like piece of plastic. 1000 Ksh for the new battery. Shame paid. The young woman snapped the new battery into place and replaced the shell of the phone.

–Do you have credit on the phone?

–I should, yes. I think so?

She pushed a few buttons to check the credit. Suddenly her eyebrows disappeared under her hijab. She looked at Benson blankly as she handed Shame his phone.

–You'll be fine now.

Shame couldn't tell if she said that to him or the driver. And Shame totally missed the elegance with which the matter of what to do with the other phone battery never arose. He hadn't even thought of it. Benson followed Shame outside.

When they got back to the car Benson sat in the driver's seat for a few moments as if Shame wasn't there.

Benson folded a few bills into his wallet, started the car and washed the window again. That was the third time he'd washed the windshield in thirty minutes. En route to the Nokia store, he'd turned off the car while stopped in traffic for about five minutes and had washed the windshield when he started the car then as well. Benson's manner was retiring, very formal but not stiff. His eyes and smile were clearly, almost brazenly, painted on a blank slate but his face wasn't hard or cold. It was simply that something was washed clean behind his face. One thing was for sure, Shame thought, "Brotherman sure loves him a *clean* windshield."

–We'll check the hotels north of the island first. Don't worry. People in Mombasa are very, very honest. Nothing can get lost here.

At that moment, a tall woman fully covered in a black buibui with shiny black beads embroidered into the trim of her veil stopped at the corner. Two lanes of traffic were turning left. Benson paused so she could cross. Looking back to watch the merging lane, the driver of a black Mercedes SUV in the lane to their right kept going. Shame braced for impact. Only the woman's eyes were visible. Under her arm, she held a sleek silver handbag. She stood unflinching in the path of the SUV. As if in slow motion, Shame watched as the woman, without turning her head, cut her eyes and aimed them into the windshield of the Mercedes. The driver turned to meet the side-gaze fixed at him and screeched to a halt as if a concrete wall had appeared in front of his car. The woman hadn't moved her head nor altered her stance. Before the Benz had a beat to settle its momentum backward she'd returned her eyes to the path before her and took two more steps to where the nose of the vehicle interrupted her path. Facing forward, she stopped at the bumper. There was plenty of room to walk around but she stopped. The offending vehicle then backed up to clear her path and the covered woman walked on without another glance. Her first glance, however, had somehow remained where it was, midair, like a suspended steel beam.

Shame didn't know what to call what he'd just seen. If asked, he'd have said, "Power." He didn't know if he'd really seen what he'd seen. He looked at Benson who smiled and nodded diagonally. Shame thought he glimpsed something there behind Benson's face for an instant, but it vanished before he was sure if he'd seen that either. They'd both seen this happen. But Benson clearly hadn't seen what Shame saw.

–Yes. She's very beautiful. If you want I can take you to have one. They're all prostitutes.

–No. That's alright.

–OK. If you need a woman. You tell me what kind you'd like, Hindu, Christian, Muslim. I'll take you to have one. Mombasa is like my hands.

As they made their left turn, the ocean appeared to the right in the distance. Shame noted that Benson discussed a new phone battery, a lost suitcase, and the purchase of any kind of woman with utterly the same inflection, or lack of it, in his voice. Mombasa, his hands. "According to Benson," Shame thought, "anything can be bought here and nothing can be lost."

After checking at a second hotel to the north of Nyali,

Benson's phone rang as he opened his door. It was Sarah. Someone had found Shame's bag. It was near Diani, south of the island. About thirty kilometers. With the ferry and traffic, maybe two hours. Maybe three. Shame nodded. And Benson:

–Yes, Sarah, thank you. I know where that is. We'll go now. Phone number?

Benson wrote down the number on the back of a business card and thanked Sarah, instructing her to settle down and stop worrying. He handed the card to Shame, who stared at it for a few seconds:

B.M. Taxi Service
For Comfort Touring & Traveling
Benson M. Kazungu
Taxi Operator

PO Box 37 Mariakani
Mwembe Tayari   Cell: 0726 324 099
Opp. Mash Booking Office   0735 608 899

Benson hung up the phone.

–Someone called Sarah to say that he has your bag. We'll go to him now.

Benson smiled blankly and blinked.

–Sarah's crying.

Shame flipped the card over and noticed something strange about the number. Distractedly, he asked,

–Did she say who it was or how they got my bag? Is it at a hotel?

–Yes. The name is Godar. No, it is not a hotel. It's at his residence to the south.

–Of course.

Shame nodded at the banal certainty of disbelief. Then he wondered what would happen if Godar had checked through his bag out of curiosity. The sweat dripped down his legs inside his pants. He decided to start caring about that when they got there, maybe.

Benson started the car and washed the windshield. He turned off the wipers after three or four quick swishes whipped away the clear fluid. After multiple washings, the windshield, of course, had been spotless when they got in the car.

–Benson, I have to say . . . you've got the cleanest windshield I've ever seen.

–Oh, you like my clean windshield, do you?

–Yes, I've noticed you wash it every time we get in the car.

–Yes, I *do*. Watch this.

Benson switched the ignition off and removed the key. Then he stared at Shame, put the key back in the ignition with his right hand and raised his left hand high, away from the controls between them. Benson held his gaze on Shame's face, smiled, and turned the key. Nothing happened.

–You see? What is it?

–What? Nothing? I don't know.

–Yes. Nothing! Exactly.

Shame stared at Benson, clueless. Over Benson's shoulder, three gaunt guards, two with rifles and one with a mirror angled on a long broom handle, stood guard near a thatch-roofed hut at the hotel entrance gate. A gaggle of red-faced tourists disembarked from a van while three men in khaki shorts and white polo shirts worked on the roof removing belts that held a mountain of luggage in place.

–Aha. Now, wait.

Benson removed the key again, held it out for Shame's inspection, and replaced it in the ignition. Then, exaggerating his gestures like a magician who was about to remove a huge clutch of flowers from his tuxedo sleeve, Benson lowered his left hand and grasped the wand attached to the steering column between the driver and passenger. Shame noticed just then that Benson's right palm was creased and gathered around a thick scar that ran like a rift across his wrist and disappeared into the cuff of his sleeve. He instructed Shame to watch closely as his left thumb depressed the button at the very end of the control wand and held it down. Benson smiled again. Still, nothing happened. Shame had no idea where this demonstration was going.

–Are you ready?

–Sure.

Benson then turned the key with his right hand and the car started, liquid shot onto the windshield and the wipers cleared it away.

–OK. I see. So what is it? A short?

–No. It's no short, my friend! I had my mechanic wire the ignition through the washer switch.

–Why?

–Why? Are you serious? This is my third car in five years, man!

–What?

–Carjackings. Robbers. Now when they come to steal my car I'll just turn it off, get out, and walk away. They'll never get anywhere.

Benson laughed now. Shame sensed an abrupt bend, if not a break, in the clean slate behind the driver's face. Call it a translation. But it was also a transaction. Benson looked at the tourists and the men in polo shirts who were now handing bags down to colleagues on the ground.

–A lot of bags coming into this country, eh?

–Yeah.

–Let's go get yours.

–Good, sure. That's great. But Benson, look, you know, I thought you said, "People in Mombasa are honest," you know, "Nothing can get lost in Mombasa," and all that. Yet here's your car wired for carjackings? Three in five years?

Shame noticed Benson's left hand rubbing his right wrist. At that moment, Benson's eyes went cold. A person in the parking lot wouldn't have seen it. But with less than two feet between them, in this theft-wired, dented Toyota Tercel, Shame felt that bent slate in back of Benson's face turn to steel. That steel wasn't cold. Something, maybe disbelief, scurried behind Benson's eyes and something else, possibly a streak of fiery contempt but just as likely a glimpse of bone-deep fatigue, sat there too. It was an instant at most. Then Benson pulled the background of his face together and, as if addressing a group of small schoolchildren:

–But the robbers aren't *from* Mombasa. They were Kikuyus from upcountry. Nairobi.

Looking as if he'd just related to Shame the most elementary information, Benson put the car in gear. Benson tipped the security guards 100 Ksh each with Shame's money, and they headed south to the tantric arts compound.

Kubwa was the family name. Over his weeks meeting the crew at the junction of paths and unloading cargo, Shame had learned one or two things about the operation. Their grandfather came from Gujarat to East Africa when the British were still ruling. His name was Chakor; no one knew his surname. One day in a rare loquacious moment Kubwa had said that Chakor meant a person in love with the moon. The man had worked as a clerk in Nairobi, but he hated the cold nights. So he'd moved to the coast, started a delivery business, and married a girl from Paté. Kubwa wasn't exactly sure in what order these events had taken place once his grandfather had reached the coast. The grandfather was a tall man and quite fat. Naturally, he'd ended up with the surname Kubwa, which meant "very large."

Shame knew it wasn't Friday. Other than that, he'd almost ceased keeping track of the days. Friday was obvious. The mosques would be packed, stacks of thong sandals piled up outside the front doors. Usually they worked a half day if that, if you could call it working at all. Most days they worked hard. Shame was used to that. Even after these weeks, the Kubwa men still watched him make circuits back and forth from the boat as if they'd been hypnotized. "A mzungu," their eyes said to him, "who *works*? A mzungu *washenzi*?" Shame knew that look well enough. He'd encountered it for most of this life in one way or another, by whatever term, wherever he went. At that moment, he thought, "What am I supposed to do, spin around until I'm dizzy?" Amina from the gallery had told him what the word "mzungu" meant. This work, however, was difficult in a very different way from what he'd known at home. When he thought that, he could feel the word "home" pulse down his arms, in his hands, and then lie down to die in his brain. At home, it was about *doing* the work, the job was a thing done. And "done" didn't mean finished, it meant enacted in a certain way, with given dimensions of one's self, part body, part something else.

At home, the labor interacted with his life in a way that gave the doing, and the word "done," its meaning. He'd never thought about it before. Shame had rarely spent much, if any, of his pay. Doing that work had meant selling his body, in time and sweat, in time *as* sweat, to the owner of the company. "Done" went beyond the dense, repeatable connection to the physical labor itself, the weight, even the smell, of the materials, went beyond the way, in the summer, his body took thirty minutes to disappear, becoming a series of waves swallowed by the heat of even the hottest jobs. He loved that feeling. No job was hot enough. "Done" went beyond the way, in the winter, it took a little longer than that to generate an envelope of warmth that erased the first painful minutes of a cold job; labor in the winter felt like flying over the surface of the worksite. In the summer it was like becoming part of the way heat disturbs the air, as if he could walk with a load of brick while watching his profile on the ground come apart into a rhythm of shadows like a distant murmuration of starlings.

Done was constant. Shame had always been glad that the crews he worked with were never idle. He felt sorry for the concrete crews, for example, who had to stand still, waiting to work for half the day, thinking about how cold or hot they were, or if their feet hurt, or wondering if they should take off their work shirt or put on long sleeves. Shame had never had to endure that kind of idle time. Putting his paychecks in the bank and living his vacant life in roadside motels, Shame had loved the way "done" meant selling his body by the hour and the physical density and variability of the time that resulted. When something was "done" it didn't mean it was over. It almost meant the opposite. The older men told him that was because he was young. In truth, for Shame, it was because work, that vacant life, was a physical alternative to a bottom-less, immaterial grief in Chicago. Mistakenly, cornered by a pain with no location in the world he knew, Shame had attempted to corral one dimension using the other. It didn't matter, though. Either way, the work worked; it was always hard work but had never felt difficult.

The difficulty with Kubwa wasn't so much doing the work. In a way, Shame never felt like he was *doing* anything. These jobs always had a strolling quality. He couldn't feel what he'd always known—without ever really know-ing—as things getting done. He felt like he coexisted with this work. The job wasn't anymore or less done when they quit in the afternoon than it had been at dawn when they arrived to find their first dusky glimpse of Kubwa's dhow low in the water, heaped with whatever load he'd set up. Shame thought, maybe this work felt saved, kind of like money felt when it wasn't meant to be spent. Or maybe these jobs were rescued more than they were done. And he knew that what he sensed about the kind of work he was doing was also what he knew about his time that, apart from the pay, which he hardly needed anyway, was really how he knew about who and what he was at any moment. If the job was done, that meant he was doing something, and if it felt rescued that meant something else. Maybe the work *was* saved?

No, it wasn't a rescue. Part of getting work done had always meant squaring off with a great adversary who moved when he moved, a kind of perfect sparring partner. Maybe a dance partner? Often enough, it was true, Shame had felt saved by his physical contest with the limits of a job, a serious game in which every second and all movements counted. He worked and watched his body eliminate needless motion. He savored the elegance, the physical intelligence, of the latest refinement, until he felt like his intricate circuits through whatever jobsite amounted to a controlled and threatened dance. It was almost grace. He felt none of that here. When he realized that much he sensed a swooping shadow, as if an invisible wing had gone over his head.

On some days, these Kubwa jobs felt like injured friends he was carrying on his back. Even these thoughts were part of it. At home, his mind wasn't thinking at work. He'd loved that. Thinking at work had been a dangerous distraction. All attributes of mind had to be physically enacted, had to be done. He couldn't afford to split the body off and let the mind travel elsewhere. Here his mind felt strangely alive and autonomous. And he'd begun, again, to hear and feel the piano. While he wasn't working, he'd realized, for the first few weeks, he hadn't thought about or felt the draw of any music at all. And, since working for Kubwa, he'd begun to wonder about Ndiya in Chicago. Maybe she was staying with Colleen or even with Kima. He knew this action in his mind was point-less. But without knowing it, he'd ceased unconsciously rebuilding that particular wall. And he wondered where he might find a piano.

■

Someone was building apartments or condos above a restaurant on the way to Shela. The tide was coming in, so the boat was docked at the shore, which dropped off steeply. Unloading here meant climbing eight feet of underwater sand at an incline of about forty-five degrees, then over the dune and down to the donkeys. The beach was full sunlight, not a stick of shade. The bow nudged into the sand. At the back of the boat, the water was over twenty feet deep. The driver had spent the morning fishing until the heat drove the fish into deeper water. Muhammad, the foreman of the crew, and the Kubwas had begun to call Shame "the Wizard," which they pronounced *Wheez-hard*. The short, squat worker from Matondoni still hadn't said one word to Shame. He might have stolen a glance at him but if so, Shame had missed that. Another with a little red under his complexion and dusty curls in his hair smiled his khat-tinted smile at Shame and wanted to feign a high five with his missing left arm every time their paths crossed on the job. He chewed continuously, working the stalks around between his teeth and gums, spitting out bits and replacing stems. He added an occasional stick of Juicy Fruit from his pocket. The gum cut the bitterness. Shame had also learned that Kubwa docked this small man 100 Ksh per day to account for his missing arm.

It was late afternoon. A gusting wind from the sea was stacking up huge clouds over the mainland to the west. The rainy season was approaching. The load was gone. The boat now bobbed like a cork and carved a ridge in the steep slope of the beach as it disappeared inch by inch beneath the rising tide. Kubwa told Muhammad and the crew they could go and they vanished almost instantly. Then Kubwa waved to Shame. "Come." He told him to take the two biggest fish they'd caught that morning and sell them to the restaurant. "1000 Ksh each. If they say no, try the hotel around the back." They could split the money, but Kubwa's tone made it clear that he wasn't asking.

Shame pulled himself up onto the wooden craft. He stepped over the bench along the side and walked on the rib-like slats to the stern. There, in a triangular opening created by the converging longitudinal beams and latitudinal slats of the boat's mangrove skeleton, three large cruise missile–looking fish lay motionless. At first the fish appeared metallic, aluminum. But the color was in transit: a blue-tinged silver moved from head to tail, passing under a lattice of vertical shadows along the side of each body. The shadows resembled windows in a train speeding past. "Fuselage," Shame thought, as if he'd never come across the term before, as if it meant "the stationary velocity of a metallic fish." Every hour, two buckets of ice from the restaurant had been poured over them, making it difficult to tell where one fish ended and another began. He saw three Y-shaped tails. A cloud of flies cavorted in the pungent air.

Barracuda. The heads were oversized like locomotives, Shame thought, as he gazed down at the strangely fixed image cast by this tangle of specialized marine engineering. Kubwa and his brothers watched Shame from behind but he had no sense of that. The eyes of the fish were obsidian discs with flecks of cobalt, none of it of much use, he figured, out of the water. He couldn't really tell which of the fish was biggest; all, he guessed, were between three and four feet long. He decided to pick the two with the largest, louvered tailfins. Every day he'd seen fisherman arrive to the Lamu Town jetty with various cargoes they'd lay out on the concrete. They sold their catch to the markets and hotels. Holding them by their gills, the tails and flanks of the biggest fish dragging in the dust of the narrow streets, kids transported the fish to the buyers' businesses. Occasionally, a shark or a sunfish would be too big to carry. These were strapped to the back of a donkey or draped over the handlebars and seat of a bicycle.

Shame stared down at the fish. In a way mocked by the incessant cloud of flies and the strobe of motion in the metallic sheen along their sides, a Pompeian, archeological fixity beamed upward at him from the sleek bodies.

Their eyes now javelins of sharpened emptiness. Standing a few feet from shore, waist-deep in the water, Shame had seen squadrons of these fish patrol the aqua currents of the sound at the tip of the island. They moved like underwater missiles. It was late in the day. He was tired and had utterly no interest in this outrage of ice and stillness. Shame removed his gloves and folded them into the back pocket of his cargo shorts. He decided he didn't really care which was the smallest. It was close enough for Kubwa. An unknown angle of shadows moved in him as the men watched from behind on the boat. He reached down for the tail and gill-lip of the nearest fish. He braced himself for leverage to pull against the dead weight.

Something spring-loaded and invisible snapped before Shame's eyes. Flies vanished and a flash of light, or something like light, slashed through the scene of soft strobe and stillness. Maybe the flies stole the stillness? An explosive hail of ice flew in every direction at once. The day spun like a mad wheel of black brightness, as if the Earth was an eyeball rolled back in its socket. Some force tossed Shame on to his back. Time took a deep breath and his mind fastened itself to a tower of gray clouds in the sky as it rolled over, passed beneath him, and then fell back into its position overhead. Shame's initial thought was that he'd been struck by lightning. Just beyond his feet he heard a tight, metallic racket as if the small outboard motor, full-throttle, had been thrown down a stone staircase. He'd landed with one of the latitudinal ribs of the boat across the middle of his back. He searched for pain. Was he conscious? Yes. He arched his back further. The horizon behind him revolved to reveal two Kubwas in his vision, upside down, laughing. "*Yes–s*. OK," he thought. He thought the pain was in his back but when he moved to get to his feet he felt a loose vibration down his left arm. He looked but didn't see his hand. A delta of blood had sprouted from his arm. An open slash from his elbow to his palm stared back at him. None of it looked or felt like part of his body.

Gush, flow, or drip? These were the first questions he'd been taught for worksite injuries. He'd seen many but he'd never been hurt on a job until this. "This?" he thought in disbelief. His hand was still there. He pulled his shirt over his head and off with his right arm and wiped off the blood, revealing a surgical, eight-inch incision on the underside of his left forearm. Pain, throb, or none? Those were the next questions. He couldn't tell just yet. So none? He wrapped his shirt around his arm, crossed the ends, bit one sleeve and jerked it tight with his right hand. While repeating the pain question, he felt a tap on his shoulder; he jumped and turned. It was Kubwa, holding a wooden-handled hammer with a steel ball-peen head.

–Would you like a wee-pon?

Shame took the hammer. Kubwa turned and absently stepped from slat to slat until he was standing with his brothers again near the bow. The three Kubwas laughed.

The sky had tilted so that it looked like a soaring, diagonal roof. Shame felt sleepy. The hammer felt heavy hanging at his side in his right hand. He felt the press of his pulse behind his ear. He held his left arm up vertical from the elbow, now definitely more throb than pain or numb. The pain would come later, followed by the fever. He looked across the sound at the shore of Manda Island, the scatter of boats docked. Fifty yards or so packed with dark bodies and children on the sand, the only stretch of public beach left in the area. He felt lucid but he wasn't. The spit in his mouth tasted like brass. He knew that was adrenaline, possibly shock.

He was also keenly aware of the urge in his upper torso to turn and go after all three Kubwas with the hammer. Instead, he stepped back to the triangle. The bodies were motionless metal. The eyes glowed blue out of black discs. One fish looked much larger now. It bent into a U shape, head faced up at Shame. Its mouth, cracked open, was bright bone-white inside. A double set of incisor fangs began a triangle from the top jaw. A single set stood like stalagmites in the front center of the lower jaw. A few dozen spikes and at least one hundred tiny shards lined the edge of the cave-like opening of the mouth. The rest was white and glowing as if the fish had swallowed a searchlight.

Shame realized two things just then. It wasn't a frozen velocity he'd been staring at stupidly; it was more like a rigorous potential—if not essential—surgery. And the hammer in his hand wasn't a weapon. It was a tool. He knew the weight in his right shoulder scaled another potential—if not essential—element. He'd always aimed violence into work. Now this? He knew nothing, really, about the weight of a weapon. On land, he thought, his brain with the essential tool had the upper hand. Removed from its element, a mouth full of essential scalpels couldn't

operate. It could only attack. Out of its element, an essential tool was reduced to a potential weapon. Shame
saw that now. And so, when circumstance reduced tools
to weapons, someone was in for a bad day. It all depended
upon which element was which. Wondering whether
he was thinking about the fish or the Kubwa brothers,
Shame knew that if they'd met underwater, it would have
been the other way around.

Shame walked back along the shore with his blood-soaked shirt tied around his left arm. He didn't like walking through the streets with no shirt so he bought a second-hand jersey from the first stall he came across: FLY EMIRATES. Then he stopped at the apothecary next to the President's Inn at the edge of town and bought sterile dressings, hydrogen peroxide. He paid 350 Ksh of the 500 Kubwa had given him for the brutal murder and subsequent sale of two barracuda. The jersey and the supplies had finished the blood-money plus some. Arm flexed and held near his body, fist closed and up near his armpit, Shame walked in the teeming main street as dusk fell like an invisible rain of ochre dust. His arm felt like a prosthesis. It signaled its own rhythmic throb to the rest of his body as if his heart had migrated to the location of the wound and was beating from there. He felt his pulse at the base of his skull. He'd known that as one of the badges and incidents of intensity. "Badges and incidents"? He'd picked up the phrase somewhere, he didn't remember where. He wondered for a moment what it meant. Then he remembered a phrase he'd come across during his first meal at Echoes: "Labor which gives form to desire takes from desire its form."

∎

Shame stepped into Echoes thinking he'd say hi to Kate, maybe toast his gullibility with a cup of something. He felt too light to be standing on his feet. He felt like he needed to sit down. He was in shock but he didn't know that. He was shaken by the momentary violence and thought maybe his career as a stevedore was over. Maybe he'd been fired? This all for some reason made him newly fearful about Ndiya's situation, wherever she was. That fear suddenly felt close by.

He entered the courtyard carrying his plastic bag, wearing his jersey. Kate was at the back table talking with Amina, the woman from Buraka, the gallery. The look on their faces when he entered made it clear that he'd made a mistake. He immediately wondered what mistake it was. In that moment, errors of all sizes and shapes rained over his head like a dome of heat lightning. He was numb to them, unable to measure what he sensed in the women's reaction to seeing him. Kate's face, her uncharacteristically hesitant greeting, clearly signaled something Shame hadn't recognized. The women stared at him as if his arm had been severed and he'd hallucinated a flesh wound. He could also feel that they weren't seeing what they were staring at. They were both staring straight at him. So what were they seeing?

His first thought was to reassure Kate that the injury wasn't that serious but Kate's hesitation wasn't exactly about his arm. He thought back, carefully and slowly, about his reaction to seeing the wound, the vibrations in his arm, his blood-washed hand. After the murder of the fish, he'd rinsed out the wound in the water. The inside of the incision was the same color as the inside of the fish's mouth. After rinsing it out he watched as tiny spots of red appeared, then they grew together, filling the channel with blood. For a moment the opening looked like it was lined with teeth. Maybe teeth had come out and stuck in his arm?

In response to their reactions to his wound, the scale of errors roared up against the eroding emergency barrier Shame had erected between himself and his previous life. Those images didn't splash like a hallucination. His arm was real. It was still there. He focused on the scene Kate had framed. He tried to see what she saw.

—Is something wrong? I know I'm a little . . .

—Maybe more than a little, sweetie, no?

—I don't know, maybe so.

—What happened?

—A fish—at work—

—A fish? Have you been *home*?

—No.

With this Kate emitted an inaudible sigh and said something to Amina under her breath. The women reclined back into the sitting positions they'd been in when he'd first seen them. They smiled privately at each other. Amina said, "Pole, Shahid, pole." Kate looked back at him, now calmly, openly. Kate wasn't seeing whatever she'd seen when he'd first approached the table a few moments ago. But he could also tell that she still wasn't really looking at *him*, either.

—Have you talked to Su lately?

—No. Not in weeks. Why?

–No reason. Just wondering.

Shame knew that was a lie. Kate wasn't a woman who asked things for no reason.

–Just wondering. Deary, if you haven't been home, I suggest you go *there*. You don't look like you're in shape to be—

Now he could feel that none of this had to with his arm, at least not anymore.

–It's not that bad, really. But, true, I should wash and change the—

He glanced down at the bloody shirt tied around his arm.

–bandage.

Holding up the white plastic bag, he turned to leave, then turned back.

–Is something wrong with Su?

–No, oh no. I was just wondering, no reason. Su's fine. You be off. You're sure you're OK?

–Yes, I'm OK.

So, that was twice Kate had insisted she'd asked something for no reason. Her concern about his arm was clearly *not* a reason. Her tone was still not her usual voice, but it wasn't the truly strange veil he'd greeted upon entering. Something about his not having yet been home had rotated the scene. Around what? He could still feel the electric charge in the air he'd entered. It hadn't begun with him. Something had already been in the air when he arrived. Whatever it was changed abruptly when they'd seen him. He felt the jolt; he hadn't recovered.

With that his mind spun outward: "Recovered from

what?" The possibilities roared, again, against the barrier between where he was and where he'd been. He'd learned long ago not to think about things at a distance, which made them general. He'd kept to details, even abstract ones, even absurd conjectures, anything but general thoughts. Far more than he knew, his life had depended, had long depended, on his body's insistence on being where it was and on his mind's eagerness, its thirst and need, to start there and deal with whatever followed from that position. That way no matter how wrong he was, it was still him that was wrong. He could take it from there.

Shame stepped back into the street behind three donkeys saddled with baskets of sand. Ali King was closing his tailor shop and the ochre dust of dusk had thickened into a low-chord, black-powdered sky filled, as if by some unseen right hand high on the keys, with bright sparks.

■

A huge red evening star was setting to the east over Manda Island. The floating bar was adrift closer than usual to Lamu Town, a string of lights along its perimeter shone like a distant suspension bridge. It was still early. All the booths along the edge were empty. The lights twitched in sync with the faint tones of the music blown ashore by the breeze. His left arm tight to his chest as if held in an invisible sling, Shame had taken his time, strolling, eventually, uphill to his room. Later for Kate and them. His mind felt loose in time, dangling from the world, the events of the day, and the roar beyond that. Somewhere close, as if following him, taking a shortcut and waiting for him to pass and then falling in behind to follow again, a vivid cross-hatching of static and color played with the edge of Shame's peripheral awareness. Something had come along with him when he left Echoes. Or maybe it had preceded him through the alleys. He felt it, could almost hear it. It was like being conscious of the frayed edge or broken border of his own mind; he wondered if he was still in shock. He was in a lot of pain. He felt that. But maybe for the first time since the you-don't-exist parade, he felt good, alive. As if those surgeon fish had been messengers or guides, as if Kubwa had been offering him a favor, he felt obscurely delivered, into what he wasn't sure.

As it did each night, the dusk had emerged from the open ocean to the east, collected over Manda, and sifted itself into the air of Lamu Town. The swallows disappeared. Bats replaced them in their paths as if substituting nighttime calculus for daylight algebra. Light from the American base would soon be visible to the north, its cloudy claims of possession sprayed into the night sky.

Shame entered his building. The smell of Mrs. Azir's curry and vegetables trailed up the stairs as he reached the lower landing. He paused and looked down at the blood-doused shirt tied around his arm. A breeze from the stairway window chilled the skin on his right shoulder, its fingers trailing diagonally across his back. Trade winds were rising; elsewhere that meant monsoon. Here it meant a season of sun splayed by dark towers of distant clouds. Shame loved the rain here, it canceled out all wind, revealing a world of perfectly perpendicular motion. "Plumb showers," he'd thought. A bazillion raindrops all aimed at a single point at the center of the earth. A silver stillness painted beyond his eyes.

His key was tied with a red string, given to him by Mrs. Azir when he'd paid her six months rent, three hundred dollars, upon arriving. With some distant sparkle in her eyes, Mrs. Azir had made a point to Shame that she'd charged him much less than others she'd rented to before. Muhammad, smiling, had told him it was more than double what he'd paid. In a way, like the silver stillness of the rain, Shame could see that Mrs. Azir's lie was true.

The key was in the left rear pocket of his shorts. It was fastened with the string wound around the button so it wouldn't fall out in the water. He stood before his door, reaching around his back with his right arm, undoing the flap and unwinding the string while his shoulder blade flirted with a cramp in the muscles beneath it. As he grasped the loop and removed the key he thought he heard a sound from behind the door. He assumed it was Muhammad on his roof across the way. He was wrong. He thought he should go see Muhammad; maybe Muhammad knew how to dress a wound properly. Maybe Shame would. Later. Just as he put his key in the door, the latch unlocked. Shame couldn't tell if the key had turned on its own.

He pushed the door but it didn't move. It was bolted from the inside. He twisted the latch again and it came to life, the knob turning against the motion of his hand.

He closed his eyes and said nothing. He whispered it to himself:

–Nothing.

Then, at eye level, he heard the iron bolt slide from its socket on the inside of the door.

ACKNOWLEDGMENTS

After beginning to write this novel on our front porch in Athens, Georgia, I worked on it over years when I could go live alone, mostly in cities (or parts of cities) that were unknown to me: Montréal, Mombasa, Nairobi, Istanbul, and the Bronx. But I wasn't alone, of course; the characters would show up wherever in the world I was. And they'd bring Chicago along with them. We walked, cooked, ate, argued, and dreamed together. Over the course of the years, often walking backward in time, we found our way to and through this story. And I was also never alone because my family was and is always with me, which is always work, the best work, at times the only work; I first want to thank Stacey Barnum for all of it, and always a little—and sometimes more than a little—more than that. And, along with their mama, thanks to Milan, Sunčana, and Mzée for life, ours.

After that, I'd like to thank a few people whose presence informed this story as well as making the writing possible through every kind of support there is: Riccardo Williams, Jr. (1965–1987), for narrating, for never never leaving; Eric Lassiter, for seeing that; Binyavanga Wainaina, for bristling, for brilliant beaming-being; Martin Kimani, for good company, for the bassline; Craig Werner, for the world of teaching; Ntone Edjabe, for a galaxy of vinyl, soundings; Tim Tyson, for soul and the paint thinner; Michael Ondaatje, for the note, surgical; Valerie Babb, for the rail at The National; Yusef Komunyakaa, for two decades of sound and / as guidance; Mikhail Iossel and Ysabel Viau, for Montréal; Billy Kahora, Angela Wachuka, Wambui Mwangi, and Sheba Hirst, for Nairobi; Suhaila Abu Cross, for Nyali / Mombasa; Peter Wheeler, for Lamu; Malik Weaver, for laughing; Tugce Mahyacilar, Shale Turkeli, Kim Fortuny, and Gulen Gulen, for Istanbul; and Jeffrey Renard Allen (and also Terrance R. Young), for the Bronx.

Many thanks, also, to the first readers who talked to me about this manuscript in parts or in the whole—Adrienne Rich (1929–2012), Jess Row, Craig Werner, and Milan Pavlić—and especially to those readers who so generously wrote notes for the book cover: Jeff Allen, Yvonne Adhiambo Owuor, Kiese Laymon, Reginald McKnight, and Emily Lordi. And thanks so much to Barbara Bendzunas for solid company in Park Hall 254.

Many thanks to many many singers and musicians, those named and unnamed, but, firstly, to Ms. Chaka Khan, whose work in song provides the basic and most fundamental—but also bottomless—logic into which the telling of this story leans for shape and direction.

Finally, thanks to the organizations that supported this work: the MacDowell Colony, the Lannan Foundation, Nicholas Allen and the Willson Center for the Humanities at the University of Georgia (UGA), the UGA Provost's Travel Grant. Most of all, thanks to Milkweed Editions, especially to Daniel Slager, who saw a horizon with this story on it and helped steer me there, and to Joey McGarvey and Mary Austin Speaker, for seeing the work into being between these covers.

Sunčana Rain Pavlić

ED PAVLIĆ is the author of eight collections of poems, including *Visiting Hours at the Color Line* and *Let's Let That Are Not Yet: Inferno*, both of which were winners of the National Poetry Series. He has published essays, poems, fiction, and dramatic pieces with dozens of outlets, including the *New York Times, Boston Review, Harvard Review, Ploughshares*, and *Callaloo*. His critical work includes *Who Can Afford to Improvise?: James Baldwin and Black Music, the Lyric and the Listeners* and *Crossroads Modernism: Descent and Emergence in African American Literary Culture*. A recipient of the Georgia Author of the Year Award from the Georgia Writers Association and a fellowship from the W.E.B. Du Bois Research Institute at Harvard University, Pavlić is Distinguished Research Professor of English and African American Studies at the University of Georgia.